Semper Fidelis

Carl O Marchi

Always Faithful: A Marine's Tale

By
CARL P. MARCHI

authorHOUSE®

AuthorHouse™
1663 Liberty Drive, Suite 200
Bloomington, IN 47403
www.authorhouse.com
Phone: 1-800-839-8640

First published by AuthorHouse 10/29/2007

ISBN: 978-1-4343-3687-3 (sc)
ISBN: 978-1-4343-3688-0 (hc)

Library of Congress Control Number: 2007937028

Printed in the United States of America
Bloomington, Indiana

This book is printed on acid-free paper.

Book designed by Ralph Sirianni (www.sirianniart.com)
Book edited by Katie Boersch.

*Dedicated
to all the
Men and Women
who served in the
Armed Forces
of the
United States of America*

Future Novels by Carl P. Marchi

Seaside Infatuations

Joe Momma

Justice in New Jersey

Unfamiliar Realm

Darker Side of Gray

Thunder Struck

Hole in the Water

Carla Keys

Waltzing Rosa

Me and My Poetry

Acknowledgements

I wish to thank Mitchell Douglas; Suzanne Douglas; Jeffrey Bialy; Cory Hellerer; Ronn Whitehead; Mariah Marchi: Robert DeCarolis; and Ralph Lugo for their help and understanding. Special mention goes to Cathy Obradovich, for showing me the way; Ann Marie D'Amico for administrative assistance and encouragement; Vincent Gallo, for giving me a part in his movie "Buffalo 66"; and last but not least, the Boys from Roma Street.

Prologue

My family make up is a framework of traditional beliefs dealing with ancestors, heroes, and events. Like many Italians who came to America in large numbers, my family came to New Jersey in the early to mid 1900's. Along with them, came a way of life known to many as a secret criminal organization. Many words describe what I am saying. Such words include the Mafia, Black Hand and La Costra Nostra.

It is not my intention to give a history lesson, but I was taught that the American branch of the Mafia is named La Costra Nostra (our affair). My family believes that the word Mafia originated during the French invasion of Sicily in the late 1200's. Morte Alla Francia Italia Anela (death to the French is Italy's cry). I am not sure about the term Black Hand, but it is believed that during the 1700's, pictures of a black hand were distributed to the wealthy by the Mafia in Italy. This was a silent request for money in return for protection. By no means am I suggesting that my family is involved in organized crime, except for my Uncle Michael that is.

My Uncle Michael Tucci is head of the Tucci crime family housed in Trenton, New Jersey. The Tucci Crime Family is a constituent of organized crime adhering to the beliefs, and practices governed by one of the five Mafia families of New York City. The majority of my family believes that the Mafia's intentions are to maintain a sense of family based on ancestry and Sicilian heritage. Many Italian people in America wear the association with members of the Mafia like a badge of honor.

My name is Joseph Mommalione. My friends call me Joe Momma for short. I graduated from high school in 1990. Between the summer of 1990 and the summer of 1991, I experienced more in life than most men do in a lifetime. I experienced the elements of a world of crime and the elements of the Marine Corps. I tried to act in conformity with both. For myself, I had no choice but to overlap between being a criminal and a person revered for my noble courage. In doing so, I created circumstances that brought about a cause.

I suppose that young men and women join the military service for a variety of reasons. Perhaps it is because their mother or father is a Veteran, maybe they had problems with the law, or they are attracted by the television commercials. Perhaps for some, it is because of rejection by friends, family or society.

I left for the Marine Corps Recruit Depot, San Diego, California on Saturday, August 25, 1990, exactly twenty-three days after Iraq dictator Saddam Hussein's invasion of Kuwait. According to the news, it was the same day that the brigade commander of the 7th Marine Expeditionary Brigade from California reported to General H. Norman Schwarzkopf, Central Command's Commander in Chief that the brigade, with the strength of more than fifteen thousand Marines, was prepared to hold a line forty miles north of Al Jubayl in Saudi Arabia.

It wasn't Saddam Hussein nor an intense feeling of heroism and valor that were the reason I joined the Marines. I enlisted in the Marine Corps because I had to prove myself, and I liked the uniforms. In addition, my friend Carmine is a former Marine. He told me that Marines identify with the Corps and remain loyal long after they complete their tour of duty. Once a Marine, always a Marine. At the time I graduated from high school, I had some petty scraps with the law, and my father was losing patience with me. I think he was worried that I would end up in jail or I would end up working for the Tooch. The Tooch is my Uncle Michael Tucci, for who my father has an unfavorable opinion of because of his gangster affiliations. My father suggested that I demonstrate my toughness in the Navy. My father is a Navy Veteran. I figured that I would show him up by joining the Marines. I didn't even know that the Marine Corps was a part of the Navy until Carmine told me. I am not certain, but I think that I was looking for some feeling of respect or approval from my old man. I could have gone to college. I am rather good with numbers. I could have gone to school to become an accountant. Nevertheless, I chose the Marines. I guess that even I could identify that I needed discipline more than schooling at that stage in my life. I figured that I could go to school on the G.I. Bill when I got out just as Carmine did.

In a short period of time, I discovered similarities between the Marine Corps and the Mafia. When it comes to loyalty, respect, honor and tradition, both organizations are alike. Both societies are keeping firm and devoted to a motive. The Mafia lives by the code of Omerta (code of honor and salience).The Marines live by a similar code. In addition, they both believe that problems in the ranks are taken care of from within. As the Marines say, "The few, the proud, the Marines," so are the Mafiosi the few and the proud.

The American people as a majority see the Mafia as a problem, achieving their goals only through illegal means. Trust me when I say that the Marine Corps is not much different. Many former Marines have a story to tell about how they were involved in an illegal operation. Such operations existed in a way to complete their mission and ensure complete concealment from the American people.

At the age of eighteen, I found myself in a state of pain and anguish that tested my resistance and character. I found myself removed from my haven and partaken on a journey that took me in a complete circle back to my family indulgence. My experiences involved two worlds. These two worlds fused together to form my life. In approximately six months, my struggle brought me home again where I waged war against a group of people that I swore to protect.

My struggles came without warning. My resolutions came within retribution.

One

I was always fond of visiting the Jersey shore and observing the scenery, ever since I was a little boy. It was always fun to comment on the strange characters and peculiar manners found on the boardwalk. I grew up at the shore. Every weekend my family and I would spend time at my Uncle Michael's beach house in Point Pleasant. I made myself familiar with every inch of that beach.

The July summers are hot, very hot. That summer day was no exception. Even after working as a bar back until three o'clock in the morning, I got up early and started my chores because I was to meet the guys at the park behind my house at ten o'clock and head for the shore. I started clipping the hedges. I really didn't mind doing it, but I wished that my father believed in trimming the hedges with an electric trimmer. It really was not that bad, because he kept the hand shears so sharp that there was some gratifying sense of doing the work by hand. I hurried, and finished the job in record time. I put the shears in the garage, threw my beach gear in the back of the Honda and headed down the street.

I stopped short of the park, watching the boys acting like mentally deficient people. They were smoking, drinking beer, shoving each other and swearing so loud that I could hear them from where I parked. There was Danny on a picnic table with a beer bottle in one hand and waving a handgun with the other. I gave myself a head slap, as I had an abrupt perception of me being with them making an ass of myself. Suddenly, I felt ashamed of them. I pulled up a little closer. Cars were slowly moving around me and people were seeing what was going on.

"Danny, get your ass out of here before someone calls the cops," I yelled as he started into the woods.

No sooner was that said when we heard sirens. The truth is I really didn't think that he would hurt anyone. He is crazy and often

1

portrays this type of behavior. I saw George Dills running toward me. "Ka-thunk" I heard, as he slapped the palms of his hands down on the car, rolled him self over the hood and entered on the passenger side.

"What's up, are we headed to the shore?"

"Let's go to the bar," George responded.

I swung the car around, got on Nottingham Way, and headed toward Trenton. The bar that George is talking about is the Casa-di-Roma, located on South Broad Street near the Court Building in beautiful downtown Trenton.

On route to the Casa, George and I made small talk about Danny Fuller. Danny did not attend high school graduation with us last month since the school system decided to hold him back. Danny is an imaginative individual who loves to be in the spotlight. He loves gangster movies and often portrays himself as a wiseguy. In a sense, George is not different, but more of a romantic. He does well with the girls. He even hooked me up with my girlfriend, Sally. George is deep, daring, and indomitable. He is dark with turbulent emotional energy. Nevertheless, he is powerful in eliciting reactions from others. The three of us have been friends since the third grade.

It was a short ride to Trenton. All the while, I wished that we were heading in the other direction on route 195 towards the shore. As I made my way down Hamilton Avenue, I was also wondering why George wanted to go to the Casa on a Sunday. Business is slow on Sundays, especially in the summer. Besides, I felt like I just left there. I worked late into the night as a bar back humping beer up from the basement and putting empty bottles into the beer cases as they came down the shoot. By the time Carmine closed and we cleaned up, I was dead on my feet. When I graduated from school, I searched all over town for a job. I was in desperate need, but a job was not easy to find. With no luck elsewhere, I asked my Uncle Michael for a summer job at the Casa, just until I decide what I was going to do about college in September.

I imagined that George wanted to go to the Casa-di-Roma with the sole purpose of making some money. George has done that before. He plays chess for money with the old men and hustles the younger guys at the pool. For only being eighteen years old, he is one hell of a pool player. Even though we are too young to drink alcohol, Carmine lets us in when he is working the bar. This is fine as long as we are only drinking sodas and we stay in the game room.

The Casa-di-Roma will arouse ones interest. It gives you an interesting yet indefinable feeling. The bar and lounge area has a 1960's setting with all the furniture, wall coverings and lighting original from that era. The dining room is something straight out of Italy, where every bit of the décor is imported from. Some might even say that the dining room is put together with unrestrained abundance. The game room is located in the back of the restaurant and has three pool tables, several dart machines, as well as chess and checkers game tables. The walls in the game room are covered with pictures of local sports figures. When I say local, I mean sport figures from Philadelphia and New York City. The Casa-di-Roma is packed on Friday and Saturday nights as the food could only be described as out of this world.

It was not even noon yet when we pulled up in front of the restaurant. When we entered, Carmine greeted us from behind the bar.

"Well if it ain't Joe Momma. Don't you get enough of this place?" Carmine said.

"Me, what did you do, sleep on the bar? George and I just stopped in to kill some time."

Carmine had the bar spotless. I found the floor swept and mopped, every liquor bottle dusted and stacked perfectly on the shelves behind the bar. He still had glasses and ashtrays drying on the bar before putting them away. I briefly peeked in the dining room and found it to be in excellent condition. One would never know that this place has been trashed the night before. I helped him clean up a little before my shift ended, but it was far from perfect. I guess that according to Carmine everything must be in good order and in clean condition. I think that Carmine's orderly ways has something to do with the way he was taught when he was a Marine. Everything must be spic-and-span you know.

"Look Joey, you know the rules. You and George must take it in the back. I will bring you sodas in a few minutes."

"Okeydokey," said George. "We appreciate it."

"Hey Carmine is my Uncle Michael upstairs?"

I have never seen the upstairs of Casa-di-Roma. Upstairs is where the Tooch has his office. I heard that it is plush, complete with a bar, hot tub, and the most expensive furnishings imported from Italy. I have personally seen grown men come down those steps with tears in their eyes. Rumor has it that some men have never returned.

"No Joey, he is at the shore and won't be back until Tuesday. That is where you two should be. What the hell are you two doing in Trenton on such a hot day?"

"We have business," George said.

"Monkey business," Carmine responded. "I hope that you two wannabe wiseguys aren't up to something."

George and I headed for the game room. There we found a couple old men back there playing chess. I paused and looked around, wondering what we were doing here on such a hot humid day.

"Hello Mr. Guido."

"Hello Joseph," old man Guido said, with his usual bright smile. "I heard there was a huge Fourth of July bash that your Uncle Michael put on at his shore house."

"Yes Sir, it certainly was." Still with a smile on his face, old man Guido proceeded to concentrate on his next chess move. I turned to George and asked. "George, what the hell are we doing here?"

"Come out back with me Joe Momma and I will tell you why we are here."

As we exited the game room and stepped out onto the patio, several people playing bocce greeted us. After exchanging hello's with everyone, I followed George to the end of the bocce court and we exited through the big wooden gate that led to Johnson Place. Johnson Place is a narrow street that runs along the back of the business on Broad Street.

"Okay George please tell me what the hell is going on?" He started to walk across the street and pointed in the direction of the Barrow Appliance Store and Warehouse.

"That is what is going on. We are going to hit it Joe Momma. You me and Danny are going to make a killing." We continued to walk and cut through some bushes and trees on the east side of the building toward the back. "You see this Joey. This wooded area cuts

4

off all views from the street and the only light is the street light in the front of the store area." George pointed to a large truck parked along the side of the building directly under a window. The truck was one of those big vans that movers use. "This is how we get in. We get on top of the truck and enter in that window."

"Wait a minute George. What about an alarm system?"

"I already cased the joint. My cousin installed the alarm system. He told me that the alarm system only covers the store area and the first floor. He said that he walked through the whole building and tried to talk Mr. Borrows into alarming the second floor also, but he would not budge. The second floor is where the warehouse is located. Trust me Joe Momma, I got a plan."

George was talking all the way back to the Casa. He was babbling about how the truck is always parked in the same spot every night.

He went on to discuss the details, which included what we are going to lift, where we were going to store the take and how we are going to move it. At the time, I really didn't pay too much attention. I figured that George was just talking out of his ass, as he usually does. When we got back inside the Casa, we found Carmine waiting for us with a couple of cokes in hand.

"What are you two up to?" Carmine asked.

I immediately recognized that Carmine was somewhat upset, and I knew not to mess with Carmine when he is upset. Even before he enlisted in the Marine Corps, he was a tough kid back on the block.

Immediately, I excused myself and made my way to the men's room. George started walking around the bar with exaggerated motions as if he was bad himself. Then he turned and said, "Fuck you Carmine."

I yelled, "Omigod George are you crazy?"

Carmine perceived George's behavior as being intentionally provocative and pounced on him. "Fuck me! Fuck with me," Carmine said as he slapped George around the bar like a rag doll. "I don't care if you screw up your life you little prick, but you leave Joe Momma out of it." Carmine threw George over a table and George got up and ran out the door. Carmine turned to me and yelled, "Get your ass out here Joey before I do the same to you."

George and I headed back to Hamilton in search of Danny Fuller. George was withdrawn as if he were in silent resentment over what just took place. As we drove down Hamilton Avenue, I noticed George lacking interest in the surroundings. He didn't even acknowledge the three young women that waved to us as we made a right onto Route 33. I knew that he was distressed and ill at ease, so I didn't say a word. We caught up with Danny on Paxon Street in Hamilton Square. He was chasing a cat across the street on someone's front lawn. He approached the car on the driver side, and he was drunk.

"Hey dude."

"Get in the car Danny," I said as I unlocked the doors and Danny got in the back seat on my side.

Danny reached over, tapped George on the shoulder, and said, "Hey what's up." George did not respond. "Hey Joe Momma, what's wrong with him?"

"Fuhgeddaboudit Danny, talk to me. Me and George, we thought the cops got you."

"No Joe Momma. I was long gone before they got on the scene."

"Jeez Danny, you better get rid of that gun. I hope you ain't got it on you now."

"No Joe Momma, I gots it hidden in some bushes, now are you gonna tell me how come George is clamming up?"

George lit a cigarette, turned and looked back at Danny. Danny could see the bruises on George's face. I put the car in drive and drove off.

• • •

I spent the next couple of weeks getting the cold shoulder from Carmine at work, and hanging out with my girlfriend Sally with whom I was getting very frustrated with when it came to sex, I was being defeated from every angle and approach that I would try. Oh, she would make out with me on the beach, in the car, or in the basement of her parents house. Nevertheless, if I took it too far, she would pull back. Her reason was that she was not ready, but I think that she was just saving herself for her wedding night. I often thought that maybe she was going to become a nun. My father raised me to respect a girl's wishes when it came to sex, but I have to tell you, she was sure making it hard. I was getting so annoyed with Sally that one Sunday afternoon, while attending Debbie's pool party, I put out the word to several girls that I was available.

I thought my efforts of making myself available were about to pay off the very next day when during eating dinner, the phone rang.

"I'll get it," I yelled. However, my grandmother picked up the phone, as she was already in the kitchen cutting some bread.

"It's for you Joey," grandma yelled.

I jumped from the table and asked, "Is it a girl?"

Grandma laughed. "It is I would be concerned because she has an awful deep voice."

I grabbed the phone from grandma. "Hello."

"Joe Momma, George Dills here, I need you to meet me and Danny at the park at 7:30."

"For what George?" I mumbled.

"The plan dude, we need to go over the plan for hitting the appliance store and warehouse."

"I haven't seen you idiots in two weeks and you still want to go through with this?"

"Don't punk out on us Joe Momma. I will see you at 7:30."

I finished dinner, helped my mother and grandmother do the dishes and I headed out to the park. There I found George drawing his plan in the dirt, like he use to do when we were kids playing army in the backyard. Danny was just sitting there eating an ice-cream cone that was dripping all over him. The first thing I thought was that these two simpletons are going to land us all in jail. I knew that Danny and George were in this for the quick score. However, for me, I wanted to take my share and pay tribute to my Uncle Michael Tucci. I wanted to show the Tooch that I was worthy of an apprenticeship position in the Trenton New Jersey, Tucci Crime Family.

"Hey, Joe Momma, you're late."

"Five minutes George. So let's hear what you got," I said. George went on to explain. Danny went on licking his ice-cream cone.

"Well, it's like this. I set a date for next Sunday, August 5th at 10:30p.m. Joe Momma, you will drive your car and either park on

Market Street or in the parking lot of the Casa. Danny, you will ride
with me in my van. The reason for this is that I will have my van
very empty leaving only one seat on the passenger side. I will pull
my van alongside the big moving van truck. Joe Momma, you will
stay with the van and load it as we hand you the merchandise. Danny
and I will climb up on the truck and enter through the window.
Danny and I will take about fifteen minutes to move the goods to the
window. During that time, you, Joe Momma, will have one of the
walkie-talkies and will be standing lookout. Joe Momma if you hear
anything, you give us a warning and get the hell out of there. Once
we have the goods to the window, I will hand them out the window
to Danny and he will drop them down to you. Keep in mind that we
are only taking small items such as, VCR's, TV's, tape players, video
cameras, microwave ovens, toasters, and whatever else we can find.
Any questions so far?"

"Yes," I said. "Are you sure about the alarm system?"

"I told you, I overheard my cousin talking about installing an
alarm system at the site. He was saying that he tried to convince Mr.
Barrows to include the alarm on the second floor, but Mr. Barrows
said no. He also said how he could get in through the window above
the truck with ease, anything else Joe Momma?"

"Where are we going to store the stuff?" I asked as I looked over
at Danny, who appeared to be half asleep.

"I have rented one of those self storage units over on Route 130 in
Cranbury. The man that we are going to unload the take to is going
to meet me there the next day, any other questions?"

"Yeah dudes," Danny mumbled. "Once we load the van, why
don't we go back in, and put another load on top of the moving van
truck. This way we can unload the first score at the storage unit and
go back for another load. We could make a double score."

George and I looked at each other with amazement as we both
thought that Danny was not paying attention to a word that we
said.

"That is brilliant," George said. "Whew, I like it, I really like it.
I will certainly consider it. What do you think Joe Momma?"

"I like it George, but I have something that needs to be
addressed."

"What is that?" George asked as if he knew what I was about to say."

I looked at Danny. "Danny, you need to leave the gun at home."

"Joe Momma is right," George said. "Danny, I agree with Joe Momma, no gun."

• • •

The following Wednesday at dinner, I noticed that my father was in one of his serious moods. "Joseph pass me the rigatoni."

"Here you go Dad," I said as I looked into his eyes. I looked into my father's eyes and he had that look. He gave me the look that he has when he has something on his mind. I just knew that I was about to hear something that I didn't want to hear. I knew I was about to get into a discussion that I did not want to engage in. Between my mother, father, and grandmother, I never knew what was going to be discussed around the dinner table.

"What have you been up to boy?" My father asked.

"I have just been hanging out with my friends, working for Uncle Michael and enjoying the summer before I made any decisions about college."

I jumped as my father slammed his hand down on the table. I watched my mother and grandmother grimace as my father yelled, "Your friends are losers, your Uncle Michael is a bum. What about you Joseph are you going to be like them? Are you going to grow up to cheat, hurt people, lie and kill or are you going to go to college and make something of yourself?"

"I'm going to go to college Dad. I am going to go to college, become an accountant and make something of myself."

"Good Joseph. I have a man coming over next week to assist you in filing papers for Rutgers. It is a little late, but there is still time to get the paperwork done so you could start school in September. Good, see me after dinner as I have a list of things that I want done around here."

• • •

9

I did much thinking over the next few days while cleaning out the garage, attic, and basement. I was having mixed feelings about pulling off the job. I didn't want to hurt my father, but I concluded that what my father didn't know would not hurt him. I figured that I would still go to college in September. College was important to me, but organized crime always aroused my interest. I viewed the appliance warehouse heist as an illegal act that would put me closer to my goal of being a wiseguy. Therefore, I decided to go through with it.

I worked both Friday and Saturday night at the Casa-di-Roma. Both nights were busy for a summer weekend. I worked hard keeping the bar fully stocked and the tables clean. I tried making small talk with Carmine, but he was still giving me the cold shoulder. It was as if he knew that I was up to no good and disapproved. I didn't like Carmine acting this way toward me, but I was fearful of confronting him. It was not as if we were really friends. Carmine Scalia is a few years older than I am and he went to school with my sister Roseanne. The Scalia family has a history with the Tucci and Mommalione families. That is why the Tooch, my Uncle Michael Tucci, hired Carmine to work at the Casa since his discharge from the Marine Corps and while he was attending school on the G.I. Bill. Carmine dismissed me early Saturday evening, which was fine with me, because Sally and I were leaving early for the shore Sunday morning.

One had to leave early for a day at the shore as parking is a real pain in the ass. It was already hot at 8:00 in the morning. August in New Jersey could be a real scorcher. It takes about forty-five minutes to get to the shore at Belmar from Hamilton Square. Sally slept all the way. I couldn't say that I blamed her. I would have done the same thing if she were driving.

"Wake up sleeping beauty, we are here," I said as I parked the car.

"Oh Joseph, I am sorry I fell asleep. Wow you got a great parking spot."

We unloaded the chairs and cooler from the car, bought our admittance badges for the day, and found a great spot on the beach. After we setup, we walked along the boardwalk for awhile before stopping for breakfast at the Oceanfront Restaurant. I ordered two eggs over easy with rye toast, sausage and hash brown potatoes. Sally ordered a fruit bowl.

While we were waiting for our order to come, Sally asked, "Joseph what are you going to do about college?"

"Don't worry about that," I said. "My father has a man coming over to the house next week to assist me with the admission forms for Rutgers."

We made small talk over breakfast. Mostly we talked about college. Not once during our conversation did Sally mention or inquire about her and I being an item in the time ahead. So, neither did I. Besides, I had things that are more important on my mind, specifically the job later in the evening. With breakfast done, I was determined to relish the day. There was not much more that I loved than being at the shore. We took a slow walk back to the beach and basked in the sun for a few hours. I took advantage of working on my tan. It doesn't take much for me to get a great tan. A few days at the shore and I have a tan that most people are envious of. While taking extravagant pleasure in the sun, a shadow cast over me.

"Joey, are you ready for some lunch?" I have potato salad and sandwiches in the cooler."

"Yes babe," I said. I couldn't resist Sally's potato salad, she makes the best potato salad in the world.

Sally touched my face. "What is the matter Joey? You have been awfully quiet today."

"I guess that I am just worried about us. What is going to happen to you and me Sally?"

Sally looked at me and smiled, "We will be alright Joey. We are both going to school locally. We will continue to see each other while we are attending school and we will continue to work on our relationship."

After lunch, we took a long walk along the shoreline. It was time well spent as we discussed in length our relationship, including sex. Sally made it very clear that she was saving herself until she is married. That was something that I certainly hated to hear. Nevertheless, I figured that is why God put bad girls on earth. We left the shore at about 3:30 p.m. Again, Sally slept most of the way home. After I dropped Sally off at her house, I headed home to get some rest myself before dinner, as it was one of the rare Sundays that we didn't have dinner at a relative's house. I felt that I needed the rest before meeting George and Danny at the appliance warehouse.

The streets were dark and desolate. I circled around the Casa-di-Roma, drove up Market Street and entered Johnson Place. Johnson Place is more of a service road than a city street, providing delivery and maintenance access to businesses located on Broad Street. Monday must have been garbage pickup day. The curbs were lined with everything from garbage cans to old worn-out furniture. Next to a hot water tank, belonging to times long past sat a couch that my grandmother would make my father and I come back for if she seen it.

As I parked the car in the rear of the Casa, I started to get a funny feeling in my stomach. I guess one would call it butterflies. I exited the car and made my way through the alley to Johnson Place. As I hid next to the old rusted fence that ran along the appliance warehouse, I tried to imagine what the old building was when erected two hundred years ago. Not five minutes had gone by when I saw the headlights of a vehicle. It was George and Danny. Just in time too, because I was getting eaten alive by mosquitoes, and sweat was starting to roll down my face and back. I knew it was him. Not by sight, but by sound as George's van has a horrible sound without equal or rival. I came to my feet and walked to the middle of the street. George pulled up alongside of me and Danny jumped out. He was jumping up and down, waving his arms like a crazy man.

"Hey dude."

"Hey Danny," I uttered as we walked to where George parked the van. George parked his van beside the large truck and removed a large canvas bag. The clanging sound of the contents of the bag told me that it was filled with tools. George opened the bag, removed a walking-talkie and tossed it to me.

The overgrowth of vines on the fence, trees and brush gave us good cover. The faint electromagnetic radiation from the 1920's corner street light gave us enough light to function.

"Joe Momma you take-up position in the front of the building. Danny and I will get up on the truck. I figured that it will take us about five minutes to open the window and enter." I headed for my position. "Testing 1-2-3, testing."

"George it's me, I hear you."

"Good Joe Momma. If you hear or see anything, give us a warning and beat it. Once Danny and me move all the swag to the window, I will contact you." George was already trying to talk like a wiseguy. Swag is Mob slang for stolen goods. Too bad he is not Italian.

I took my position in front of the building and waited what seemed like forever when in reality it was not even ten minutes. "Breaker breaker, good buddy," Danny said over the walkie-talkie.

"Knock it off Danny," I said. "Let's take our conversation seriously. Are you guys in?"

"Joe Momma, this is George. That is affirmative, we are in. I will check back with you in about twenty minutes, over and out."

The waiting was killing me. It was hot as hell and after a half hour, I was getting bored. I was getting antsy. I wished that I were up in the warehouse with them. I put the walkie-talkie to my mouth and was just about to make contact when I heard sirens, many sirens. Then I seen headlights from vehicles, many vehicles and they were racing right toward me. I pressed the button on the walkie-talkie, "Abort, abort, we got cops." I then put the walkie-talkie to my ear as I beat feet across Johnson Place.

"Joe Momma this is Danny. I thought that we were going to make all communication serious communication?"

"I am you dumb ass. We got cops. Get the hell out of there."

As I looked back, I could see flashing lights getting closer. I lost my bearings for a moment. I didn't even realize how far I ran when I found myself running down an unfamiliar alley that took me out on Broad Street. There I saw several cop cars and fire engines. Holy shit, they were responding to a fire call. That is why there were vehicles with flashing lights on Johnson Place. The police and firefighters were responding to the fire call in front and behind the building. They were not after us after all, I thought.

In a panic, I ducked into the doorway of two businesses. On the right side of me as I faced the street, was the Trenton Bail Bond Company. On my left was a Marine Corps Recruiting Office. The life-size poster in the window of Uncle Sam pointing at me scared the bejeezus out of me. After standing there for a few minutes directly across the street of the court building, I realized that the Casa was only one city block to my left. I took a deep breath and thought that George and Danny must be okay when suddenly the van came flying by me swaying from the left to right with the Trenton police in hot pursuit. In an attempt not to run into the fire trucks or police cars, George jumped the curb and smacked into a utility pole. Everything was happening so fast yet it seemed like slow motion. There was a sudden sharp and explosive noise. The impact was so hard that the van burst into flames. The force of the crash was so extreme that Danny was thrown from the vehicle and thumped his head on the pavement. His lifeless body lay in the middle of Broad Street. Then, George came staggering around the back of the van. Even from where I was standing, I could see that his face and shirt were covered with blood. He stumbled over to where Danny was. By now, a pool of blood formed around Danny's head. George dropped down to one knee and then the other. The cops watched with their guns fixed on George. George gave out a long and loud piercing cry. He reached into Danny's waistband, pulled out Danny's gun and cranked off two rounds into the air. The police never said a word. In a matter of seconds, George dropped from a hail of bullets. His body was slumped over Danny. I jumped from the doorway looking in the direction of my dead friends with my mouth wide open. I was about to let out a scream when a hand covered my mouth and pulled me back into the entrance of the two businesses. Carmine had a hold of me.

"Easy Joe Momma, I got you." Carmine had me wrapped up in his arms. I was shaking all over. "Relax boy and calm down." I wanted to talk, but I was lacking the faculty of speech. I stooped down against the door. After a few minutes, I was still shaking but I was able to talk.

"Carmine, do you think that they are dead?"

"Joe Momma, there is no doubt in my military mind. Those two boys are dead."

"How did you know that I was here?"

"Carmine knows everything. Look man take a few minutes and collect yourself then we got to get out of here." Carmine helped me to my feet. "Now get a grip boy. Then, we are going to make our way back to the Casa." Carmine was very patient with me. I thought that he was going to kick my ass for sure, but he did no such thing. After about three more minutes, we stepped out onto the sidewalk. As we did, a uniform police officer greeted us.

"What is going on here?" He asked. "Carmine Scalia is that you?"

A smile of relief came to Carmine's face. "Well if it isn't Tony Gianadda. Or, should I say Officer Gianadda? How long has it been?"

I knew this cop too. He hung out with my sister when they were in high school, and his father is friends with my dad.

"Since high school," Officer Gianadda said. "Carmine I heard that you joined the Marines and seen combat in Panama. I heard that you were even awarded a medal for bravery."

"No medal Tony, I did my part although others did more."

"It's good to see you Carmine but I must ask again, what's going on here?"

Carmine was cool. "Oh, we just come by to see what was going on. What happened here?"

"We were responding to a fire call. My unit responded to the back of the building on Johnson Place. As we came upon our location, that smashed up van over there sped out of the yard of the Barrows Appliance Warehouse and clipped the front of our unit, which led to a high-speed chase. Well, you could see the results." Officer Gianadda looked at me, and then he looked at Carmine.

"What's wrong with him?" He asked Carmine. "He looks like he seen a ghost. Could it be that his two friends lay dead over there?"

"Tony it was good seeing you after all these years, but we must go. Come on Joey we gotta get back to work." Carmine put his hand on my shoulder and gave Officer Gianadda a nod. We walked about fifteen feet when the walkie-talkie in my back pocket sounded off.

"Freeze, I am not done with you two yet."

"Uh-oh," I said.

Carmine looked at me, "Did your ass just speak or am I imagining things?" We did an about face and froze. "Don't say a word Joey. Let me do all the talking." We stayed put and Officer Gianadda came to us. As I reached for my back pocket to retrieve the walkie-talkie, Officer Gianadda drew his gun.

"Hands on your head." Carmine and I looked at each other and did what Officer Gianadda ordered. Officer Gianadda came within five feet of us. "Up against the wall." Again, we did what he commanded. Officer Gianadda searched us both for weapons. The only thing he found was the walkie-talkie.

"Carmine had nothing to do with this officer. He came looking for me after he spotted my car parked at the Casa-di-Roma, and found me hiding. I was involved. Me and my friends George Dills and Danny Fuller were burglarizing the warehouse. We panicked when we seen the flashing lights and heard the sirens. We thought that you were coming after us."

Carmine interrupted. "Shut up, Joe Momma. Tony listens to me. Do you know who this is? This is Joseph Mommalione."

"Mommalione," Officer Gianadda said. I know that name. Do you have a sister named Roseanne?"

"Yes Officer, I do."

Again, Carmine interrupted. "That is not what's important here Tony. Joseph Mommalione is the nephew of Michael Tucci."

Officer Gianadda had a look of fear on his face. Carmine are you telling me that this boy is related to the Tooch, the crime boss, the Godfather of Jersey!"

"Yes," Carmine said. "All the above and I work for Mr. Tucci. Look Paisano I am asking for a favor on behalf of the Tooch and the Mommalione family. I am asking you to look the other way on this one."

Officer Gianadda looked back at all the interruption of public peace. By now, the fire was in full force, smoke filled the air and the firefighters and police offices were very busy. In addition, reality really set in on me. My friends were dead and the thought of it brought tears to my eyes.

Carmine looked at me. "Stop crying Joe Momma. If Tony doesn't cooperate here, you will really have something to cry about; so will he."

"I don't appreciate the comment Carmine. I have every right to arrest Joseph Mommalione for accessory. I could arrest you too for the threat and obstruction of justice. But, I won't do either on account of us being Italian and all. However, I have two conditions. One is that I take Joseph home and explain this incident to his father. I owe him that respect. Mr. Mommalione and my father grew up together, and they are still friends. If my father finds out that I did not inform Mr. Mommalione, he will kill me. Two is that you put in a good word to Mr. Tucci on my behalf. I am not looking for any gesture of appreciation or expression from Mr. Tucci. I just want him to know, that's all."

I looked at Carmine and knew what he was thinking. The proposal from Officer Gianadda had nothing to do with being an Italian thing. Officer Gianadda was scared of the consequences of not doing what Carmine requested, but he wanted to save face. I didn't like the part of Officer Gianadda taking me to my father, but somehow my father would have found out anyway and I will have caught hell for it. Shit, even if I were not involved, I would be guilty by association in my father's eyes. In about an hour, the events of the night will make its way to Chambersburg the Old Italian neighborhood that my mother and grandmother come from. Five minutes later, my parents will know. Anyway, I figured what Officer Gianadda offered was better than the alternative. However, little did this stupid know that my Uncle Michael will put him in his file bank and use him for some deed later? It is not that the Tooch will not be grateful for what Officer Gianadda is doing for me; it's just the way it is.

"Okay Tony." Carmine said. I agree and thank you. How are we going to do this?"

Officer Gianadda handed Carmine both walkie-talkies, took off his hat and wiped his forehead with a handkerchief. "Damn it's hot. Carmine you take Joseph and wait for me at the Casa. My shift ended when I got the call for the fire. I will make my verbal report to the shift supervisor and request my banged up unit be towed to the garage. I will meet you guys at the Casa in about thirty minutes. Joseph will drive his car. Carmine I will ride with you to the Mommalione house. Afterwards I will need a ride home. We could catch-up on old times. It is getting late. I suggest you call Mr. Mommalione so he is expecting us."

Officer Gianadda went in one direction. Carmine and I went in another. "Listen to me," Carmine said. "Let's walk and you listen while I talk. The first thing that you have to come to terms with is the fact that your friends are dead. They are dead and you are not. Be grateful to God for that. When we get to the Casa, I'm going to do like Tony suggested. I am going to call your father. You wait by the car and think. When we get to the house, Tony is going to take your father into the kitchen and explain what went down. You had better come up with some answers. You had better admit your participation and show a strong feeling of regret for what happened. And, you better come up with some quick and convincing answers for what you are going to do with your life."

With some hesitation, I asked, "Carmine are you going to tell the Tooch what happen?"

"I have to. I gave Tony Gianadda my word." Carmine said with some regret. "Besides, your Uncle Michael would be highly upset if I held this from him."

I wondered what I feared most, a beating from my father and being thrown out of the house, or loss of respect from Uncle Michael. When we reached the Casa, Carmine went inside to call my father. I waited by the car reflecting on what happened. Did I desert my friends? Did I overreact causing the fatal outcome? My hands were shaking and I felt like I had to vomit.

Carmine came out after about fifteen minutes of talking to my father. I looked at him and he shook his head. "What did he say? How is the mood?" I asked.

"Your father said that he is coming here. He is on his way." Carmine then turned to greet Officer Gianadda, as he approached.

I sat on the hood of my car while Carmine and Officer Gianadda talked. It took about a half hour for my father to arrive to the Casa. He parked the car and approached the others without even looking at me. I couldn't hear what they were saying, but I stayed put. The meeting was short. My father shook their hands and approached me.

"I'm sorry Dad."

"Just shut that mouth and listen to me Son. I told your mother and grandmother that you found out what your friends, George and

Danny were up to and you came to the scene to try to talk them out of it. They do know that both boys are dead. Now that is your story and stick with it. That pertains to everyone. People will form their own opinion, but so what. Carmine and Tony gave me their word that they will tell no one. The only one outside this circle that will know the truth is your Uncle Michael. Now get home. We will talk when I get home from work tomorrow. By the way, it is late so I instructed your mother and grandmother to go to bed. Therefore, you do not have to face them when you get home. Oh, one more thing, I am taking off from work on Wednesday and we are going to talk to the Navy Recruiter. You want to be a tough boy, let us see how tough you are in the Navy. This is your third strike in the last four years with breaking the law. This one could have cost you your life or time in prison."

I knew that my father was serious about me joining the Navy. I knew that he was fed up with me and I was confident that if I failed to do what he said, I would be kicked out of the house. I also knew that my Uncle Michael would not intervene on my behalf. Maybe the Navy would not be so bad.

My father and I arrived at the house at about the same time. We both entered without saying a word to each other. I went directly to bed and had a hard time sleeping. Every time I started to doze off, I saw the faces of Danny and George. Although I went to bed very late, it seemed to take forever for morning to come. It was eight o'clock when I heard my bedroom door open.

"Joseph, are you awake?" I heard in a low voice. "Joseph, it is your mother." I didn't answer. She leaned over and kissed me on the top of my head as I pretended I was asleep.

I waited about fifteen minutes before I got out of bed. I took my time brushing my teeth and taking a shower in hopes that by the time I got downstairs, my grandmother would be out with one of her senior friends getting their hair done or something. After my shower, I was dressed, made my bed and straightened up my room. I exited my room only to find grandma waiting at the bottom of the stairs.

"Joey, get your culo down here. I made pancakes and bacon."

I trotted down the stairs and kissed grandma on the cheek. "I'm not very hungry Grandma, but thanks anyway."

"You never mind Joey. You sit and eat. I got questions."

I took a seat at the kitchen table and grandma put a stack of pancakes and crispy bacon in front of me. "Pray tell, what happened last night?" I heard that your two friends were killed and that you were there?"

I dove into the breakfast, as I was starving. "Well Grandma, I will tell you what I know. My friends were up to no good. By no good, I mean they were burglarizing the Barrows Appliance Warehouse and it went bad. I tried to talk them out of it, but they would not listen."

"Are you sure that you were not involved?"

"I am sure Grandma. I tried to stop them and I was not successful. I was on my way to retrieve my car from the Casa when I heard sirens. You know the rest."

"Joey you know that people are going to talk."

"That is my story Grandma and I am sticking to it," I said as I got up from the table. "Thanks for the pancakes, Grandma. Now, I got to go."

"Where are you going in such a hurry?"

"I have an appointment with Sam."

"Who in the hell is Sam?" Grandma expressed.

"He is my uncle."

"Joseph, you don't have an uncle named Sam."

Two

I found the recruiter's office to be somewhat frightening, as well as lacking liveliness, and charm. Not that a Marine recruiter's office should be charming, but this place was dull. The sign read, "Take a seat and someone will be with you momentarily." I sat in the outer room of the store front office facing Broad Street thinking of the events of the night before. Only a stone throw away is where my good friends George and Danny died. I thought that if they were important people, someone would put up a memorial. As it is, they were not important people so the soiled spot where the van crashed must serve to keep their memory alive.

A young man entered the door. I figured that he was maybe two years older than me. His uniform consisted of blue trousers with a red stripe running down the outside of each leg. His shirt was khaki and it had two stripes with crossed rifles under the stripe on each arm.

"May I help you?"

"Yes Sir, my name is Joseph Mommalione and I want to join the Marines."

"Please step into my office Mr. Mommalione." I followed him into his office and took a seat. I was impressed in the way he addressed me. No one ever called me Mr. Mommalione before. "Mr. Mommalione do you have any identification that includes proof of age and education?"

"Yes Sir," I said as I handed him a large envelope containing my driver's license, social security card, birth certificate, and high school diploma.

"You do not need to call me sir. My name is Corporal Graeber. I will be right back. I am going to make copies of these vital papers. Once I stamp them as certified copies, I will have you fill out some forms and then you will meet with Gunnery Sergeant Stubbe and he will talk to you."

As I waited, I looked around Corporal Graeber's office. The walls were covered with Marine Corps memorabilia. The Corporal had a small desk. One wall was lined with the file cabinets and there was a table along the back wall. The table was larger than the corporal's desk. I took a seat when Corporal Graeber entered the room. He sat at his desk, punched holes in all the copies of my papers and made up a file.

"Mr. Mommalione will you please take a seat at the table and fill out these forms I have for you?" I did what the Corporal asked. It took me about twenty minutes to complete the forms. I handed Corporal Greaber the forms and it took him just as long to look them over as it did me to complete them.

"Are there any questions?" I asked.

"No Mr. Mommalione. Everything seems to be in order. Now, if you will follow me. I will introduce you to Gunnery Sergeant Stubbe."

Gunnery Sergeant Stubbe wore the same uniform, but he had three stripes on each arm and under the crossed rifles there were two more upside stripes. I figured the older the Marine, the more stripes he has, and the more stripes, the bigger the office and desk. His office was dark. He sat behind a big gray metal desk with an American flag to his right and a Marine Corps flag to his left. The wall had wooden paneling with a big Marine Corps emblem centered between the two flags. Gunnery Sergeant Stubbe looked over the file that the Corporal made up on me. While he did, I looked around the office. The walls were covered with prints of Marines in Combat. There were no file cabinets, or tables in the Gunnery Sergeant's office. It finally came to mind that the whole place looked like the office of a private detective that you would see in a black and white American classic movie.

"Please have a seat, Mr. Mommalione."

"Yes Sir," I said as I sat directly in front of the Gunnery Sergeant's desk.

"Mr. Mommalione, in any language the word Marine defines something more than a soldier. As you could see in the pictures around my office, a Marine is a warrior. Tell me why you want to be a Marine?"

"Sir, I just want to be a Marine that's all. If I am going to join a branch of the service, I might as well join the toughest."

"Mr. Mommalione, in looking over your forms that you filled out, I see that you did not complete the items asking for knowledge, skills, or abilities. I realize that this is a tough question for someone eighteen years old, but I was wondering if you may have overlooked anything pertaining to this."

"Sir, could you give a for instance?" I asked.

"The name Mommalionme, is that Italian? Perhaps you speak Italian?"

"Yes Sir, I am Italian. However, the only words I understand of the Italian language are the bad ones."

"Gunnery Sergeant Stubbe laughed and said, "I also see that you did not express an interest in any military occupations. We have several jobs in the Marine Corps. An example of some jobs include, clerical, truck drivers, mechanics, instructors, cooks, infantry, intelligence, supply, and many more."

I paused for a moment and responded with, "Sir as I stated. I just want to be a Marine. Infantry will be just fine with me."

The Gunnery Sergeant made some notes in my file. "You will be taking some tests next week. You will take more tests when you enter boot camp. I think that we will let the results of those tests dictate your placement. I am still not convinced why you want to be a Marine Mr. Mommalione. Was your father a Marine?"

"No Sir, my father was in the Navy."

"Again Gunnery Sergeant laughed, "And you want to show him up by joining the Marines. Am I correct?"

"Something like that," I said.

"When would you like to leave for boot camp?"

I looked at the Marine Corps calendar on the wall. "Sometime this month would be good." However, I have one request Sir. I would like to go to boot camp at San Diego instead of Parris Island, South Carolina."

"Mr. Mommalione, this is an unusual request. We send all of our recruits from the east coast to Parris Island. Despite what you may have heard, I can assure you Parris Island is no harder than San Diego."

"That is not the reason," I said. "I have my reasons for wanting to go to San Diego."

The Gunnery Sergeant made a notation in my file. "Please excuse me, Mr. Mommalione. I will be back shortly."

I walked around the office while Gunnery Sergeant Stubbe was out. I looked at the prints on the wall and wondered how I could hold up in a combat situation. I knew that there was talk about America going to war in Kuwait. I took my seat when the Gunnery Sergeant entered the room fifteen minutes later. He took a piece of paper from his desk and wrote something on it

"I will grant your request for San Diego, Mr. Mommalione. Here is the address and room number for the Federal Building in downtown Trenton. You will need to be there at 0800 hours on Friday August 10, 1990, to take a series of tests and your medical physical. Report back here to me at 0800 hours on August 15, 1990. At that time, I will set a date for you to report to boot camp at the San Diego Recruit Depot. I wrote it all down. Do you have any questions?"

"Yes Sir. What time is 0800 hours?"

"That is eight o'clock in the morning for you civilians, Mr. Mommalione."

I thanked the Gunnery Sergeant and Corporal for their time and assistance. I assured them that I will keep my date for my tests and physical and that I will see them on the fifteenth. When I exited the building, I avoided looking at the spot where George and Danny were killed the night before. I turned left, went to where I parked at the Casa and then headed for the shore at Belmar.

I arrived home just in time for dinner. Everyone was sitting at the table when I entered the dinning room. A day of rehearsing how I was going to break the news about my enlistment made me hungry.

"Where have you been all day?" my father asked.

"Are you okay, Joseph?"

"I am fine Mom." I said as I sat at my usual spot. "I have something to say before we start dinner. To answer your question Dad, I joined the Marines today."

"Oh no Joseph," my mother cried.

"It will be fine Mom. For a long time I let this family down. I am going to go in the Marines and when I get out, I am going to go to school on the G.I. Bill."

My grandmother slammed her hand down on the table. "Damn, now I get it. You were talking about Uncle Sam when you said that you had an appointment with your uncle named Sam."

"What in the hell is she talking about?" my father asked.

"Never mind that for now. When are you leaving?"

"I am not sure Mom. I am taking tests and my physical on the tenth. On the fifteenth, I meet with the recruiter and he will give me a date. It will be sometime this month. The good news is that I will be attending boot camp in San Diego."

"Oh that is good news. You will be close to Roseanne and Mark. I will call them right after dinner. In addition, you must let me know when you get a date so I could call everyone. We will have a going away party. I must tell you Joseph, I am not happy about this Marine Corps enlistment. I hear that we may be at war in Kuwait soon."

"Please don't call my sister and Mark just yet Mom. I prefer that nobody knows for now. I want to get a reporting date first and no party Mom."

"The hell with that," Grandma said as she jumped from the table. "This is news. I got phone calls to make."

"Sit down," my father yelled. "We will respect my son's wishes. And keep silent about this until he is ready to let everyone know. After all, he is a man now. Now let us eat before everything gets cold."

"I heard that the boys will be laid out for viewing on Wednesday at Urso Funeral Home," Grandma said.

The next few weeks were difficult. I attended the viewing of Danny Fuller and George Dills. I couldn't believe the guilt I felt. Moreover, people looked at me as if they knew that I was involved. Both boys were laid out at the Louis Urso Funeral Home on Nottingham Way in Hamilton Township. Urso's is not far from where George, Danny, and I grew up. The Funeral Home always reminded us of a haunted house. The house is a very large old farmhouse. Bushes run along the long driveway that led to the garages in the back. One day when we were eleven years old, we crawled along those bushes and entered the basement of Urso's Funeral Home from an outside entrance. Once we were in, we opened the door to the room where the embalming is done. Danny dared us to go in, so George and I did, with Danny following. Behind a curtain, we discovered the very dead and naked body of Mr. Ippolito. His skin was gray, and his lips were black. I will never forget what happened next. We all stared at Mr. Ippolito as if we were in shock. Then, at the exact moment, the three of us let out a scream and ran around the room bumping into each other and knocking things over. We looked like the Three Stooges. In confusion, we ran up the stairs and ran down the red-carpeted hall past the viewing rooms and out the front door.

I attended both viewings during the day so not to confront many people. My parents and grandmother went to the funeral home at night. I did not attend the funerals.

On the tenth, I reported to the recruiter's office at the Federal Building and took my test and physical. On the fifteenth, I met with Gunnery Sergeant Stubbe. He informed me that I would report for boot camp at the San Diego Recruit Depot on August 25, 1990. I told my mother that she could call my sister and tell her, but no going away party. I had daily talks with my mother concerning my enlistment. She had been spending a lot of time watching the news at work and was troubled by the American buildup of troops in Saudi Arabia since the August 2, 1990 invasion of Kuwait by Iraq. My father on the other hand kept his thoughts to himself.

This time in my life was definitely marked by disturbance. To make things worse, Sally's parents had forbidden her from seeing me or talking to me. She did have a chance to tell me that her parents where convinced that I took part in the burglarizing of the warehouse with Danny and George.

I was now spending most of my days and nights at the shore wandering like a lost soul. I love the shore, but by then, not only was I anxious to be a Marine, and see my sister and her husband, Mark, in San Diego, but I was excited in knowing that I was going to see the Pacific Ocean. I was ready to move along in my particular course in life.

I met my mother, father, and grandmother for dinner at the Casa on the eve of my departure for boot camp. They each ordered their usual Friday night fish fry for dinner. I broke the habitual course of action by ordering Spaghetti Carbonara, which is known as the pasta breakfast meal. It contains pasta with bacon, olive oil, cheese, onions and eggs. Some people like grated parmesan sprinkled on top, but not me. My father looked at me as if I was nuts for my dinner selection. I had expected him to have a talk with me about my decision to join the Marines, or at least address what I was to expect, but thus far he said nothing. I hoped that it didn't come during dinner.

By then, the word was out about me leaving for the Marines and people were coming to the table to wish me luck. This went on during dinner too, so it was hard for us to make conversation amongst ourselves. I could see that my father was getting a little frustrated with it. It made me feel good considering most of these people had suspicion about my involvement with Danny and George on the night they were killed. I was disappointed that my Uncle Michael was not in the restaurant. I knew that he was in the city on business, but I was hoping that he would be back from New York to see me before I left. We were eating dessert when Carmine took a seat at the table.

"Hi Carmine, you handsome devil," Grandma said.

"Where are my manners?" Carmine said as he stood, approached mom, then grandma kissing them on the cheek. "Mr. Mommalione would you mind if I keep your son for awhile? I am really busy here and could use a hand."

"Not at all," my father said. "Joseph, why don't you excuse yourself and give Carmine some help."

My mother looked at me. "Joseph what time do you have to be at the Federal Building in the morning?"

"I have to be there at eleven o'clock. I will be home early Mom."

We had a pretty good night considering business is slow in the summertime. It was about eleven o'clock when Carmine sounded off with last call. At eleven thirty, he closed the bar. He then cracked open a couple of beers.

"Follow me, Joe Momma." I followed Carmine to the game room and took a seat as Carmine slid a beer in front of me. "Now put on your listening ears because I have a lot to say."

"What about cleaning up?" I asked.

"Don't worry about that. I want to review the elements of boot camp with you. I want you to know what you are in for. First, I would like to say that I think you are doing the right thing by going in the service. Your father is proud of you for making this decision."

"Well he sure has a funny way of showing it," I said. "Maybe he is disappointed that I didn't go in the Navy like he did?"

"I don't think that is it at all Joe Momma. I think that he will be proud of you no matter what branch of service you join." Carmine had a smile on his face. "Technically speaking, you did join the Navy. The Marine Corps is a part of the Navy."

"What," I said with a confused look on my face.

"The Marine Corps is not its own branch of the armed forces. It comes under the jurisdiction of the Department of the Navy. You will learn about that in boot camp during history and traditions classes. I learned many things in boot camp. Besides history and traditions of the Corps, I learned about leadership, as well as discipline and courtesy. I learned about rank insignia, and interior guard. I learned how to march. Boy did I learn how to march. Drill for foot troops is the first step to learning to work as a member of a team. I learned about clothing and equipment. I learned about first aid, sanitation, and hygiene. I was educated in small arms to include the M-16 rifle as well as familiarization with the pistol, machine gun, and other infantry weapons. I almost pissed my pants the first time I tossed a hand grenade as well as during gas mask training. We had demonstrations in demolitions, mine warfare and camouflage. Boot camp training touched a little on basic communication and navigation. I learned how to shoot a rifle and kill without regret by using a bayonet in hand-to-hand combat. Boot camp is tough Joe Momma. It is based on massive regimentation. You will experience an extreme change in your freedom as if you are in prison. You will be isolated where humiliation is a way of restraint. All of this treatment is designed to give you a new identity."

I must have had a dumbfounded look on my face as Carmine snapped his fingers. "I'm sorry," I whispered. "I can't believe how you remember all this."

Carmine picked up my beer. "Take a drink. I gotta tell you Joe Momma. What I learned in boot camp will remain with me for the rest of my life. Boot camp is not designed to make you become an expert in combat. That will come in the form of infantry training after boot camp. But if your job assignment takes you in a non-combat or non-infantry direction, you will have learned enough in boot camp to survive if the shit hits the fan." Carmine stopped talking and looked at his watch.

"Crissake Carmine don't stop now. I don't care how late it is. Tell me what Marine Corps recruit training is really designed to do and what I am to expect from the first to last day there."

Carmine took a moment to take a well deserved sip of his beer, cleared his throat and continued. "Let me sum it up by saying that boot camp training is intended to install physical stamina with emphasis on mental attitude. Besides, all the things I said that I learned, I also learned respect for authority, and the men and women around me. I learned the broad and basic rules, which it takes to be a Marine. It is hard to explain unless you have been there. But, I could give you the course of action that you will follow in each phase of training. I will get started once you run and get a couple more beers."

I only took a couple of sips out of my beer, but I did exactly what he said. I was so intrigued by what Carmine was telling me that I ran to get the beer. "Whew, Carmine this is good stuff you are telling me. Please continue."

"Okay Joe Momma, here we go. When you arrive at the San Diego Airport, you need to find the Marine Corps Recruit Podium. Look for the military information area. There you will submit your orders and board the bus to the Recruit Depot. You may have to wait an hour or so before you board the bus, but I suggest that you report to that location as soon as you arrive. You will be told this when you go to the Federal Building tomorrow. Busses roll into the Recruit Depot all hours of the day and night. Do not bring anything other than the clothes on your back. You will be able to keep your wallet, but everything else will be boxed and shipped home within a couple hours of your arrival. The D.I. (Drill Instructor) will enter the bus before everyone is allowed off. He will give instructions. I must inform you that he will do a lot of yelling. There will be much confusion. He will order each of you to take your position on the painted yellow footprints. After he walks up and down the ranks, you will enter the Receiving Barracks. You will immediately be instructed to stand in line for haircuts. After you get your head shaved, you will be taken to a room. There you will stand in front of large tables where you will be ordered to empty your pockets. Do not wear any jewelry. Once this is done, the D.I. will come around and inspect. You will be amazed what some of these idiots bring with them. After that, you will be ordered to strip down to your birthday suit and enter a line for clothing. After you receive your clothing, you will go back to your spot at the table. You will be instructed what to put on. Next you will box all your civilian clothing, and address the box so it could be mailed home. Wear clean underwear because your mother will be getting it in the mail. Then, you will be in another line to get your I.D. picture taken. If you are lucky, you will get to make a short call home. You will only be in Receiving Barracks for a day or two."

"Could I bring money?" I asked.

"Yes, but I wouldn't bring much. When you are done at receiving, you will enter Forming, where you will spend about a week. Forming is a period of adjustment. In Forming, you will learn to move as a platoon. It is a hectic week. You will take medical and dental exams, draw rifles, and take I.Q. tests. In Forming, you are given your general orders. Study your general orders, and memorize them. Any questions so far?"

"No Carmine," I said. I was too confused to ask any questions.

"Once you complete the first week of Forming, you will be assigned to a platoon where you will meet your Drill Instructors. The D.I.'s are tough sonofabitches. They will cuss and kick your ass. The D.I. is now your mother, father, and God during your thirteen weeks of basic training. His language is vulgar and he is unemotional. This is the beginning of Phase I. In Phase I, you are introduced to the obstacle course, and classes. Classes consist of first aid and Marine Corps history. You will do a lot of drill, running, and physical training also known as P.T. You will take part in your first physical fitness test. There is much training in care for your uniforms and gear. Your progress is measured by inspections. Bayonet training is given in Phase I. Bayonet training comes in the form of Pugilstick fighting which is designed to teach you without injury."

"What the hell is a Pugilstick?"

"A Pugilistic looks like a giant Q-tip. One end represents the butt of the rifle and the other the bayonet." I didn't get it, but Carmine expressed amusement as he told me this. "You will see Joe Momma. Your second phase of training will bring more classes on cleaning and breakdown of the rifle. This segment of training will take you to the rifle range. This is where you will qualify and earn your shooting badge. It is necessary that you qualify. You will spend about two weeks at the rifle range. During the first week, you will be snapping in. And, the second week is for firing the rifle and qualifying. From the rifle range, you will go to mess duty. I think that mess duty lasts a week. The hours are long and the work is tiring, but in a way, it is a break from training and the constant harassment from the Drill Instructors. Infantry training is also conducted in this Phase. You will get to wear combat gear, learn to use a gas mask and throw a hand grenade. Infantry training includes training in combat formations, small arms, and camouflage. Pay close attention to infantry training. If your M.O.S. is not infantry, you may not receive any additional infantry training. As I stated earlier, what you learn of infantry training in boot camp will be enough to save your ass if the shit hits the fan even though basic training touches very little on destroying the enemy."

"What is an M.O.S.?" I inquired.

"M.O.S. stands for Military Occupational Specialty. Before you leave boot camp, you will be assigned an M.O.S. Say you become a Supply Technician. When you leave boot camp, you will attend training in Supply. If you find yourself in a war and you are in a convoy delivering supplies and your convoy comes under attack, you are going to grab your rifle and kick ass. Boot camp infantry training will enable you to react to and defend yourself or survive in the field, no matter what your M.O.S. is.

"What was your M.O.S. Carmine?"

"Well I'll tell you. I am proud to say that I was a Grunt, an infantryman."

"I hope I'm a grunt," I said.

"One thing you need to remember. Every swinging dick and shirt in the Marine Corps is a rifleman. Honor, courage and commitment are installed in every Marine no matter what your M.O.S. is. You will receive your Military Occupational Specialty in your third phase of training. Other than water survival training, things lighten up some in Phase III. You will find there is no formal physical training. Your physical training comes more in the form of morning runs and hand-to-hand combat training, as well as a lot of close order drill for drill competition and final parade. You will spend much time in preparation for the Company Commander inspection. There is much concentration and groundwork for final exams and graduation. A few days will be spent on maintenance duty and clothing alterations. Platoon pictures will be taken, and your biggest challenge will come in the form of the crucible."

I raised my hand as if we were back in school. "What is the crucible?" I whispered as if I dare to ask. Again, Carmine chuckled.

"You will see. The Crucible is a three-day ordeal that tests your physical and mental endurance. Look Joe Momma, I just threw a lot at you. Keep in mind that training is conducted by the Drill Instructor through such tactics as degradation, pain, scolding, humiliation, and molding. Boot camp is not easy. As I said, boot camp is like being in prison with the Drill Instructors acting as the jailer. Boot camp is brutal and intense, causing tremendous pain both mentally and physically on the recruit. To be a Marine, you have to believe in yourself. If you make it through Marine Corps Basic training, you can make it through any obstacle that you experience for the rest of your life. No matter if you go to combat, or serve in peacetime, you are ready and willing to defend America. You are even ready to die for Country and Corps if necessary. As a Marine, you are a part of the finest fighting organization in the world. Former Marines remain loyal to the Corps forever, and a former Marine is one bad motherfucker who is respected by all."

Before we said our goodbyes, Carmine explained the few jobs that are held by recruits in a boot camp platoon.

• • •

"Joseph it is time to get up. Wake up and what is that dog doing in your bed."

"What Mom?" I said as I put the pillow over my head.

"Wake up, you need to be at the recruiter's office at the Federal Building to get sworn in and pickup your orders and ticket for your flight to San Diego."

I got up and stumbled around my bedroom until I got my bearings. I made my bed and put out a pair of jeans and cotton shirt. As I made my way to the shower, I could hear my mother yelling at the dog to stop begging for bacon that my grandmother was cooking. I stayed in the shower for about twenty minutes. No sooner did I step out of the shower and wrap a towel around my waist when my mother entered the bathroom.

"Jesus, Mom, I'm almost naked here."

"You never mind, Joseph. You are not naked; you have a towel wrapped around you. Besides, you have nothing that I have not seen before. You will always be my baby," she said as she started to cry.

"What Mom, what's with the tears?"

"You are my son, my only son and now you are going off to the war."

"I'm not going off to war Mom. I am going off to the Marine Corps. We talked about this."

"There will be a war, Joseph. I watch cable news. There will be war in Kuwait. Our boys are already there."

I hugged my mom and wiped away her tears. "Don't worry Mom. I promise you that I will not be going to war. I will be hanging out with Roseanne and her husband in California."

Roseanne is my older sister. She was married a year earlier and moved to California where she is working as a hairdresser while her husband Mark is going to school and working part time.

Just then, my grandmother entered the bathroom. "Jesus Christ," I said. "Don't I get any privacy around here?"

"Don't you swear at me? Did you come home drunk last night?"

"No Grandma, I did not. I was with Carmine and he was filling me in on what I am to expect at basic training."

My grandmother is a character, all ninety-five pounds of her. She is always on the go. I think that she has more energy than all of us. My father should take lessons from her.

"Farsi Bello."

"Okay Grandma. Now you go downstairs and I'll doll myself up."

By the time I got dressed and made my way down to the kitchen, my mother had a full breakfast waiting. It was as if it was my last meal or something. In a way, I guess it was. I looked around for my dad and did not see him. I heard the dog barking outside and when I looked out of the window, I saw my father cutting the bushes. Him and his obsession with those damn bushes.

"Mom, is Dad going to eat?" I said as I dove into my stack of pancakes. My pancakes were only the appetizer.

"No, Joseph, he is being a little quiet. I think that we should just leave him be now."

I had no intentions of bothering him. All I was thinking about for the moment was eating.

"What should I pack for you?" My mother said.

"You need not pack anything Mom." Carmine said that I was not to bring anything with me. He said that they will only make me send everything home."

I was about to dive into the bacon and eggs when my father came through the kitchen door. "Eat up Marine, I am going to drive you to the Federal Building."

I figured that finally we were going to have that father to son talk concerning my enlistment. "Okay Dad," I said as I shoveled more food into my mouth.

"Stanley Wozniak's grandson left for the Marines last year and he went to South Carolina for boot camp." Grandma said.

"Oh Mother!" My mother said. "It is the most amazing thing. Joseph told the fine recruiter that his sister lives in San Diego and they asked Joseph if he would prefer to attend boot camp in San Diego so he could be close to Roseanne." My mother thought that the Marine Corps must be a compassionate organization for honoring my wish.

It was about fifteen past ten when we left for downtown. Traffic was light because it was Saturday. I had to be at the recruiter's office in the Trenton Federal Building at eleven o'clock to take my oath and pick up my orders as well as my airline ticket. I already had the flight information from when I met with Gunnery Sergeant Stubbe the second time. I was scheduled to fly out of Philadelphia at twenty minutes past six in the evening. I was happy because it was a direct flight to San Diego with one stop in Chicago. My dad drove and we took my car. I have a 1986 Honda Accord. My dad liked driving it because it was fully loaded and newer than his. It is hardly a Goomba's car, but he liked it. My sister left the Honda to me when she moved to San Diego.

My dad did not say two words all the way downtown. We pulled up in front of the Federal Building, and parked. "Dad I will call you at home when I am done."

In his stern voice, he responded with, "I will be right here when you get out Son."

All I could think of was my father while I was with the recruiter. I never saw my father cry. I think he was doing his best to hold back the tears. It was about one o'clock when I was finished. On the other hand, I should say thirteen hundred hours, which in military time is one o'clock in the afternoon. Sure enough, my father was waiting in the same spot where he had let me off. He was leaning against the car smoking a cigar and talking with two men with whom he works.

As I approached the car, one of the men said, "Hey kid, I hear that you joined the Gyrenes. I was in the Army, and went to Vietnam too."

"Yes Sir," I said. "I leave for the Marine Recruit Depot in San Diego in a few hours."

"San Diego, what are you a Hollywood Marine?" The other man said. Both men started laughing as my father and I got in the car.

"How did it go?" My father asked.

"It went fine Dad," I said as he drove off. My father made his way to I-295 South when we headed out of Trenton.

"Dad, where are we going?" I asked with some concern.

"We are going to the airport. I know that we will have a few hours to kill, but we will have lunch and that will give us some time to talk and I can fill you in on some things."

"But Dad, I didn't say goodbye to Mom and Grandma."

"Don't worry about that, I will say goodbye for you. Besides, this is how a man does it."

I just sat there and shut up, as I wanted to avoid an argument with my old man. It would have killed me to leave that way. It took about forty-five minutes to get to Philadelphia from Trenton, so I just closed my eyes and eventually fell asleep.

I woke up when we got to the airport. I had no luggage to check in. All I had was a small bag containing a toothbrush, shaving cream, razor and soap that I got at the recruiter's office. I think the Red Cross gives them out. I was very sad not to say goodbye to my mother and grandmother. After we got through security, I gave my dad my watch and school ring to hold.

"Okay Son, I will hold these, now wipe those tears from your face or I will give you something to cry about."

"I just miss mom that is all."

"I understand Joseph; now let's get something to eat."

Of course, my father picked the only Italian restaurant in the airport. As we approached the restaurant, I was shocked when everyone started yelling. There was my mother, grandmother, and some of my aunts, uncles and cousins. There were about thirty people there. I couldn't help it, I just busted out in tears. I looked at my dad, and he was in tears too. Everyone gathered around, patting me on the back and smothering me with kisses and hand shakes. I was face to face with Grandma Tucci when the dust settled.

"Grandma who set this up?" I asked as she handed me a glass of red wine. She gave me a palms up as if to say, "I don't know."

"Your Uncle Michael did," my mother said.

I went up to Uncle Michael, gave him a kiss on both cheeks and thanked him. He gave me a big hug and patted me on the back.

"When you get out, you come and work for your Uncle Michael."

"The hell he will," my father said.

We all sat down to eat, and boy did we eat. We started with wine, antipasto and baskets of Italian bread. Then, the waiters brought out the family style bowls of spaghetti and meatballs. We sat around eating, laughing, and drinking. Time went quick. Before I knew it, it was time to go. Everyone walked me to the gate. Mom was really struggling with me leaving.

"Now remember, your sister and Mark will meet you at the gate when you get to San Diego." I hugged my mother so hard that I felt like I was going to break her, she is so skinny. Sometimes if I look at her the right way, she looks like a kid. My mother has the body of a teenage girl, and she is so pretty. I remember that all the boys I hung around with while growing up had the hots for her.

"I love you Mom." She just looked into my eyes without saying a word.

"Hey boy, Marines don't cry. And remember, you are a part of the Navy," my father said as we hugged.

"Watch out for the Culattina. California is loads with gay guys," Uncle Michael said.

Everyone in my family thinks it is okay to say something bad or bad words, as long as they say it in Italian. I cannot speak much Italian, but I know enough to figure out what people are saying. I am good with the parolaccia (dirty words).

I said goodbye to grandma last. "Tell Carmine I said that I will make him proud."

Take care of the ceffo," grandma said as she pinched my cheek. I laughed. This morning she told me to doll myself up, and now she is telling me to take care of my ugly mug. "Joseph where is your Saint Christopher metal that I gave you?"

"I took it off Grandma. Carmine told me not to wear any jewelry so I took the Saint Christopher metal off and put it in my wallet. Carmine told me that we are allowed to keep our wallets."

"Put it on for now, Saint Christopher will carry you. Whoever shall behold the image of Saint Christopher shall not faint or fall on the day."

I did as she asked and then gave my grandmother a hug and avoided looking back as I walked through the gate. I could hear everyone yelling. The tunnel to the plane seemed like it was a mile long. I was starting to get a little nervous because it was the first time that I was on a plane. I found my seat and sat down, trying to hide my tears. I looked out the window when we started to taxi down the runway, knowing that my family was still hanging around until the plane was out of sight.

Three

I held on for dear life as the plane took off. After my stomach did a couple of flips, I realized that flying was not as bad as I thought it would be. I had a window seat and thought that it was somewhat cool to be able to look out while flying. I enjoyed looking at the buildings and roads from the sky as we took off. The feeling that I got was better than the feeling I got from any of the rides on the Jersey shore boardwalk at Seaside Heights. I immediately fell asleep. The plane was only half-full, and there was no one sitting next to me so I was able to stretch out a little. I figured that not too many people flew from Philadelphia to Chicago on a Saturday night. I was asleep less than half an hour into the flight. Falling asleep may have had something to do with getting to bed late or maybe it was because I had a few too many glasses of wine before I boarded the plane.

I had a dream that was deviating from the customary dreams I have. I dreamt that I was walking along the shore. This beach was not Belmare, Point Pleasant, or Seaside Heights. I am not sure that I was even in New Jersey. In this dream, I was walking along the beach with my feet in the water. There was no boardwalk, or buildings in sight. However, a large pier complete with amusement rides stood off in the distance. The rides were still, and the only sounds I heard were the waves crashing against the shore. There was only one person in sight. As I was walking along feeling the water break against my legs, I noticed a woman walking toward me. She had long black wavy hair and wore a long black dress. I stood still until she came within an arm length away. She was a plain looking woman who judging from the lines on her face had a rough life to some extent.

"Hello Joseph. Your friends are waiting on the pier for you."

"She spoke with an accent and quality that indicated emotion. "My friends?" I asked.

She placed her left hand on my back and guided me forward as she pointed toward the pier with her right arm extended. "Go Joseph. Go to your friends."

I took a few steps toward the pier. When I looked back, she was gone. The next thing I remember about the dream was that I was walking on the pier and came face to face with Danny and George.

"Hey dude. How come you didn't come to our funerals?" Danny said.

George interrupted with, "Joe Momma you are about to embark on a journey that will take you to faraway places. In a three day period, you will experience more in life that most men will experience in a lifetime. Now we need to go. You will not see us again, but we will give you a sign that everything will be okay. Oh yeah, Joe Momma, you are going to meet two new friends to take our place."

"Wait, wait," I cried out and both of them started to fade. Then there was a booming sound as the pier starting to crumble beneath me. I started to fall. I looked down only to see debris from the pier floating in the water. Then there was a thump as I hit the water and I woke up just as the plane landed. We were in Chicago. I was startled and covered with sweat when I awoke.

"Are you okay young man?" An elderly woman sitting in the isle seat asked.

"Where did you come from?"

"I was sitting here all along, since I boarded the plane."

"No you weren't," I said.

"Oh yes I was young man. You had a bad dream. Who are George and Danny? You were talking to them."

"They are friends of mine."

"Well good luck to you young man. This is where I get off. Where are you going?"

"I am going to San Diego to attend Marine Corps boot camp."

"Once again I wish you good luck." She looked back and smiled as she exited the plane. I wondered where she came from. I swore that no one was sitting next to me. What a weird experience. First, I had the dream and then the woman sitting next to me came from nowhere. I was happy to be on the ground.

We sat for about forty minutes in Chicago. I stayed on the plane and watched people get on. I noticed that a few of the young people that boarded had those little blue bags. I figured that they would be attending Marine Corps basic training in San Diego, since the Navy had basic training in Great Lakes Illinois. The flight attendant came to me and asked me if I would like a coke and snack since I was sleeping when she came around while we were in flight. I told her that I would like that very much. I tried to keep my mind off my mother, as well as the dream about Danny and George that I just had.

Again, I held on for dear life when we took off. I started a little conversation with a woman sitting next to me. She was in Chicago on business. We talked a little about her job and family. It turned out that she has a son that is a year younger than I am. She seriously expressed her desire for her son to go to college. She admired my decision to go into the service, but she said that was not an option for her son. Not with the war that was about to come. All this talk about war made me think that maybe I should have reconsidered about college. The flight attendant came around and served dinner about two hours into the flight. I really was not hungry, but I took the beef dinner anyway and ate some of it.

Once more, I fell asleep for a couple of hours. It was about 12:30 in the morning, California time when we landed in San Diego. I was happy that I awoke well before we landed and realized that I had no more dreams. I was excited and scared at the same time.

I was excited that I would be seeing Roseanne and Mark, but scared to enter basic training.

I was anxious to get off the plane, but I had to be patient. It seemed that everyone in front of me had an item to retrieve from overhead storage. Finally, I was able to move.

"Goodbye and I wish you well," the woman sitting next to me said.

I shook her hand as she extended it to me, and said thank you.

My heart beat rapidly as I exited the plane and walked down the tunnel. Roseanne ran to me and jumped in my arms. She started kissing me all over my face, just like my mother and grandmother do.

"Sorry I kept you up so late," I said.

"Never mind that Joey, she slept most of the time while waiting," Mark said.

"Hi Mark, it is good to see you."

"Mark gave me a hug and three pats on the back. "Hello kid. On the other hand should I say hello Marine."

"I'm not a Marine yet. That reminds me, I need to find the Marine Corps podium to check in."

Roseanne grabbed my arm. "It is downstairs. Come, we will take you there. Do you have any luggage?"

I let Roseanne lead the way. "No luggage, Carmine told me not to bring anything."

"How is Carmine doing?" Mark asked. Mark and Carmine graduated from high school together.

"Oh, he is doing fine. He is going to school and working part time for the Tooch at his restaurant."

"You should not refer to Uncle Michael Tucci as the Tooch," Roseanne said.

I found the Marine Corps station and checked in. A Marine told me that I had about an hour before the next bus left for the Recruit Depot.

"Sorry for the short visit Sissy."

"That's okay Joseph. I am glad that I got to see you. Mark and I will come to your graduation and I was thinking of making a trip home with you when you start your leave from boot camp. You do get to go home on leave after you finish the three months of boot camp, do you not?"

"I'm sure that I do. The recruiter told me that I would get at least ten to fourteen days before I'm assigned to my duty station for training. Carmine told me the same thing. So I assume that I will get leave at the end of boot camp. Unless…"

"Unless what, Joseph? Unless America goes to war and they send you directly from boot camp to your next duty station. I hear more and more about war in Kuwait."

"Relax Roseanne. Just like I told Mom, I am not going to war."

We sat around and talked. Mark got some cokes out of the machine. Before I knew it, there were a lot of people gathering around the Marine Corps check in station holding those little blue bags of bathroom items that we received from our recruiter's office. I threw mine in the garbage. A few minutes later, the call came out over the loud speaker for all Marine recruits to assemble in front of the podium.

I looked at my sister and her at me. "Well you guys, it is time for me to go." I hugged my sister very hard. "Here Sissy hold my Saint Christopher medal for me."

"Joseph, why don't you put your Saint Christopher metal in your wallet along with my card that has our phone number on it. You are allowed to keep your wallet, are you not? You call us as soon as you can." Mark then gave me a hug. "You take care of yourself my brother. Make your sister and me proud of you."

"I love you little brother." Roseanne always called me little brother even though she is only three years older than I am. Roseanne and I always got along when we were younger. I cannot remember one time that we ever had a fight or even a heated discussion. I always felt blessed to have a sister like Roseanne. She kissed me on both cheeks and we said our good-byes. I think that I felt all cried out by then, because I didn't shed a tear. Roseanne was rubbing her eyes as she and Mark turned and walked away.

I took my place in line. A Marine checked my name off a list and directed me to the bus. I was surprised when I saw a Grey Hound bus waiting for us. I guess that I was expecting a military type of a bus. I got on the bus and took a window seat toward the middle. I was surprised to see how many recruits had luggage with them. I guess that no one informed them that they would be sending every item back home. The recruiter as well as Carmine informed me to travel light. I was looking out the window when I heard a quiet voice.

I looked up to see a scrawny kid standing there with a suitcase in hand. "Scuze me," I said.

"I was wondering if it's okay that I sit here."

"Yeah, take a friggin load off." This guy looked at me as if I were from another planet. I presumed that he did not understand what friggin means. Hell, I am not sure that I really know what friggin means.

After he struggled to secure his suitcase, he took his seat and extended his right hand for a handshake. "Hi, I am John Pryce."

"Hello John Pryce," I said as we shook hands. "My name is Joseph Mommalione. My friends call me Joe Momma for short. It is a pleasure to make your acquaintance. John didn't your recruiter tell you about not bringing any luggage?

"Yes he did, but my mother insisted. You know how mothers can be."

"Oh yeah, I know how mothers can be all right. Where are you from John?"

"I am from Northern California."

"Why did you join the Marines?" I asked.

"I don't really know. I have been weak and pushed around all my life. I guess that I just wanted to prove myself to my family and friends, so I joined the Marine Corps."

"Why did you join the Marine Corps?"

"Oh pretty much for the same reason," I said.

"I doubt that very much Joe. Joe, do you think that boot camp is going to be as tough as they make it out to be?"

"That depends on who they are. I happen to know from the best, that boot camp is not only going to be physically tough, but it is going to be mentally overwhelming as well. Just stick with me John Pryce and you will make it." Little did I know that I would never see John Pryce again?

I looked around at all the guys as the bus started to move. Some were sitting still with a blank look on there face, but the majority of them were smoking and joking. I knew that would change soon. The bus trip was short as the base is next to the airport. Almost before I knew it, the bus approached the gate where the sign read, "U.S. MARINE CORPS RECRUIT DEPOT, SAN DIEGO, CALIFORNIA." It was very dark outside. I quickly saw some Quonset huts and H shaped buildings before the bus stopped at a building marked receiving. The Receiving Barracks looked like a Mexican style building similar to the Alamo or something to that effect.

I looked over at John. He looked sick. "Hey are you okay man?"

"I don't know Joe. I don't feel so good."

"Try and stick with me when we get off the bus," I told him as he retrieved his luggage.

44

Again, I looked around the bus. Most of the guys looked tough. I could tell that a good number of them came from the bad part of town and had nothing going for them. They had attitudes. The quiet ones looked like psychos. I am not an authority on the subject, but I could imagine men entering the Navy, Army, or Air Force come from all lifestyles, but the young men on the bus with me, with the exception of John Pryce and maybe one or two others, came from back on the block. The majority of the guys looked as tough as the mean streets. They looked like they were without a doubt, Marine material. There was even a guy sporting motorcycle club colors on the back of a leather vest.

The bus came to a stop and just sat there. I looked out the window and seen a group of Marines huddled against a wall. They all had clipboards in their hands and wore Smokey the Bear hats so I assumed they were Drill Instructors.

Carmine Scalia told me that buses come through the Recruit Depot gates all hours of the day and night. However, he did not tell me about the waiting on the bus once we got here. Maybe it was the Drill Instructor's way of messing with our minds. If that was the case, I think it was working because it had become noticeable that it got quieter with each minute of waiting.

Well, this is it. There was no turning back now. In a few minutes, all hell is going to break loose, I thought. One more time I looked around. The recruits lowered there voices from yelling to mumbling. As I turned to face the front of the bus, the door opened and a Drill Instructor entered. This Marine stood about five feet nine inches tall and looked as solid as a mountain. He took a few minutes to talk to the bus driver. Some of the recruits were still chattering when the Drill Instructor yelled out, "Shut the fuck up. You are presently at the Marine Corps Recruit Depot at San Diego California. And, this is Receiving Barracks. You shitbirds have twenty seconds to get your fatbodies off this bus and plant your motherfucking feet on the yellow shoe prints outside. Now move it, assholes."

Everyone grabbed suitcases, bags and whatever belongings they had with them and like cattle, herded out of the bus. I didn't realize that another bus pulled up behind us until I got off the bus. I wondered where this one came from as I thought that we all got on the one bus at the airport. Perhaps that explained the long wait before we exited the bus. Recruits ran from both buses at the same time. This made total confusion out of the situation. We were all bumping into each other as we tried to find an empty set of footprints. The lack of order made me loose sight of John Pryce. Eventually we all firmly positioned ourselves on the yellow feet, which put us in perfect aligned ranks.

Several Drill Instructors walked up and down the ranks with one yelling out information. "Listen up you scummy pigs. You are about to enter Recruit Receiving Barracks. This is your first calculated action in becoming a part of the finest fighting organization in the world. You sorry hunks of crap will be under my command and the command of the other Drill Instructor's here for the fist day of your miserable lives in basic training. After that, you..." He paused, turned and then approached a recruit. "What the fuck is that on your back?"

"This is my biker club colors," the recruit said.

The D.I. was furious. He grabbed the recruit by the throat and yelled out. "When you address a Drill Instructor, the first word out of your filthy mouths will be sir, and the last word out of your mouth will be sir. Is that clear, scum?" Everyone just froze. We really didn't know what to do or what to say. "I can't hear you." We were still silent as if we were traumatized. "You ladies better answer me before I kill this motherfucker."

All together we yelled, "Sir, yes Sir."

No one was looking straight ahead. We really lacked the meaning of standing at attention. I noticed all the recruits intensely sweating. The hot summer night didn't bother me. I was used to the heat from living in New Jersey. I always say that people do not realize how hot and humid it gets in Jersey. Jersey heat is a bitch. It is common for summertime temperatures in New Jersey to reach the mid to high nineties. I could recall many August days reaching the one hundred plus mark.

My eyes made their way back to the D.I. and the recruit with the leather vest. The recruit was sweating like a pig. The D.I. was not. The D.I. just stood there with a mean look on his face, staring at the recruit. Then, he broke his silence. "So you had the balls to wear your motorcycle club colors to boot camp? You must think that you are a real badass?"

"Sir, no Sir," the recruit replied. The D.I. cold cocked the recruit in the side of the jaw and the recruit went down. The D.I. was on him like a wild animal that just took down his prey. He jumped on the recruit and stripped him of his colors. He threw the vest to the ground and started jumping on it.

"Now listen up you motherfuckers. We have one emblem here and that is the eagle, globe and anchor. The Marine Corps emblem represents our capability to fight in the air, on the land, and at sea. We have one color here and that is green. All you bastards will become green amphibious monsters. Is that clear?"

"Sir, yes Sir!" The D.I. then pulled out a big combat knife and cut off the recruit's ponytail.

I knew that I was in for a world of shit right from the get go. I got some comfort in reading the sign over the building.

"TO BE A MARINE
YOU HAVE TO BELIEVE IN:
YOURSELF...YOUR FELLOW MARINE
YOUR CORPS...YOUR COUNTRY...YOU'RE GOD
SERMPER FIDELIS."

I could recall Carmine telling words of that nature, but Carmine was not here. I realized that I was on my own.

"Now let me continue ladies. After a period of approximately one day at receiving barrack, you will be turned over to your instructors. They will have you for the next thirteen weeks. Is that clear?"

We all sounded off with, "Sir, yes Sir."

The D.I. took us inside where we stood in front of tables. He instructed us to take everything out of our pockets, suitcases, or bags and place them in front of us. The D.I. then came around with a wastebasket, looking for contraband. Contraband included gum, candy, obscene pictures, etc. Wallets and wedding rings we could keep. We had a choice, either the illegal items were dropped in the wastebasket or it was boxed up with our civilian clothes to be sent home. Once that was done, we were lined up for a more vivid act of destitute. Several barbers were waiting to shear off our hair. It seemed like every sixty seconds, a bald recruit came running out and down the hall for identification portraits and then back to their position at the tables, where we had box lunches waiting for us. After we received our uniforms, the remaining hours spent in receiving were pretty much hassle free. We were even issued stationary as well as stamps and were told to write letters home. The only time we went outside is when we were taken to chow. We ended our time at Receiving Barracks by drawing towels, soap, shaving cream, razors, clothing marking kit, brass cleaner, and shoe polish. During my first day at boot camp, I managed on less than three hours of sleep, had my head shaved, took a cold shower, and waited two hours in line for utilities to cover my nakedness. Utilities are the Marine Corps version combat uniforms. I believe the Army calls them fatigues.

• • •

Some of us were sitting on our sea bags, and some of us were sitting on the floor. We were wearing utility trousers, combat boots, sweatshirts, and had our covers tucked in our belts. It was 1300 hours in the afternoon. I sat on the floor reading my guidebook trying to decipher rank and insignia. All of us were tired and silent. All the recruits were wondering what was coming next, when our speculating was interrupted by the explosive noise of a steel garbage can that was thrown down the middle isle.

"Grab your socks and grab your cocks. You have ten seconds to fallout. Move it, move, move, and move! Get out on the yellow footprints recruits." We did not hesitate, nor did we analyze what the D.I. meant by socks and cocks. We knew what he meant as we clutched our sea bags containing clothing and beat feet outside.

After standing at attention in the late afternoon heat, I saw two D.I.'s approach from my right. As they got closer, I could see that one was a Sergeant and one was a Staff Sergeant. The recruits around me didn't have a clue what was coming next, but not me. I knew what was next. We were about to be picked up by our Drill Instructors, and enter a week or so of Forming. Forming is a period where the recruits become suitable to enter training. Carmine told me about this. He said that it is not only a period of processing, but the week of Forming is also designed to prevent the recruits to think and act for themselves. The week of Forming is designed to pound a new way of thinking into our minds. The endless shouting and staring down is to get us to think as one. During my first day at boot camp, I immediately started to learn a new vocabulary. Such words as head call, eyeballing, running your mouth, maggot, shitbird, sweet pea, are used daily. Sometimes all these words are used in one sentence or breathe.

The sun was hot, as we were now standing at attention on the yellow footprints for about a half an hour, but I was okay. Some of the other recruits were not, but they did their best to hang in there. All sixty plus of us stood there with a great deal of anxious concern. The D.I.'s came closer and stopped to talk to the Receiving Barrack D.I. They talked for about ten minutes. I didn't realize it yet but I was having my first experience at playing the hurry up and wait game.

Both of the D.I.'s started walking up and down the ranks. One of them stopped at a recruit two rows in front of me.

"What is your problem maggot?" The D.I. asked.

"Sir, I have to go to the bathroom Sir."

"How could you refer to yourself as I? Did I not just call you maggot? Well answer me maggot."

"Sir, the Private has to go to the bathroom Sir."

"Private, you are not a Private. Marines who complete boot camp are called Privates."

"Sir, yes Sir, the maggot has to pee Sir!"

The boy was shaking very much. I felt bad for him. It was clear that the D.I. was just messing with him. Too late, the recruit went allover himself. The D.I. went berserk and started beating the recruit with his clipboard. "You little bastard, you pissed all over yourself. Everyone listen to me. From now on, this recruit will go by the name as Bedwetter. Sergeant Rippen will you please have this motley crew fall in?"

With that command, Sergeant Rippen grabbed three recruits and pulled them up front. "On my command people, I want each of you to fall in on the three recruits, and one behind the other. Put your sea bags on your right shoulder, extend your left arm forward placing your left hand on the shoulder of the recruit in front of you. Now move it!"

We looked like three rows of elephant's as we headed down the road. The sound of the D.I. calling cadence echoed off the buildings that surrounded us. "Leh rite a leh, ado leh rite a leh." Once we arrived at our barracks, we lined up in front of our bunks.

"My name is Sergeant Rippen. You are now proud members of Platoon 3105, a seventy man platoon, which is part of a series of four platoons. When you address a Drill Instructor, the first and last word out of your mouth will be sir. We are now your mother and father. There is two ways of doing things around here. There is your way and the Marine Corps way. Guess what way you turds are going to do things?" Under your bunks, you will find a footlocker. Pull them out and place them in front of the bunks. When I give the word, you will remove from your sea bag, two pair of utility trousers, two pair of utility shirts, all skivvies, all T-shirts, all toilet articles, one sweatshirt, all socks, one pair of combat boots, one pair of sneakers, writing stationary, towels, your guidebooks, brass cleaner, shoe polish, two cover's and marking kits. Place all items on top of out footlocker. Once that is done, you will be storing your sea bags in the walk-lockers. Later this evening, you will receive instructions on how to store items in your footlocker and how to properly make your bunks."

All the while the Junior Drill Instructors were talking to us, the Senior D.I. just stood there with his hands on his hips. Carmine told me that they like to play good cop, bad cop routine, with the Senior D.I. being the good cop. No matter what Carmine told me, the Drill Instructors were extremely disgraceful and grossly offensive and I knew that the worst was yet to come.

The Junior D.I.'s came around with the list of items on their clipboards to make sure we took the proper items out of our sea bags as instructed. There was a lot of yelling going on. Some recruits didn't get the assignment right and were getting cussed out for it. Once we stowed our sea bags, we were instructed to stand at attention in front of our bunks and the insults began by the Junior D.I.'s as they walked up and down the barracks, spitting out words intended to ridicule every recruit, even assigning nicknames like, Buttface, Dogbreath, Mary, Snowflake, Stickman, etc.

Oh God, please do not let him stop at me, I thought. A sense of ease came over me when I figured with sixty recruits in the squad bay, what were the odds? The D.I. walked by me three times and on the forth, he stopped, turned and looked directly in my eyes with his nose about a half of inch from mine.

"Are you eyeballing me asshole?"

"Sir, no Sir," I yelled out as loud as I could.

"I think that you were, you fucking asshole. What is your name, you worthless maggot?"

"Mommalione, Sir." With that response, I caught a right punch to the stomach that buckled me over.

"Stand tall recruit. That was just a little reminder that the first word out of your mouth when addressing a Drill Instructor is Sir. So your name is Momma-lee-own-ee?"

"Where are you from Momma-lee-own-ee?"

"Sir, the recruit is from Trenton, New Jersey Sir."

"Are you Eye-talian?

"Sir, yes Sir."

The D.I. looked around and addressed the entire squad bay as he waved his arms in the air and said, "So what we have here is a dago from New Jersey. Are you a tough guy? Are you in the Mafia? Do I have something to worry about here? Today, Momma-lee-own-ee, I would like an answer today."

It was as if I froze for a second or ten when I received a slap upside my head. "Sir, no Sir." The Drill Instructor has nothing to worry about Sir." I grimaced, as I was not sure if I should have put a Sir on the beginning of my last sentence, I was expecting another slap in the head or something to that effect.

"What do your friends back in Wop land call you?"

"Sir, the recruit's friends call the recruit Joe Momma, Sir!"

"Well here, you are called Meatball. Recruit Meatball is what I will call you. Is that clear?"

"Sir, yes Sir!"

"I like what your friends call you. I think that you would make a good mother. On the other hand, should I say house mouse? Maybe I will make you our house mouse. The duty of the house mouse is to care for the cubical where the Drill Instructor on duty stays. You know, clean up after us, and make our coffee and things like that? It is a very important job, usually given to the smallest recruit. How high is your shit stacked, Recruit Meatball?"

Again I stood there with a puzzled look on my face.

"How tall are you recruit?"

"Sir, five feet and ten inches Sir!"

"How about it Recruit Meatball would you like to be my house mouse?"

"Sir, no Sir! It is the recruit's intention to be the bearer of the platoon guidon Sir."

"The Platoon Guidon? That is usually reserved for the most physically superb recruit. Hey Meatball, how do you say you are a worthless maggot in Eye-talian?"

"Sir, one would say ciucciami il cazzo, Sir." This Redneck was really pissing me off by now so what I told him was to suck my dick. At least that is what I think I told him. My Italian is not as good as it should be, especially under stress.

"Okay Meatball, it is yours to lose. When I march this mob to chow this evening, you take up the position of bearer of the Platoon Guidon. Don't fuck it up. I am giving this honor to you because I think that you got balls. How do you say balls in Eye-talian?"

"Sir, the word would be conjones Sir."

The Platoon Guidon is the recruit who carries the platoon flag. This is done during drill or when the platoon is in movement. The flag is red with the platoon number printed on it.

I was surprised that the D.I. didn't ask me how I knew about the Platoon Guidon. I was happy that this honor was bestowed on me and couldn't wait to write home and tell everyone, especially Carmine. Nevertheless, I think that I was just as happy to see the D.I. move to the other end of the squad bay and hear him say to another recruit, "So what do they call you numbnuts."

I was starving when the order came to fall out for chow. Our second attempt of marching as a platoon was no better than our first. I took my position as Platoon Guidon. We mobbed out awkwardly and clumsily to the Drill Instructor yelling "leh rite a leh,ada leh rite a lehada.." The cadence did not sound like left right left, but we got the message. At least most of us did. I looked down at my feet when the D.I. barked out, "Your military left asshole."

When we entered the mess hall, we were asshole to bellybutton as we waited holding our medal trays to our chest and taking baby steps as we move forward. We were warned that we only had a few minutes to eat, and that we had to eat every single crumb on the tray, or else. I had the privilege of being first to enter the mess hall. As I did so, I stood face to face with Platoon 3105 Senior Drill Instructor. We got our chow and stood at attention in front of our seats until the last man arrived. We then waited for two orders. One order that we waited for was to sit, the second order that we waited for was to commence eating. We ate like animals as we shoveled our food into our mouths. One recruit attempted to swat away a fly and the D.I. was on him like a fly on shit. "Let my flies eat," he yelled. "I am watching you, you fuck up. I am watching all of you. You make a wrong move and I will get your ass." One by one, we finished eating. We were under the watchful eye of one of the Junior D.I.'s as we turned in our trays, and ran out the door to formation.

We didn't do any better in our attempt to march on our way back to the barracks. We spent the remainder of the evening learning how to make our bunks, mark our name on our cloths, and how to properly place our clothes and items in our footlockers.

• • •

During the remainder of our time spent in forming, we drew rifles, took a series of aptitude tests, and received medical and dental exams. The morning physical training and the abundance of verbal abuse, as well as the occasional physical abuse were brutal. I quickly realized something that Carmine told me. The Junior D.I.'s took on the role of the bad guys. The Senior D.I. had the higher rank and took on the role of the father figure.

The twelve days of forming became one mass so that the constituent parts were beginning to work together. We were all placed in permanent squad positions and started to move as one. In the evenings, we learned how to salute, make our rack, and mark our clothing. We learned our general orders, and we got time to write letters home. Another thing we did in the evening was to learn the basics of the manual of arms and close order drill. The D.I.'s made us repeat a single movement over and over again. When one recruit referred to his rifle as a gun, the D.I.'s made him run around the squad bay holding his rifle above his head with one hand. With his other hand, he held his crotch. He had to shake each item with each hand as he yelled out, "This is my rifle, this is my gun, this is for fighting and this is for fun." We had to name our rifles. I named mine after my girlfriend Sally. On the command of the D.I. before lights out, we had to say good night to Chesty Puller. Chester Puller is the most decorated Marine in History. He rose from the rank of Private to General. One of his famous quotes was, "ALL RIGHT THEY'RE ON OUR LEFT. THEY'RE ON OUR RIGHT, THEY'RE IN FRONT OF US, THEY'RE BEHIND US...THEY CAN'T GET AWAY THIS TIME."

• • •

Moving onto our first phase of training, I knew that the time will come when the D.I.'s will feel that sterner treatment, more than verbal abuse will come in the form of kicking ass and taking names on an individual basis. I was determined that it would not happen to me.

It was a Sunday, shortly into our second week of formal training when the D.I. called us up to the front of the squad bay and had us sit on the floor. Sunday's were normally a little relaxed. On Sunday's we received an extra hour of sleep, went to mass, did our laundry, cleaned the squad bay, shinned our shoes etc. I watched the Senior D.I. as he was holding a group lesson in-between our long daytime classes that we attended thus far. "You have been here for only a little more than three weeks and five of you are already gone. You are months away from becoming Marines. You will need to work even harder as you complete your first phase of training. You need to lean on each other more and work as a team. Some of you are already showing informal leadership skills. Follow the example of Recruit Meatball here. In just a few weeks, Recruit Meatball has proven himself as Platoon Guidon and holds the highest score on the Physical Fitness Test, as well as the aptitude tests."

I was shocked when he mentioned my name. I was proud that I was making a name for myself in such a short period. At the same time, I had doubts if it was such a good idea to draw this much attention on myself.

The Senior D.I. went on to say, "I know that the morning runs and physical training are trying, but the more you sweat in peacetime, the less you will bleed in wartime. I got news for you. It looks like some of you are going to get the chance to go and kill some Ragheads. There is no doubt in my military mind that we are only a few months away from war with Iraq, and some of you will be going. Those of you that do go will have a good chance of coming home alive and in one piece because of your training. It will not be your duty to die for your country. It is your duty to make the enemy die for his. Over the remaining time at boot camp, you will become killers. That is your job people. You are a killer, and you will remain killers for the rest of your life. That is why you joined my beloved Marine Corps. Go over there with your head up you're ass and I guaranfuckintee you, you will become a casualty. Maybe your M.O.S. will not take you to war, but remember this. No matter what your military occupational specialty is, you are a rifleman first, so be ready. In Vietnam, many a Marine who was not grunt had to pick up a rifle and kill Gooks. Once you complete basic training, you will be assigned a M.O.S. and receive training in the M.O.S. If you are lucky enough to be infantry Marines, you will be assigned to an additional four to six weeks of infantry training. Pay attention to detail recruits."

I went back to my bunk and looked out the window where I could see the airport. One of the toughest things about being in basic training at San Diego was being so close to the airport. All day long, we could see what we come to call freedom birds flying. The thought of going to war was weighing heavy on my mind. I promised my mother that I would not be going to war. I tried to dismiss it from my mind once I hit the rack. I figured that if I had to go, I had to go. At least I will be ready for it.

• • •

The daily routine of training in phase one began with P.T. (physical training) and ended with drill. I particularly enjoyed the obstacle course. We were soon aware that we were a part of a four platoon series, as we seen what the D.I.'s called our competition out on the parade ground or in physical training. The D.I.'s were hard on us. If we messed up as a unit, we had to go to the sand pit and make it rain, or we received P.T. on the spot. If you messed up individually, you personally paid for it by the hand of the D.I.

We came in the barracks one evening after several hours of drill and found a footlocker turned over in the middle of the barracks with its contents scattered all over the floor.

"Stow your rifles check your footlockers and get at attention in front of your racks," the D.I. yelled. We did exactly what he said. "Whoever belongs to this mess better step forward and sound off."

"Sir, the footlocker belongs to Recruit Baker Sir."

The D.I. walked up to the recruit. With a slap to the recruit's head, the D.I. said, "Look around you hogs. This is what happens when you don't lock your footlockers. Now we believe that all you ladies are honest here, but locks are intended to keep you honest. Is that clear?"

"Sir, yes Sir!"

In addition to an enormous amount of physical training, and drill during the first phase of training, we attended four weeks of training classes in Marine Corps history, military customs, courtesies, breakdown and cleaning of rifles, weapons, first aid, hygiene, military gear, as well as standing inspections.

It was extremely hot in San Diego during the months of August and September. Marching and doing calisthenics in the hot summer heat caused sharp and often prolonged discomfort on the recruits. It was ninety-four degrees the day we received bayonet training. A pugilstick looks like a huge Q-tip. One end represents the bayonet and the other end represents the butt of the riffle. We wore the protective gear and used the pugilsticks to prevent injury to the recruits. Two recruits were paired off against each other. The reward I got for winning my matches was that I had to fight until I was defeated. I fought four rounds until the D.I. stepped in to fight me.

"So, Recruit Meatball is a bad motherfucker?"

"Sir, no Sir," I sounded off with.

He took out his frustrations on me and beat me up before he struck the killing blow. We also had to stick dummies and boards with our bayonets fixed to our rifles and yell out things like I must kill, I must defend my country, die motherfucker, and I love to kill.

From bayonet training, we went directly to the obstacle course. By then, we were half-dead. We were all happy when that day was over, and we received our ninety minutes of free time before taps. Free time was a period when we hit the shower, shaved, stood daily hygiene inspection, wrote letters, and received our mail. My father never did write, but my mother always told me that he is proud of me. I was a little disappointed not to receive a letter from Sally. I had been in boot camp for a little over a month and had not received a letter from her.

During the last week of Phase one, I drew guard duty. In the middle of the night, the officer of the day approached me. "Recruit, what are your first, second, and third general orders?"

I sounded off correctly and gave a verbal account of each general order he asked.

We had a field meet on the last Sunday of our first phase of training. The competition was against the other platoons in the series and consisted of sprints, push-ups, pull-ups, baseball, and a tug of war.

Platoon 3105 did not win overall competition, but I could tell the D.I.'s were proud of us as we marched back to the barracks. The look of approval on the face of the Senior D.I. made us all feel proud that day.

"I'm very proud of you today," the Senior D.I. said as we marched back to the barracks. "You worked as a team out there. Keep up the good work. What a way to end your first phase of training. Gung ho recruits, gung ho."

Four

It was now near the third week of September, and I had been in boot camp for little over five weeks. By the time we entered our second phase of training, we lost several more recruits. Some were set back, discharged, or sent to a motivation platoon.

The weather in San Diego was just beautiful. Someone said that it never rains in Southern California and this was correct thus far. The days were still hot, but the humidity was low. Not like New Jersey. When it is ninety degrees in New Jersey, it feels like it is one hundred and twenty, and that is in the shade. I could see why Roseanne and Mark loved this area so much.

We were on the eve of starting our second phase of training. We just finished hygiene inspection and packing our sea bag for our journey north to Camp Pendleton and the rifle range when the squad bay was called to attention. We all scrambled to the front of our bunks and like statues, we froze at attention.

"At ease recruits," the Senior D.I. barked out as he walked up and down the squad bay with a rifle in his hand.

We all looked at each other wondering what this crazy bastard had on his mind, when he stopped in front of me. Oh. Shit. I immediately snapped to attention.

"Recruit Meatball, what is the maximum range of this weapon?"

"Sir the maximum range of the M16 rifle is two thousand six hundred and fifty three meters Sir."

"What is the effective range?" He then asked me.

"Sir the effective range is four hundred sixty meters Sir."

"You are right on both accounts Recruit Meatball, at ease."

I let out a sigh of relief as I assumed the at ease position. The Senior D.I. gave me a look of approval before he walked away.

In a blaring voice, the Senior D.I. continued. "You have all attended classes on the nomenclature and operational characteristics of the M16 rifle. You have spent numerous hours disassembling and assembling this weapon. In addition, you have spent numerous hours at close order drill with this weapon. But you have never fired it."

He was right. As a unit, we were starting to click as one. During close order drill, you could actually hear only one pop with each rifle movement. Nevertheless, marching with rifles and firing rifles are two different things.

"Listen up recruits. Tomorrow starts your first day of your second Phase of training. Phase two of your basic training will be launched at Edison Rifle Range."

The Senior D.I. walked with the rifle in his right hand in total silence. He placed his left hand to his chin and he looked as if he were considering in length what to say. We were standing at ease so we were able to watch his actions. He turned and faced a recruit.

• • •

"Recruit Shitbird, what is the semiautomatic maximum rate of fire of this weapon?"

"Sir, the semiautomatic maximum rate of fire of the M16 rifle is forty-five to sixty-five rounds per minute, Sir."

"Amazing, Recruit Shitbird, simply amazing. We may have to change your fucking name. The M16 rifle is a five point fifty six milometer, magazine fed, gas-operated, in line stock, shoulder weapon, with a muzzle velocity of three thousand two hundred and fifty feet per second. When you were issued your weapons, you were instructed to give it the name of a woman. Treat her with the respect that you would give a woman who will not fail you."

With that said, the lights started to rapidly go off and on. That was the signal for lights out. In five minutes, you had better be on your back at attention in your bunk awaiting instructions on which Marine legend in addition to your god, you were going to give a formal gesture of appreciation and admiration. However, on this particular night and for the next couple of weeks, we recited the Rifleman's Creed at lights out.

In a panic, we hurried to get all our gear stowed, make a final head call and get in our bunks. We lay perfectly still at attention as we heard a recruit being chewed out for not making it in his bunk on time.

"Listen up pigs," the Junior D.I. said as he stalked up and down the barracks. "Tomorrow you will board buses where you will embark on a new location and new type of training centered on rifle marksmanship. In celebration, we are going to sound off the Rifleman's Creed."

We all sounded off with, "THIS IS MY RIFLE. THERE ARE MANY LIKE IT, BUT THIS ONE IS MINE. MY RIFLE IS MY BEST FRIEND. IT IS MY LIFE. I MUST MASTER IT AS I MASTER MY LIFE. MY RIFLE WITHOUT ME IS USELESS. WITHOUT MY RIFLE, I AM USELESS. I MUST FIRE MY RIFLE TRUE. I MUST SHOOT STRAIGHTER THAN MY ENEMY WHO IS TRYING TO KILL ME. I MUST SHOOT HIM BEFORE HE SHOOTS ME. MY RIFLE AND I KNOW THAT WHAT COUNTS IN THIS WAR IS NOT THE ROUNDS WE FIRE, THE NOISE OF OUTBURST, NOR THE SMOKE WE MAKE. WE KNOW THAT IT IS THE HITS THAT COUNT. MY RIFLE IS HUMAN, EVEN AS I BECAUSE IT IS MY LIFE. THUS, I WILL LEARN IT AS MY BROTHER. I WILL LEARN ITS WEAKNESS, ITS STRENGTH, ITS PARTS, ITS ACCESSORIES, ITS SIGHTS AND ITS BARREL. I WILL KEEP MY RIFLE CLEAN AND READY EVEN AS I AM CLEAN AND READY. WE WILL BECOME PART OF EACH OTHER. BEFORE GOD, I SWEAR THIS CREED. MY RIFLE AND I ARE DEFENDERS OF MY COUNTRY. WE ARE MASTERS OF OUR ENEMY. WE ARE THE SAVIORS OF LIFE."

It was before dawn when the buses pulled up in front to the barracks to take us to Edison Range at Camp Pendleton. I don't know why, but I was pleased to see that the buses were green military buses, not like the greyhound buses that took us from the airport to the Recruit Depot. With our bellies full from early chow and our sea bags stowed, we took our seat on the bus. We sat at attention of course. One of the Junior Drill Instructors stood at the front of the bus with his hands on his hips and his Smokey the Bear hat tilted slightly to one side.

"Listen up assholes. You could sit at ease. I will allow talking at low voices. I will not allow any fucking off. So do not abuse the privilege. At ease girls!"

I sat next to Recruit Draper and he immediately started a conversation. "Hey Mommalione, I got to tell you man. I am a little scared."

"What are you scared of?" I asked while looking out the window.

"I never fired a gun before."

I turned and looked at Recruit Draper. "The hell you say. A brother who never fired a gun in his whole life, go figure."

I started laughing when Draper said, "I wish I could be like you Mommalione, Nothing scares you."

The Recruit could not be more wrong. Everything about boot camp scared me. Within minutes, Draper was asleep along with almost everyone else. As I looked around the bus, I made eye contact with the D.I.

"Did you loose something, Recruit Meatball?"

"Sir, no Sir.

"Then why are you eyeballing?"

"Sir, no reason Sir."

I sat back in my seat and looked out the window. My eyes widened. There sat the Pacific Ocean. I was emotionally aroused. Nothing excited me more than the ocean, any ocean. I sat back in my seat thinking and daydreaming of the Jersey shore when I too fell asleep, only to be awoken by the abrupt instructions of the Drill Instructor.

"You hogs have thirty seconds to fall out and get in formation outside the bus."

We all beat feat off the bus. It reminded me of the time we exited the buses upon arrival at boot camp. The difference being this time we needed no yellow feet to stand on to form ranks. I took my position as Platoon Guidon. I stood proudly as Platoon 3105 scrambled off the bus and joined the formation. We were given the remainder of the day to settle in our new barracks as well as draw our rifles, shooting jackets, scorebooks and rifle magazines.

• • •

Before dawn on our first day at Edison Range, we finished chow and marched to the rifle range. We were instructed to place our rifles down on the grass to our right. We then filed into the bleachers and waited for the Senior PMI (Primary Marksmanship Instructor) to address us.

"Good morning recruits. Thus far, you have received instruction in physical conditioning, drill, first aid, history and discipline, to name just a few subjects. During the next two weeks, you will be taught to fire the M16 rifle and qualify in rifle marksmanship. It does not matter if you have never fired a weapon before, because you will be taught. You will learn the various firing positions. By now, you are aware that you are an element of a platoon. The platoon is made up of squads. The squads are made up of fire teams. Platoon 3105 is a member of four other platoons that make up a series. The rifle range is the first time you will work as individuals and not as a member of a platoon. You will start your day one hour earlier at 0400 hours. You will learn new terminology such as sight alignment, chambering, ejection, cocking, clicks of elevation, bull's eye, locking etc."

• • •

We spent the first week at the range performing what is known as snapping in. Snapping in is doing dry runs in the firing positions. We sweat beneath our shooting jackets and sweatshirts. There was no excitement in firing empty rifles, and there was no let up of harassment and ridicule from the D.I.'s despite being at a new location and new phase of training. The rifle holding exercises even continued at night in the barracks. Except for the teaching of the Primary Marksmanship Instructor, the first week at the range was tedious and full of fatigue. At the end of the week, we spent the weekend doing laundry and even more snapping in.

On the following Monday, we got to fire the .45 caliber pistol. We only fired the pistol for familiarization. They were so worn and old we hardly hit the target. I had to aim at the lower left corner just to hit near the center of the target. The same day, we fired our rifles for the first time. We first fired our rifles to get our dope. Dope means the number of clicks that we set our sights by. One click of elevation moves the strike of the bullet one inch on the target for every one hundred yards of range. Daily, for a week, we fired our rifles in the sitting, kneeling, prone and standing positions, and at different intervals up to five hundred yards for the prone position. When we were not firing, we were in the pits marking targets for those recruits who were. We marked targets by putting a plug in each hole and then raising the target. A long pole that had a disk on the top is then raised over each plug to show the recruit where he hit. If the recruit missed the target, the pole was waved across the target. This is known as a Maggie's drawers. Each day for a week, we fired for qualification.

A few of the recruits went unqualified to that point. We called those types of recruit's unqs. One evening while cleaning our rifles, I overheard one of the Junior D.I.'s addressing the unqs. He was screaming up one side of them and down the other. Finally, the D.I. planted a rifle butt into the shoulder of one of the unqs.

There are three types of metals you were awarded by qualifying. They are marksman, sharpshooter and expert. On record day, I qualified and received the expert metal. I felt sorry for the unqs. They would probably be set back or something, I thought. You cannot be a Marine if you cannot qualify with a rifle.

• • •

The squad bay was called to attention as the Senior Drill Instructor entered.

"At ease and listen up Recruits. Tomorrow is Sunday and this particular Sunday is a day of R&R. R&R means rest and relaxation. Tomorrow after morning chow and religious services, you will do laundry and we will draw equipment in preparations of infantry training. In the afternoon, you will write letters, and call home. Lights out in five minutes."

The Junior D.I. on duty conducted the usual hygiene inspection. I could tell that all the recruits were delighted about the opportunity of calling home. I slept well that night.

After chow and Sunday morning mass, we were marched to supply where we were issued a haversack, mess gear, canteens, cartridge belts, gas mask and helmet. The thought of calling home was giving me butterflies in my stomach as I was eating afternoon chow. It was 1300 hours when we marched to the pay phones, and one of the Junior D.I.'s had us stand at attention as he gave us instructions concerning our phone calls.

"Each of you will have exactly three minutes to complete your calls. The base telephone operators will complete your collect call. This is your one and only call while in boot camp, so make it count."

I waited in line for about twenty minutes before it was my turn to make my call. The phone rang three times before my father answered. I started talking as soon as he accepted the collect call. "Dad, it's me, can you hear me?"

"Slow down Son, I can hear you just fine. How are you doing?"

"Dad, I only got three minutes. I really miss everyone. How are you doing?"

"I am doing just fine. Your mother and grandmother are fine as well."

"Dad, let me talk to them."

"I can't do that Son. They are at church."

I didn't give the time difference a thought. My mother and grandmother always go to 10:00 mass. I immediately felt loneliness inside.

"Son, tell me how are you getting along."

"I'm doing okay. It is hard Dad. Sometimes I don't think that I can make it."

"Just hang in there Son. You can do it. You are halfway there. The Marines sent us a schedule of graduation day ceremonies. Rosanne and Mark assured me that they would be there. The Corps also sent your mother and me a progress report concerning you. I read nothing but good things."

"Tell Carmine that I said hi, and tell mom and grandma that I am sorry that I missed them, I said in a sad tone.

"I will Joey and you keep your chin up. You will be home soon."

I hung up the phone without saying goodbye, double-timed it back to formation and fell in with the recruits who already completed their calls. Some of the recruits seemed happy and some of them seemed like they were sad. I was one of the sad ones.

• • •

It was no surprise that the next two weeks at Camp Pendleton consisted of prolonged discomfort, yet I found it to be interesting. Infantry training brought out the most basic structure of the individual recruit as it pertains to the transformation of a civilian to a Marine. Infantry training gave us our first perceivable indication of the dedication and training it takes to become a warrior.

Re-emphasis and repetition were the order of the day during the first week of infantry training in the field. The Drill Instructors pounded combat formations and squad tactics into our minds and bodies. We literally had our dicks in the dirt. The second week was less physical, but nonetheless mental. The outside classrooms educated us on probing for land mines, sanitation and hygiene in the field, live fire simulation, chemical attack protective gear, camouflage, proper handling of the use of hand grenades and introduction to infantry battalion weapons.

I almost wet my pants the first time I tossed a grenade. Many recruits did wet themselves during gasmask training where we were exposed to chemical warfare as if we were instructed to remove our gasmasks in the gas chamber, and sound off with name, rank, and service number. In doing so, we instantly lost control of most of our bodily functions as the chemicals set in. The most interesting element of infantry training came in the form of demonstration of large caliber machine gun fire. Mortar fire, handheld antitank rocket fire, as well as demolitions on mine warfare were interesting. I personally enjoyed the live fire simulation, where we crawled under barbwire as explosives detonated around us and machine guns were fired overhead.

We spent the last week of our second phase of training on mess duty. It was a sweaty interval during training phases where continuity was suspended. Although the pressure of the D.I.'s eased up, we were at the mess hall hours before breakfast and stayed for hours after dinner. The days of mess duty were long and tiring. We spent up to fifteen hours a day working in the galleys, store rooms, pot washing, serving and cleaning. It was not fun, but it was somewhat of a break.

Not much conversation took place among the recruits. There were days on end throughout boot camp where neither I nor the other recruits talked to one another, especially during training. The same applied during mess duty. On the third day of mess duty, I was surprised when Recruit Lochinger approached me while I was mopping the floor of the scullery. Lochinger held the position of Platoon Clerk.

"Hey Meatball, while picking up the mail today, I noticed a letter addressed to you. It is from a girl named Sally. I remember you talking about her when we were back in Receiving Barracks."

I was stunned and stood there with my mouth open. By the time I could respond, Recruit Lochinger was gone. I finished mopping the floor and did everything I could do just to control my emotions.

At twenty hundred hours, we fell out for formation. I was very anxious as we marched back to the barracks. I knew that once we were back in the barracks, we had approximately forty-five minutes to shit, shower and shave before hygiene inspection, followed by mail call. To receive mail, the recruit must yell out his name when called, run down the squad bay and stand tall in front of the Drill Instructor. He then had to repeat his name beginning with and ending with sir and clap the letter between his palms. Once that is done, he had to take a step backwards, do an about face and run back to his bunk. Once at our bunks, we could immediately open our mail. My heart was pounding as the D.I. called my name. Once I received my letter, I raced back to my bunk. I was so excited to get a letter from Sally that I tore it open at once and began reading it. My bubble burst as it turned out to be a Dear John Letter. It couldn't have come at a worse time. I sat in disbelief at my footlocker. Then, I got a thought. I opened my foot locker, took Sally's picture from my wallet, walked up to the bulletin board that hung on the wall next to the head (bathroom) and stuck Sally's picture up on the hog board. The hog board is made up of pictures of females that are close to the recruits.

This included pictures of girlfriends, sisters, even mothers. There was no way I ever considered putting a picture of my mother or sister on the hog board. In addition, I always thought that Sally's picture was too pretty to share with the others, but now they could have her.

I felt like I was going to die. I could not eat or sleep. I had a feeling in my stomach that I never experienced before. I found the remainder of days spent on mess duty to be even longer and more mentally exhausting, which gave me more time to think about Sally and my hurt. I couldn't wait for Phase III to start and get back to training. I couldn't wait to drown my sorrow by means of recruit training.

Five

The bus ride back to the Marine Corps Recruit Depot at San Diego was less impressive than the ride from there to Camp Pendleton. The Dear John Letter from Sally really had me in low spirits. I did what the other recruits did; I slept for the entire ride. I could care less about getting another glimpse at the Pacific Ocean. The only thing on my mind besides Sally was starting the first day of phase three of training which brought me another day closer to the last day of boot camp.

We spent our first day back at the Recruit Depot settling in, minus four more recruits. We did laundry, and posed for a platoon picture. That evening after we shit, showered, shaved and before hygiene inspection, the Senior D.I. addressed the platoon.

"At ease recruits," the Senior commanded.

We all assumed the position and waited for him to speak. I suddenly realized that when the Senior Drill Instructor spoke, he impart courage, inspiration, and resolution to the recruits. Therefore, I was somewhat relieved that he was the one doing the talking and not one of the Junior D.I.'s. The Junior Drill Instructors always degraded us when they spoke. I watched, as the Senior D.I. walk was marked by extraordinary superiority and importance.

"I am extremely pleased. Not only am I pleased with the way you demonstrated your marksmanship skills, abilities and knowledge at the range, but also as well as how you conducted yourselves as recruits in my beloved Marine Corps. You have now entered your third phase of training. This is your last phase of training before you take your place in the world as United States Marines. This phase of training involves water survival, drill, and preparation for graduation. It will also include hand-to-hand combat, final exams, the crucible, final inspection, and finally, graduation. All of this will take place in the next several weeks, and there will be no formal physical training. P.T will mainly consist of morning runs. Pay attention to detail, do not fuck it up now recruits. You are not home free yet. It doesn't take a genius to look around this squad bay and count the number of empty racks. Just remember, each one of those empty racks represents a recruit who has been set back. You all know what that means. Being set back could add weeks if not months of additional time spent in basic."

I couldn't help but to notice the look of approval the Senior D.I. gave me as he walked by.

• • •

Our first week of phase three training included daily runs. After the runs and morning chow, we visited the pools for classes in water survival. We learned how to remain in the water for hours, using our clothing as floats. The recruits that couldn't swim had to attend special classes. Again, I was determined to qualify. There was no way I was going to get set back, not at this stage of training. You cannot be a Marine if you cannot swim and survive in the water. After water survival, three more recruits got set back.

It was at the end of our first week of training when I was sitting on my footlocker reading my guidebook during free time when the house mouse came to me and told me that the Senior Drill Instructor wanted to see me. Oh shit, what was this all about, I thought. I ran up to the cubical in front of the squad bay and shouted out, "Sir, Recruit Meatball reporting as ordered Sir!"

"Get your spaghetti eating ass in here Recruit Meatball," the Senior D.I. shouted.

I took three paces through the door, made a right face and stood at attention. The Senior D.I. sat there with both elbows on the desk. He looked all business like. Yet, he looked casual sitting there in a tee shirt. It was my first time in the Drill Instructors cubical. It really was not what one would expect. One single bunk stood against the wall. The metal desk was small, and the only other piece of furniture was a cushioned metal chair with arms. The only thing on the wall was a clock in military time. His uniform hung on a hanger hooked to a standing coat rack. The most exciting thing about the cubical was a cigar burning in an ashtray on the desk next to a computer. It was amazing what I could see with my eyes fixed forward.

"Stand at parade rest recruit." Parade rest is a more relaxed version of standing at attention. When given the command of parade rest, the recruit moves to a position where his feet are placed shoulder length apart and his hands are cupped behind his back with his head and eyes fixed forward. "Sergeant Rippen tells me that you have not been yourself for the last week or so."

I searched my mind for what to say.

"Well spit it out man."

"Sir, the recruit received a Dear John Letter from his girlfriend Sir."

"Now listen to me recruit and listen closely. You are going to have many women in your life. Treat each one like we taught you in class, with feeling of respect, approval, liking, and with each one, you will gain new experiences. After you get out in the world as a Marine, you are going to get so much pussy that you are probably going to catch some disease and die anyway. Knowing you, you probably will not wear a raincoat while doing it, which is another thing we taught you. Take a load off Mommalione."

"Sir, yes Sir," I said as I snapped to attention before I took a seat and even then, I sat at attention.

"I need you Private Mommalione, the Platoon needs you. I have watched you helping the recruits who are lagging. I watched you excel in every interval of training thus far. We still have a ways to go here, and you are my informal leader. We still have more close order drill, exams, hand-to-hand combat training, preparation for graduation, final inspection, and the crucible. I will not have some Mary Jane Rottencrotch back in New Jersey fuck up my recruits. Is that clear?"

"Sir, yes Sir!"

"Just to inform you Mommalione, I have recommended you to Battalion for Platoon Honor Man and Series Honor Man, and it has been approved. However, don't fuck this up because you will make me look like a fool. What this means Private Mommalione is that while every Private goes home in his dress green uniform, you will be going home in an issued set of dress blues with a stripe, as you will not be leaving here as a Private, but as a Private First Class. You will be leaving basic training with rank. It will take each of those men out there a year or more to achieve that. Don't let me down Private First Class Mommalione, and don't let your sister down. I want her to see you standing above the rest in your dress blues and a stripe on your sleeve. Now get the fuck out of my house, and keep this conversation to yourself."

I immediately jumped to attention, and stood tall in front of the Senior D.I.'s desk. "Sir, I will not let you down Sir." I did an about face, pivoted left and ran out the door back to my footlocker. Fuck Sally, I was on a high. For the first time, a D.I. called me by my name. For the first time, a D.I. referred to me as a Private.

The next day we were being fitted for uniforms and I fitted for a set of dress blues. I wondered how the Senior Drill Instructor knew that my sister was coming to see me at graduation. It seemed like the Senior Drill Instructor knew everything. In the evening, I sat down and read a letter from my sister. She told me that she will see me on November 10th, at graduation, but she was not going home with me while I am on leave, because she decided on going home for Christmas.

• • •

After two weeks of hand-to-hand combat training, we were able to kill a man in ten seconds using the palm of our hand or using our fingers as gouges, or our hands and arms in a chokehold. We could even bust his face open by using our knees, or elbows. Hand–to-hand combat incorporated training in how to defend ourselves unarmed against an opponent who has a rifle with a bayonet attached, to various ways of taking out an enemy when neither of us has a weapon. We went through a variation of training that consisted of one recruit with a pugilstick and the other without, as well as a series of knife fighting maneuvers.

Hand-to-hand combat was not limited to structured classes. It continued in the evening whereas the Junior Drill Instructor taught us to distract our opponent by spitting in his face or out of nowhere, kick his teeth in. We learned how to kill with a lead pencil, a piece of glass, and a variety of natural weapons. We learned to strike an opponent where he is vulnerable, in the eyes, face, kidneys, or solar plexus. I could now snap the enemy's neck or tear out his Adam's apple. Of course, his family jewels are very vulnerable. Even our teeth are weapons. You cannot be a Marine if you cannot kill with your bare hands.

• • •

It was late in October when we were down to our last few weeks of basic training. During our second to last week, we took a series of tests on everything we learned, which included every element of operations in basic training. Everyone did well. By now, physical training was limited, but we still had our final physical fitness test to take. It consisted of pull-ups, crunches, and a three-mile run, which had to be completed within a thirty-minute period. I completed the run in twenty minutes.

Our final test of physical readiness came in the form of the Crucible. The Crucible is a fifty-four hour ordeal each recruit must go through before earning the coveted eagle, globe and anchor emblem and the right to be a United States Marine. The Crucible demanded teamwork. We literally had to carry each other. We marched for hours, dragged ammo boxes filled with sand through mud, crawled under barbwire, evacuated wounded, overcame obstacles, and we did it. You cannot be a Marine without physical and mental endurance. Fifty-four hours later, we could barely stand to receive our eagle, globe and anchor emblem to become Marines. I could see the men readily stirred by emotion as the Senior D.I. congratulated each one of us and called us Marines for the first time as he placed the Marine Corps emblem in our hand. Some responded with, "Aye, Aye Sir." Some could not respond at all, and some of the new Marines were just unable to hold themselves up.

As I received my emblem, I couldn't help but to think of my friend Carmine Scalia. The advice that Carmine gave me was priceless. Not only did Carmine complete basic training, but he was involved in the weeklong operation in Panama. The December 1989 intervention in Panama was aimed at deposing drug dealing Dictator Manuel Antonio Noriega. During the operation, two Marines died and three ended up wounded.

• • •

The next couple of weeks were grueling. We drilled on the parade deck daily for hours in preparation for drill competition. We cleaned rifles, shined shoes, worked on our uniforms, shined our brass belt buckles, and reviewed our general orders, as we were primed for final inspection. The D.I.'s accepted nothing less than razor sharp creases in our uniforms and our shoes and belt buckles had to shine like a diamond in a goat's ass. Those were their words exactly. The D.I. on duty even looked the other way after lights out as some of us sneaked into the head to put final touches on our belt buckles, and shoes.

Finally, we reached our last week of boot camp. The pressure was still on though. We still had drill competition, final inspection, and graduation. drill competition was the highest point to the D.I. A team of Senior Drill Instructors judged each platoon for freedom of error performed in a series of drill movements. Although Platoon 3105 did not win the drill competition, the customary overwhelming flow of harsh insulting language from the D.I.'s did not come.

The night before final inspection was crazy. We spit shined our brass buckles, shoes and weapons for what seemed like the hundredth time. In the morning, we got up an hour earlier than usual and went to chow. After chow, we were dressed in our dress green uniforms and stood outside the barracks in formation, and the Drill Instructor's looked us over. Other than a few crooked ties, we were ready. Just before the Company Commander, Series Commander and the Series Sergeant Major came to inspect us, the Senior D.I. came around with a bottle of Listerine mouthwash. He made each one of us take a small mouthful, swish it around in our mouth a few times and swallow it.

I was nervous as I took my position of Platoon Guidon. Being that I was the Platoon Guidon, I was the first of the recruits inspected. This was the only time in platoon formation where I did not carry the platoon colors, as I had to hold my rifle for inspection. I felt the sweat roll down the middle of my back when approached by the Series Commander, Captain Carter and his party. I immediately brought my rifle to port arms. A port arms is a two-count movement from my right side where the rifle is raised diagonally across the body with the right-hand, the left hand grasps the rifle at the balance and holds it so that it is four inches from the belt. The left elbow is held down without strain. On the second count, the rifle is regrasped with the right hand at the small of the stock, fingers and thumb closed around the stock. The right forearm is horizontal and the elbows are against the sides. During the movement for inspection purposes only, the chamber is opened. In one movement, Captain Carter snapped the rifle from my hold, and I assumed the position of attention. Once the rifle inspection was completed, the rifle was handed back to me whereas on command, I closed the chamber and lowered the rifle to my right side at the attention position.

"State your name Private?"

"Sir, Private Mommalione Sir."

"Where do you hail from Private Mommalione?"

"Sir, Trenton, New Jersey Sir."

"Private Mommalione, what is your eleventh General Order?"

"Sir, the Private's eleventh General Order is to be especially watchful at night and during the time for challenging; to challenge all persons on or near my post, and to allow no one to pass without proper authority, Sir."

"Very good Private Mommalione and congratulations on your promotion to Private First Class, as well as being selected Platoon and Series Honorman."

I sounded off proudly with, "Sir, thank you Sir."

It took almost two hours for the inspecting officers to complete the most rigorous inspection that most Marines will ever take part in while on active duty.

The next day was graduation. I was fortunate to arrive at the Recruit Depot when I did. I joined a group that was ready to form a platoon. Some of the recruits arrived ten days or so earlier and waited around receiving barracks for enough recruits to form a platoon. Not only was the next day graduation, it was also the Marine Corps birthday. That meant that it was going to be like a holiday around the Depot. We spent the remainder of the morning turning in our rifles and equipment, as well as doing grounds maintenance. After that, the Senior D.I. brought us together for a final sit down in the barracks. We were about to receive our military occupational specialty.

We sat in a semicircle in front of the squad bay. "Now listen up," the Senior Drill Instructor commanded. You are about to take the initial step in your Marine Corps mission. Most of you are assigned the military occupational specialty of 0300. Zero three hundred is infantry. An infantry man is the backbone of the Marine Corps. I can't stress this enough, no matter what your M.O.S. is, you are all rifleman. All 0300's will go on to infantry training school at Camp Pendleton. Throughout your enlistment, as an infantryman, you will receive training in basic communications, land navigation, combat formations, and signals, protective measures, scouting and patrolling, prisoner of war survival, desert warfare, jungle survival, squad tactics, small arms, amphibious raid, mountain warfare, etc. Basically, you will go on to become better killers. Remember what I said, all of you no matter what your M.O.S., you are riflemen first. And, if you make the Marine Corps a career, no matter what your M.O.S., most likely you will spend a good portion of your career in the infantry. I would like to share something with you, and if any of you motherfuckers laugh, I will kick your ass. I am a cook, and here I am training you bastards. I have twenty-three years in the Marine Corps. During the Tet Offensive, my base was overrun by the North Vietnamese. When I left the kitchen, I grabbed my rifle, and took a position on the perimeter of the base. I had twenty-three confirmed kills. To make a long story short, I was twice wounded. I wear my bullet hole scars like a badge of honor. I have another interesting point for you. Your company commander is a pilot and here he is at Marine Corps Recruit Depot. I think you get my point. Trust me when I say, the Marine Corps is the finest fighting force in the world. Obedience to orders, training, and discipline is what makes you a warrior, and a part of the finest fighting force in the world. If you find yourself in a hostile situation, remember what you learned here. Whether it is in combat, a bar, or back on the streets, you learned enough in basic training to survive any unfriendly situation."

The Senior D.I. really had our attention. The man spoke like a preacher. I was pumped. At that moment, I wanted nothing more than to be half the Marine he is. I watched as the Senior D.I. walked and pondered what he was going to say next. He stopped, pulled a card out of his wallet and proceeded to read from it.

"Marines win over the hearts and minds of the people they are liberating. If we cannot win over the hearts and minds of the people, we burn their damn huts down. Marines fight wars, start revolutions, plot assassinations, quell uprisings, organize orgies, and convert virgins etc. Many military occupational specialties are needed to accomplish this. Reed-0300 infantry; Sanz-0300; Mixon-0300; Hollingsworth-0300; Enright-2500 communications; Jones-0311 infantry on the job training; Bates-0100 clerk; Vargus-0300; Owen-1800 engineers; Thomas-0311; McDonald-0300; Mommalione-0200 intelligence; Draper-0300; Fisher-0300."

Everyone listened eagerly as the Senior Drill Instructor continued to read out names and their related M.O.S. After afternoon chow, we marched over to administration to receive pay, orders, and airline tickets. In the evening, we packed our sea bags, and got ready for graduation the next day.

• • •

Graduation was a formal act dictated by ritual. We passed in review. It was amazing as three hundred or so newly dubbed Marines marched before an audience of family, Battalion Officers and Marines in attendance. I marched proudly as I knew that my sister and Mark were in the crowd and there I was in my dress blues leading my platoon. After the Battalion Commander gave a speech, he dismissed us. Some Marines ran to their families, others ran to the telephones and some of the new Marines ran to the base restaurant to get a long waited cheeseburger and fries. I ran to Roseanne and Mark. Roseanne jumped in my arms and I spun her around with ease.

"Wow," she said. "I think that you got a lot stronger in boot camp. You look so handsome in that uniform. I am really proud of you Joseph."

"That goes for me too Marine," Mark said. Both of you stand under that tree so I can get a picture of you. After that, we could find a picnic table. Roseanne packed a terrific lunch."

Mark took the picture, and then Roseanne gave me another big hug. "Wait until mother, father, and grandmother see you in that uniform; they are going to be so proud."

"Let me tell you something," I said. "I am proud to be presented this dress blue uniform and to be promoted to Private first Class."

"Was it real tough?" Mark asked.

"I found it to be extremely hard. Ten times harder that anyone could imagine," I said as we sat down to lunch.

Roseanne prepared a large platter antipasto accompanied by a nice loaf of Italian bread. We ate lunch, had a few cokes and talked about home before I took them around a little and showed them the obstacle course, barracks, parade deck, and we stopped at the P.X. where I bought a candy bar. As we walked around, a platoon was running by chanting, "I don't know but I've been told Eskimo pussy is mighty cold." I started to laugh. Roseanne and Mark looked embarrassed.

The base liberty was just about to end when I told my sister and Mark to wait by the car, as I needed to go back to the barracks to change my uniform, and get my sea bag and orders. They walked to the parking lot, which was located behind the barracks.

I was one of the first back to the Barracks. "Private First Class Mommalione," the Senior D.I. called out.

"Sir, yes Sir," I responded.

"Pfc. Mommalione, you don't have to call me Sir anymore. You may call me Gunny Brown. No more Sir, I work for a living. It has been a pleasure awarding you that set of dress blues and promoting you to Private First Class."

"Thank you Gunny, I will never forget you," I said as he offered me his hand.

"Shoot straight Pfc; kill without regret. Killing a human is not like stepping on ants. Remember what you learned."

His words were powerful as usual and sent a chill down my spine. It was as if he knew something and was trying to give me a warning. We shook hands and he walked off. I quickly dismissed the thought from my mind as I was in a hurry to change into my green dress uniform as well as look over my orders one more time before meeting Mark and Roseanne.

I was pleased as I finished reading my orders. I took one more look around the squad bay, and I suddenly had a feeling of relief. I grabbed my sea bag, as well as my clothing bag containing my dress blues and I got out of there without saying a word to anyone. I was so happy to be finally done with basic training, I ran to the car.

"Here, let me give you a hand with your bags," Mark said.

I elected to sit in the back seat. As Mark drove closer to the gate, a strange feeling came over me when a bus of new recruits passed us. My eyes followed the bus. I starred out the back window until it disappeared. As we approached the guard shack at the base entrance, I watched a platoon of recruits cleaning the grounds for the festivities later in the day. Mark handed in his pass and drove off. Once again, I looked out the back window knowing that I will never forget my stay at Marine Corps Recruit Depot, San Diego, California.

Six

It is amazing how much could go through the mind in a matter of minutes. Moments earlier, I ran to the car, as I was so happy to get to out of boot camp. Once in the car and on my way, I was not so sure. My mind was racing as Mark and Roseanne engaged in a conversation about a party they were invited to on the upcoming weekend. I remembered the last time I was outside the gates of the Recruit Depot. It was on the bus ride back from Camp Pendleton. I remembered how the only thing on my mind was getting back to the Marine Corps Recruit Depot to start the third phase of my training which brought me one-step closer to getting out of boot camp.

As we drove, I was thinking that only a few minutes prior, I felt a sense of relief, finally being done with basic. I felt a certain uneasiness come over me as we exited the gate. As brutal as boot camp was, I no longer had the security and structure of being in there. My life had definitely changed over the previous three months. Life for me was no longer about hanging out back on the block with my friends. Life for me was no longer about deciding about college or getting a job. Life for me was no longer what I was going to do with myself.

I knew that I was now a Marine and I had to measure up as a United States Marine. I had no clue as to what the future had in store for me, but I knew that it was more than what I had mastered in boot camp. I also knew that being a Marine, meant that I am a warrior, and a member of the finest fighting force in the world. I knew that the Marines take benefit from a reputation that I must live up to.

My thoughts switched to what the Senior Drill Instructor told me about killing without regret, and shooting straight. What was he saying? Did he know something? Was there going to be a war? Moreover, was I going to be in combat? How would I hold up? My daydreaming suddenly came to an abrupt end by Roseanne.

"A penny for your thoughts?"

"Oh I'm just sitting here reflecting on what I have gone through at basic training."

"Are you thinking of that or are you thinking about what is yet to come."

"Damn it Roseanne, you are just like mom. I swear she always knows what I am thinking."

"You really miss her don't you, Joseph."

"I miss everyone, I miss mom, dad, grandma and I even miss that dumb dog."

"Well you will see them tomorrow, along with…" Roseanne hesitated. I think that she was going to say Danny and George.

Mark cut in with, "I'll bet you are looking forward to seeing that cute girlfriend of yours. What's her name?"

"Her name is Sally and we are no longer an issue as she sent me a Dear John Letter."

Mark and Roseanne looked at each other as if to say oh shit, we really put our foot in out mouths. I thought that I would change the subject.

"What are the beaches like out here?"

"They are beautiful," Mark said. "However, they are lacking something in comparison to the Jersey Shore."

"In what way are they different?"

"What my husband is saying is the beaches out here are lacking a distinctive element. There are no boardwalks. Boy I have to tell you, I really miss that atmosphere. I miss that distinguishing smell and taste of Italian sausage with peppers, cotton candy, and french-fries, as well as the ice cream. I miss the games and the rides. I miss the air, mood, smell, taste and feel of the boardwalks at Point Pleasant, Seaside Heights, Ocean City, and Atlantic City."

"It sounds like you need a trip home Sissy."

"We both need a trip home," Mark added. "I also miss the Jersey shore."

"Well if things go as planned, I will be in New Jersey tomorrow. I just wish it were summertime."

"Why shouldn't things go as planned," Mark asked.

"I don't know; just a saying I guess."

All that talk about the beach had me thinking back when I was younger. It was only a few years ago, but it seemed like a lifetime has gone by when my family would spend summer weekends and weeks at a time at my Uncle's beach home at the shore. Again, I was daydreaming which brought me back to Point Pleasant and running on the boardwalk with George and Danny. I was once again riding the Ferris wheel, roller coaster and eating saltwater taffy. I was once again in my favorite arcade, riding the rides and playing games. The bumper cars were our favorite. Once again, Roseanne interrupted my daydreaming.

"Did mother tell you about Uncle Joe?"

"What about him?" I asked as I leaned forward.

"He died. I thought for sure that mother would have written you with the sad news."

"No Sissy, mom only told me about happy things. I guess she didn't want to upset me."

"What about your father? What did your father write to you about?" Mark asked."

"Fuhgeddaboudit," I said. "My father never wrote to me. He's not that kind."

"Sissy, what did Uncle Joe die of?"

"He died of heart failure. From what I hear, he had a huge funeral with hundreds in attendance. He was cremated, and Uncle Michael seen to it that Uncle Joe's ashes were spread up and down the entire boardwalk."

"Roseanne, I remember you telling me about Uncle Joe, but how was he related?" Mark expressed.

I intervened. "Uncle Joe was not really our uncle. He was every kid's uncle. He owned an Arcade off the boardwalk on one of the side streets in Point Pleasant. It was one of our favorite hangouts at the shore when we were kids. Uncle Joe was charming, accepting, and secure. He took in many kids who were runaways. He straightened out many kids who had drug problems. You could go to Uncle Joe with any problem and he would help you out. Uncle Joe had a vivid imagination. We spent many evenings sitting around the Arcade listening to Uncle Joe's stories. He had some great ones. He was involved in the community and church. He was truly satisfied with his life and he experienced a kind of happiness unknown to most people, except for those who come in contact with him."

"Hey little brother, we did not discuss where you go from here?"

"Well Sissy, I'll tell you. Every recruit takes aptitude tests before basic training starts. In boot camp, every recruit is taught the basics, as well as the basic techniques of infantry ground combat. Infantry and marksmanship training among other training received in basic training qualifies each recruit to be a Marine. In theory, each Marine is a rifleman. Each Marine is a rifleman, no matter what their M.O.S. is. The rifleman part means that each Marine must be prepared to fight at any given time. In addition to the aptitude tests, the recruit's progress is measured. His or her qualifications are classed as a Military Occupational Specialty, M.O.S. for short. After basic training, each Marine is sent for training in their M.O.S. Upon completion of Military Occupational Specialty training, the Marine is assigned to a duty station to perform their duty."

With much interest in her voice, Roseanne asked, "What is your M.O.S.?"

"I got good news," I said as I looked over my orders. "I have been assigned to Intelligence and will receive my training at the Marine Corps Base located at Twentynine Palms. My training will last approximately three months, and I will probably be stationed at Camp Pendleton afterwards."

"Where is Twentynine Palms?"

I turned the page on my orders. "It says here that Twentynine Palms is one hundred and forty two miles north east of San Diego."

"What about going to war in Kuwait?" Mark inquired.

"I don't understand, what about Kuwait?" I said with a little more than some concern.

"I hear that things are really heating up over there. That is all Joey. I hope I didn't upset you?"

"No Mark I'm not upset. It's just that I lost touch with what's going on in the world. I need to catch up on current events. Anyway, getting back to my orders, I have two weeks leave starting tomorrow. I have to report for duty at Twentynine Palms by 1800 hours on November 25th."

• • •

The ride to Roseanne and Mark's apartment lasted only about twenty minutes. A lot went through my mind during those twenty minutes. I thought about my two-week leave at home. I thought about leaving boot camp behind. My mind was racing with those thoughts, but most of all, I thought about going to war. How would I hold up and how would I feel the first time I kill a man. Not every Marine sees combat, but every Marine is willing to kill for God and their country or make the enemy die for his. As I rode in Mark's car, a feeling came over me. I knew right then and there that I would be going to war. I just knew it.

We drove down a side street on a continuing hillside that went on for miles until we parked at the curb. Mark helped me by carrying my sea bag as Roseanne ran ahead of us. We walked down a long sidewalk with one-floor apartments on either side. All the buildings looked the same. They were beige color and separate from one another. I viewed it as San Diego's version of Philadelphia row houses. Roseanne met us at the door with a smile on here face and a huge ricotta pie in her hands. My eyes widened, as ricotta pie is my favorite type of pie, usually reserved for holidays.

"Come on in little brother. Look what I made for you. I'll just put the pie in the kitchen for now and save it until after dinner."

Roseanne gave me the grand tour while Mark went to talk to his neighbors about something. The apartment was small with southwestern décor. There were much iron and color tiles. I was not sure that mom, dad, grandma or anyone in the family would approve, but I said nothing. After all, most Italians couldn't distinguish Spanish from nineteen fifties interior decorating. However, they do know Italian, and if any house does not have Italian furnishings, with plastic covering on the furniture, than fuhgeddaboudit. I was impressed to see a picture of the pope though. I was also happy to see a print of the Trenton skyline on the wall. I froze though when I came to a picture of a pier on the bedroom wall.

"What is wrong Joseph? You look like you seen a ghost."

"Sissy, where did you get this picture?"

"I took it," Mark said as he entered the bedroom. I took the picture at Oceanside Beach. Actually, Oceanside is located just outside the Marine Corps Base at Camp Pendleton. Why do you ask?"

"Because, I had a dream that took place while on the plane ride out here. I dreamt that I met a woman while walking on a beach and she took me to this very pier where George and Danny were waiting for me. It was weird. I know that Danny and George were killed in that shootout with the cops, but the dream was so real."

"That was it?" Roseanne asked as she put her arms around me from behind.

"Yeah, I woke up when the plane landed. How about feeding me some of that pie now?"

"Not a chance. I have a big dinner planned for you. Mark has to work tonight so it will be just you and me. No pie until after dinner."

Mark worked as an evening manager at a department store. He goes to school during the day and is studying to be an accountant. I always viewed Mark as a good person. Everyone did. We all knew that he would do well in school and would never do Roseanne wrong. Mom and Dad were counting down the days when Mark is done with school and they will come back to New Jersey, but I felt that they would stay in California when he gets out of school.

Mark and I sat and talked before he had to leave for work and while Roseanne prepared his dinner. The apartment was consumed with the aroma of sauce that reminded me of my mother's kitchen.

"Did Carmine go to boot camp at the Marine Corps Recruit Depot?" Mark asked.

"No, Carmine received his boot camp training at Parris Island, South Carolina. I really miss him. If it wasn't for his advice and guidance, I don't think that I would have made it through boot camp."

"Speaking of Carmine," Roseanne yelled from the kitchen. "He called and you need to call him. He said that he is going to meet you at the airport. I have his phone number here on the refrigerator."

Oh shit, what is going on now, I thought. I bet that my Uncle Michael had something to do with what ever is going on. All I wanted to do was have my father pick me up at the Philadelphia airport and quietly slip into the house and then into my civilian clothes.

Mark stood and walked toward the sliding glass door in the dining room. "Joey come here, I want to show you something."

I got up and followed Mark out onto the patio. I couldn't believe my eyes. I had a bird's eye view of the Marine Recruit Depot and the Naval Base. Roseanne came out and joined us.

"This is awesome," I expressed. "Roseanne how come you never told me about this?"

"I wanted to Joseph, but we thought that we would surprise you."

"Joey, every day we would sit out here and look at the base wondering what you were doing," Mark said as he set up a telescope mounted on a tripod. "Here Joey take a look through this. You will be amazed at what you see."

I looked in the telescope and focused in. Mark was right. I was amazed as I saw the parade deck, receiving barracks, and theater. What a view. I even zeroed in on a platoon drilling on the parade deck.

Roseanne poked me in the ribs. "Come on Joseph, you need to call Carmine. You could come back out here later." I really didn't want to leave as I followed Roseanne back into the apartment. Roseanne smiled as she handed me the telephone and Carmine's phone number. "Here Joseph, call Carmine. He is concerned about you."

Mark approached me just as I sat down to make my call to Carmine. "Joey I have to go to work now, but before I go, I just want to say that I am proud of you. We are all proud of you. You need to keep in mind that we are all worried about war and the fact that you could be involved in it."

I stood and gave Mark a hug with three or so pats on the back. This is the typical Goomba hug. Mark was by far not a Goomba, but he understands the hug. "Don't worry my brother. I still have training to go through and all we could do is take it from there."

"Okay," Mark said. "I am going to be late. Enjoy your dinner, and I will see you in the morning."

Mark left for work and I called Carmine. "Hello, city morgue."

Carmine always displayed a complete lack of forethought and good sense when answering the telephone. "Carmine, Joe Momma here."

In a vociferous manner, Carmine responded with, "Hey Bro, I see that you made it. Baby Joe Momma is now a United States Marine, go figure."

Carmine was only a few years older than I was. Nevertheless, being a Marine Corps Veteran who seen limited combat, he became a Mentor to me. Little did I know at this time, what a role he would play in my life after my enlistment in the Marine Corps?

"Yeah, I made series Honor Man and received a dress blue uniform and the rank of Private Firsts Class too."

"I heard and congratulations to you Joe Momma. I explained what that all means to your mom and dad."

"How about you Carmine, how are you doing?"

"I am doing fine. I am keeping busy going to school, as well as working for your Uncle Michael. Listen, I'm going to meet you at the airport with a limousine, courtesy of the Tooch, I mean your Uncle Michael. Sorry Joe Momma; I don't mean no disrespect."

I started to laugh. "That's okay; you could call him the Tooch. Sometimes I slipup and do the same thing." Even though I was not happy with the fact that Carmine was picking me up at the airport, I said. "Here, let me give you my flight information."

"I got it, just enjoy your flight." With that said, Carmine hung-up. Jesus, it seemed that everyone knew what I was doing before I could even tell him of her.

No sooner did I hang-up, Roseanne was all over me to call our parents. "Joseph, you better call home."

"Yeah sissy, I'll call them later. I don't want to get nausea and ruin my dinner."

Roseanne stood at the approach to the dining room with her hands on her hips and her eyes narrowed. Uh-oh, I seen that expression before. I have seen it on my mother and grandmother. That expression has become to be known as the look, or the evil eye. Beware of the look. Suddenly I felt like a little kid again. "Okay," I uttered. "I'll call home now."

"Good boy Joseph."

I am not a boy; I am a Marine, I thought as I dialed home. I was happy that my mother answered and not my grandmother. "Hi Mom, its Joey."

"Joseph it is so good to hear from you. Where are you? Are you okay? Did Mark and Roseanne come to your graduation? How was the ceremony?"

"I'm fine Mom. I am with Roseanne at her apartment. Mark had to go to work. Everything is okay. Here, Roseanne wants to talk to you. I love you Mom and I will see you tomorrow." Again, I got the look as I handed the phone to Roseanne.

As soon as Roseanne took the phone, I sat down to watch television. I couldn't believe how much I missed television. Besides, I wanted to watch CNN and see what was going on over in Kuwait.

A few minutes later, Roseanne was standing in the archway holding the phone with her hand over the receiver. "Are you going to say good-bye?" I just waved her off, shaking my head no.

Afterwards, Roseanne and I sat down to dinner, and what a dinner it was. She started out by serving Italian bread with provolone cheese, salami, mozzarella, proscuitto, and a bowl of pasta fazool. "Wow Sissy, this is just like home," I said as I dug in.

"I wanted to give you a treat. Just eat slowly; I do not want you getting sick on all the spicy food I prepared. I know that your system will take time to adjust to this type of food. Joseph are you okay?"

"What Roseanne, what are you talking about?"

"I am just concerned about you Joseph. You seem different that is all. I did not like the way you avoided talking to mother and father. It is not like you to behave in such a manner. I know that I cannot begin to understand what you have gone through for the last three months, but you know that you could talk to me. Is something bothering you?"

"No Sissy, I'm just a little scared that's all and I didn't feel like explaining things to mom and dad right now and have to go through it all again tomorrow."

"Are you scared bout going to war?"

"No not really. After my military occupation specialty training, I will be prepared to go to war and even die for my country if I have to." I could tell by the expression on Roseanne's face that she didn't like that comment. "Roseanne, I just feel a little unsure. I have to prove myself as a Marine. I have to prove myself to dad, and I am scared that I will not live up to everyone's expectations."

"I do not understand Joseph, what expectations?"

"Well," I said with some hesitation. "Three months ago I left New Jersey as a boy, and now I leave California as a man."

"I think I understand what you are saying," Roseanne conveyed. "Now enjoy your appetizers and save room for the main course."

After eating the appetizers, I cleared the table, rinsed off the dishes and placed them in the dishwasher while Roseanne put the main course on the table. She served spaghetti and meatballs, the classic Italian meal. It was definitely mom's recipe, better than you will find in any restaurant. I had to take off my blouse (jacket) and shirt for this meal. You can only eat this kind of meal in your tee shirt.

"Joseph, I must tell you, Mom and Dad are planning a huge party for you upon your arrival home. This is supposed to be a surprise to you, but I feel that I must inform you of this because I want you to be prepared."

I put down my fork, leaned back in the chair and gave my sister a palms up. "Jeez Roseanne, why do they do this kind of stuff? All I wanted to do was to go home, and collect my thoughts for a couple of weeks before reporting for training."

"I know little brother. I cannot begin to understand what basic training was like for you. Carmine explained to me that Marine Corps boot camp could in perspective be compared to prison. I think that the welcome home party is mother's idea. Remember, father was in the Navy, and I think that he understands what you went through."

"Yes," I said. "Dad might understand, but remember, the Marine Corps is a part of the Navy, but the Navy is not the Marine Corps."

• • •

Roseanne avoided talking about the Marine Corps, or war for the remainder of dinner. Most of our conversation was about our mother, father, and grandmother and how they were while growing up. After dinner, we did the dishes.

"Joseph, are you ready for some ricotta pie?"

"Ricotta pie, now there is something we did not get in the mess hall. Come to think of it, we didn't get to eat any sweets during boot camp."

Roseanne came back quickly with the ricotta pie and a large glass of milk. "What are you looking at?" She said as she put the pie and milk on the table.

"I'm looking at this real estate paper," I said as I picked up the pie and shoved it in my mouth."

"Use the fork Joseph. We are not looking to buy a house yet. I just pulled the real estate section out of the newspaper to browse through it. There is no way we could afford to buy. Mark gets nervous every time I bring up the subject."

The hours went by without even realizing it. "Speaking of your husband, where is he? It's getting a little late, ain't it?"

"My wonderful husband is working late. He is getting in some overtime, stripping and waxing the floors after hours at the store."

• • •

My sister and I sat up late, as if we were kids getting away with something. In addition, I ate half of the pie. We were still up watching CNN and talking when Mark came home.

"What are you guys still doing up?" Mark asked.

"We are looking at what kind of house you and Roseanne are going to buy."

"That is a long way off. Buying a house won't happen until I am done with school and Roseanne gets her college degree."

I knew that they made out like fat rats at the wedding. They received a large sum of money in wedding gifts. A large portion of the money came from Uncle Michael and Mark's parents who are well off. Weddings are a big deal for Italians. The ceremony, as well as the reception is where family and friends come together. As in many nationalities, wedding receptions go on all night long with traditions honored. However, there is one difference in Italian weddings. People do not bring kitchen appliances, picture frames, or any gift other than money to an Italian wedding. Therefore, I figured Mark and Roseanne are in good shape. I admired their plan to live off their wedding money as well as work menial jobs until Mark was done with school. Then Mark could start his career while Roseanne went to college. He is correct in saying that a house is a ways down the road.

"I hear what you are saying Mark. I just hope that it don't take too long. I wouldn't mind being an uncle soon. Well I guess it is time to get some sleep since we have to be at the airport in a few hours." Both Mark and Roseanne agreed.

"I will set the alarm," Mark said as Roseanne and I opened the couch bed for me.

• • •

I couldn't sleep. I guess I was too excited about going home. I think that I was too excited or afraid I would not get up, and I would miss my flight. Roseanne must have sensed this too, because she came out of her bedroom and sat with me while Mark got some sleep. I had nothing to pack so I took a quick shower and shaved while Roseanne changed her clothes. A shave, that was uncalled for. After three months of shaving daily, I still didn't have even a whisker on my face.

No sooner did I get in my uniform, and Roseanne was clicking away with her camera again. In what seemed like no time at all, we got Mark up, threw my sea bag, and clothing bag in the car and we were on our way to the airport. The airport was only a short distance from Roseanne and Mark's apartment so it didn't take us long to get there.

Mark turned to me, "Hey Joey, will you stop by and see my parents if you get a chance? I know they would love to see you."

"Yeah Mark, you know I will."

I always viewed Mark's parents as great people. Mrs. Lorenzetti has old fashion ideals just like my mother. Mr. Lorenzetti is a kind man who made his fortune as a contractor. He built homes all over New Jersey. He is a sophisticated, dynamic, original, self-made man. He is a man who can do the impossible and make it look easy. Mr. Lorenzetti has no Mafia connections. He is not a wiseguy. Hell, he is not even a Goomba. As far as I was concerned, Roseanne married into a class family.

"Joseph, do you have your airline ticket?"

I turned, faced the back seat and waved my ticket in Roseanne's face.

Mark laughed. "I guess he has his ticket. I am really going to miss you Joey. Sometimes I wish that I had a brother. I can't wait until you come back."

"I could Mark. Training is one step closer to going to war."

"Do you really think that America is going to war?" Mark inquired.

"I just got a bad feeling," I said. We rode in silence for the last ten minutes. Either we were tired or the reality of war was setting in.

Mark pulled up front of the terminal where the sign read loading and unloading. "Joey I will say my goodbye now. Roseanne will go in with you."

We shook hands. "Mark, you no longer have to wish for a brother. I am your bro; bro."

Roseanne and I checked in my sea bag outside the curb, and I carried the clothing bag with me in the terminal. We checked in at the gate and had a few minutes before boarding.

Roseanne put her hands on my shoulders, and pulled me in for a hug. "I will call mother in a few hours and tell her that her Marine is on his way."

"Okay Sissy, I will call you when I get home," I said just before I turned and made my way through the gate.

• • •

I was not on the plane for ten minutes when I fell asleep. I was so tired that I didn't even know that we were airborne until I woke up two hours later.

"Did you have a good rest?"

I looked over to see an elderly man sitting next to me. "Oh yes Sir. I guess I was pretty tired," I said as I bent down to pick up my cover that fell on the floor. In doing so, I noticed the special orthopedic shoe that the man was wearing.

"My name is Fred Cooper. My friends call me Coop. It's funny how nicknames could stick with you. So much so, I refer to myself as Coop. I served in the Army, and over in Korea too."

"Hello Coop, I know something about nicknames. My name is Private First Class Joseph Mommalione, and my friends call me Joe Momma."

Coop laughed and extended his hand. "Well hello Joe Momma it is a pleasure to meet you," he said as we shook hands. He also said to my embarrassment, "I see that you took a good look at my corrective shoe when you bent over to pickup your hat. Go ahead son ask, I know that you want to."

"With some awkwardness, I asked, "Did you get wounded over there in the Korean War?"

"Yes young man, I guess you could say that. I lost half of my right foot due to frostbite. We were so ill-equipped for the winter that we suffered much from the cold."

We spent the remainder of the flight, even during our meal, talking about boot camp, the military in general, and Coop's experiences in Korea.

• • •

It was about 4:30p.m., Eastern Standard Time when we landed in Philadelphia. I looked at my watch; it was still set to west coast time. It felt good to be home, I thought as I exited my seat to depart the plane. As I stood, I noticed a young sailor that was seated a couple seats behind me. Marines and Navy personal are natural born enemies. Like cats and dogs, they just do not mix. We set that rule aside as we made eye contact and gave each other a look of approval. In front of me were three teenage boys who were goofing off in the isle of the plane. They reminded me of Danny, George, and I. There they were in their leather jackets with their hair long and one with his slicked back. I ran my hand over my baldhead and laughed. I might be minus my hair I thought, but thus far the Marines have been good for me. Just a few months ago, I was a self-indulgent kid just like them who spent their time hanging out avoiding responsibility, work, or any useful action. A real wiseguy wannabe was I.

I said goodbye to Coop. My stomach was churning as the line moved slowly forward and it had nothing to do with the flight dinner. I was excited to see Carmine. It took about ten minutes to exit the plane, and there stood Carmine, waiting for me with a huge smile on his face. We gave each other the typical Goomba hug including the kiss on the cheek and the pats on the back. The kiss and pat on the back was to tell each other that you are an okay guy, but I don't want to fuck you. It is an Italian thing.

"You did it," Carmine said.

"I could not have done it without you."

"Oh yes you could. Come on; let's get your sea bag. The limo is waiting."

"Could we stop at your place first so I could change into my blues before going to my parent's house?"

"You are reading my mind," Carmine said.

We got my sea bag from baggage and went out to the limousine. I have never been in a limo before. I had seen one at my sisters wedding, but I didn't ride in it. As soon as we got in, Carmine popped open a bottle of champagne. I thought it seemed odd that I could go and fight for my country, but it is illegal for me to drink alcohol.

Carmine raised his glass. "Here's to you Joe Momma."

"Semper Fi," I said. Semper Fi is short for the Marine Corps motto Semper Fidelis, which is Latin for always faithful.

As the limo pulled off, Carmine asked, "So what did you think of those Drill Instructors?"

"The senior was okay, but those juniors were real bastards."

"I know what you mean Joe Momma, but I'll tell you, you will never forget them."

Carmine offered to refill my glass, but I pulled my glass back. I felt a buzz after only one drink, so I stopped with the champagne. Carmine must have understood because he did not push it.

• • •

An hour after we left the airport, the limo came to a stop in Chambersburg. Carmine grew up in the Old Italian quarter of Trenton and is now living in an apartment above a liquor store owned by my Uncle Michael, A.K.A. the Tooch, Crime Boss, and Godfather of Trenton as well as most of Central New Jersey.

"Carmine, could we loose the limo? I would rather you drive me to the house."

"I understand," Carmine said as he went to tip the limo driver. The driver refused the tip. I guess that the Tooch must have had it covered.

As we went upstairs, I asked. "How is my uncle treating you?"

"Oh great, he is a real friend of mine."

I thought, he must mean that my uncle is a real stand up guy. Because, if you refer to someone as a friend of mine, in Goomba lingo, it means that he is a member of the Mafia. I already knew that about Uncle Michael. Then again, the term "stand up guy," is used to describe someone who will not rat on someone. Sometimes I get confused with all this mob slang. As Carmine continued to explain, I was able to understand what he was saying.

"I hold your Uncle Michael in the highest esteem. He has me working as a cook and tending bar in his South Broad Street Casa-di-Roma restaurant, while I attend school for hotel management. I do other things for him too. I do some collecting, body guard and tough guy work for him."

We were sitting at the kitchen table when I asked, "What Skipper (crew boss) does the Tooch have you reporting to?"

Carmine put a Pepsi in front of me. With some hesitation he said, "I account to Vito (Big Nose) Barbero, that stonzo di merda."

Again, I was confused. I really must brush up on my Italian. I was not sure if Carmine called Vito a fucking bastard or a fucking shithead. The important thing was that Carmine knew what he said and it was not nice. I just shook my head up and down and responded with, "Vito is a real motherfucker. He is so tough, that he could make a Marine Corps Drill Instructor look like a boy scout." We both laughed.

"Come on Joe Momma let me show you around."

Carmine's apartment lacked the Goomba look. He had roosters in the kitchen wallpaper, lace in the curtains, and knickknacks all over the parlor. His bedroom looked like a dollhouse. The place looked too sweet. The apartment did have its share of luxuries in the way of furniture, appliances, and electronics. I figured most of the costly items were swag (stolen goods). Most of those things probably fell off a truck. I just gave Carmine a confused look accompanied with palms up and shook my head side to side.

"I know, I know," Carmine said. "My girlfriend decorated it. What could I say, she's Polish. Wait until you see her, she is a real good-looking woman. How is Sally doing? When are you going to see her?"

"I'm not going to see her. She dumped me," I said.

"Oh man Joe Momma, it don't mean nothing. Wait until you get on a cruise to the orient and you visit the Philippines, Thailand, Hong Kong, Japan and Singapore. Perhaps you will land a med cruise, and visit all the Mediterranean countries. When you do, you will be fucking so much that your dick will fall off."

"Perhaps I will end up in war and die before I ever get a chance to fuck at all."

Carmine changed the subject. "Come here Joe. Let me show you something more characteristic of Carmine (the Collector) Scalia." Carmine took a key out of his pocket and unlocked a bedroom door.

I was shocked when I walked in. He had a huge Marine Corps flag hanging on one wall. On another, he had several assault pistols and assault rifles. On a third wall was antique rifles, shotguns, and swords. On the door sidewall, he had a bookcase with Marine pictures and his honorable discharge. In the middle of the room was a big wooden desk with an American and Italian flag on it. I was truly impressed. He took a minute to show me his Marine Corps sword and a stereo system that he shipped back from Japan. He had Marine Corps memorabilia all over the room. I was convinced that one day, I would have a den just like his. I reached over and picked up a picture from his desk. This picture was of a beautiful sexy girl at the shore.

"Carmine, is this your girl?"

"Yeah bro, that is my girlfriend, Holly."

"I see what you mean," I declared. "She is gorgeous. If I was waking up next to a woman like this, I would let her decorate my apartment anyway she liked, except for my den that is."

"Come on, change your uniform and meet me out back in the garage. Just make sure the door is shut and locked when you leave."

I changed into my dress blues and went in the backyard to meet Carmine. "Do you want to see something hotter than Holly?" Carmine said as he opened the garage door.

There stood a new dark blue 1990 Pontiac Firebird. She had slender and graceful lines with a satiny polish. "Whatta car, this car is ravishing." I said. "You are doing good Carmine. Maybe one day you will be a crew boss."

"No not me, I have no desire to be a made man. I must say tough, I am enjoying the juice (power) my position has given me. The hotel management is where it's at for me. One day, I will be working in Atlantic City or maybe Vegas. Vegas will be better yet. Of course, I will pay tribute to the Tooch for helping me get there. Besides, I think that it is you who will be groomed for a middle management position in the family. If that is the case, I will be at your service if you need me. Perhaps one day, you will be Godfather of Trenton, and all of New Jersey. Imagine, Joseph (Joe Momma) Mommalione, head of the Jersey Mafia. It has a ring to it. Your Uncle Michael has big plans for you Joe Momma. You are going to be a boss one day."

I gave Carmine a dumb look as if to say what are you talking about. He slapped me upside the head. "Don't worry about that right now," he said as he hand me the keys and put my sea bag in the trunk. "Go ahead, you drive."

"I can't," I said. "I haven't driven in three months. What if I wreck it? No Carmine, I can't." Carmine clamed up as he got in the car on the passenger side. I slowly pulled out and made my way to Hamilton Street, which I took over to Nottingham Way. I knew that his car was fast and powerful, but I drove slow as I headed east toward Hamilton Square.

Seven

Hamilton Square is a suburb of Trenton. I love American history, and this area of New Jersey is loaded with history. Being that I love American history, I made it a point to learn as much as possible about my family's history as it pertains to them coming from Italy and settling in New Jersey. My mother's maiden name is Tucci. My Uncle Michael is her younger brother and my Aunt Theresa is her older sister. Aunt Theresa is married to my Uncle Angie who is a part owner of an Italian restaurant in Princeton. Of course, his partner is Uncle Michael. Grandma Tucci lives with us. My grandmother is one who is traditional, especially in an old fashioned Italian way, even though she was born in America, as were her parents. The Tucci's arrived in America back in the 1880's and settled in the Chambersburg neighborhood of Trenton which was a rather small part of the city's geographic unit. I learned that there were so few Italians in Mercer County back then, that the United States census did not even count them. The population of Trenton was more than one quarter foreign born by 1910. By then, most of the Italian immigrants were passing through Ellis Island. It is obvious that Italians were not alone among Trenton's foreign population. There were Germans, Irish, Polish, Jewish, Hungarians, Puerto Ricans, Africans, Slovaks, and others. Chambersburg was largely an Irish and German borough before the Italians settled there. I was told that Italians settled on such streets as Chambers, Butler, Elmer, and Bayard as well as others with non-Italian names in the Burg. I always wondered why there were no streets with Italian names in Chambersburg, now I know why.

Even though so many Italians had left the Burg for the suburbs, many of them along with those who are not Italian go to Chambersburg weekly to eat at the many Italian restaurants. I am happy by the extent to which Italian-Americans as well as other nationalities in this area still help each other out by patronizing business in the Burg.

My grandfather Tucci owned a grocery store on Chambers Street. He was also a laborer, working in construction, as well as a barber. Grandpa Tucci died of heart failure. He said the reason he died was that he drank too much and he was nasty. I am not sure if I agree with all that, but rumor had it that Grandpa Tucci had a barbershop where illegal gambling took place in the backroom. Rumor also has it that he ran numbers too.

My mother and father bought their house in Hamilton Square in the late seventies. My parents married before my father went into the Navy. During the time that my father was away, my mother went to college for journalism. Her job includes a company car, she is employed as a news writer for a local talk radio station.

When my father got out of the Navy, he went to college on the G.I. Bill. My father works for the State of New Jersey. He does planning and design of highways and city streets. His work also includes traffic requirements, safety control, drainage, and sub grade structure. It seems like my father has a great job, but according to him, the state does not pay very well. I know that he could afford a better car though. He is so cheap. My father did not grow up in Chambersburg. In fact, he was born in Sicily. He came from Sicily when he was only eleven years old. He is one of four brothers who came to America. He came first. He came to America and lived with his aunt and uncle, who lived in North Trenton. It seems that southern and central people from Italy tended to settle in Chambersburg in those days, while the Sicilians settled along the railroad tracks in North Trenton. My grandmother and grandfather on my father's side still live in Sicily. I have never been there, but my mother, father, and uncles, as well as their wives go every couple of years or so and my grandparents come here often. They tried to settle in America, but did not like it so they went back to Sicily. I think that their decision to go back to Sicily had something to do with not liking New Jersey. All my father's brothers are here in New Jersey, except for my Uncle Frankie, who teaches at the University in Ithaca, New York, which is only about a four-hour ride from Jersey. My Uncle Pauly is a lawyer in Newark and my Uncle Mario has a funeral home business in Freehold.

• • •

I could not believe the number of cars parked on the street when I drove by the house. It looked like a funeral was about to take place with Uncle Mario's Cadillac parked in front. It has Mommalione funeral services painted on the doors. I told my mother and father that I preferred that no fuss be made when I came home. I should have known that they would not listen. Even Roseanne tried to tell them that I didn't want a reception when I got home. Maybe it would not have been like this if it were not a Sunday, I thought.

"Jesus Christ, do you believe this Carmine?"

"This is wild Joe Momma. Pull down the side street and we will surprise everyone by sneaking in the back door. Besides, there is nowhere to park anyway." We did exactly that. I pulled down the street and there was still nowhere to park. I was lucky that Mrs. Kozinski was standing in front of her house.

"Hey beautiful," I said as I put the window down. Could we park in your driveway?"

"Well if it isn't Joseph Mommalione. Aren't you a sight for sore eyes? You sure could park in my driveway."

I pulled in the driveway and was in Mrs. Kozinski's arms as soon as I exited the car. After talking with Mrs. Kozinski for a few minutes, Carmine and I crossed the street and cut through the yard to the back door. It was a cool day so all my little cousins were playing inside. The smell of tomato sauce was so potent that we could smell it outside. We opened the back door between the house and the garage apartment and quietly entered. I felt as though we were on a reconnaissance mission. My dog, Lucky, almost gave our position away. She came running up the stairs from the cellar. She barked a little until she realized that it was me. I bent down to greet her, as I did not want her to jump up on my uniform. She is really Roseanne's dog, but we would not let Roseanne take Lucky with her when she moved to California. In the kitchen, I could hear my grandmother talking. We have a huge kitchen with a restaurant stainless steel stove in it. Everyone else was in the parlor or dinning room. In the background, I could hear Italian music playing.

No one is allowed in the kitchen when my mother and grandmother are cooking. Grandma was on the kitchen phone talking to an old woman from her singles club or beauty parlor. I could hear her talking about a dance she attended on Friday night. "That old cornuto, he put his hand directly on my culo as we were dancing," she said into the phone. I peeked around the wall and noticed that she had her back to me. I was watching her as she was talking about some old man. All the while, she was talking; she was making a gesture with her free hand. She had the forefinger and little finger extended like a pair of horns.

I stepped into the kitchen, "What old bastard put his hand on your ass. And, what a bony little ass it is."

Well, she turned and let out a scream that sent everyone running to the kitchen. "Joey is home," she yelled as she jumped into my arms and kissed me all over my face. She took off my cover and started rubbing my brush cut head. "Look at you, you look so handsome. And, is that Carmine Scalia with you?" Come over here Carmine and give Grandma a big kiss, you good looking hoodlum you."

Grandma is so crazy. Carmine went to give her a kiss, and she planted one on his lips. "You know that I use to date your grandfather?" Carmine didn't know what to say.

There must have been about forty people in the house and they were all jammed in front of the kitchen door. Suddenly, just like when Moses parted the Red Sea, everyone stepped to either side and my mother walked through. There she stood in one of her Sunday dresses, with her long black hair pulled over her right shoulder.

"Joseph."

"Hello Mom."

She held her arms out and open to me. She looked like a movie star. "Come to me Joseph."

I ran across the kitchen to her. I put my hands around her tiny little waist and lifted her above my head. As I put her down, she kissed me on the corner of my mouth. I wiped a tear from her cheek with my white gloves.

I felt like I was going through a gauntlet when my mother led me to my father. A friendly gauntlet that is, as I got many pats on my back. My dad was standing in the parlor looking out the window.

"Hi Dad," At first, I thought that he was mad at me. When he faced me, I put my cover on, snapped to attention and gave him a hand salute. Everyone started to cheer when my father hugged me and kissed me on both sides of my face.

"You look sharp in that uniform Son. Carmine told me what it means to be awarded a dress blue uniform. Oh yes, I need to pin those stripes on for you."

"Yes Sir," I said as I gave him my right shoulder. He gave me a punch in the arm that almost knocked me over. I was a little hesitant to put my left shoulder forward.

"Joseph," my mother yelled out.

"Both my father and I responded with, "What!"

"Do not hit your son."

"I have to dear, it would be bad luck not to finish," my dad said as he punched me in my left arm. My dad turned and faced his guests. "Let us sit down and eat, my son is home from the Marines."

Uncle Michael came to greet me. "It is good to have you home Joseph."

"Thank you Uncle Michael and thank you for getting me a limo, I felt like a rock star riding in it. Sorry I didn't bring it to the house. I just wanted to surprise mom."

"My sister is lucky to have a boy like you. Now go and greet your guests. I will talk with you later. I am proud of you young man." My Uncle Michael is also my godfather and because he has two daughters and no sons, he is very fond of me.

I went around and talked with everyone. Carmine was in the kitchen with my mother and grandmother. I think he was dipping bread in the sauce. I guess that because he is Carmine, my mother made an exception to the no one in the kitchen rule. I bet that if I were to have gone to the kitchen, my mother would have kicked me out. It was not long before we were going to eat anyway, so I stayed out of the kitchen. I passed the mirror on the wall in the dinning room and realized I was so happy to be home and in my dress blue uniform too. I would have been just as proud in my green uniform, but the blues made the feeling a little bit more special. I was making my rounds when my mother came up to me and gave me a tight hug.

"Joseph, we will not be eating for a little while."

"Will you need help serving?" I asked.

"With all your aunts here, I should say not. Why not go up to your room for a minute?"

My mother was reading my mind. I was dying to go to my room, but I didn't want to appear rude if I were to disappear. I was only gone for a few months, but I really missed my room. However, I was disappointed when I entered. It looked like a little kid's room, except for one thing. Over my bed hung a Marine Corps poster that I assumed my father hung up. I took off my blouse, hung it over my desk chair, and plopped on the bed. Lucky followed me up the stairs. She knew that she was pushing the envelope as she is not allowed upstairs, but I guess she really missed me. Lucky jumped up on the bed and we started rolling around. It didn't last very long as there was a knock at the door.

"Joey, it is Bria, are you decent?"

Bria is the daughter of my Uncle Mario and Aunt Nina. She is so hot. She was seventeen at the time and a year younger than me. If she were not my cousin, I would have hit on her a long time ago. "Yes Bria, come on in."

"Your mother sent me up to get you. Dinner will be ready in about twenty minutes." She was staring at me as I put my blouse on. "You look so sexy in that uniform Joey. I am a sucker for a guy in uniform. You think that maybe we could go to the movies some time while you are home?"

"Sure Bria, how about one night next week? I will call you."

"Yeah Joey that will be swell, will you wear your uniform?"

"Sure I will, but not this one. This is a ceremonial uniform. I will wear my green uniform. Now come on, we had better go downstairs before my grandmother thinks something is going on up here."

We had to fight our way through the crowd. Being the dining room was not large enough to hold everyone, my mother had tables set up in the parlor and family room, which is where my cousins sat.

I was looking for Carmine as I ran into my dad. "Dad, where is Carmine," I asked.

"Don't worry about Carmine. He is in the kitchen with your grandmother. He already ate enough to feed a horse. Come, today you will sit at the head of the table."

A proud man I was. My father sat at my left side and there was an empty chair for my mother on my right. My mother does not sit much when we have a dinner like this. She is always bringing food to the table or filling up empty bowls. Uncle Michael sat directly across from me at the other end of the long table. No sooner did we sit when all my aunts came out of the kitchen carrying a bowl or plate. It was like a friggin parade. I laughed when I saw Carmine. He was the line leader. I sat there with my hands clinched to the armrests.

It don't get any better than this. When I get out of the Marines, I am going to go to college and then I am going to marry an old-fashioned Italian girl just like mom, I thought.

I sat at the table thinking that growing up in this family has always been fun. Most Sundays we had dinner at one of my aunt and uncle's houses. In the summer months, the dinners were held at Uncle Michael's beach house. No one spoke normal when we got together for Sunday dinner. You have to yell if you wanted to be heard because everyone is screaming. The food is always great, especially when grandma and mom are doing the cooking. This was the first time that I didn't help with getting dinner together. Before anyone arrived, I always helped set the table and put out the bread, wine, salami, provolone cheese, prosciutto and fruit. When dinner started, we would eat and argue. Later, after we rested and my uncles took naps, it would start all over again when my mother and grandmother served the Italian sausage and roasted peppers with garlic.

What a great feeling. My cousin, Nino, took his place between the dining room and parlor. Nino is an alter boy at St. Anthony's. He will probably grow up to be a priest. After my cousin Nino said grace, everyone started to dig in. Moreover, the arguing began. Italian kids are no different from the adults. I could hear them arguing from the other room. My cousin Nino was the loudest. We were only a few minutes into the eating and hollering when my father stood up and demanded everyone's attention. It took what seemed like five minutes to get everyone to quiet down. "A toast," my father said. "I would like to make a toast to my son, Private First Class Joseph Michael Mommalione of the United States Marine Corps."

I saw my Uncle Michael's face light up when my father used my middle name. I wish that one day, my father and Uncle Michael would come together for a sit-down. A sit-down is a big meeting between fighting families or members of a family usually reserved for the mob, but I thought to myself that a sit-down would do them good. My mother always says that we should be grateful that they even tolerate each other.

My father went on with the toast. "I wish my son well as he goes off to defend our wonderful United States of America. May he defeat the enemy? With the grace of God, may he come home safe."

Everyone raised their glasses to me and said, "Salud." I enjoyed everyone's gesture of appreciation and admiration for my achievements. Nevertheless, talk of war had me a little concerned. My plans were to get my training in California and then be assigned to a Navy ship in the orient. All I could say is lucky mom was in the kitchen and didn't hear dad's toast.

• • •

My grandmother cornered me in-between rounds of eating. "Joseph, I am sorry to hear what your girlfriend did to you, and while you was away too."

"That is okay Grandma. I will be fine."

"I only worry about you Joey. She is nothing but a battona (whore)." I changed the subject and asked. "Did Roseanne call yet?"

"Yes Joey. She called twice earlier in the day and then again just before dinner. I think you were upstairs in your room when she called. Joey, I don't know why she had to marry that boy and move to California. Now both of your mother's children are away."

"Grandma, you have been told a hundred times, Mark had to go to California. His scholarship is at the University of San Diego. Did you want Roseanne to run off to California with Mark and not be married?" She married Mark just as mom married Dad before he went away to the Navy and the war in Vietnam. She did the right thing."

"I didn't like your mother doing that either. Joey, are you going to war?"

"I don't know Grandma, but if I do, I will be ready."

I gave grandma a big hug. "I love you Grandma. I will talk to you later." She then handed me a folded plastic booklet. On one side was a St. Anthony medal and on the other was the prayer of St. Anthony.

"Keep this on you at all times."

"Okay I will Grandma."

My mother and father were in the basement getting some wine. Most of my uncles were sleeping. Carmine and the Tooch were talking business. Since all my aunts and female cousins were cleaning up and getting ready for the Italian sausage with roasted peppers and garlic, I went upstairs with the intention of making some phone calls to my friends. I ended up lying on the bed and I fell asleep just like the old men.

I was out like a light when I was awakened by a soft touch on my face. At first, I thought I was dreaming, but when I focused, I was staring at a pair of long silky legs in a short skirt. It turned out to be Bria. She sat on the side of my bed and said, "Come on Joey. It is time to eat."

"Already," I said."

"Yes Joey. You slept longer than you think."

"Did my mother send you to see me?"

"No, I came all on my own," she said as she bent over and kissed me. It was a long passionate kiss with a little tongue. I couldn't believe that I gave into her. She then slowly rubbed my face with the back of her hand and left the room. I hurried up, put my blouse and shoes on, and started down the stairs. I was lucky that I had my cover in my hand. I was able to use it to cover my crotch as I had a boner.

Once again, a pleasant odor filled the house. This time the arguing started before the food made its way on the table. I couldn't quite understand all the words because this time, most of the yelling was in Italian. Uncle Michael did respond in English. "If you do not like it here, go back to Italy." They must have been arguing about the government, foreign policy, or something like that. They stopped arguing when the food came. Then they went on to argue about something else. All through dinner, I was thinking about Bria.

• • •

All the women started cleaning after the sausage and roasted peppers. It was getting late, so we did not have dessert. Grandma was making dessert bags for everyone to take home. The men were watching football and I walked Carmine to his car.

"Carmine, how come you spent so much time in the kitchen, where you checking out my mother?"

We both started to laugh at what I said. "Actually, I was having fun. I like to cook and your mother and grandmother were giving me some tips. I have to tell you though, when I was a kid, I use to call on your sister just to get a look at your mother."

"Don't worry, I won't tell anyone," I said. We started to laugh again. All my friends had a thing for my mother. I remember getting in fights with the guys over it when I was younger. To me, she was just mom. I didn't understand all the excitement over her at the time. I took their excitement over my mom as an insult.

"Enjoy your leave Joe Momma. Call me. I would like to discuss where you are going from here. I have more advice for you." We hugged, and patted each other on the back before he got in his car and drove off.

I went inside and tried to help cleanup, but I was yelled at for the good intention. I was going to go upstairs and change out of my uniform, but I decided to sit with my cousins and uncles to watch some football. Besides, I was afraid that Bria would follow me.

One by one, everyone started to leave. I waited by the door and got so many kisses and pats on the back that it started to hurt. Bria did give me a cousin type kiss when she left, but whispered, "Call me."

I walked Uncle Michael and his family out to their car. "You are my favorite nephew Joseph. You are like a son to me. Make sure you come and see me before you leave."

"Okay Uncle Michael, I will," I said as I received more hugs and kisses from my Aunt Connie and my cousins as well as from the Tooch.

• • •

I spent the first few days of my leave hanging around with my friends. Things just were not the same. Most of these kids were going nowhere fast. I joined the Marine Corps to get away from this way of life. Some of my friends were in meaningless jobs. Many of them were doing petty crimes, and some were getting high, or doing both. The smart boys and girls I graduated with went to college either locally or away. A couple of my friends were still in high school so they couldn't even come out at night. I was not having much fun. Sally called a few times, but all I could think about was the Dear John letter she sent me, so I refused to talk to her. The boredom got so bad that on Wednesday, I volunteered to take grandma to the beauty parlor to get her hair and nails done. Afterwards, we stopped at a diner on Route 1 and had lunch. Then, we went to the Quaker Bridge Mall, where Grandma did some shopping. We had a blast. Grandma flirted with every man over forty. I laughed because she was enjoying every minute of it. We were walking past a men's shop when she stopped.

"Joey, I want to buy you some clothes for when you go out on liberty."

"I have money Grandma." I dreaded the thought of my grandmother buying me clothes.

"No, this is on me Joey. I insist and I don't want to hear another word about it."

Grandma is a lot of fun. My mother and father would never take any money from grandma for household expenses, so she is always buying food or things that we might like. She ended up buying me a couple of outfits that consisted of two pull over short sleeve shirts and trousers to match. She even bought me a light three quarter length black leather jacket and a pair of Italian made shoes. She bought dad a real sharp looking Goomba shirt. My father by no means is connected with the Mafia, but he enjoys dressing like a Goomba. Not every Italian man is a Goomba, not every Italian man is in the Mafia.

One does not have to be Italian to be associated with the Mafia, but one has to be Italian to be a Goomba. Explaining the Goomba is a difficult thing, because it is an Italian thing. Only an Italian can understand the definition of a Goomba. He may not be able to explain it, but he understands it. In addition, only Italian-American men are Goombas. There are no Goombas in Italy. Go figure. My dad is definitely a Goomba but he was born in Italy. All he needs is a Goomba car and he would be a perfect Goomba, minus the cheating on my mother part that is.

• • •

It was about 5:30 in the afternoon when we got home. I noticed Uncle Michael's car parked in the driveway. I also noticed a car parked in front of the house with white U.S. Government license plates. I knew why Uncle Michael was at the house. He always stops by and brings mom some food. She particularly likes it when he brings prosciutto because he always slices it very thin at the restaurant before bringing it over. What puzzled me was the government car parked out front. I pulled in behind the government car and ran to the front door.

Grandma yelled out, "What is the matter?"

I didn't respond, as my mother was waiting by the door with an unusual look on her face. "What is wrong Mom?"

"Joseph, there are two men from the service inside."

Grandma yelled from the front of the house, "What is going on? Joey come and help me with the bags."

I followed my mother in the house, and there stood a Staff Sergeant from the Marine Corps, and a Lieutenant, Junior Grade, from the Navy waiting to see me. I shook hands with both of them and the Marine spoke first.

"Good evening Private First Class Mommalione. I am Staff Sergeant Walker, and this is Lieutenant Meadow. Lieutenant Meadow is a Liaison Officer. I also work for the Department of the Navy Liaison Office in Philadelphia. Lieutenant Meadow will take it from here."

Just then Grandma came busting through the door. "What the hell is going on here?" She made the Lieutenant jump a little.

"Grandma these men are from the Department of the Navy Liaison Office and are here to speak to me on official business."

I looked at the officer and said, "Please speak Sir."

"Pfc. Mommalione I regret to inform you that new orders have been cut for you. Due to training requirements and a timetable that needs to be met, you are to report to the Air Ground Combat Center at Twentynine Palms on November 18, 1990 at 1800 hours to begin your training in Naval Intelligence. Your current orders are void. Here are your new orders."

"That means he has to go back a week early," my mother cried out. Michael, can you do something?"

Uncle Michael gave palms up with both hands. "I have much pull in Trenton, but when it comes to the Department of the Navy, I am afraid my hands are tied. All I could say is that my nephew must be a very important man for the Marines to want him back early, and be assigned to intelligence too."

"Lieutenant Meadow handed me an envelope containing my orders and said, "Good day ladies." Then he and Staff Sergeant Walker shook hands with Uncle Michael and I led them to the front door.

"Lieutenant Meadow, is there more to this?" I asked.

"What do you mean Pfc?"

"Are we going to war Sir?"

"I am not at liberty to say any more than the probability of war is likely."

"Will I be going Sir?"

The lieutenant put on his cover and nodded his head up and down. He then grabbed the brim of his cover and conveyed, Good evening Ma'am. I turned to see my mother standing behind me.

Staff Sergeant Walker hesitated, turned to me and said. "Pfc. you are a Marine. Your military occupational specialty is intelligence. You must have scored high on your tests to have that M.O.S. Wherever your duties take you, you will serve your Unit, Corps, God, and America gloriously. Make your family proud." He then shook my hand, did an about face and exited the house.

By then, my mother was hysterical. "I told Joseph not to send our boy to the Marines. I told him that our boy will be going to war."

"Mary, calm down," Uncle Michael said. He grabbed my mother by the arms. "Joseph reporting early to training has nothing to do with war. They probably have men sitting around doing nothing and want to start a class with everyone present."

Uncle Michael then took my mother into the kitchen to talk to her. Grandma came by me in the parlor. "What is your mother so upset about Joey?"

"Oh, I asked the officer if we were going to war and mom overheard me."

Grandma put her hand on my shoulder. "Anyway Joey, your Uncle Michael brought us a big pot of pasta fazool and Italian bread for dinner."

"That is good Grandma," I said and we went to the kitchen.

When we reached the kitchen, I could hear Uncle Michael talking to my mother. "Now Mary, snap out of it. Do not let your husband see you like this when he gets home."

"I'm sorry Mom," I cried out.

"Joseph come and give your mother a hug."

As I hugged, mom, dad came in the back door leading to the kitchen. Everyone tried to act like nothing was wrong, but I knew that dad could see through the act. "What is with the long faces?" dad asked.

"Oh some men were here from the service and it turns out that Joey has to report to duty a week early," grandma said.

"Is that all, that happened to me once, but then again, there was a war on."

Well, that is all my mother had to hear, and the tears started to flow again.

"What did I tell you Mary," Uncle Michael whispered.

"Joseph, Michael brought some pasta fazool for dinner," grandma said.

Uncle Michael yelled out, "I'm going now. Enjoy dinner, and I want everyone at the restaurant for dinner Saturday night. Joseph, do me the honor of seeing you before you go back Sunday."

"No party Uncle Michael."

"No party, just dinner," Uncle Michael said as he kissed mom and grandma before leaving.

I think that my father knew there was more to the events of the visit from the Navy Liaison Office than he was told, but he never said a word about it all through dinner. That is the way my father is. Neither my grandmother nor mother said anything about my conversation with the Naval Officer about going to war.

The only conversation about the visit was when grandma inquired, "Joey why didn't you salute that young officer?"

My response was, "Because Grandma, you only salute an officer when you are in uniform and you never salute when inside unless you have a cover on. You only have a hat on indoors if you are on guard duty or if you are a member of a color guard." I then laughed and said, "Do you understand?"

"I think so," grandma declared with a puzzled look on her face. Dad started to laugh and mom even smiled a little.

After dinner, grandma and I did the dishes and cleaned up while mom and dad went upstairs. I am sure they were talking about the visit from Lieutenant Meadow and Staff Sergeant Walker.

Once grandma and I finished the dishes, I called Carmine. I was lucky to catch him at home. A girl with a sweet voice answered the phone.

"Hello, may I speak with Carmine please,"

"You sure may," she said in a sexy voice.

I waited a few seconds for Carmine to come to the phone. All he said was, "Yo."

"Carmine, Joe Momma here. Did I interrupt anything?"

"No Joey, not at all. What's up?"

"Today I got a visit from the Naval Liaison Office in Philadelphia. They informed me that my leave has been cut short and that I have to report to duty one week early."

"Joe Momma, I know all about it. The Tooch called me a little while ago. Listen, I still have some friends in high places in the Corps. I am going to see what I can find out about this war stuff. Meet me at the admissions building at Mercer Community College at 1:00 tomorrow afternoon."

"Okay Carmine and thank you."

• • •

113

The next day was Thursday. I got up early and made my airline reservations. I then called my sister.

"Hello," she said in a sleepy voice."

"Sissy, it's me Joey. Did I wake you?"

"No Joseph. It is about 8:30 here. What is wrong? Is everything okay?"

"Oh yes, everything is okay. It is just that I have to report a week early for duty, so I will arrive in San Diego at about 11:00 on Sunday."

"That is okay Joseph. Mark already has the directions to Twentynine Palms. It is about a three-hour ride from San Diego. We will pick you up at the airport and go directly there."

"Thank you," I said. "Mom will call you with my flight information. It will give her an excuse to call you. Not that she needs one."

"Okay Joseph and do not worry about anything. Just enjoy what time you have left at home. I love you."

"Love you too," I said as I hung up.

I met Carmine at 1:00 o'clock at the college. "Ciao Joe Momma."

"Ciao Carmine", I said.

"Joey, I have an hour until my next class. Come, we will go to the cafeteria and get a bite to eat while we talk."

I couldn't help but to notice that Carmine was unusually quiet as we walked. We ordered a couple of hamburgers and fries and took a seat at a table in the corner.

"Listen up Joey. This is what I found out. By the first of this month, while you were still in boot camp, the 7th Marine Expeditionary Brigade from California had been stationed in Saudi Arabia. The 7th MEB is at strength of some forty-two thousand Marines. That is a quarter of the Corps. By the middle of January, the strength is expected to be at ninety-thousand. We are going to war bro."

I looked Carmine in the eyes. "Is that all," I said as I felt he was holding something back.

"No, Joe Momma. That is not all. I have much to tell you. Almost all the Marine reservists are being called up to active duty. The 2nd Marine Division and the remaining aircraft groups from the 2nd Marine Aircraft Wing are heading for the Gulf at the end of

December. They are to be followed by the 5th Marine Expeditionary Brigade in January. You will most likely be going with the 5th Marine Expeditionary Brigade."

"Carmine, how did you find all this out in one night?" I probably should not have asked I thought, but I was curious.

"I saved an Officer's life while we were fighting in Panama. He is now stationed in Washington D.C. Need I say more?"

"No Carmine, does the Tooch know?"

"Yes, I briefed him this morning, and that is as far as this information goes. As for now, this is still top secret information, capeesh?"

"Don't worry Carmine, I won't say a word."

"I know you won't, because Joe Momma is a stand up guy. You told me that you are going to Twentynine Palms, which I know is a desert training area, but I can't remember if you told me what your M.O.S. is?"

"Intelligence is my military occupational specialty."

"This is good news Joey. You will probably be stationed at headquarters. It seems like you will be gathering information from combat and air groups. You will probably gather the information, code it, and brief the brass. You may have to update troop movements on maps or prepare maps and brief troops on enemy movement. Now, I am just assuming it is going to go this way."

At that point, I was thinking of my mother. I was worried how she was going to feel when she found out that I am going to war. I was only hearing half of what Carmine was saying. Suddenly, I felt a slap upside my head. "Are you listening to me Joe Momma? What I have to say is very important, so listen up. I said that I assume things are going to go as I stated, but you never know. Joey, if you find yourself in a combat situation, I want you to think. It only takes a few seconds to think. My military occupational specialty was infantry. As a grunt, I received three months additional infantry training. I also received infantry training on a daily basis after that. You will not have that type of training, but you learned enough in boot camp to cover your ass if the shit hits the fan. You must be a smart man to have the M.O.S. they gave you. Too bad you aren't a college boy, you are probably officer material. Trust me if you find yourself in a combat situation, you will have no fear. Just think baby. Those few seconds it takes to think will save your life and the lives of fellow Marines. Do you hear me Marine?"

I could tell that Carmine was very concerned for me. "Yes Carmine, I hear and understand what you are saying."

"Wait, I got more. Do everything that you can to avoid becoming a prisoner of war. Never surrender. Marines never surrender or retreat. If you do become a P.O.W., give only your name, rank, and serial number. Look directly in the camera, because they will film your ass. Don't break down or say anything wrong. You couldn't say anything wrong if you only give your name, rank, and serial number. Remember, you are a Marine. People will be watching you on the news. Do not embarrass your family or the Corps, because when the war is over and you are back in the world, you will look back on disgraceful behavior, and you will wish you were dead. And, any sign of weakness will only get you a bullet in the head from them motherfuckers. Trust me; I was trained in P.O.W. survival. If you are tortured, and I don't mean just slapped around, you need to think positive. Think no pain. Think of a happy place. Think about the fact that you are still alive at the moment. Remember the code of Conduct and that it is your duty to escape. If you become a P.O.W. and are asked, why are you in Iraq, what do you say?"

"I will tell them that I was just following orders," I said in a confident way.

"Carmine yelled out at the top of his lungs, "What the fuck did I just tell you Joey? You give your NAME, RANK, AND SERIAL NUMBER, and that is it. Do you understand?"

All the kids in the cafeteria were looking at us. "I understand," I said.

"Good Joey. Now recite the Code of conduct to me. Come on, start with article one."

"Okay Carmine here goes. Article one. I am an American fighting man. I serve in the forces, which guard my country and our way of life. I am prepared to give my life in their defense"

"Now give me article two."

"I will never surrender of my own free will. If in command, I will never surrender my men while they still have the means to resist."

"Article Three."

"If I am captured, I will continue to resist by all means available. I will make every effort to escape. I will accept neither parole nor special favors from the enemy."

"You are doing good Joey. Continue with article four."

"If I become a prisoner of war, I will keep faith with my fellow prisoners. I will give no information nor take part in any action, which might be harmful to my comrades. I can't remember the rest," I said nervously."

"Close enough Joey. You only have two more to go. Give me article five."

"When questioned, I am bound to give only my name, rank, service number, and date of birth. I will evade answering further questions to the utmost of my ability. I will make no oral or written statements." I hesitated for a few seconds. "I can't remember the rest of article five Carmine."

"You are doing great," Carmine said with a pleased look on his face. "Continue with the final article."

"I will never forget that I am an American fighting man, responsible for my actions. I will trust in my God and in the United States of America."

"You did good Joey. Never forget the Code of Conduct. I will pray that you never have to use it."

"Carmine, how did you remember all the articles of the Code of Conduct?"

Carmine smiled. "I didn't Joe Momma, I don't need to remember the Code, but you do. With that said, I must be off to class. I need to make a stop at the baccausa (outhouse / bathroom). I had dinner with my parents last night. Mom served bacala (fish) with polenta and snails. I will see you Saturday night at the Casa. I'll be tending bar and I will slip you a drink. Sorry I was so tough on you Joe Momma."

"It's okay Carmine. You would have made one hell of a Drill Instructor."

"I have one last piece of advice for now. Keep yourself physically and mentally fit, and force yourself to think when you are tired." I just sat there watching Carmine walk away. Carmine is only a few years older than I am, but I couldn't help but to think how mature he is.

• • •

I stayed close to home for the remainder of my leave. On Friday and Saturday, I got up early and went on a two mile run. Saturday evening we went to the Casa-di Roma for dinner. I ordered the New York steak smothered with onions, and my dad poured me a glass of red wine. I think that this was the first time I sat down to dinner with my mother, father, and grandmother where hardly a word was said. Uncle Michael came over to the table and sat with us for awhile. "Joseph," he said. "You take care of yourself out there in California."

I knew what he really meant. He really meant take care of yourself in Kuwait. Then, my father and Uncle Michael started to argue over the bill. My father always insists on paying, and Uncle Michael would not hear of it. This is typical every time we eat at the Casa. Even if Uncle Michael is not present, my family never pays. It is a standing order. I knew what the outcome was going to be, so I went to the bar and talked to Carmine.

"Hey Joe Momma, what could I get you?"

"Nothing Carmine, I had wine. I am fine."

"Joey I'm going to the airport with you in the morning."

"Wow," I said. "I thought that my father is taking me. Won't you be tired from working late?"

"No, I'll be fine. Besides, it is all set. The Tooch got us a town car and driver. I won't even go to sleep. I will be at your house at 4:00 in the morning."

• • •

When we got home, Dad took me to his den. After Roseanne moved to California, he turned her bedroom into a den. I was never in his little hideaway before. Dad always kept the door locked. I just assumed that he kept the room locked because he stored his guns in there. When my grandfather Tucci died, he left all his guns to my father. The collection included several old guns. Some are antique shotguns and pistols dating back to the Civil War era. I use to enjoy looking at them when I was a little kid. I always wondered why the guns never went to Uncle Michael, since they belonged to his father, but I imagine that the Tooch has his own collection of guns.

My eyes opened wide when I entered the den. Dad had one wall covered with pictures of when he was in the Navy. I reached up and took one picture off the wall so I could get a closer look. "Dad, what are you doing in Marine Corps combat gear?" I asked.

"Son, I never told you this before, but I spent sixteen months on a river boat conducting patrols and transporting Marine reconnaissance teams in South Vietnam."

Wow, my old man was full of surprises. "Dad, if you wanted to do that, why didn't you join the Marines?"

"I always regretted not being a Marine. But, at the time, my heart was with the Navy so volunteering as a gunner on a boat let me be a little of both."

I put the picture back on the wall and looked at my dad. "I always thought that you were stationed on a ship? Did you see any action?"

"I saw action Son."

"You never told me Dad."

This was the second time I have seen my father with tears in his eyes. I caught him with tears when I left for boot camp and at this moment. All of a sudden, I saw him in a different light. Now I understood why he acted withdrawn at times.

"Listen to me boy. If you did not go in the service, you would have regretted it for the rest of your life. I say this because you had serving your country in your blood. It is the greatest honor a person could have. You will always remember your time in the Marine Corps. I mean this, no matter how successful you will be in life. Now I could only pray that your decision will turn out to be a constructive one. I have seen so many young men come back all fucked up from Vietnam."

That was the first time I have ever heard my father use the word fuck. "I'll be okay Dad," I said as I gave him a hug.

"I know you will Son. Now go and pack your sea bag. And, send me a picture of yourself in combat gear so I could proudly hang it next to mine."

When I walked into my room, I found grandma and mom putting my folded uniforms in my sea bag. "What are you doing?" I yelled. I think that I startled them, because they jumped a little and Lucky started to bark at me from downstairs. "I am sorry, I didn't mean to yell, but we do not place our uniforms folded in the sea bag."

"Well how do we do it?" Grandma said in a sarcastic way.

"We roll them. Look, I will show you."

"Joseph, how come these shirts do not have the stripes on them?"

"Because Mom, they only issued me one set of uniforms with my rank on it. It is up to me to sew the chevrons on the others. I need to take my uniforms to the base cleaners to get them pressed and starched anyway. They will put on the stripes for me."

I think that I hurt my mother's feelings. I could see it in her face. She would have loved to press my uniforms and sew on my chevrons. I am surprised that she didn't insist.

"Look guys, I appreciate what you are trying to do, but I will take it from here."

"Okay Joseph. Here is a suitcase for you to put the clothes in that grandma bought for you, as well as any other clothes you would like to take."

"Would you like us to fold your civilian clothes for you?"

"No Grandma. The Marine Corps taught me how to fold my clothes. Thanks Mom. Thanks Grandma," I said as they exited my bedroom. My grandmother slapped me in the back of the head. I suppose that was her way of letting me know that I hurt my mother's feelings. As soon as they left, Lucky jumped up on the bed. She must have been hiding, and waiting for Mom and Grandma to leave. Lucky started to pull my clothes out of the suitcase. She looked at me as if to say, "Do not go."

• • •

Carmine was not the only one who was going to stay awake. I tossed and turned all night. Before I knew it, it was time to get up.

I took a shower, shaved, and got dressed. Everyone was up when I went downstairs. Mom and Dad were sitting at the table drinking coffee, and Grandma was cooking breakfast.

"How would you like your eggs Joey?"

"Looking at you Grandma."

"Good morning Joseph."

"Good Morning Mom."

"Where did that dog sleep last night Joseph? I recall a rule that states the dog will not sleep upstairs."

"Oh Mom."

"I will let it go this time."

"What are you going to do about it anyway? He is leaving in a few minutes," Grandma said.

That grandmother of mine is such a smart ass. My father still did not say a word. I was pleased when he said, "Pass the salt Son."

I hardly started breakfast when we heard a horn beeping. Very calmly my father got up and put his coat on, and grabbed my luggage. The horn went off again. Grandma stuck her head out the front door.

"The horn blows, how about you? You are going to wakeup the whole neighborhood for crissake," Grandma yelled as she shook her fist at Carmine and the driver.

"Not already," Mom said. "Joseph you finish your breakfast, they will wait."

I slapped my ham and eggs between my toast, took three bites and washed it down with a glass of milk. I gave Lucky a kiss good-bye and we all put our coats on and went outside. Lucky was looking out the window barking. I was freezing. I decided to travel in civilian clothes and the leather jacket that Grandma bought me.

"Give my little girl a hug for me."

"Okay Dad, I will."

I kissed and hugged my dad and then my mom. "I love you Joseph. Call me when you get on the base."

"I will Mom," I said as my mother quickly turned and went inside.

Grandma was the last one I hugged. "I love you Joey, and don't pick your nose in the Marines."

"I won't." I said as I got in the car.

I looked out the window and watched my father and grandmother walk into the house. The driver put my sea bag, suitcase, and clothing bag containing my dress blues and pressed duty uniform in the car. Carmine fell asleep and didn't wake up until we hit I-95.

"Sorry I fell asleep bro."

"Oh that is okay. Did you get any sleep last night?"

"No man! Once I got home, I was stroking until the driver came to get me." Carmine then stuck his fingers under my nose. "Here, did you ever smell pussy before?"

"You are crazy Carmine," I said as I pushed his hand away.

"That's okay bro. You will get plenty soon."

"Carmine, were you with a lot of girls?"

"Oh I would say about thirty, give or take a few."

"Get the fuck out of here," I yelled.

"Yes Joe Momma. While I was stationed in California, I went to Tijuana a lot. Counting the girls in California, Mexico, Panama, the Orient, and the girls I was with once I got home, I would say that thirty sounds about right."

"Did you get any pussy before you went in the Marines?" I asked.

"No I did not. And, if you tell anyone, I will kick you ass."

I looked at the driver. He was laughing. Knowing that Carmine was a virgin when he went in the Marine Corps made me feel a little better. With that thought, I fell asleep until I felt a shake of my arm.

"Come on Joe Momma get up. We are here."

"We are where?" I mumbled.

Carmine let out a hardy laugh. "We are at the airport Marine. You are on your way to report to your duty station."

I got my wits about me and said, "You don't have to come in with me Carmine. I'll be okay."

"I wasn't planning on it Joe Momma. I prefer to say good-bye here."

As the driver pulled over to the curb, Carmine handed me a plastic coin holder with a four-leaf clover in it.

"What is this?"

"It's a four-leaf clover. I carried it with me all through my enlistment. Hey, it works for the Irish."

"Thanks," I said as we got out of the car and gave each other the Goomba embrace. "Thanks for everything Carmine."

"Don't mention it Marine. Just remember me when you are mobbed up and I'm calling you sir." I just looked confused, as if I did not comprehend what he was saying. "Call me from California and let me know how things are going. And, one last piece of advice. If you do have to leave for war, it would be best that you do not come home first."

As I picked up my bags, the driver said, "Good luck man."

I nodded, turned and walked toward the terminal. I heard Carmine yell, "Joe Momma, you are a warrior. You are a natural born killer. You are a Marine. If you have to kill, kill without regret." I did not look back.

Eight

Surprisingly, *I found the terminal* to be quite lively for that time of the morning. I checked in my sea bag, suitcase, and held onto my garment bag. I bought a large cup of coffee before I went to the gate and once there, I checked in and took a seat.

"Hello Marine."

I turned and looked, "Hello to you," I said to an elderly cleaning lady. "Excuse me Ma'am but how do you know that I am a Marine."

"I just know Pfc. Joseph Mommalione."

"Okay lady, this is getting a little freaky."

She pointed to my garment bag. "Your name is on your clothing bag."

"So it is."

"I'll bet that your friends call you Joe Momma. Am I correct?"

"Yes Ma'am you are correct."

"Why did you join the Marine Corps, Joe Momma?"

"Oh I guess I am a patriotic type of a guy."

"That's bullshit," she said with a mean look on her face as she took a seat next to me.

I was stunned by her remarks. "Excuse me!"

"Joseph, do you come from a good family?"

"Yes Ma'am, I come from large loving family. My mother, father, sister and grandmother are the best."

"You are blessed to have such a loving family. Mommalione, is that Italian?"

"Yes it is."

"Well then tell me what went wrong?"

"Wrong?"

"Yes, the way I figure it is that you got into trouble with your no-good friends or you just had to prove something to your old man?"

125

She was right on both accounts. "How do you know all this? Are you physic or something?"

"No Joseph, I had a boy who was a Marine. He joined the Marine Corps for those very reasons."

"You said that you had a boy!"

"Yes, he was a real hell raiser. Always in trouble, he was. His father and I were good parents, but my boy and his father clashed all the time over my little Eddie's behavior. He joined the Marines in December of 1966. How old are you Joseph?"

"I'm eighteen years old Ma'am."

"That is how old my Eddie was. He went away in December and by May he was dead."

Before I could think about it, I asked, "Where did he die?"

"Did you ever hear of a place called Tam Ky in Vietnam?"

"No, Ma'am. We studied about the Vietnam War during Marine Corps history classes in boot camp, but I never heard of that place."

The announcement came to board the flight. She hugged me and gave me a kiss on the cheek. "Good luck Marine."

"I am sorry about your son," I said. When we parted, I realized that I failed to get her name. Not that it mattered, but it did.

I was full of sadness when I took my seat. I was sad that I was leaving home for a very long time. In addition, I was sad for the woman that I met before boarding. I felt sorry for her. She will never come to terms with the loss of her son and she will carry that to her death.

Just before the plane took off, I downed my cup of coffee. It was cold, but I was hoping to stay awake knowing the pre-dawn darkness would not last long and I wanted to see the night turn to day. Maybe I was trying to prolong the flight not knowing what to expect once I reached my destination or maybe I was scared of failure. I really didn't know. Sure enough, I fell asleep anyway and didn't awaken until we landed in Chicago.

I had to change planes. Once I got off the plane, I located a monitor listing outgoing flights and located the gate where I needed to be. I felt like I was on a three-mile hike. I ran the lengthy distance to that gate. I only stopped to get a breakfast sandwich. This time I purchased a soda instead of coffee.

Once I checked in at the gate and received my seat assignment, I took a seat and had about twenty minutes before we boarded. I was sitting there enjoying my breakfast when I noticed a kid with long hair sitting across from me. He was holding one of those little blue bags issued by the Red Cross that some of us received from the recruiter's office. The bags contained soap, a razor, shaving cream, toothpaste, and a toothbrush. Little did he know that it would go in the garbage once he arrives at the receiving barracks. I knew he was on his way to boot camp, but which one. It was obvious that he was going to San Diego, and I ruled out the Navy because the Navy has a basic training facility at Great Lakes, Illinois, which is where my father attended basic. Therefore, he had to be going to the Marine Corps Recruit Depot, San Diego, California.

Jesus H. Christ, as my father would say. Do I go talk to this guy? Should I give him a heads-up on what to expect? I had to go over and talk to him. I felt it was my duty to do so. After all, Carmine helped me out tremendously with the advice he gave me. I stood, disposed of my food wrappings in the trash, and approached him. "Hey man, how you doing?" I said as I extended my hand for a handshake.

"I'm doing okay." He looked very nervous.

"My name is Private First Class Joe Mommalione, United States Marine Corps."

"Jim Levir, nice to meet you Joe."

"Where are you headed Jim?"

"I am headed for Marine Corps Boot camp in San Diego."

It was just as I figured. "Come with me Jim." Jim followed me to the gate desk where we arranged to sit together on the plane.

• • •

The plane took off as scheduled. Jim looked like he was even more nervous than before. I wondered if he was nervous of flying, or because of what was waiting for him when he landed and reported to the Recruit Depot. I really wanted to help this guy, but I was not sure where to begin. Jim broke the ice.

"I'm really not sure if I did the right thing by joining the Marines?"

"Tell me about your family," I said.

127

"I have a good family. We are very close. I have two sisters who are two and four years older than I am. My father works construction, and my mother works in a school cafeteria."

"Tell me a little about yourself."

"Well Joe, I played little league baseball, as well as high school baseball. My grades were average and after I graduated, I took a job in a box-making factory. I never got into smoking, drugs or alcohol, or anything like that."

"What about friends?"

"I have good friends, but after summer, some went on to college and others seemed too busy for me. Summer was great, as we all had a lot of fun. But, after summer, they were all gone. I found myself all alone, and being that college was not an option at the time, I decided to enlist in the Marine Corps. I didn't see any future in the box-making assembly line."

"Jim was your father in the service?"

"Yes, not only my father, but my mother was in the army too. My father was drafted and was sent to Vietnam. My mother was stationed in Germany and the states."

"Okay, both of your parents were in the Army, so why the Marines?"

"Well I originally wanted to join the Air Force, but I didn't do so well on the entrance exams and the Air Force recruiter suggested that I try the Marine Corps, so here I am. I must have had a disgusted look on my face because Jim said, "Why do you have a disgusted look?"

"No man it don't mean nothing. I was just thinking that it would have been good if the Air Force thing would have worked out. That's all." I was really hoping that his friends would have turned out to be shit like Danny and George, God rest their souls. Moreover, that he only joined the Marines to show up his old man. I guess people join the Marine Corps for a variety of reasons.

"Why do you say that about the Air Force? Joe you gotta fill me in on what I'm in for at boot camp."

I took a long look at Jim. He seemed to be physically fit being athletic in high school, and it seemed like he came from a good family. However, was he mentally strong?

"Jim, I got to tell you, brutality is the way of the Drill Instructor. In addition to physical violence, the Drill Instructors have methods to demean, and degrade recruits uniformly. Usually though, the only time a Drill Instructor will single out a recruit is if the recruit gives them a reason. So, don't draw negative attention to yourself. Don't fuck up. Don't be a shitbird and pay attention to detail. You need to be mentally strong. Are you mentally strong Jim?"

"Yes Joe, I think that I am. I mean I will be if I have to."

"Good, because the Drill Instructor will talk to you and the other recruits, using terrible language. He will use curse words to address you, especially the fuck word, which is used to describe everything. Nevertheless, after time cursing by the Drill Instructor becomes normal to you. Physical training is used as another form of punishment. The humiliating is mind-boggling. Didn't anyone fill you in on what boot camp will be like?"

"No man, I just joined and left home without any information on what to expect. I heard the Marines are tough. They have that reputation you know."

I could tell that Jim was hungry for information about boot camp. "Yeah Jim, I know," I said with a smile. "Now just sit there and relax as I give it to you by the numbers." Once again, I briefly addressed the thought of not telling Jim anything else, thinking he may be better off not knowing, but I knew how much I appreciated Carmine briefing me on what to expect.

"I won't lie to you Joe. I'm scared."

"Processing begins upon your arrival at the Recruit Depot. Before you exit the bus, all hell breaks loose. The Drill Instructors will be screaming for you to move as fast as you can and plant your feet on the yellow footprints painted on the pavement. Soon as things calm down, you will enter the Receiving Barracks."

"What is Receiving Barracks?"

"Receiving is where the Marines welcome you with open arms."

"What about war?" Jim asked with much concern. "I hear a lot about America going to war in Kuwait."

"Don't worry about war man. You have to get through boot camp first. Trust me when I say if you have to go to war, you will be ready. As I was saying, Receiving Barracks is where the Marines welcome you. In your first day or two, you will be in Receiving. There, you receive your haircut, pack your clothing that you are now wearing and send them home. You will be issued clothing, identification cards and your first taste of Marine Corps chow. It is good that you don't have any luggage. You will only be sending it home anyway. You don't have any contraband on you do you?"

"What is contraband?"

"Contraband is weapons, drugs, food, pornography, and things of that nature."

"What about wallets, could I keep my wallet?'

"Yes, you could keep your wallet. After you complete your short stay at Receiving Barracks, you will be part of a platoon and start a week of Forming."

"What about calling home? Will I get a chance to call home?"

"Sorry, I forgot to tell you about that. Sometimes they will let new recruits make a call home as well as write a letter on the first day of Receiving. Now let me continue telling you about Forming. Forming is a period of adjustment whereas you will start to move as a platoon. In Forming, you will draw rifles, and take I.Q. tests. You will also receive medical and dental exams."

By the time we landed, Jim was well briefed on Marine Corps boot camp, and I was focused on seeing Roseanne and Mark.

"It is so good to see you again." Mark said as we exchanged hugs.

"Who is this young man with you?" Roseanne asked as we exchanged hugs and kisses.

"This is Jim Levir," I said as I patted Jim on the back. He is reporting to the Recruit Depot to begin his training.

"Well hello James," Roseanne said.

"Jim, this is my sister Roseanne and her husband Mark."

"Hello," Jim said.

"Hey guys, I am going to walk Jim over to the Marine Corps podium, I'll be right back."

"Okay," Mark said.

"Good luck to you Jim," Roseanne added.

I walked Jim to the podium. "Remember everything I told you Jim and you will do just fine. Maybe I'll run into you again."

"You think so Joe?"

"Yeah, sure, the Marine Corps is small. Anyway, here is my home phone number. Call home and my mother or father will give you my military address." Jim and I shook hands and I left him.

It felt good to see Roseanne and Mark again. "How was your flight?" Roseanne asked as we made our way to baggage claim.

"Oh it was fine. It seemed quicker this time. Maybe it had to do with meeting Jim. I filled him in on everything about boot camp. I told him just like Carmine told me. In fact, talking to Jim made me think of Carmine."

"Speaking of Carmine, how is he doing?" Mark asked.

"Oh he is doing fine working for the Tooch, and going to school. He has one fine looking girlfriend too. Carmine has big plans for himself."

"Big plans my ass. He is being groomed for the family business and one day he will be reporting to you."

Roseanne snapped, "Do not talk like that. Joseph is not going to be a part of that criminal element. Our father will never allow that."

"Well everyone knows what your Uncle Michael has in mind for Joey. I didn't mean anything bad in what I said. Rumor has it that your Uncle Michael is under investigation by the federal government for racketeering. Rumor also has it that your Uncle Michael plans to retire early from his business and he has Joey in mind for taking over the family."

"Sissy, is Uncle Michael in trouble?" Is he going to go to jail or something?"

"No Joseph, Uncle Michael is not going to jail. It is true that he is under investigation, but it is something that he has faced before. Father says that Uncle Michael is under a lot of pressure from the F.B.I., but he will be okay. Everyone seems to think that Uncle Michael is going to groom you to take over one day. Even father is a little worried about it. Grandmother told me that she heard father and Uncle Michael arguing about it just before you went home."

Everyone seems to know better than I do what course my life is going to take. "That's okay Mark. I take what you said as a compliment."

"Joseph, you better not take it as a compliment and you better get that way of life out of your head. As I said, father will never allow it."

It didn't take us long to get to baggage. I was thinking about Jim. I supposed he would be okay. Once again I felt that it was good to see Mark and Roseanne again. Roseanne was already carrying my garment bag and Mark picked up my sea bag and suitcase as we made our way to the car. Roseanne planted a big kiss on my cheek. "How was your reception when you got home?" I heard from Aunt Connie that mother and father went all out."

"Oh my God, It was great. The house was packed. It reminded me of Christmas, and the food was awesome." I seen the disappointment is Roseanne's face, as if she really missed something special. "Everyone asked about you guys," I said. "They all wanted to know how you two are doing."

"What did you tell them?" Mark asked.

"Of course, I told them that you are doing great and I am very proud of you. I told them about your apartment and how beautiful San Diego is."

"How are mother and father?"

"They are fine. Dad never misses a day of work and is always complaining about local and state politics. Mom goes above and beyond at her job and still manages to keep everything in order at home."

"How is grandmother doing?"

"Grandma is Grandma. You know how she is. She couldn't understand why you and Mark are out here in California. I tried to explain it to her, but I don't think she understands."

"Your grandmother is a trip," Mark said. "I just love her. Remember the time when she farted so loud in church that people in the back even heard it, and last New Years Eve when she shot your grandfather's old shotgun at midnight and ended up flat on her ass."

"Yes she is a trip alright. I had fun hanging out with her when I was on leave. At times, Mom just throws her hands up and shakes her head in disgust or disbelief at what grandma does."

"You are correct Joseph, and there are times that Dad just wants to kill her."

"Mark, I'm sorry that I didn't get a chance to visit with your parents." I said as we approached the car. Mom and Grandma have a big dinner planned for them this week. They are all still getting together, only I won't be there."

"That's okay Joey. I understand with your leave cut short and all. Let us put your things in the car and be on our way. We have about a three hour ride."

"I really appreciate you guys being here for me," I said with all sincerity. We put my bags in the car and we were on our way.

"Are you hungry Joseph?" My sister asked.

"No, I'm okay for now."

"We will stop on the way," Mark said.

We spent the first hour talking about home, Uncle Michael's problem with the feds, and more about grandma's antics.

"Oh yeah sissy, wait until you see what Dad did with your bedroom."

"What did he do to my room?"

"Oh you will see. Dad turned it into a small sitting room of sort. He turned it into a den. It houses his antique gun collection and his Navy memorabilia. Actually, it is cool. Dad even has a computer in there."

"Father is on the computer! That is interesting."

"I found out another interesting fact about Dad. Did you know that Dad spent time as a gunner on a river boat and seen combat in Vietnam?"

"I thought your father was in the Navy?" Mark said.

"He was, but he was stationed on a river boat. He transported Marine reconnaissance teems deep into enemy territory. He even wore a Marine Corps combat uniform and combat gear. He said that he really wanted to be a Marine, but his heart was with the Navy. I think that this was the closest he could come to serving with the Marines, short of being a Corpsman that is."

"What is Corpsman?" Mark asked.

"A Corpsman is a Navy man who serves as a medic with a Marine platoon or unit. I don't know if I explained it or not, but the Marine

Corps is a part of the Navy. Technically speaking, all Marines are in the Navy. The history of the Marines dates back to the late 1700's. When the Navy ships did battle, the Marines boarded the other ship and did close quarter's, mostly hand to hand combat."

"Getting back to my room, where will we sleep when we go home? We cannot stay in the garage apartment as the utilities are not on."

"We will stay in your brother's room or at my parent's house," Mark said.

After driving for over an hour, we merged onto CA-60 E toward Beaumon/Indo. We stopped at a small Mexican diner. I couldn't help but to notice how much the server looked like my cousin Bria. We ordered our lunch and I asked Mark, "Where exactly is Twentynine Palms located?"

"Well Joey, we have about an hour and half to go. It is located in San Bernardino County on highway 62 at junction highway 247." Mark then pulled a paper out of his back trousers pocket. "It says here that it is where the Mojave Desert meets the Colorado Desert. Twentynine Palms is a small desert community. It has a military base and national park nearby. Nearby towns are Joshua Tree, Desert Hot Springs, Palm Springs, and Yucca Valley. That is all the information I got."

It was not long before the food came. I looked at the waitress. "She looks like our cousin Bria. That reminds me, I need you to call Bria for me. I promised her that I was gong to take her to the movies this week. Please call her and tell her that I cannot make it on the account of I had to leave so sudden."

"I think that she already knows that Joseph. Besides, I do not think that you should hang out with her. Mother told me that she was toying with you when she was at the house."

Damn, that confirmed the fact that my mother could see through walls and could read minds. "Oh her intentions weren't serious," I said.

"Nevertheless, do not encourage her. She is bad and she is your cousin for goodness sake," Roseanne yelled.

I decided not to take the topic of Bria any further. We ate our lunch and were soon back on the road. I really enjoyed the ride. Mark talked about school and Roseanne talked about her work and her plans to attend college in September of 1991.

I was really enjoying the ride. The natural surroundings and backdrops of the desert made for a dramatic presentation. Talking made the remainder of the ride go fast. I was pleased that the topic of war never came up. My father must have talked to the both of them and told them not to bring the subject up. Once we entered the city of Twentynine Palms, we were all strongly impressed. We took a little time to see the city. The city is geographically separated by a mountain range creating a small town living environment.

"One could see that the City of Twentynine Palms is dedicated to securing the quality of life through development and preservation," Mark said. After riding around for awhile, Mark drove up to the front gate. "Joey, do I let you off at the gate or will they let us go in with you?"

Being new at this, I was uncertain as to what to advise him. "I don't know Mark. Just pull up at the gate and I will ask the Military Police." We pulled up to the gate and the M.P. directed me to pull off to the side and park. Mark and I went inside and filled out a visitor pass. After that, I received a small map of the base and directions to the Administration Building. We drove to the Administration Building and once again, it was time to say good-bye.

We got out of the car and unloaded my bags. "Well guys, it was really good seeing you again," I said. "Once again, thank you for greeting me at the airport and bringing me here."

"Joey, I want you to take this." Mark handed me a card. "This is our telephone calling card. Just follow the directions as stated on the card. Call us at least once a week or anytime you are feeling lonely. Do not worry about the cost. It will be automatically charged to our telephone bill."

"Yes little brother. Like Mark said, call us at least once a week and let us know how things are going."

I put the card in my wallet and gave Roseanne a kiss and hug. "I love you sissy. I will call you soon. Thank you for everything." I then turned to Mark, "You are the best. Take care," I said. We shook hands, gave each the Goomba hug with three pats on the back that say, you are my bro, but it doesn't mean that I want to fuck you. We ended with a group hug and I waited as they got in the car. "Make sure you hand in the visitor pass on your way out," I said as I waived good-bye.

There I stood, outside the Administration Building of my first duty station at Twentynine Palms Air Ground Combat Center. I bent down to retrieve my orders from my suitcase, and looked up at a pair of the best-looking legs that I have ever seen in my young life.

"Are you reporting in Marine?"

I jumped to my feet and snapped too with a hand salute. "My name is Private First Class Mommalione Ma'am."

"At ease Pfc. Mommalione and we do not salute when we are not in uniform."

I was embarrassed. I should have known this, being I recently had this conversation with my grandmother.

"My name is Captain Gutterman. Please come inside with me and we will get you squared away."

"Yes Ma'am," I said as I followed her. Once inside, Captain Gutterman led me to a conference room.

"Pfc. Mommalione, you can stockpile your gear over in the corner and be at ease. I will be with you in a few minutes." She took my orders and left the room.

I walked around the room and looked at pictures of the base on the walls. The room reminded me of the Recruiter's office back in Trenton, only more modern. The Captain came back in the room about fifteen minutes later. "Take a seat Pfc. and I will brief you."

I took a seat and sat at attention.

Nine

"*Relax Marine; this is going* to take some time. Please feel free to ask any questions during the briefing. Private First Class Mommalione, I welcome you to the Combat Center. The Air Ground Combat Center at Twentynine Palms is primarily a mechanized desert training center. When I say mechanized, I mean several types of vehicles coming together in support of one another to complete a mission. Such military vehicles include the Hummer, Bradley Fighting Vehicles, Abrams Battle Tanks, Light Armored Vehicles, etc. This training is in conjunction with SeaKnight Helicopters, Huey Helicopters, Super Cobra Attack Helicopters, Harrier Jets, C130 Planes, F-18 Fighter Jets, and then some. Infantry training is also linked with air and mechanized units for training purposes."

I liked what the Captain was telling me. Her briefing brought me back to when I was a kid and my friends and I would play army in the yard. We would pretend to have tanks, helicopters, and fighter jets all around us.

"Pfc. Mommalione, I see here that your Military Occupational Specialty is 0200, Naval Intelligence. I know that you are aware that at the conclusion of basic training, every Marine is assigned an M.O.S. However, I am going to take a few minutes to explain how the Marine Corps completes training. Once a recruit completes boot camp, he or she is assigned to a training facility to begin training in their assigned M.O.S. Training is usually a three month assignment."

"Excuse me Ma'am, but do I get liberty during training?"

"Yes you do. You are no longer in boot camp, but while here, you will be conforming completely to established training. You will get liberty, but it will be limited over the next three months. In your case, you will be receiving most of your training in a classroom setting. The hours will be long and the training will be demanding."

"What happens when training is completed?" I asked with the idea of war on my mind.

"Once you complete your training, you will be assigned to one of several bases where you will work in your Military Occupational Specialty while continuing to receive training. Pfc. Mommalione, according to your records, you are single. Is that correct?"

"Yes Ma'am. Why do you ask?"

"I ask marital status because I am about to explain living quarters to you. The rule is you must be the rank of E-5 or married to live off base during training. You will be housed in the F section billets. I think that you will find the barracks comfortable. They are three person rooms in a platoon size setting. You are assigned to the third platoon in Mike Company. Each platoon has an E-5 or an E-6 who will serve as platoon sergeant. At the rank of Private First Class, you may find yourself serving as a squad or fire team leader."

"Excuse me Ma'am; will everyone in my platoon be receiving the same training?"

"No Pfc. Mommalione. The platoon setup is only for military function. Reveille will be at 0430 each morning. The platoon will fall out for formation at 0500. The Platoon Sergeant will take roll call and then conduct physical training. After P.T., the platoon will shower, dress in the uniform of the day, assemble as a platoon once again and march to chow. After chow, each Marine will go to his or her perspective M.O.S. training. The platoon will assemble each evening for formation. That is when the Platoon Sergeant will give out cleaning assignments, guard duty, and other assignments such as work details. At times, your training may deviate from the schedule. If this happens, you must let the Platoon Sergeant know. Rely on your Platoon Sergeant or their assistant. He or she may be a big assistance to you. Do you have any questions?"

"No Ma'am."

"Good, you will spend your first two days here getting situated. On Wednesday, you will attend orientation. At orientation, you will receive a tour of the base, city of Twentynine Palms, and the base hospital."

The Captain completed her briefing and handed me a binder that was loaded with information. "Are you sure you do not have any questions Pfc. Mommalione?"

"No Ma'am," I said as the Captain called the Corporal of the guard. A couple minutes later, a tall lanky Marine entered the room. He stood tall in front of the Captain and gave her a sharp hand salute, as he wore a cartridge belt and cover because he was on guard duty and could salute indoors.

"At ease Cpl. Gordon and I would like you to meet Pfc. Mommalione."

Corporal Gordon turned and extended his hand. "How are you Mommalione?"

"I'm doing fine," I said, as we shook hands.

"Corporal, I would like you to take Pfc. Mommalione to Mike company barracks."

Once again, the Corporal saluted the Captain. "Yes Ma'am," he said and within a minute, he exited the room with my luggage in hand.

"Good luck to you Pfc. Mommalione. I have a feeling you will not be standing much guard duty or working on many work details, as your training will be intense."

"Thank you Ma'am," I said as I almost made a fool of myself by saluting her again. Instead, I extended my right hand. We shook hands and I went out to meet the Corporal. He already had my things in the back of the pickup truck.

"So where are you from?" Corporal Gordon asked.

"I'm from Trenton, New Jersey," I said rather proudly.

"Mommalione, is that Italian?"

"Yes it is," I said even more proudly. "Where are you from Corporal Gordon?"

"I'm from Cincinnati, Ohio and I am being discharged next month. Three years of the Marine Corps is enough for me."

It didn't take us long to reach the barracks. I was lucky to be located in the administrative area. I had the mess hall, base store, Movie Theater, and dry cleaners all within walking distance. The barracks were nice. My room was located on the first of three floors. Being that it was Sunday, the barracks were quiet. The room was set up for three men. Each of us had a small desk, footlocker, and wall locker next to our bunks. On each floor was a large head (bathroom) with showers.

I sat down on my bunk and a minute later, there was a knock on the door. "Welcome Marine. My name is Sergeant Woods, and I am your Platoon Sergeant." Sergeant Woods explained the barracks regulations, morning and evening platoon formations and P.T (physical training).

"Where do I draw my desert camouflage utilities (combat uniform)?" I asked.

"After morning P.T. Corporal Haddon will take you to supply, where you will draw your uniform, and she will show you where you need to report for orientation on Wednesday. Corporal Haddon is my assistant, and she is one squared away Marine. Don't hesitate to call on her or me if you have any questions. I will be back in twenty minutes and take you to the mess hall."

On our way to chow, we stopped off at the exchange and I bought a pair of red shorts and a yellow Marine Corps tee shirt for P.T. Chow was not bad. While we were eating, Sergeant Woods shared more information about the base with me. After chow, I went back to the barracks, and hung my uniforms. About an hour or so later, Sergeant Woods came back with another Marine.

"Pfc. Mommalione, I would like to introduce you to Lance Corporal Merlino. You and Lance Corporal Merlino are the only personnel assigned to this room for the time being."

"Nice to meet you," Merlino said. We talked until lights out. It turned out that L/Cpl. Merlino is a tank crew member, and he is from Harrisburg, Pennsylvania, which is not far from Jersey.

Monday morning before formation, Sergeant Woods approached me with a female Marine. "Pfc. Mommalione, this is Corporal Haddon."

"Hello Pfc. I will be helping you get acclimated."

"It is good to meet you Corporal Haddon," I said.

I spent the next two days with Corporal Haddon. On Monday, after physical training and chow, she took me to supply, where I received my camouflage uniforms. That took all morning. After lunch, she took me to the dry cleaners and I dropped off my uniforms to be starched and pressed. I also left instructions to have my stripes sewed on. Later in the afternoon, she showed me where sickbay was. From there, we went to check in at the library, swimming pool and the enlisted personnel club. Before I knew it, the day was over, and we went to the mess hall for dinner and then fell in for formation. I spent the evening ironing my uniform and shinning my boots for the next day. Lance Corporal Merlino came in the barracks and we talked for awhile.

On Tuesday, after formation, physical training and morning chow, Cpl. Haddon took me to the location where I will report for training. The building was two levels. It looked like a modern high school. After that, she took me to check in at the gym. I had the afternoon to myself so I went to the barracks and washed my physical training shorts, along with my underwear and socks. I then went to the base store and bought another pair of shorts and some other items I needed. Afterwards, I went to the barber where I got a high and tight haircut. In the evening, I wrote a short letter to my parents and grandmother.

After two days on the base, I started to feel like I was adjusting. Wednesday morning, I reported for orientation. The first thing we did was view a film about history and tradition of the base. The remaining agenda for the day included a lecture from the Chaplain, the mission of training on the base, discipline, courtesy, administration, emergency leave, and liberty. Thursday morning, Thanksgiving Day, we took a bus tour of the entire base. It was interesting to see all the mechanized training facilities, family living quarters, hospital and the urban buildings combat training facility. In the afternoon when orientation continued, we discussed dependents information, interior guard, personal hygiene measures, and clothing allowance. After evening formation, and a turkey dinner at the mess hall, we were ordered to field day (clean) the barracks. What a way to spend Thanksgiving, I thought. We cleaned the barracks from top to bottom. Sergeant Woods was to conduct an inspection on Friday morning after breakfast formation. Friday morning orientation started out with information on off duty education and car registration. After that, we took a bus tour of the City of Twentynine Palms. And then the instructor dismissed us early. Later in the afternoon, I went and picked up my uniforms from the cleaners. My evenings were a little boring. I worked on my uniforms and wrote letters. I had liberty on the weekend, but I didn't do much. I went to a movie on Saturday night. Sunday morning, I attended mass and hung around the barracks reading a book. In the evening, I called my sister and talked with her and Mark. After I called Roseanne, and was yelled at for not calling home for Thanksgiving. I then called my mother and father. I was only able to talk to Mom because my father was out taking Grandma to bingo.

"What do you mean, dad took grandma to bingo. What the heck is that all about?"

"It is your father's time to do volunteer work at the church so he decided to set up and serve refreshments at bingo. I convinced him that he could kill two birds with one stone by working bingo. I would make him either take or pickup your grandmother anyway. How was your Thanksgiving Joseph?"

I laughed. "Poor Dad," I said. "Thanksgiving was great Mom. We had the day off and a large turkey dinner." I was lying through my teeth, but I figured the truth would only hurt her. I was thinking of what lie to tell if she wanted to know why I failed to call home on Thanksgiving, but to my surprise, she never asked, nor did she explain how their Thanksgiving Day was.

"Your father is going to be so disappointed that he did not get to talk to you Joseph."

I went on to explain to her how life on the base was so far and when I will begin my training.

My concern about training the next day really had me in a state of uneasiness. I had my uniform ready to go. The uniform of the day for me was my dress green trousers, open short sleeve shirt, and piss cover. I did manage to fall asleep, but I was up earlier than I had to be and was dressed for physical training and then chow. I reported for training at 0845 hours and there were only two Marines in the class besides me. I expected a lot more. At 0900 hours, the instructor entered the classroom. The Marines were called to attention.

"As you were Marines, my name is Major Berwick. I will be the one who educates you over the next five weeks. I know that you are already doing the math in your heads, and it does not add up. I have only five weeks to jam in twelve weeks of training." Well, that explained the reason why they cut my leave short, I thought. "I am going to be perfectly honest with you. At this point, approximately one hundred thousand Marines are in Saudi Arabia. You are a very special group of young men, chosen as intelligence personnel who will be assigned to a Light Armored Reconnaissance Battalion in Saudi Arabia." Major Berwick then pointed to a poster of a light armored vehicle. "This is a LAV-25. This vehicle has the capacity to hold one driver, one gunner, one commander and six troops. Your existence will be that of commander. As commander, or intelligence specialist, you are the person in charge of the vehicle up until the recon team is dropped off at the designated drop point. In addition, that goes from pick up point back to base or other designated stops as well. I do not care if there are officers or non commissioned officers aboard. You are the commander. Are there any questions up to this point? I will explain your mission as intelligence specialist in a minute."

This answered my question about going to war. "Sir, my name is Pfc. Mommalione. When will we be shipped out and with all due respect, will we be prepared?"

"Those are two good questions. Remember, there are no dumb questions. Ask me any question at any given time. You will fly, via C130 cargo aircraft from Norton Air Force Base to Dover Air Force Base in Delaware on December 31, 1990. It is my understanding that you will make one stop to refuel and pickup personnel that are reporting to Dover. You will travel with your team. Your team will include one LAV, one driver and one gunner. From Dover, you travel by convoy to Norfolk Virginia Naval Base. You will board a cargo ship and set sail for Saudi Arabia on Wednesday January 2, 1991. The estimated date of arrival in Al Jubayl, Saudi Arabia will be on Thursday, January 17, 1991. Moreover, you will be prepared. Your days of training are going to be long. We will work late daily. I will try to give you Sunday's off. You will be exempt from physical training, guard duty, etc. You will attend early chow at 0500 and report for training at 0630. I will clear it with your Platoon Sergeants. I will advise you of the uniform of the day, on a daily basis."

I couldn't take notes fast enough. "Sir, could we let our families know of our date of departure to Saudi Arabia?" One Marine asked.

"Not at this time Marine. I will let you know when you could divulge that information. Now I would like everyone to take a fifteen-minute break. Get some coffee or juice and introduce yourselves to one another."

Major Berwick had a table set up with coffee, juice, coffee cake and soda. During the short break, everyone in the class took the opportunity to introduce themselves to one another. Fifteen minutes later, Major Berwick came back in the room. Again, one Marine called the others to attention.

"Let me have everyone's attention," Major Berwick commanded. "During the Vietnam War, all infantry Marines were sent to infantry training school. Normally, ITS, is a three month course. This was not always the case during most of the Vietnam era. ITS, was completed on an average of seven weeks. Thus, is the situation that we are in. The aerial campaign against Iraq is scheduled to begin in the middle of January. Any negotiations you may read or hear about to prevent this, means nothing. It will happen. I for one have never experienced war, but I am a student of the subject matter. I have not known a war that has been entirely won by aerial combat. Eventually a ground war will take place. One of the key components of a successful ground war is intelligence. Military intelligence gives us the power to determine the outcome of a battle or even a war. Personally, I do not view the war to free Kuwait to be another Vietnam. This has all the makings of a quick conflict. America has not taken part in a desert war since World War II. Much was learned of the experience, from tank combat formations and air support to the maintenance and movement of equipment, supplies, and personnel. Does anyone know what intelligence means?"

"Sir, intelligence is a form of knowledge," Private Dombrowski said.

"This is true," Major Berwick said. "Intelligence is knowledge about a specific subject or situation. Alternatively, it is new information, especially about recent events and happenings. It is the faculty of thinking, reasoning, acquiring and applying knowledge. There are many individual entities contributing to military intelligence. A Marine with the 0200 Military Occupational Specialty could find themselves working with the most sophisticated equipment in a command center, the Pentagon or an American Embassy. In doing so, he or she would be compiling information, analyzing information, plotting maps, or documenting enemy troop movement. Former Marines with intelligence backgrounds have found themselves working in the C.I.A., State Department, F.B.I. and other government agencies, working out a secret plan to achieve a legal or illegal end to a threat against America. Take Private Swartzburg here. He speaks German. Private Dombrowski speaks Polish. Private First Class Mommalione speaks Italian."

Everyone laughed when I said, "Sir, I only know the bad words in Italian."

"Yes Pfc. Mommalione, but you demonstrate the skills and abilities to be taught how to speak fluent Italian. "Don't you think so Pfc?"

"Yes Sir," I said.

"Who knows where any of you will end up after the hostilities in the Gulf? I have mentioned and pointed out the Light Armored Vehicle. You will be assigned to a Light Armored Reconnaissance Battalion. Keep in mind that a battalion is a ground force unit composed of a headquarters and two or more companies. This regiment will be made up of LAV's as well as Marine Reconnaissance Teams, Navy Seals, and two companies of grunts (infantry). Your responsibility is to transport a recon team to a drop off point where that team will conduct their mission. They will make a search for useful military information by examining the area. Your job will be gathering facts, and news. Upon completion of the recon mission, you will debrief the recon team. This debriefing will start inside your LAV."

Major Berwick held up a keyboard. "All of you are familiar with this device. In boot camp, you all went through a battery of tests. Your intelligence quotient, IQ tests scores combined with your ability to type at a high rate of speed is why you are here. Your high school records indicate that all of you have worked with computers. Your LAV will be equipped with a computer. However, you will not have a monitor. Computers defy description. I am not going to explain the inner workings of this system, because this system is more along the line of a word processor anyway. Each keyboard is fitted with a floppy disk drive. This keyboard is plugged into an uninterruptible power source that is compatible with the electrical system of the Light Armored Vehicle. You need not remember this, but each LAV has twenty-four bolts of positive ground and waterproof radio suppressed system, wiring, connectors, and breakers. It also has a 220 amp alternator, four batteries and a 550 amp slave receptacle. You will be trained in the operation of the communication equipment which consists of two radios."

"Sir, I'm afraid that my typing is a little rusty," Dombrowski said.

"Don't worry about that private, you will be fine. As I was saying, you will immediately start debriefing your recon team upon retrieval of the team. If the debriefing of your recon team is not completed by the time you return to headquarters, you will continue the debriefing in a debriefing room. If headquarters is in the field or desert, the debriefing room will be set up in a tent or building. When the debriefing is completed, you will print a hard copy via computer system in the debriefing room and attach any handwritten notes including hand drawn maps from the recon team."

Being that I lacked confidence in my typing, as well as my spelling, and punctuation, I asked, "Sir, will we be able to proof read our reports?"

"No, you will not be able to read the hard copy, because it is encrypted. Don't worry about things like typing, grammar, or even spelling. It is the report that is important. You will attend typing and report writing classes. Once you complete your report, you will conceal the printed report and attachments along with the floppy disk in an issued envelope. You will then seal the envelope and call for a courier. Under no circumstances will you leave the debriefing room with the contents of the envelope. You will be trained repeatedly in the procedures of submitting reports. Each light armored vehicle will be equipped with a shredder and lighter fluid. If you are in danger of being captured, you will shred and burn all hand written notes, and floppy disk. We will go over that when we learn all the operating elements and functions of the LAV. Now listen up people.

Everything I covered is only a part of your responsibility. As I stated, you are responsible for getting your team from point A to point B, and you will function as commander of your light armored vehicle. Therefore, training will include leadership, basic communications, land navigation, scouting, and patrolling. You will also receive training in nuclear, biological and chemical warfare. I understand that all of what I discussed may seem overwhelming. Trust me when I say that everything will fall into place. Are there any questions?"

• • •

We spent the remainder of Monday through Wednesday typing until our fingers were numb. Major Berwick put us through the grinder. We typed simulated reports to include printing hard copies, and attaching recon team notes. Everyone did very well in performing the assignments. Each day was long, ending at 2100 hours.

On Thursday morning after typing for only two hours, the Major brought us all together in the classroom. "Today, you begin classes on leadership. Such training is normally set aside for noncommissioned officers of Corporal and above. Let me begin by saying that every private in the Marine Corps is a potential squad leader."

• • •

From Thursday through Saturday evening, we studied leadership. I learned that integrity means that when you give your word, keep it. Knowledge is knowing your job and putting confidence in those around you. Courage comes in two kinds, physical and moral. If you are in a tight place and feel fear, recognize it. Then get control over it. Carmine also told me that.

Major Berwick taught us to be decisive. Get all the facts make up your mind and issue orders. The major summed up dependability as getting the job done no mater what the obstacles are. This is done by improvising and by completing your mission to the best of your ability. We were educated on initiative. A Marine must think. He or she must stay mentally alert and physically fit to be ahead. I already knew some of what we were taught from Carmine.

We were taught that tact is as simple as doing the right thing at the right time. In addition, we trained to give orders in a courteous manner. In our class on bearing, the Major disciplined us to master ourselves before we try to master others. The Major instructed us on the danger of losing our temper. Moreover, Marines are judged on behavior and how we carry ourselves.

Leadership training also included classes in endurance, unselfishness, loyalty, and judgment. Training closed with discussions on teamwork, decision-making, and responsibility.

• • •

Major Berwick had us fall out for physical training at 0600 on Sunday. We went on a three-mile run and the Major granted liberty for the remainder of the day. After morning chow, I attended mass and then I did my laundry and brought my uniform to the dry cleaners. In the afternoon, I called my sister.

"Joseph how are you?" My sister asked.

"I'm doing fine. Things are going okay. I spend many hours in training on a daily basis."

Mark got on the other line. "Hey Marine how is it going?"

"I'm doing great Mark. How are you doing?"

"Oh, I'm fine. I'm busy with work and school you know."

"Wow it is so good to talk to you guys. I miss you very much."

"What have you been doing?" Mark asked.

"Oh, Marine stuff," I said not knowing what to say.

"Joseph have you talked to Mother and Father?" Roseanne asked.

"No, I was planning to call them today. Where are they?"

"I do not know who they are having Sunday dinner with, but call them at about six o'clock our time and they should be home."

"Okay, I'll do that. I'm going to go know. I'm calling on your calling card and I don't want to run-up your phone bill."

"You take care of yourself and call anytime," Mark said.

"Joseph, make sure that you call home, and I love you."

"I love you too," I said before hanging up.

I waited until 6:30p.m., California time before calling home, which made it 8:30p.m. in Trenton. I heard the operator ask if they would accept a collect call from Pfc. Mommalione.

"Mom, it's me."

"Joseph, how are you?"

"I'm fine Mom. How are you?"

"I'm doing well."

I went on talking to my father and my grandmother too. I explained what my first week of training was like. The topic of war never came up. The discussion of war not coming up was good, because this way I didn't have to lie. My mother always knows when I lie. I then relaxed for the remainder of the day.

On Monday, December 3, we started a week of basic communication training. Again, the days in the week were long. The daily communication training included hands on use of radio, visual, and sound communications, and taking messages. We also learned the Phonic Alphabet, A-alpha, B-bravo, C-Charlie…..We wrapped up basic communication classes learning numeral pronunciation. 1-won, 2-too, 3-thrh-ee,…..70-seven-zero,….84-eight-te-for-wer,….500-f-yi-hundred etc.

• • •

Sunday was the same as the previous Sunday. Sundays were like déjà vu around the base. Again, I called home, as well as, Mark and Roseanne. Once again, I avoided the subject of war. After talking to everyone, I was sad, so I was determined to do something entertaining the next Sunday.

Monday came quicker than I would have liked it to. Major Berwick ordered us to muster in room 54. We entered the room and found the walls covered with maps and aerial photographs. We were all walking around looking at the maps on the walls when Major Berwick entered. We all snapped to attention.

"Take a seat men. As you could see, this week we are going to learn all about land navigation. However, first I want to say a few words. I am very pleased with the progress that you have made thus far. So much so that I am granting a forty-eight hour pass that will commence on Friday at 1800 hours and conclude on Sunday at 1800 hours."

We all let out a loud uh-rah. This granting of a long liberty couldn't have come at a better time. We all needed it.

"Let me have your attention, Major Berwick commanded. "Effective December 15th, you could inform your loved ones of your orders after training is completed. In addition, I have requested and received permission to promote every one of you one grade upon each of you receiving your security clearance."

Wow, this was good news I thought. I was going to be a Lance Corporal, an E-3. All the Marines I graduated from boot camp with are still an E-1 Private. The good news from Major Berwick inspired us. In addition, Major Berwick seemed proud as he began class.

"If you are visiting New York City and are confused as to where you are going, it is common to ask a stranger or pull out a map to get directions. In combat, Marines find themselves in an unfamiliar environment. If you find yourself in such an unfamiliar place or need to plot a destination, or call in an air strike, you will turn to your map. A map is a drawing of the land and surroundings. At times, you may be working with overhead aerial photos. However, the difference between a photo and a map is that the map has signs and symbols on it. These signs and symbols represent various things on the ground. This class is going to teach how to read a map. We are going to cover signs; symbols, elevation, and contour beginning at sea level. We are going to commit to memory, measure distance, determine location, and learn how to use grid lines and the use of the compass. You will not only use the compass to find north, south, east, and west. You will master the compass as it pertains to aligning the map with the ground. We will use the compass in the day as well as the night. In addition, we will analyze aerial photographs. You will focus on the limits of tone and color as well as size and relation. Identifying military symbols on the map will become a natural for you."

• • •

The week of land navigation was interesting and overwhelming. I couldn't believe that I was that smart. Maybe I should have gone to college and then joined the Marines as an officer.

On Friday morning, Major Berwick instructed us to fall out for physical training before going to chow and class. Just as I was leaving for physical training formation, there was a knock at my door. I opened the door and found Corporal Haddon standing there.

"Good morning Pfc. Mommalione. I hear that you have a weekend pass and I was wondering if you would like to have dinner with me tonight at my husband's restaurant."

"Your husband owns a restaurant?" I asked with surprise in my voice.

"Well it is his family's restaurant. I met my husband two years ago at his restaurant while on liberty. Six months ago we were married."

"Please excuse me if I'm out of line, but I must ask. Are you Italian?"

"Yes, my maiden name is spelled Rocchi. It is pronounced Rocky. No one at home ever called me Pauline. I was always known as Rocky."

"My friends call me Joe Momma. Where is home?"

"I am from Cleveland. Where are you from Mommalione?"

"I am from Trenton, New Jersey."

"So tell me Mommalione, is it a date?"

"How could I pass this up? I was going to sit in the barracks and write letters. Going to dinner sure beats writing letters. Sure, it's a date."

"Okay then Joe Momma. I will pick you up here at 1900 hours." All day long, I was looking at the clock. When class was over, I ran to the barracks to get ready. I dressed in an outfit that Grandma bought for me. It was a little cool out, so I brought along my leather jacket, which contained a razor, toothbrush, and toothpaste in the pockets. I also threw an extra pair of sox and underwear in a bag. Rocky picked me up right on time.

"Rocky, I was wondering if I could check in at a motel before we go to your restaurant. I would like to stay in town until Sunday and then I will take the shuttle back to base."

"You are welcome to stay with us. We have plenty of room."

"Don't think that I don't appreciate that Rocky, but I think a couple of evenings in a motel would be good R&R (rest and relaxation) for me."

"I understand," Rocky said with a smile on her face. "But don't think you are going to be spending your days alone. Now come on lets get to the car."

The first place Rocky took me to was the motel. I checked in and then she drove me around town, showing me the sights. We got to the Canyon Restaurant at 2030 hours. Rocky gave me a tour of the restaurant. I liked the southwestern décor.

"I was never in a place like this," I told Rocky.

"You won't find anything Italian on the menu, but I could recommend the steak."

"Steak sounds great." I was amazed at the size of the steak when it came to the table. It was huge and thick.

"Twenty-four ounces," Rocky said. Needless to say, they would not let me pay for anything.

• • •

After a great night of eating and talking, I slid between the sheets and fell asleep as soon as my head hit the pillow. The next day we attended an art festival. We stopped at a small café in Joshua tree for lunch. When I went to the bathroom, I cornered the waiter and paid the bill. Roger was okay with me paying the bill, but invited me to dinner Saturday night at the Canyon. I had the steak. Saturday night was just as terrific as Friday night, with fantastic food and conversation. Roger seemed a little uncomfortable though. I was not sure if it was because Rocky and I were Marines or was it because we were both Italian. We did carry on talking as if were back on the block.

• • •

I spent Sunday afternoon doing my laundry and ironing my shirt. I decided not to call Mom and Dad or Roseanne. I wrote to them instead. It was easier to explain my going to war in a letter than it was on the phone. There were no emotions involved that way.

152

I felt refreshed on Monday and was ready to put in a good week on learning about scouting and patrolling. The lessons for the week came under the titles of cover, concealment, camouflage, and the principles of movement in the desert. In addition, we studied scouting by night, which included working with night vision equipment. Reporting was another factor of scouting. We worked with written messages and the type of written messages that the recon teams use to report. Written facts on the messages included size, activity, location, unit, time, and equipment of enemy forces. From messages, we worked with sketches, and overlays. In addition, we concluded the week of training on reconnaissance patrolling. We learned that Marine Recon and Navy Seals usually only engage in combat when it becomes necessary to accomplish their assigned mission or in order to protect themselves. On Friday, Major Berwick brought us together for an informal meeting.

"I am granting leave to commence today, December 21, 1990 at 1600 hours through December 25, 1990 at 1600 hours. Enjoy your holiday Marines. And, thank your Jewish, Orthodox Christians, and those Marines of other faiths for volunteering for duty over the Christmas holiday."

I was baffled as to what I was going to do for Christmas. I knew that my sister and Mark were going back to New Jersey for the holidays and Rocky and Roger were going to Cleveland. As I was going to afternoon chow, Rocky approached me with a note.

"Mommalione, I took this message from your sister, she wants you to call her. Merry Christmas, I will see you in ten days."

"Merry Christmas," I said accompanied with a hug. I then read the note. Instead of going to lunch, I went to the pay phones and called Roseanne at her place of work.

"Joseph, why did you not call this week? Mother and I are so mad at you. You are in big trouble little brother."

"I thought that you were going home for Christmas," I said.

"No, Mark and I decided to have Christmas with you. If you had called, you would have known that. After receiving your letter detailing your deployment, I see we made the right decision."

"I didn't even know if I was going to get liberty for Christmas."

"I knew, Joseph."

"How did you know?" I inquired.

"I will give you one guess."

"The Tooch," I said with confidence.

"No, Carmine found out for me. He still has friends in the Marine Corps you know. Now listen to me, there is a bus leaving at 5:30 p.m., be on it. Mark will pick you up at 9:30 in San Diego."

"I have to be back here at 4:30p.m. on Christmas day."

"We have that all worked out Joseph. We are having dinner on Christmas Eve. Mark and I will bring you back Christmas day."

"Okay Sissy, I will catch a taxi here on base and take it to the bus station."

"I love you Joseph," Roseanne said before hanging up.

I still had time before I had to be back at class so I went to the exchange to buy Christmas gifts and grab a sandwich. I bought Mark a backpack for school and I bought Roseanne a stuffed bear dressed as a Marine in dress blues. When class let out, I went and packed my small suitcase. I stayed in my dress uniform and had no trouble making the bus on time. I had a good ride to San Diego and Mark was at the bus terminal to meet me.

All the way to the apartment, Mark was telling me how mad everyone was at me, and how sorry he was that I was going to war. When we got to the apartment, my sister was waiting.

"Hi Sissy, the house is decorated beautifully and I just love the tree," I said with the biggest smile I could muster, but she did not respond. "Do you know that you look just like Mom when you are mad?"

"Never mind how I look. Go call Mother and Father, and then sit down and eat."

"Damn Roseanne. I don't even get a hug or anything?" Roseanne slapped me in the back of the head and pointed to the phone.

I called home, and my mother scolded me for not calling. Even my grandma got in on it by yelling at me from the background.

"Mom don't be mad at me for not calling."

"Joseph, I am mad at you for not going to college. Now my baby is going to war."

"Mom, I will be okay over there. We still don't know if there will be a war for sure."

"Joseph, I will call you on Christmas Eve."

"Okay Mom I love you," I said as she hung up. She was mad, I thought. My mother never hangs up without telling me she loves me. I didn't even get a chance to talk to my father.

• • •

Mark spent the next couple of days working long hours. Roseanne and I spent the next couple of days at the San Diego Zoo and Disney land. We stayed up long into the night talking while we made sauce and ravioli. It was my job to roll the dough and close the sides of the ravioli, by pressing the edges down with a fork. I have been doing this every Christmas since I was four years old.

Roseanne and I got up early on Christmas Eve. We took our showers and cleaned the house. Mark was already off to work. When we were done cleaning, I sat in the recliner and smiled when I noticed a stocking with my name on it hanging from the fake cardboard red brick fireplace. I felt blessed to be with family at Christmas time. I knew that so many people serving in the armed forces were not so lucky. The house was filled with the aroma of tomato sauce, and Christmas music was playing, all of which was sung in Italian.

"Hey little brother we are far from done here. Come and help me set the table."

"Mark is going to meet us at the church for 4:30 mass. We need to hustle back here after mass, as my company will be here at 7:00 for dinner."

The church was just beautiful. An old Spanish church set high on a hill. No sooner, did we get back and my mother called. I could see the frustration on Roseanne's face when Mark answered the phone. I quickly came to the rescue as I took the phone from Mark.

"Merry Christmas," I said.

"Merry Christmas to you Joseph, now put your sister on."

"She can't come to the phone right now Mom. She is getting dinner ready. Her company is coming soon. Could we call you later?"

"I suppose so. How are you doing Joseph?"

"I'm doing good Mom. I was a big help to Roseanne in preparation of Christmas dinner and getting the house ready."

"That is good. I have the whole family coming in an hour and I am ready. Here talk to your father." I heard her tell my father that Roseanne couldn't come to the phone because she is getting dinner ready."

"Hey Dad," I said.

"Hey to you Marine, I heard the news about you going over there. You are going to be just fine. Thank you for the detailed letter. Call me if plans change." I couldn't even respond when Grandma got on the phone.

"Joey, I'm going to spank you when I see you. Are you coming home before you go off to war?"

"I don't think so Grandma."

"Don't be a hero Joey, just come home safe."

"Grandma, I'll talk to you before I go. Have a Merry Christmas and tell Mom that Roseanne will call later."

Roseanne and Mark's company arrived at 6:50 p.m. By 7:15, Roseanne and I put the wine, bread, and antipasto on the table. At 7:20, my mother called again. I answered the phone and once again, I saved the day.

• • •

Roseanne set the alarm for 8:00 a.m. We got up and immediately exchanged gifts. Mark and Roseanne gave me a Bulova wristwatch. We then cleaned the apartment, made breakfast, called Jersey and hit the road for the Marine base at Twentynine Palms.

The ride was quiet, as no one was talking. Mark let me drive for the last hour. That is when Roseanne started crying.

"Sissy, what is with the tears?" I said.

"Because this is the last time Mark and I will see you before you go over there."

"What are your plans for New Year's Eve?" Mark asked trying to change the subject.

"We are scheduled to be in the desert on maneuvers from the 28th to the 30th. I fly to Dover Delaware on the 31st, and we board ship and leave for the Gulf on the 1st or 2nd of January."

"You better call home and tell Mother and Father what is going on," Roseanne said.

"Roseanne, you need to tell Mom and Dad that I will call as soon as I could, and remind me to give you your phone card as soon as we get to the base."

"No Joey, you hold on to it," Mark said.

"What are your plans for New Year's Eve?" I asked Mark.

"Well we are going to New Jersey on New Years Eve."

"That is great," I said. "Why didn't you guys tell me?"

"We did not want to make you feel sad or upset," Roseanne said.

"I'm not upset. I am happy for you guys. Thank you for giving up vacation time to spend Christmas with me. Believe me when I say that I am grateful."

We were all quiet for the remainder of the ride. When we got to Twentynine Palms, I got a pass for Mark and Roseanne to come on base. We sat at a picnic table in the pavilion and had a Christmas dinner of meatball sandwiches and macaroni salad that Roseanne packed for us. It was nice until it was time for them to leave.

With tears in his eyes, Mark hugged me, and went to the car without saying a word. Mark is a great guy. He is one of the few Italian men I know that does not have an ounce of Goomba in him. That is why I know he is right for my sister.

Roseanne had tears in her eyes. "I love you little brother and I will talk to you before you leave for Saudi Arabia."

"I love you too Sissy," I said as I gave her a hug and then watched as she walked to the car.

I spent the rest of Christmas day getting my uniform ready for class on Wednesday.

Ten

Wednesday morning Major Berwick entered the classroom. "Good morning men. I trust everyone had a good Christmas. We have a busy two days ahead of us. Today and tomorrow, we will learn about nuclear, biological and chemical warfare. Unfortunately, for humankind, nuclear biological and chemical operations are a factor in today's war. Iraq has nuclear biological and chemical weapons in their arsenals, which may be used at any time. For this reason, you must be familiar with the effects of those weapons, and the defensive measures necessary to counter them."

"Sir, you are not putting us through the gas chamber, are you?" One Marine asked.

Major Berwick laughed. "No, that is one experience kept for boot camp. The next time you have that experience it will be for real. "Today, we will review the hazards of nuclear warfare. We will examine the defense of nuclear attack, effects of nuclear explosions to include radiation, and types of injuries caused. Tomorrow, we will study biological and chemical warfare. We will pay careful consideration to the matter of biological and chemical warfare, which will include protective measures, detection, and decontamination. You all learned how to use a gasmask in boot camp to protect yourselves against chemical agents. We will learn the behavior, neutralization and effects of chemical agents."

Major Berwick was not lying when he said we had a busy two days ahead of us. Again, classes went late into the evening. On December 27th we received our certification of promotion notices and security clearance. Luckily Major Berwick told us in advance of the promotions. This gave us time to get our stripes sewed onto our uniforms. I felt proud to receive a promotion to Lance Corporal in such a short period. As a Lance Corporal, I still had one stripe, but now I had one stripe over crossed rifles on my sleeves.

On Friday, December 28, 1990, we all assembled in our desert camouflage uniforms. We reported to one of the desert training facilities on the base. It was then, that I met my team members for the first time. Private First Class Noah Smith was my nineteen-year old gunner from Buffalo, New York. My light armored vehicle driver was twenty-year old Corporal Patrick O'Neill from Boston, Massachusetts. We stayed in the desert for three days, taking part in war games.

Training in the desert included everything that I learned during the five weeks I was at Twentynine Palms. We covered everything we needed to know. I had to plot maps, deliver and pick up a recon team, and file a report from that team just back from a visual observation mission. Everything went off without difficulty. It did feel a little funny acting as Light Armor Vehicle Commander with a Corporal aboard, but Corporal O'Neill had no problem with it.

"A Black American Marine, and Irish American Marine, and an Italian American Marine, what a mixture of individuals united in a common cause," Major Berwick said.

I finally had some time to myself Sunday morning when we ended maneuvers. After doing laundry and getting my uniforms in order, I called home.

"Joseph, how come you do not call?" My mother asked. "I wait and wait for your call."

"Mom, I can't always call. I have been very busy and I didn't have the time."

"Here, talk to your father. I am so upset with you right now that I cannot talk."

"Hello Marine. Are you ready to go?"

"Yeah Dad, I am mentally and physically ready. My sea bag stayed packed. I only had out the uniforms that I used on a daily basis. Dad, I have been very busy and we just came off maneuvers. Please try to explain to Mom."

"I understand boy. I went months without calling home. Do the best you can in writing though. Now that you are going over seas, I don't expect to hear from you for awhile. I will explain to your mother."

"Dad I will try and call when we land in Delaware."

160

"Okay Son. We will be home so call whenever you get a chance. Would you like to talk to your grandmother?"

"No Dad, I got shit….stuff to do. I will talk to her when I call from Delaware."

"Listen Son, just in case we don't talk, I would like to say Happy New Year, and stay alert over there."

"Save it for later Dad. I will call."

"Okay Son, I will talk to you then."

I spent the rest of the day collecting my thoughts and putting the final touch on things. After chow on Monday morning, New Year's Eve, there was a knock at my door. "Open up Pfc. Mommalione."

I quickly opened the door. "Corporal Haddon, I wasn't sure if I was going to see you before I left."

"Oh excuse me; I see that it is Lance Corporal Mommalione now. You take care of yourself over there. Don't be a hero. Here is my address and the restaurant phone number. Keep in touch, and call, I am discharged next month and we are buying a ranch outside of town. You are always welcome."

"Thanks Rocky. I will keep in touch," I said as we gave each other goodbye hugs and kisses.

I left my suitcase on the bunk as I managed to pack all my uniforms as well as my civilian clothes in my sea bag. Two hours later, after checking out at supply, the armory, sickbay, etc, I headed to the staging point dressed in my camouflage uniform, and met up with Pfc. Smith and Cpl. O'Neill, as well as Major Berwick, who was also there. I greeted the Major with a salute.

Major Berwick returned the salute. "At ease Lance Corporal Mommalione, and be advised that I am very proud of you. I am so impressed with your potential, as well as your skills and abilities you demonstrated as a Marine in my command, that I am recommending you to Officer Candidate School at Quanico, Virginia. It is rare that someone gets to go to O.C.S. without a college degree, but I am making the recommendation. It is true that enlisted men at the rank of corporal and above provide the most direct and personal leadership found in the Marine Corps, but I feel that you could serve the Corps better as an officer. Go with God speed Lance Corporal Mommalione."

"Thank you Sir," I said as I saluted him and watched him walk away.

Cpl. O'Neill, Pfc. Smith and I hung around for about an hour before the truck came for us. It was not that long of a ride, being that Norton Air Force base was also in San Bernardino County. When we got to the base, we went directly to the C141 Starlifter. The plane was large. Cpl O'Neill briefed us on the plane. "Men, this is a cargo plane with four Pratt and Whitney Tf33-P-7 Turbofan engines. The wingspan is 160 feet. This plane will hold 200 troops."

I was impressed with the Corporal's knowledge, and was eager to hear more, but an Air Force Sergeant interrupted us. He instructed us to board, before our light armored vehicle was loaded. There were 14 seats up front of the plane. It took about a half of an hour before the plane was completely loaded with our LAV and freight. When it was time to take off, Pfc. Smith, Cpl. O'Neill, and I took a seat with two flight engineers, and one loadmaster. It felt like the plane would never get off the ground as it rumbled down the runway.

• • •

The flight was long and loud. Both Pfc. Smith and Cpl O'Neill fell asleep shortly after we took off. Rumor has it that a Marine could fall asleep anywhere, but not me. The smell of fuel and oil was killing me. In addition, I was freezing as well as hungry. My field jacket was not warm enough, and my box lunch sucked.

We stopped for about an hour at an Air National Guard Unit in Jackson, Mississippi. Still, nobody talked. Maybe it had to do with the seating arrangement, or maybe it had to do with the noise on the plane, but nobody talked. It was about 9:00 p.m. when we landed at Dover, Delaware. It was killing me that I was so close to home and couldn't see my family.

We had about two hours to kill before the convoy was to leave for the Norfolk Naval Base, and it was cold so the authorities took us to a terminal that had a snack bar with tables and booths in it. I downed a sandwich and a bowl of chicken soup before I called my parents. Grandma answered the phone.

"It's Joey, Grandma, Happy New Year."

"Joey, where are you?"

"I'm in Delaware, Grandma."

"Come home, Roseanne and Mark are here. We are going to the Casa Di Roma to bring in the New Year."

"Grandma, I don't have much time. Please get Mom and Dad."

My mother came to the phone. "Joseph, how are you?"

"I am fine Mom. I am in Delaware, but I cannot come home. We are moving out soon."

"Where are you going?"

"Mom, I am going to Norfolk Naval Base where I am going to catch a ship headed for the Gulf."

"Hello Son," my father said from the other line.

"Hi Dad, I think that I am going to be an officer. Major Berwick is recommending me for Officer Candidate School. If it is approved, I will be attending O.C.S. when I get back from Saudi."

"That is great, but listen Son, you cover your ass over there. Do not try and be a hero. Pay attention to detail and your basic Marine instincts will take over. I love you, don't hang up. Say good-bye to your mother."

"Good-bye Mom, I love you. And, don't cry Mom. The guys are standing here. You don't want them to see me crying, do you?"

"It is not right Joseph. You are my baby boy. You are too young to go to war."

"Mom it is us young men and women who fight the wars. I am proud to serve my country. I am a Marine, Mom. You know what that means. We are the best Mom. We are the toughest. I need you to do something for me. Please tell Carmine, Roseanne, and Mark that I am thinking of them. Tell Carmine I am sorry that I didn't call him."

"Happy New Year Joseph, we will pray for you. I love you Joseph."

"I love you Mom," I said as I hung up the phone.

I sat in the furthest seat to try to collect myself before I joined the guys. I looked up to see Private First Class Smith and Corporal O'Neill sitting at separate tables. This was odd I thought. I just figured that it would take some time for us to get comfortable with each other. I studied the faces of each man. I tried to detect any emotion. I was not comfortable with the looks I was getting, so I focused on the window and the darkness outside and began to feel sorry for myself. I wished that I were home with my family bringing in the new year. My thoughts turned to my mother who tried to discourage me from being a Marine. I guess being a mother; she didn't understand things like honor, commitment and duty to your country.

"Hey," said the Black Marine. You aren't going to cry, are you?"

"No bro, I'm not going to cry," I said with anger.

"I'm not your bro," Pfc. Smith said. "Mommalione is that Eyetalian?"

"No, it is Italian and don't worry about me, I am not a sissy or a coward. When the shit hits the fan, you can count on me. I won't run. I am ready for the fight."

"Where are you from Mommalione?" Pfc. Smith then asked me.

"Trenton, New Jersey, I said with much pride."

"I guess there are a lot if Eye-talians there. I myself am from Buffalo, New York.

"I guess there are a lot of Blacks there, and I suppose that you are the badest," I said in a smartass way.

"Well let me put it to you like this Eye-talian. I am the nigger with his finger on the trigger and I'm gonna get me some kills."

"Well let me put it to you like this bro. I'm the Italian that is going to kill the raghead man."

"Knock it off. If both of you are done testing each other, let me remind you that there is only one color in this team and that is the color of our desert uniforms. We may not even get into the fight. There are hundreds of thousands of troops over there that have been there for a hundred days or so. They are all thinking the same thing as you are only they have had more time to think about it. This is going to be an air war and the whole thing will be over with in a matter of a couple of months."

The red haired Marine really impressed me. He suddenly reminded me of Carmine with his wisdom. "Corporal O'Neill have you ever seen combat?" I asked.

"Yeah Mommalione, I have seen about three days worth. I was part of the Marine Barracks at an Embassy in a South American country during the drug wars a couple years ago. An American was killed execution style. Naval intelligence said that the culprits were hiding in a jungle village. A squad of us went to that village with the mission of bringing them to justice or killing them. The operation turned into a disaster. We found ourselves in a firefight against about two hundred of them bastards. We couldn't even call in air support because we weren't suppose to be there."

Cpl. O'Neill then became silent and just sat there looking at the floor. "Well, what happened man?" Pfc. Smith asked.

"What do you think happened? I'm here aren't I? The guerrilla's retreated into the jungle and we went berserk killing everyone in the village."

"Where was this?" I asked with much interest.

Cpl. O'Neill looked at me somewhat crazy like. "It was in South America. That is all I can say. I signed a confidentially agreement. Forget that I said anything."

"Did any Marines get killed or wounded?" Pfc. Smith asked.

"Six were wounded. The headlines read six Marines wounded in support of local government trying to oust a Drug Lord, the massacre at the village was blamed on the Drug Lord. Don't be in such a hurry to kill. Just being over there will haunt you for the rest of your life."

It wasn't long before notice came that we were moving out. We boarded a Navy bus that was in front of the convoy of flat bed trucks hauling light armored vehicles and other equipment. We had a several hour ride ahead of us, so I curled up in the seat and went to sleep. I woke up when I heard someone yell, "Three minutes to midnight." The next few minutes were extremely quiet when we heard someone yell out, "Happy New Year." Everyone started yelling and whistling. I fell back asleep and woke up when we stopped for a head call. I presumed that the others could tell that I was feeling down.

When we got back on the bus, Pfc. Smith asked, "Hey Lance Corporal Mommalione, are you okay?"

"Yes," I said. "I'll be fine."

• • •

It was too dark to see much of the base. It seemed like we drove for quite a distance once we got there. I had no idea of what ships they were, but we passed some big ones. Finally, we got to our destination. It was a well-lit area. We immediately went aboard the transport. The quarters were tight, but the chow was okay. I have never been on a ship before, so to me it was exciting. After spending most of New Years day loading supplies aboard ship, we were ready to set sail. It was a nice January day. Every inch of the ship was loaded with vehicles and equipment. It seemed terribly crowded.

"Have you ever been on a ship before?" Corporal O'Neill asked me.

"No," I said. "The only thing close is when my father took me on fishing boats at times, if that counts."

"It doesn't," Cpl. O'Neill said.

Pfc. Smith already looked sick. "I don't like the water. That is why I joined the Marines. The closest I ever came to an ocean was riding on a boat on Lake Erie."

"That don't count either," Cpl. O'Neill added.

We stood on deck and watched as the ship shoved off. The cold air willingly passed from land to sea. I knew that the travel aboard a ship to the other side of the world was going to be a great adventure for me. I understand that a cruise ship carries people out of reality and in to fantasy. I also understood that this was no cruise ship. This ship carried Marines from fantasy to reality.

"Yes, finally the moment had come," I said after watching ships file past us out to sea.

"Yes, it is our turn," Pfc. Smith said.

It was early in the afternoon, and the harbor was empty as our ship slipped away from the pier. Everyman except for those on duty was on deck to take a last look at American soil. Once we were on our way, I walked around on deck and came across a group of Sailors talking about how grateful they were not to be Marines. When one noticed me, he asked, "How do you feel about going to war?"

I didn't answer. It was not that I was stuck-up or anything like that, it was simply that I had no answer for him. I guess that the ship was like home to them whereas I was about to make a tent in the desert my home.

Our first day at sea was somewhat relaxing. The sun was out and although the air was cool, the water was smooth as silk. I pretty much kept to myself on the first day collecting my thoughts and trying to focus on the situation at hand.

After a few days on ship, I started to get adjusted. It seemed terribly crowded though and some of the Marines complained of the food, but not me, I thought the food was okay. The worst thing for me was the crowded quarters and sleeping arrangements. Another thing, was that we only had three minutes of hot water to shower. We were allowed to go anywhere on deck that we wished though.

I found a little corner on the ship that I liked. It looked over much of the cargo. Even when the sea became rough, I went up on deck as much as possible. Some of the men became sick. Both Corporal O'Neill and Private First Class Smith became seasick.

"Fuck this," Pfc. Smith said. "Now I know why I didn't join the Navy."

"Were you ever on a Navy ship before?" Pfc. Smith asked Cpl. O'Neill.

"Yes," Cpl. O'Neill answered. "But it was only for a week of training in San Diego."

There was only a small number of Marines aboard ship. Mostly there were sailors aboard. All of which had a specific duty to do on a daily basis. The few Marine Officers aboard were assigned to rooms that I think were called cabins. The enlisted men were quartered below. The mess area was filled with long tables with benches on each side. We were fed in shifts. There was a small ship store where one could buy the basic hygiene necessities as well as other needs. I stocked up on candy and I bought some stationary with the ship logo on it. I wrote several letters to my mother and father as well as Roseanne and Mark. I was able to mail my letters at the ships post office.

Everyday during the first week aboard ship, we attended classes on the customs of the people in the region that we were going. We were even issued small booklets that explained such things as the laws and religion of Saudi Arabia. We also received instructions on what to do incase the ship was attacked. I thought it was odd that no ships escorted us. However, who was going to attack us anyway. Battle station instructions for the Marines were simple. Marines were to stay below deck. We were also warned about throwing debris overboard. It had something to do with enemy submarines being able to detect a ship that had passed hours ahead. I thought they had radar for such things. Moreover, I was almost sure that the Iraqis did not have submarines. I could say that there was absolutely no anxiety aboard about our safety.

It didn't take me long to see the rivalry or opposition between the Marine Corps and the Navy. Mostly I seen this in the distance kept between the two groups. Marines and Sailors are about as different as night and day. Being in the company of both, one would not ever know that technically speaking, Marines and Sailors are one of the same branches of service. I had met many Sailors on ship, but almost all of them were merely through acknowledgement of existence.

I must say that I didn't find them to be at all as crude as the Drill Instructors made them out to be when I was in boot camp. Actually, I found them not to be as unpleasant as Marines were. I was surprised to find them to be quiet, and almost humble. They seemed to have respect for the Marines aboard, but if a Marine confronted a group of them sitting around for example, they would ignore him. If a Marine would engage in laughter with them or comment on something they were talking about, the Sailors would most likely turn their back on the Marine. Sailors did seem foreign to me, but I couldn't understand the dislike Marines have for Sailors and visa versa. One thing that the Marines and Sailors had in common other than being a part of the same branch of the service was that each was proud of where they came from. A lot of talk was heard of hometowns, as well as nationalities. There was no fighting or quarreling on the ship between the Sailors and Marines. There was no contempt toward each other. Furthermore, I didn't witness any sarcasm between the two groups either.

One Sailor the Marines have the utmost respect for is the Corpsman. The Corpsman is the medic who lives, as well as serves with the Marines and is a member of the Marine infantry platoon. He is the authority on cuts, blisters, colds and any minor ailment. He takes care of his Marines and goes into combat just like a Marine, without hesitation. He shares our hardships and when a Marine is wounded, the Corpsman is right there administering medical attention. The medical attention that he provides is more important than that of a doctor. If it were not for the Corpsman, the casualty in many cases would not live to be treated at a military hospital. However, when a Corpsman is not available, it is the responsibility of every Marine to provide medical treatment from his first-aid packet.

One thing I discovered while on guard duty, as I got to eat at the mess during naval personal chow, was that when it came to food, the Navy ate better. It was early in the morning when I came off guard and before the Marines reported for morning chow when I reported for chow held in reserve for Sailors. To my surprise, I was served real eggs and real milk instead of the powdered milk and eggs. I also had a steak with my egg that was to die for. It sure beat the thin slices of ham that the Marines were served. I was also served fruit and juice, which Marines never tasted while on the voyage.

Being of Naval intelligence, I first found guard aboard ship to be somewhat lacking in intelligence. My thoughts changed as while on guard duty, I came across an incident that involved gambling. I was doing my rounds when I came upon three Sailors beating up another Sailor for cheating in a card game. They were threatening to throw him overboard when I appeared.

"What the fuck is going on here," someone said.

I turned to see Cpl. O'Neill standing behind me. All the Sailors scattered upon first sight of Corporal O'Neill.

"Where did you come from?" I asked Cpl. O'Neill.

"Hell. I come from hell."

"What are you doing here?" I asked with relief in my voice.

"I am watching over my Marine. You may be the Marine in charge when we are in the light armored vehicle on a mission, but I am the ranking Marine of the group. Now let's get this man up."

We helped the trampled young man to sickbay and I entered the incident in the logbook, minus the appearance of Cpl. O'Neill. Besides that incident, there was no real trouble at all among the troops during the voyage that I experienced.

We got radio news broadcasts twice a day. The news was not good from the Gulf. The days were purposeless and without duties, but Cpl. O'Neill made us P.T. daily. As we progressed, the weather became warm and the seas even more calm.

By the end of the first week, I was no longer fearful of being at sea. Sailing upon a great ship somewhat put me at ease and I found it impossible to be afraid. Even though we had a couple days of rough weather, the last days of the first week were calm. The daytime on the sea was serene, but the days were also very long and lonely. They gave me too much time to think. I started spending a lot of time alone and thinking about my role in the Marine Corps. I concluded that my job was an important one and only a few men could accomplish it. That is why I was chosen for it I thought. I wondered how it would feel to become a killer if in fact I would have to kill anyone. I was not looking for pity, because one does not pity a man willing to fight at any given time and who is willing to give his life for his country. Besides, there was no one to pity me anyway. Never the less, I was starting to feel sorry for myself.

I attended mass on Sunday, but felt no relief from my loneliness. By the end of the first week at sea, I started thinking of my mother, father and grandmother too much. I worried about how my mother was holding up. I thought back to being back on the block and running the streets of Trenton with George and Danny. Their tragic deaths ran through my mind consistently. I thought of Sally, and tried to understand why she dumped me. I was really missing Mark and Roseanne too. I think that I missed Carmine more than anyone. Not having Carmine to turn to for advice made me feel a little insecure. I was sure glad that Cpl. O'Neill was a part of the team.

I became a devoted reader by the second week at sea. It was not that I liked to read, because reading was actually one of my least favorite things to do. I was just so bored, that I read everything I could get my hands on. My favorite things to read were old magazines and newspapers.

Even though I took up reading, the ship was starting to close in on me. Even the food was starting to taste worse. I came to respect the Sailors for living in such conditions. I was getting sick of the overcrowding, as well as the fact that it took several sittings three times a day to feed everyone. My bunk was in one of the lower living quarters. The Sailors referred to it as sleeping quarters because that is the only time they spent there. They were the lucky ones aboard because they had jobs to do. Living conditions just seemed abnormal.

I was always hot and sweaty when I tried to sleep. I actually thanked God that I didn't join the Navy.

I think that the officers started to notice the dreariness, or they were feeling it too. We were ordered to attend classes on a daily basis. These classes were focused on the history and traditions of the Marine Corps.

"We just finished class on culture and laws of the Arabic people, now we got to go through these fucking classes again. Fuck this, I had that shit in boot camp," Pfc. Smith said.

Cpl. O'Neill laughed, "Do you remember any of it?" He asked Pfc. Smith.

"No"

"Me neither," I said. "They should be giving us refresher classes on first aid. That is something that could come in handy when the shit hits the fan."

"They are just trying to keep us busy and our minds off of what we are about to face," Cpl. O'Neill said. "Besides, your first aid training will come back to you when the time comes."

• • •

I became gloomy as the days passed by. Because of that feeling, I found myself drawn closer to Pfc. Smith and Cpl. O'Neill. Actually, the three members of our special little group finally got to know one another and we became close.

I discovered Pfc. Smith to be powerful and street smart. I am no authority on the subject, but I thought of Pfc. Smith as a young man with psychological problems due to his upbringing and exposure to drugs and violence while growing up. Being able to understand the nature of the man had become necessary for me if we were going to work together. This understanding of him went beyond training and dedication. I seriously thought he needed counseling. Despite that, I was confident in Pfc. Smith. I became certain that he could overcome personal difficulties and focus on the mission where his violent emotions could come in handy. I found his humor having a mocking quality. The man impressed me as one who kicked ass and took names on the streets. I didn't view him as a man of heroism, but more of a man of rough determination. Pfc. Smith could sense what is wrong with someone and almost immediately suggest the best remedy. He exposed himself as being combative, which made him a quality Marine. There was no doubt in my military mind that Noah Smith was one badass motherfucker, on the mean streets of the east side of Buffalo.

I found Cpl. O'Neill to be dependable. The Marines would not have made him a noncommissioned officer if he were not. My one concern was that Patrick O'Neill had a knack for instilling fear or anxiety in the most powerful opponents. This is a good quality to have in battle though. I could tell that the dynamism of Cpl. O'Neill carried him through difficulties. I found him to be a serious individual, as well as intense and goal minded. His strengths seemed to be purposeful and influential. Cpl. O'Neill demonstrated great responsibility. He had been in the Marine Corps for a few years, since he was seventeen and demonstrated the capacity of enduring hardship or inconvenience without complaint. His energetic, gutsy and aggressive manner really impressed me. His talent for organization also impressed me. He also confirmed his ability to listen to his peers, which is a quality that would be helpful to me during a mission. On the other hand, he verified that he would not tolerate any serious threat to his authority.

As we drew closer to voyage end, Cpl. O'Neill, Pfc. Smith and I acquired a feeling of connection as if by kinship or a common origin. We no longer looked like we were eighteen, nineteen, or twenty years old. We looked like men. We looked like, Marines.

Eleven

We arrived in Saudi Arabia on January 16, 1991. It was a hot January day. We picked up our clothes from the ship laundry, turned in our blankets, packed our sea bags and were instructed to report to the briefing room.

"What do you think this briefing is all about?" Pfc. Smith asked Cpl. O'Neill and me. Before Cpl. O'Neill or I could respond, Pfc. Smith continued to talk. "It sounds like we were in for another one of those bullshit lectures if you ask me. If I hear another sermon on the customs and laws of the Arabic people, I am going to shoot someone."

"Don't ask me," I said. I gotta tell you, I don't have a clue. I have to agree with you though. If I hear another officer addressing the laws and way of life of the fine people of Saudi Arabia, I am going to lock and load on his ass."

"He is probably going to inform us on the events that are going to take place once we embark," Cpl. O'Neill said as the ship really slowed down.

"Look at that stone wall," Pfc. Smith commented. It looks just like the waterfront at the Marina in Buffalo. It reminds me of where the Niagara River and Lake Erie meet.

"I never seen Niagara Falls," I said. "It must really be cool to see the Falls. I heard that the Canadian side has a better view because you could see the American Falls as well as the Horseshoe Falls."

Pfc. Smith nodded. "That is not entirely true Mommalione. There is a walk out on the American side. This takes you out over the falls and allows you to see the Horseshoe Falls as well. I'll tell you what, if you don't get killed or seriously fucked up over here, I will take you there someday."

Cpl. O'Neill looked at Pfc. Smith. "If you are done with the geography lesson, let's get a move on."

The briefing room reminded me of a miniature Movie Theater or something out of a World War II Air Force movie where pilots were briefed before a flight mission. We took our seats, along with about thirty other Marines, and were soon called to attention when an officer entered the room.

"As you were Marines." All the seats clattered as we sat back down. "My name is Captain Morgan, and I am here to instruct you on what you need to do once the ship docks. By now you, all have your gear stowed on deck and are ready to go. In order to avoid a clusterfuck, you will all assemble on deck in some sort of formation. All Marines will disembark at the same time, before any supplies or equipment. Flags mark designated staging areas. If you are assigned to a particular piece of equipment or vehicle, you are to assemble in the red flag area. If you are assigned to supply, you will assemble in the green flag area, and if you are part of a medical hospital team or medical supply, you will assemble in the yellow flag area."

A Marine in front of us jumped up from his seat waving his arms. "What is it Marine?" The Captain asked with a smile on his face.

"Sir the Private is not with any of the groups that the Captain just mentioned."

"Well who are you with?"

"Captain Sir, the Private is with the United States Marine Corps."

Well, everyone busted out in laughter, including the Captain. "What is your Military Occupational Specialty, Private?"

"Sir the Private's M.O.S. is that of a Cook."

Again, everyone started to laugh, including me. I laughed and was in tears from laughing so hard. However, I suddenly stopped laughing when I remembered the story about my Senior Drill Instructor. I remembered the story the Senior D.I. told us abut when he was a cook in Vietnam; he picked up his rifle when the shit hit the fan, and commenced on killing the enemy.

"At ease Marine," the Captain said. "All of you who do not fit in any of the groups that I just mentioned are to report to the blue flag area. There will be hot chow, hot coffee, and bottled water. Make yourself comfortable as you may be there for some time." An aid to the captain called us to attention and instructed us to fall out into formation with our sea bags.

We assembled in ranks of four as ordered and were called to attention by ranking sergeant. "Left face," he barked. "Move out by ranks, and good luck men."

We all marched down the gangplank and went to our assembling points.

"I want you two to get some chow," Corporal O'Neill said.

"Where are you going?" Pfc. Smith asked the Corporal.

"I am going to scout around a bit."

"What are you looking for?" I asked.

The Corporal gave me a look as if he were annoyed with the question. "I don't really know. Just do as I said and get some chow. I don't know how long it will be before we eat again."

Pfc. Smith and I looked at each other and sort of shrugged our shoulders. "What about you, are you going to eat?" Pfc. Smith asked Cpl. O'Neill."

"Yeah, I'll eat when I get back."

Pfc. Smith and I eagerly took our place in line, and we filled our plates. "Why don't we get some chow for the Corporal," Pfc. Smith said.

"Yeah, it sounds good to me. By the time he gets back, the line will be long and the food may be gone." We each grabbed another metal tray and got some chow for the Corporal. The food was good. They served hot roast beef, corn and mashed potatoes with gravy, as well as rolls. We had our choice of hot coffee, milk, water or soda to drink.

We found a couple crates to sit on and began eating our chow when Cpl. O'Neill came back.

"Here," I said. "We got you some chow. I didn't know what you wanted to drink so we got you some water and a coke."

Cpl. O'Neill took the tray and chugged his coke. "It is fucking hot over here," he said. "I found out that we will be leaving here in about two hours. Our light armored vehicle will be among the first to be unloaded. I will be going in about an hour to get the LAV, and the convoy will be moving out in about two hours."

Cpl. O'Neill had a concerned look on his face. I felt as if he were holding something back, Pfc. Smith noticed it too. "What else did you find out?" Pfc. Smith asked.

The Corporal really looked concerned as if he were in a state of uneasiness. "I found out that the shit already hit the fan. I confirmed the rumors that I heard aboard the ship." Cpl. O'Neill took a seat on a crate and began to eat.

"Well what is it, what did you find out?" I asked in an anxious tone.

"Okay, I found out that this morning we started bombing the shit out them fuckers."

"Where are we going?" Pfc. Smith inquired.

Cpl. O'Neill stood and pointed. "We are going that way. We are going to a small base located northwest of a town by the name of Al Jubayl. That is all I found out. We are in for a long ride. Now if you two don't mind, I would like to finish my meal, so shut the fuck up."

Just then, we heard an explosion. In a split second, Pfc. Smith and I were face down in the sand. We were not alone. Everyone was face down in the sand with their hands locked together over their heads, everyone except, Cpl. O'Neill. He was still sitting there eating his chow.

I slowly got to my feet and as I was dusting myself off. I said, "What the hell was that?" Cpl. O'Neill pointed behind me. I turned to see a big puff of black smoke rising in the horizon.

"What the hell was that?" Pfc. Smith yelled.

Cpl. O'Neill shook his head from side to side. "Oh, it was nothing. Probably a camel stepped on a land mine."

"Are you for real?" Pfc. Smith asked.

Again the Corporal shook his head. "No I'm not for real. How should I know what it was? Besides, it's way the hell over there anyway."

• • •

We had to wait for for the ship to be unloaded. The quantity of material flowing off the ship was grand. As I stood and looked around, I realized that this was only one ship being unloaded, which was a drop in the bucket compared to the amount of supplies already sent. Cpl. O'Neill secured the vehicle. Cpl. O'Neill looked cool in his special helmet when he popped his head out of the hatch. Pfc. Smith and I jumped on and took position behind the turret. Cpl. O'Neill lined up at the ammo depot where Pfc. Smith stowed 25mm ammunition for his chain gatling gun. He also stowed 7.60mm ammunition for his machine guns, mounted coaxial to the main gun.

Pfc. Smith continued to make ammo ready for all the guns as Cpl. O'Neill and I checked the communications system and Nuclear Biological and Chemical warning system, which included the M8A1 ventilated facemasks and M543A1 detector alarm. I then proceeded to check the navigation system, which consisted of a precision lightweight GPS receiver (AN/PSN-11). The electrical system was fine and once Pfc. Smith gave us the word that his work was complete, we took our place in the convoy. The Arab kids swarmed the road for about two miles outside the secured area. They were yelling for chewing gum, chocolate, and cigarettes.

A large military convoy moving across the desert is something that I will never forget. The place we were in reminded me of Twentynine Palms. Even the weather and climate reminded me of Twentynine Palms. Once we were underway, we were surprised how good the roads were. They were macadamized much like the roads in the United States. We drove on the outskirts of Dhahran and Ad Damman, which are big cities and well populated. The costal highway stretched north, between cities, pastures, wells, and petroleum reserves. It looked very much like our own Southwest. It was lacking trees. However, it was not exactly desert either? Parts of the landscape were very fertile and under cultivation too. I remembered reading that dates are a product grown in Saudi Arabia. We were impressed by the elegance of the part of the country that we seen. Once we passed Al Jubayl, the convoy headed northwest and we started to see sand ridges, as well as sand dunes. I was looking for camels, but I didn't see any.

When we reached the Marine Base, Cpl. O'Neill broke away from the convoy, and military police directed us to report to the rear echelon, which was a subdivision of headquarters. We were instructed to park our light armored vehicle in a large paved area and report to the administration building, which was only a short distance away. The building was small and made out of plywood. Cpl. O'Neill presented our orders to the Second Lieutenant seated at a desk. This man looked like a high school kid. He was a good-looking young man who looked a little nervous.

"Sir, Corporal O'Neill, Lance Corporal Mommalione, and Private First Class Smith reporting for duty."

The Lieutenant took a few minutes to look over our papers. "Welcome to Camp Bulldog, my name is Second Lieutenant Rizon. I am going to take you to the briefing room. Master Sergeant Gaskin will join you momentarily and he will brief you."

The building was well air-conditioned. The cool air felt good. It was a busy place with Marines moving in a rapid pace down the narrow hallways, ducking in and out of rooms. We followed Lieutenant Rizon to the briefing room.

"I have never seen so many officers in one place." Cpl. O'Neill said. "Lucky we don't have to salute indoors, my arm would fall off."

When we entered the room, I noticed a huge bulldog painted on the wall. He was in the sitting position and was wearing a Drill Instructor Smokey the Bear hat. The British bulldog is the mascot of the Marine Corps.

There we found six Marines huddled around a small television set. They were all yelling and cheering.

"Yeah, he got that motherfucker."

"Holy shit, did you see that?"

"This is awesome."

"What is going on?" Cpl O'Neill asked.

"We are fucking them up. We are bombing the shit out of them," one Marine said.

Stupid me, at first I thought these guys were watching the taping of a football game. Cpl. O'Neill was right with the information he found out when we disembarked from the ship. The shit indeed hit the fan I thought. Desert Storm's aerial campaign began before dawn on January 16, 1991. A Marine in the room told me that the entire world watched on cable television. All I could think about was my mother, and how she must be freaking out.

My curiosity, as the same for Cpl. O'Neill's and Pfc. Smith's set in as we muscled in position to see the small television screen. The men were very good about letting us in to see. I was flabbergasted as to what I saw. The segment we were watching showed the Air Force bombing the hell out of certain targets. Their targets were mainly buildings.

"Look at this shit," Pfc. Smith said. "We are putting a hurting on their ass."

"Yeah," I said. "I can't believe that my mother is watching this. She writes the news for New Jersey radio talk station. She must be having a cow."

"She will be fine," Cpl. O'Neill alleged. "Just keep focused on what our job is over here. I hope that this war will be over quickly and we could get the hell out of here."

What a day to arrive. My eyes were glued to the television. The devastation created by the aerial campaign was unbelievable. Everyone's eyes were fixed on Master Sergeant Gaskin when he entered the room. The room was not called to attention because the Mater Sergeant is not an officer, but I knew that he must command respect. He was the highest ranking enlisted man on the base. He looked leather tough and rock hard as he chewed on a big fat cigar.

Master Sergeant Gaskin looked at all the men sitting around the television set. He then looked down at the clipboard he was holding in his hand. "The only devil dogs I want in this room are Corporal O'Neill, Lance Corporal Mommalione, Private First Class Smith, and I. And, shut off that damn T.V. You will all be in the shit soon enough."

Everyone beat feet out of the room. Cpl. O'Neill approached Master Sergeant Gaskin. "Master Sergeant Gaskin my name is O'Neill." He then pointed to Pfc. Smith and me. "This here is Smith and Mommalione."

"Welcome Marines. You are assigned to this command post and will be housed in headquarters billets, in the rear of this building. As you could see, people are running around here like chickens with their heads cut off. This is because the aerial campaign has begun.

Despite what you just seen the Air Force doing on television, Marine pilots are also involved. The 1st Marine Aircraft Wing, which has one quarter of the fixed wing tactical aircraft in the theater, did its share of the strike, but they are more concerned with preparing the battlefield for Marine Expeditionary Brigade up coming ground operations."

The three of us looked at each other. What the Master Sergeant was saying, told us that it would not be long before we see action in the way of a mission.

"Master Sergeant, may I take the LAV to the motor pool before we get started?" Cpl. O'Neill asked.

"Yes Corporal. It is getting late, get your gear, go get chow and report to me at 0730 in the morning for orientation. As we started to exit, Master Sergeant Gaskin grabbed me by the arm. "You two go on ahead, I need to talk with Lance Corporal Mommalione a moment."

"We'll bring your sea bag," Pfc. Smith said as he and Cpl. O'Neill exited the room.

Cpl. O'Neill slapped me on the shoulder. "Yeah, we'll meet you in the barracks."

"Come with me Mommalione. I will walk you to the barracks. You and your group are lucky to be in the barracks and not a tent. Major Berwick is a good friend of mine and he tells me that you are one squared away Marine."

"Woe Sir, you know Major Berwick! He is a great Officer and taught me well."

"Yes, I trained him at Quanico. I had fun training them college boys to become officers. I really busted their balls. In addition, years later we served together in Okinawa. He is responsible for me being promoted from Gunnery Sergeant to Master Sergeant. I agree with you, he is a great Administrative Officer. The Major sent me a message telling me that I was to expect you."

"Sir, what a small world."

"The Marine Corps is small young man. I know because I have been around the block with it more than once in the past thirty years. People don't realize that there are only about 170,000 of us. And don't call me Sir. I work for a living."

The barracks was not what I expected it to be. It reminded me of a scene out of an old World War II movie. It certainly was not like the quarters back at Twentynine Palms, which that was like a hotel. However, as the Master Sergeant said, it was better than living in a tent.

"I will see you in the morning." Master Sergeant Gaskin said as he turned and walked away.

I was looking at a Navy Seabees logo on the wall. The logo was a bee carrying a gun and a wrench, and it read, "WE BUILD, WE FIGHT." Pfc. Smith and Cpl. O'Neill came in and joined me.

Cpl. O'Neill stopped and looked at the logo. "Do you guys know the earliest Seabees were recruited from the civilian construction trades and were placed under the leadership of the Navy's Bureau of Yards and Docks? The Seabees went on to play a big roll in WWII, Korea, and Vietnam. They even took on a civil role in Vietnam by building schools and infrastructure. They also provided healthcare services."

That Cpl. O'Neill, he knew everything I thought. The next day, we met with Master Sergeant Gaskin. He showed us around headquarters and then we drew rifles, and ammunition, as well as smoke and hand grenades. We also drew gear such as helmets, canteens, etc. I immediately set my dope (sights) on my rifle.

• • •

We attended physical training and orientation for the next two days. We were all disgusted with the fact that we had to sit through culture and customs of Saudi Arabia again. It seemed like our hundredth time. Orientation briefly described the history and geology of the Arab countries. A big part of orientation was the "Do's and Don'ts." The instructor warned us never to enter mosques. In addition, never to loiter, smoke, or spit in front of a mosque. He said that bread is holy to the Muslims. We were never to cut bread, but always break it with the fingers, and not let any drop on the ground. The instructor cautioned not to give Muslims alcoholic drinks, not to bring dogs into a house and not to kill snakes or birds, since many Arabs believed that the souls of departed chieftains resided in them. We studied Arab culture and were told that under no circumstances were we to fraternize with the women. Orientation concluded with a lecture on conduct, and the limitations of picture taking.

On Sunday, we had base liberty. I went to mass and did my laundry. In the evening, we watched CNN. The highlights of the aerial campaign were astonishing.

From Monday, January 21st through Wednesday, we had physical training in the morning and attended classes on the land elevation and contour. I received maps and it felt like I was at land navigation classes all over again. On Thursday, I got to sit in on a recon team debriefing while Pfc. Smith and Cpl. O'Neill took out the LAV to test the vehicle and fire the guns.

Friday was interesting. Cpl. O'Neill pulled guard duty while Pfc. Smith was assigned to some shit detail. I had the privilege of sitting in on a top-secret briefing of the headquarters staff. A benefit of having a security clearance I supposed. We learned that the ground attack was scheduled to take place on February 24th. The first Marine Division was to break through the line near the A1 Wafrah oil fields. The second Marine Division was to continue the attack, possibly linking up with an amphibious landing against the Kuwait coast.

Both Pfc. Smith and Cpl. O'Neill could not wait to get the scoop when we all met at the Enlisted Man's Club in the evening. I was already there nursing a Coke when they arrived.

"Well what's the word, and don't leave anything out," Pfc. Smith said as he pulled up a chair.

Cpl. O'Neill gave me a light slap in the head as he took a seat at the table. "Yeah, like the man said, don't leave anything out."

I looked at the both of them like they were nuts. "The information I got was that the second Marine Division was planning an amphibious landing against the Kuwait coast and the First Marine Division is to break through the line at A1 Wafrah oil fields."

"That's it?" Cpl. O'Neill asked.

"Yeah, that's all the information I got."

"Where does that leave us?" Pfc. Smith asked.

"Hell man, I don't know," I said as I took a sip of my coke.

On Saturday, I spent the day in the planning room reviewing maps. Pfc. Smith and Cpl. O'Neill went to the range to fire their weapons. Afterwards, they went and fueled the LAV. On Sunday, we had base liberty, but we were on standby notice. Command allowed us to leave the barracks, but we had to sign out as to where we will be. We had to sign back in and out again for everywhere we went.

"Something is up. I could feel it. I'm just going to sit here and wait for the word to move out," Cpl. O'Neill said.

"Well I'm going to church. Then I will sign back in and sign out to the laundry."

"I'm going with you Mommalione. I could use some religion," Pfc. Smith said.

Nothing happened that Sunday. I went to mass, did my chores and wrote letters home. However, Cpl. O'Neill was right. On Monday, January 28th, after physical training, and morning chow, we were called to the briefing room.

"This is it," Cpl. O'Neill said.

Pfc. Smith looked puzzled. "What do you mean this is it?"

"I told you that I had a feeling something is up. It is time for us to earn our pay."

"Mommalione, what do you think this is all about?" Pfc. Smith asked. I said nothing as we entered the room and where greeted by the Master Sergeant.

"Gentlemen please take a seat," Master Sergeant Gaskin said. We all sat down around the conference table. "I have a mission for the three of you. Tomorrow afternoon, you are to pickup a recon team outside the Saudi town of Al Khafji. Here are your maps. The recon team consists of four Marines. They were dropped off four days ago. They have no radio. The pickup point was specified before their mission."

I had a knot in my throat as I put my maps in my map pouch, and checked my wallet to make sure that the four-leaf clover Carmine gave me was still there. No one was talking when a Saudi Arabia officer entered the room. The Master Sergeant called us to attention.

The Master Sergeant greeted the Saudi officer. "Marines, I would like for you to meet Mr. Hadad. Mr. Hadad is a Lieutenant in the Saudi Arabia Army. He will be bunking with you men tonight and will accompany you on your mission."

We introduced ourselves to Lieutenant Hadad. The Master Sergeant continued to say, "Lieutenant Hadad comes from a military family. His father comes from royalty and is a General in the Saudi Army. You have your orders Marines. It should be a routine mission, but be on your guard out there."

We were all quiet, as if stunned. Cpl. O'Neill broke the ice. "Everyone grab your combat gear, including rifles and meet at the LAV. After the inspection, we will assemble in the planning room and plan our mission. Are there any objections?"

We all shook our head no, and then we got our gear and met at the light armored vehicle. It took us about fifteen minutes to assemble. "Fall in, that is with your approval Lieutenant Hadad," Cpl. O'Neill ordered.

"That is fine Corporal," Lieutenant Hadad said in his best English.

Cpl. O'Neill walked around us as we stood at attention. "Each one of you check your equipment. Make sure you have your helmet, ammunition, grenades, smoke grenades, gas mask, canteens, first aid kit, NBC kit, bayonet and rifles."

This was an informal inspection. It was true that I was the LAV Commander while we were on a mission, but I would never have thought of what Cpl. O'Neill did. He exercised his rank as a noncommissioned officer and leader.

Cpl. O'Neill looked pleased. "Good job Marines. I will draw rations and then meet you in the planning room."

Lieutenant Hadad, Pfc. Smith, and I took our place in the planning room and I looked at the maps while we waited for Cpl. O'Neill.

I shook my head up and down. "Yes, from what I could see, they are in order," I said outloud.

When Corporal O'Neill entered the room, he said, "Okay men, Mommalione will review the route with us. As well, as discuss the details of the mission. Afterwards we will initial the mission orders once we understand Mommalione's instructions."

We spent the remainder of the day going over the mission. On the morning of January 29th, we fell in for physical training. After chow, we went over the mission again and stayed at it most of the morning. I was not feeling scared, I just wanted everything to go okay. As the Master Sergeant told us, it should be a routine mission.

I was mostly concerned about making sure that I didn't mess up the operation.

Al Khafji is a desert rich Saudi costal town. It was 1445 hours, and we were a few minutes away from the collecting point. While I was looking through one of the seven periscopes in the LAV, I noticed smoke on the horizon. I immediately called it in on the radio, and we continued on course. We reached our destination five minutes early, and found a Marine helicopter burning about forty yards from us as we stopped outside the town. Again, I called it in. We were facing the back of the square dwellings that were sectioned off with block walls. Cpl. O'Neill stuck his head out the hatch. Pfc. Smith immediately took position behind his gun. Lieutenant Hadad and I exited the vehicle.

"I can see one body lying outside the helicopter," Pfc. Smith cried out.

"It is your call Mission Commander," Cpl. O'Neill said as he handed down the radio to me. "Do you want me to drive up along side?"

"No Corporal. I need you to stay in position for the recon team. We cannot jeopardize anything happening to the LAV. Listen up, I'm gonna check it out. You guys cover me."

"Wait a moment Marine," Lieutenant Hadad said. "What if it is a trick? That could be the enemy lying there. It could be an ambush."

I looked at the Lieutenant. I could see the fear in his eyes. "I appreciate your concern Lieutenant, but with all due respect to your rank, I'm gonna check it out. I can't leave that man there. He could be wounded very badly. Please stay put." I handed him the radio and turned toward the burning chopper.

"May your God be with you Marine?"

"Thank you Sir," I whispered.

"Heads up Lance Corporal," Pfc. Smith said as he threw me a smoke grenade." I felt for my smoke grenade, and it was not there. I had two hand grenades on my belt, but no smoke grenade. Pfc. Smith must have noticed that. "This is in case you need to mark the position of the helicopter. I will call in our situation."

I was sweating a great deal. I held on to my rifle as if I had a death grip on it. My palms were sweaty and I felt sweat rolling down my back and from under my helmet as I started running toward the objective.

"Weave and bob Mommalione. Weave and bob," Cpl. O'Neill yelled out.

I would say that it would be hard to say that I was petrified or confused at that point, but anxious would be high on my list of defining how I felt. I ran about thirty yards when I heard an explosion. It came out of nowhere and scared the bejeezus out of me. I looked back and seen that our LAV was hit. "Oh, shit! Oh, shit!" I yelled. I hit the ground as fast as I could. At that time, I started receiving small arms fire from my right flank. It was coming from behind a wall. Fuck, what do I do? Think Joe Momma. You must think. My men were wounded or dead, a helicopter was down and I was under fire. Suddenly, my training came back to me, as I fired several burst in the direction of the enemy. My only option was to attack. I was laying face down in the sand, and I was facing my attackers. Sweat was rolling down my face and my heart was pumping even faster at that point. I rolled over on my side, pulled the pin and hurled the smoke grenade that Pfc. Smith gave me. Bullets were hitting the sand in front of me. I waited a long thirty seconds and rolled over about seven times to my left side, knowing that the smoke would give me cover.

My plan was working. The smoke was giving me the cover I needed. I slapped another magazine into my rifle, and locked and loaded. I then jumped to my feet, dropped to one knee and placed my rifle on the ground. I then took the two grenades off my belt. The smoke grenade was fading and my position was becoming exposed. I pulled the pin on one hand grenade. My hand was shaking, but I let it fly. As I threw the second hand grenade, I was hit in the left arm. "Son of a bitch, you mother fucker," I cried out. As I lay in the sand bleeding, I realized the shooting had stopped.

I put yet another magazine in my M-16 rifle and ran at the wall firing like a maniac. When I reached the wall, I found two dead Iraqi soldiers. I went crazy as I spit on them several times, and kicked one in the side for good measure. I noticed a trail of blood and footprints in the sand, leaving the area. I had too many men down to investigate where the remaining Iraqi soldiers ran off. Besides, the rumble of a tank moving about in the town interrupted the moment.

I slid down and observed through a hole in the wall. I could see Iraqi personnel carriers and T-55 tanks moving through the street. I then crawled on my belly just as I learned in infantry training and stopped near the spot where I was wounded. My arm was hanging motionless. I could barely move it and blood was dripping from my fingertips. I was feeling faint, but I knew that I must suck it up and move on. I staggered to my feet and looked around. Where is that recon team? I sure could use them now, I thought. I figured that I must have run into Iraqi forward observers, and the recon team that we were to pick up must be trapped in the town. I knelt down to collect my thoughts. My arm was killing me. It felt like I was stung in the same place by a hundred bees. I figured that the bone in my forearm was shattered. My sleeve was soaked with blood. At that point, I couldn't tell how bad my wound was. The bullet entered just above my wrist on my left hand and by examining my shirt, I could tell that the round did not exit. My mind was racing. I should have had nothing but my predicament on my mind, but I couldn't help but to think how pissed off my mother was going to be when she found out.

I was so confused, but I remembered Carmine telling me that it only takes a few seconds to think before I react. The whole firefight lasted only a few minutes, and I knew that a major Iraqi force was about to enter the town, or was already there. I knew that I must gather the men and tend to their wounds including my own. I prayed aloud, "God, please let the men be alive. Dear God, give me the strength to get through this. Moreover God, please do not let me die here as a virgin. Carmine will ridicule me every time he'd visit my grave."

I had to make a decision. I decided to go to the helicopter first. I was closer to the chopper and who knows how long that man was lying there. I wondered what if the man is dead. I also wondered if I would be wasting time on him that I could be spending with my men. In the time I spent tending to the Marine at the helicopter, could I be saving one of my men's lives. Fuck, it I told myself and I ran to the chopper. I got to the chopper and found two men. One was lying outside the chopper and the other was inside. Both were still alive but unconscious. The Marine inside was burned badly and in shock. I pulled him out and positioned him in a firefighter carry, disregarding my wound. I took him to the wall near the Light Armored Vehicle and placed him in the yard behind it. I then tore a piece of his uniform and tied it tightly around my arm just above the wound. I was tempted to go to the LAV. It was about twenty-five yards away from me. I looked over at it. Pfc. Smith and Lieutenant Hadad were on the ground, and Cpl. O'Neill was on the vehicle. However, I knew that the other Marine at the chopper was still alive, so I ran back to the chopper, retrieved the Marine, and laid him next to the first one I brought back. I hurried to the LAV. I started to realize that it was a real pain in the ass to run in the sand. Pfc. Smith noticed me and tried to crawl to me.

"Easy Marine."

"Mommalione, take one of the others, I was only hit in the leg and I think they are worse."

"No, I'm taking you and your rifle. I need you to provide cover for me." I said as I picked him up and brought him to the yard. I quickly went back and got Lieutenant Hadad and then Cpl. O'Neill. Once I got everyone behind the wall, I removed their first aid kits from their cartridge belts and put them next to Pfc. Smith.

"Stay put," I told Smith. Not like he was going anywhere.

"Here Mommalione, take some water, you look faint."

He was right. It has been awhile since I had water and I could not afford to get heat stroke, and pass out. I couldn't imagine where he got his strength. Hell, I couldn't imagine where I got my strength either. I figured God must have heard me and intervened. My arm was not bleeding as much. I figured I must have formed a blood clot or something.

I chugged the water and poured the remainder of what was left in the canteen over my head. "Smith, I'll be right back."

"Where are you going Mommalione?"

"Stay cool Marine, I'm going to get the other rifles and the radio. Keep an eye open. We have a whole lot of bad guys out there, and they know our location."

When I got back to the yard, I knew that I must act quickly in addressing their wounds, as well as my own. I had all the wounded men lined up against the wall inside the yard and went to work. I attended the burn victim from the chopper first. Again, my training came to mind. I didn't tear away his clothes. Instead, I cut the clothes with my bayonet and lifted them. I didn't break the blisters or touch the burns on his legs as I covered them with sterile dressings. I then treated him for shock.

Cpl. O'Neill had a jaw wound. He came to as I was working on him. I stopped the bleeding by exerting pressure with a sterile dressing. I than sat him up and instructed him to tilt his head forward to allow the blood to drain from his windpipe. I also instructed him to apply pressure.

As I went to attend to Pfc. Smith, he waved me to the others. "Okay bro, you just sit there. I will be back," I said. I did look at his leg and grimaced. I seen bone sticking out and it was ugly.

The other officer from the chopper had a belly wound. His guts were actually outside of him. The man started to come to, and asked for water. I knew not to give him any water because anything taken orally will pass out from the intestine and spread germs through the belly. Again, I used a sterile dressing as I gathered his intestines and shoved them back into his belly before wrapping him. He grunted and passed out again.

Lieutenant Hadad had a chest wound. I was taught in boot camp that the chest wound itself is not as dangerous as the air, which travels through it into the chest cavity. The air squeezes and compresses the lung and prevents proper breathing. I covered the small hole with a piece of tape and plastic, that I tore from the garbage bag I had put my maps in inside my map pouch. I was a little nervous, wondering if I were giving the proper treatment, but I knew if I did what I was trained to do, I would be okay.

I went back to Pfc. Smith. "Hey Mommalione I was standing up watching you when we were hit. I think my leg is broken. What do you think?"

"Yeah bro I think so too?" Moreover, I knew that is was worse than just broken. I checked him out. He had pain with movement. One leg had an open wound with bone sticking out of it. There was also swelling and discoloration. I treated him with care as I dressed his wounds and tied his legs together. I used wood that I found in the yard as splints, and sat him up against the wall.

"Mommalione, what are we going to do? I wonder if we could get the LAV working. I think a RPG (rocket-propelled-grenade) hit us. Maybe it only hit the top of the LAV and it will still run. What do you think?"

"I think that we should stay put. Besides, we need to wait for the Reconnaissance Team. Furthermore, none of you guys are in any condition to travel. I am going to finish my first aid and then move everyone into the house. This place is crawling with bad guys. Keep your finger on the trigger and provide cover.

After I finished treating Pfc. Smith, I went back to Cpl. O'Neill and finished my first aid on him by binding his jaw sound. He looked like a character in a cartoon that had a toothache. "How are you doing?" I asked.

"I feel like I have a major toothache."

"I should say so, your jawbone is devastated."

"How about you Mommalione, how are you doing?" Cpl. O'Neill mumbled.

"I was hit in the arm. I'll be okay."

"No, I mean how are you doing? What happened back there?"

"I got my first kill."

"How do you feel about that?"

"I feel like I just hit a dog with my car."

I was finished with everyone and Cpl. O'Neill helped me make a tourniquet out of my belt. We put the tourniquet above the wound and roughly bandagedmy wound. We managed to stop my bleeding all together. I was weak from loss of blood, but I was okay considering the circumstances.

I was telling Cpl. O'Neill about my encounters with the Iraqi troops when we heard a deep reverberating sound outside the wall. I got on my belly and peeked around the end of the wall to see a tank coming by. I watched as the tank blew the hell out of our LAV.

"There goes our rations," I said.

Cpl. O'Neill commented with, "Trust me Mommalione, your not missing much."

Two minutes later, I looked over the wall which was about chest high and spotted three Iraqi soldiers. I fired and scared the hell out of them. They ran into the next yard. As Cpl. O'Neill and I moved along the wall, the Iraqi infantrymen made a break for it and Cpl. O'Neill cut them down. I turned around and found six more coming toward us. They were holding their rifles above their heads. I didn't know what to do. We were just receiving fire from the front, and I had wounded men behind the wall. I had no choice I thought, but to kill them. Afterwards, I just stood there thinking about the Senior Drill Instructor saying, "Killing people is not like stepping on ants."

My hands were shaking and my bottom lip was quivering as if I were cold. I shook it off after I heard firing coming from where the wounded were. I looked over the wall and seen two dead Iraqi soldiers. Pfc. Smith shot them both. I froze in place. Then, Cpl. O'Neill grabbed me and pulled me behind the wall.

I approached Pfc. Smith, as I felt like I was going to toss my cookies. "Snap out of it Mommalione. Killing is not easy. Look at me, my hand is shaking. You, O'Neill and I did what we had to do. Come on man, you and O'Neill need to get me and these men inside that house. Once we do, get on that radio and call in our situation and location."

Cpl. O'Neill cranked off a round and when I turned to look, I noticed three women in the yard. "Marine, Marine, do not shoot."

"Is this your house?" I asked the woman who talked.

"Yes it is. We will help you."

We got all the men in the house and I asked Cpl. O'Neill, "Should I go out and move the dead Iraqi soldiers?"

Cpl. O'Neill could barley talk by then. "No Lance Corporal, leave them. If a patrol comes by, hopefully they will think that we engaged in a firefight and took off," he said just before passing out. One of the women attended to him. I approached the woman that talked with us. "Excuse me Ma'am, how is it that your English is so good?"

I was stunned as she took off her hood and let her hair down. I thought it was her. It was her. She was the woman in my dream that I had on the flight to boot camp. This was the woman walking along the shore. She had on the same long black dress, and she had the same face and wavy hair. She had lines on her face that had the signs of a rough life. Oh my God, she was without a doubt, the woman in my dream. In that dream she took me to a pier where I seen George and Danny. It was in that dream that George told me that I was to embark on a journey that will take me to faraway places. In that dream, he told me that in a short time, I would experience more than most men will experience in a lifetime. He also told me that I will not see him or Danny again, but we will give you a sign that everything will be okay. Another thing he said was that I will meet two new friends that will take his and Danny's place. The woman was the sign, and Pfc. Smith and Cpl. O'Neill were the two friends that would take the place of Danny and George, but, would everything be okay? After all, it was only a dream.

"My name is Amber," she said.

"Amber, Amber is an American name."

"No Marine, Amber is Arabic. It means jewel."

Amber was not exactly a jewel, but she was an angel. So far, God was answering my prayers. It is funny how strange thoughts could go through ones head, especially in my predicament. I actually wished that the three women were prostitutes instead of angels. I had this fear of dying as a virgin. Moreover, for some stupid reason, I was hornier than I was hurting.

"You speak good English," I said

"I was educated in America."

"Why did you come back here?"

"I am a teacher. I come home to teach my students."

"Amber, I thought that this town was empty."

"Most people left, but not all. Go upstairs and rest Marine. I will soon attend to your wound and feed you."

I grabbed the radio and went upstairs. I had a good view of the town, and heard only distant gunfire. I called in our position and gave a brief report of our circumstances, as well as the missing recon team and enemy strength that I have seen. Afterwards, I fell asleep for awhile only to wake because of the pain in my arm. Now that things were calm, I was starting to be concerned about getting the men out.

Amber came up with one of the other women. They brought me soup and bread. They also had a washbasin and bandages.

"How are you doing?" I asked.

"Everyone is sleeping except for the Black Marine. He is guarding the door. I am going to attend to your arm before you eat something."

I almost fainted when she loosened the tourniquet and removed my blood covered watch that Mark and Roseanne gave me for Christmas. She put the watch in my breast pocket. My arm was numb until she touched it. She washed my wound and put some kind of balm on it before bandaging it good. We were very lucky to have Amber and her people looking over us. Their aid included bathing, feeding for those who could eat, toileting, as well as first aid and overall comforting.

• • •

The next day was long. I was happy to have the comfort of running water and a toilet. I checked on the men often. It was a long night and everyone was still alive. Cpl. O'Neill was still out of it. Pfc. Smith still didn't sleep. He took it as his personal responsibility to stay awake and protect the men. Not me, I was fading in and out. Again, I wondered where Pfc. Smith got his stamina. I knew he was worried just like me, but I said nothing to him about it. I figured that you do not mess with a man's fear as he does that for himself. Amber changed my dressing and gave me more food. It was late afternoon of January 30th, and I was full of fear for the men, as well as myself, but I tried not to show it.

"You are like a mother to your Marines," Amber said.

"Well at home, they do call me Joe Momma, but my name is not spelled Mama. It is spelled Momma as my last name is spelled, MOMMALIONE."

Amber laughed. "So, your friends call you Joe Momma for short."

I spent the day talking with Pfc. Smith and a Warrant Officer from the helicopter. Pfc. Smith was in much pain but he refused to get any sleep as he guarded the others. We were trying to figure a way out, but according to my radio conversations with command, we had no choice but to sit tight. I stood lookout from the second floor. I saw a lot of troop and tank movement on the streets. I called it in to command. The day ended as it did the day before.

• • •

The decision to retake the town came on the morning of January 31st. All hell broke loose. I was in constant radio contact with headquarters, as I kept them briefed on our situation and called in air strikes on Iraqi tanks. I never doubted that the Marines would win the battle, but I was worried that we were going to be shelled and killed by friendly fire or by some Iraqi soldiers who tried to take shelter in the house. From what I could see, no Saudi or Marine troops entered the town yet, but the bombardment had started. Moreover, it was hellacious. At that point, I was apprehensive and started praying again. A blast shook the house. I was careful not to cuss in fear that Jesus would not help me. Another blast shook the house and sent me to the floor. I was getting to my feet, when I found a cord that led to a telephone under the bed. I picked up the receiver and got a dial tone. I dialed some numbers. I don't know which numbers I dialed, but I heard a voice. It was in Arabic.

"Hello, hello," I yelled.

The women then switched to English. "This is the operator may I help you?"

I was so excited. "Yes, could you please connect me with an overseas operator in America?"

"Yes, please hold. It will take a few minutes to connect you with an operator in New York City."

I yelled down to Amber, "Are you okay down there?"

"Yes Joseph, we are okay."

"Is this the overseas operator?" I said with excitement. "I am a Marine and I am in Saudi Arabia. I would like to place a call to Trenton, New Jersey. Could you help me out here?"

"No Marine, not from this connection. Do you have long distance service on the line from which you are calling and if so, I will need that information?"

"You don't understand. I am trapped in a house. We are under fire and I want to talk to my parents. I may die today." I paused for a few seconds. "Wait, I have a phone card. Will that work?"

"Yes Marine, I believe it will. I will tell you what I am going to do. I will connect you from here, charging your card for the call from New York City to New Jersey. However, the line you are calling from may be charged with a long distance overseas call."

I couldn't get the phone card out of my wallet fast enough. I was nervous and excited at the same time. As I took out the card, I also took out two one hundred dollar bills that I had tucked away. Goomba's always have money on them, even in combat. I put the money on the table and gave the operator the information from the card, along with the area code and phone number in Trenton. As I did so, I looked out the window, more bombs fell and the Iraqi solders were running around like rats. They were running into buildings and I was worried that they were going to come in the house that we were held up in.

"Please wait while I connect you. Good luck Marine, I hope you make it okay." The bombing and shelling stopped. I looked at my watch. It was 1115 hours Saudi time on Thursday, January 31st. My calculations put the time at about 3:15 a.m., Wednesday in New Jersey. I was getting all choked up as the phone started to ring. It rang two times and then on the third ring, I heard, "hello."

"Dad, it is me, Joey!"

"Son, where are you calling from?"

"I'm in Saudi Arabia. I used Mark and Roseanne's phone card to make this call, so I won't talk long. Listen to me Dad. I really love you guys."

"Joseph," I heard my mother say from the other line.

"Hi Mom, I really love you guys."

"I'm in a bad situation Dad. I have five wounded men. I tended to their wounds the best I could, but we are trapped in a house. Our own men have been bombing the town and the Iraqi soldiers are taking cover wherever they can. It is just a matter of time before they come in here. It is a miracle that the phone is still in order too."

"How long have you been there Son?"

"Two days Dad." I could hear my mother gasping in the background. She was hysterical. "I panicked Dad. I'm sorry I called you. I didn't stop to think what affect my calling could have. I improvised Dad, just like the Marine Corps taught me to do."

"Do not worry about that Son, now calm down and listen to me. First of all, are you hurt?"

"Yes, I am shot in the arm. It must have been by a big caliber bullet, because I could see the bone coming through my arm and it is splintered." I heard my mother screaming on the other phone. I just wanted to talk with you guys one last time. Please don't be mad at me."

"Son it is okay. Listen to me. This will not be the last time you will talk to us. Now stop crying. Marines don't cry. I want you to take a deep breath and calm down. Now take a few minutes and tell me what happened."

"Okay Dad, here it goes. We were on mission to pick up a reconnaissance team from a town. The town is on the Saudi boarder near Iraq. We found a helicopter burning by the collection point. I went to check it out and my team stayed with the Light Armored Vehicle. I made it about half way when a rocket hit the LAV. I started receiving small arms fire from my right flank. I attacked the position, by firing my rifle and throwing hand grenades. I was successful by killing two Iraqi soldiers, but I was wounded. I collected the wounded men and brought them to the backyard of a house where I performed first aid on their wounds. We were attacked again. Corporal O'Neill killed three soldiers and Private First Class Smith killed two Iraqi soldiers, and I killed...I killed six more. Three women took us in a house and helped us. Dad, I think that the soldiers were trying to surrender, but I killed them. I killed them all! I think that I murdered them."

Just then, Amber called to me. "What is it Amber?" I yelled.

"Marine Joe, I must tell you that the Black Marine has passed out."

"I will be right down," I said.

"Joseph, focus on me a minute," my father commanded. "Everything is going to be okay. I am so glad that you told me about the six Iraqi soldiers. But, do not ever repeat that the soldiers were trying to surrender. Never ever, repeat that. Do you hear me? If the authorities get wind of this, you could be charged with war crimes and murder. You did the only thing that you could do. You could not care for your Marines and take on six prisoners of war at the same time."

My mother was crying vigorously. "I love you Mom," I said as I was sobbing. "I am sorry that I have upset you. Tell Grandma, Carmine, Roseanne and Mark, and the dog that I love them too, and it is okay if I die today, because I love my country and the Marine Corps."

"I love you too Joseph. Just listen to your father."

"Son, your mother and I are not upset that you called. Remember, you are only eighteen years old, and you made some good decisions over the last couple of days. Now I want you to come to terms with your fear and find a way to get yourself and your men out of there. You can do it. Do you have a radio?"

I heard a lot of firing and explosions going on outside. "Yes Dad, I do. I called in our position and situation I also called in some air strikes that took out several tanks and one armored personnel carrier. It is only a matter of time when the Marines and Saudi Army retake the town, but I really think that our luck is about to run out."

"Just hold on Son. Do everything that you could do."

"It is weird Dad. I'm not really scared. You cannot be a Marine, if you are really scared. Please don't tell anyone that I was crying. I was only sobbing. Sobbing is not exactly crying."

"Not a word Son, I promise."

All of sudden, I heard three bursts of automatic gunfire. In addition, I heard yelling from outside the house. "Marines, we are United States Marines. Do not fire. I repeat, we are United States Marines. We are Marine Recon. Are there any Marines in the houses?"

The women were cheering. "Dad it is a miracle," I said with much excitement. "The Marines have landed. The situation is well in hand."

Twelve

With so much going on, I hung up from my parents without saying good-bye. A sense of relief came over my body as I stood at the top of the stairs. The sense of relief that I felt was soon overcome by a sense of sorrow for the men though. Every man in the United States Marine Corps is born a mother, as it pertains to the care of other Marines. This was evident in the comments made by Amber when she praised me by telling me that I was like a mother to my Marines.

I know it sounds crazy, but I was becoming sad with the thought of leaving my situation. I had become attached to Amber's drab but comfortable house. I could bet that there were no other men of any branch of service that could fix himself a home away from home like a Marine can. I felt this because we were taught to overcome, adapt, and improvise. For two days, we made Amber's house, a home away from home. In boot camp, we were taught how to prepare living quarters, whether it is a hut, barn, house, or even a foxhole. I would bet that my story of our temporary living quarters would rank high of the situations that men were in during the many wars America fought.

My reasons were twofold. First, we were lucky to have Amber and the women come along and offer such shelter and medical assistance that made our stay bearable. Second, I didn't have to piss behind a bush or a tree. For that, I felt blessed, because in that part of the desert there was not a bush or tree to be found anywhere. There were however many buildings or alleyways to go to the bathroom in, if we wanted to get our dick shot off, or shot in the ass.

"Welcome," I yelled down the stairs. "I am Lance Corporal Mommalione. I will be down in a minute."

I turned to the telephone and picked up the receiver. I had all attentions of trying to contact my parents again, but this time, there was no dial tone. I knelt beside the bed with my hands folded as a child does when he says his prayers before going to sleep, and I prayed. I thanked God for listening to me and answering my prayers. I thanked Mary for a live phone line when I needed it, and I thanked Jesus for sending us the angels to aid us. I didn't really pray to Mary, but I felt that she had something to do with the active phone line, because she would be most sensitive to my need to talk to my mother and father. I took one last look out the window. I saw Marines all over the place. Those beautiful jarheads, I thought as I picked up my rifle, as well as the radio and headed down the stairs. As I did so, I came face to face with a Sergeant. I was the only Marine walking and talking, so he didn't bother trying to talk to the highest-ranking Marine.

The Sergeant extended his hand and said, "Lance Corporal Mommalione, I presume. I am Sergeant Dower, of Marine reconnaissance."

I extended my hand and shook his. "You are correct Sergeant. I am Lance Corporal Mommalione. I am with intelligence. It is so good to see you Sergeant Dower. I am the team leader of the light armored vehicle that is blown up out back. I assume that you guys are the recon team that we were to retrieve."

"We sure are Lance Corporal. We were caught up a few blocks away and had no way of getting to you. I had a chance to look at the wounded men. I will call in a medavac. We will have choppers here in a matter of minutes."

I handed the radio to the Sergeant and sat at the bottom of the steps. Amber came up to me. "It was a pleasure meeting you Marine Joseph."

"It was a pleasure meeting you too, my jewel." I wrote down my address, as well as a phone number to my parent's house, and gave it to Amber. "Give me a call anytime, or look me up if you are ever in America. Amber, you and your people saved our lives, and that is something that I will never forget."

"You saved them Joseph. By the way, they have all awakened, as if they knew it was time to go."

"That pleases me Amber. Lucky Private First Class Smith passed out before the Marines came to rescue us. It could have been a disaster if we opened fire on each other. It would have been a classic case of friendly fire if you know what I mean." By the way, Amber looked at me; I could tell that she did not know what I meant. "I must tell you Amber, I used your telephone to call America. I left some money up in the bedroom for the call."

"You did not have to do that Joseph." I was surprised when she kissed me on the cheek, before walking off.

I walked out of the house with Sergeant Dower. "I see numerous dead Iraqi soldiers. You men must have had one hell of a firefight."

I shook my head up and down. "Yes, it was one hell of a firefight." I said, as I looked up to see three helicopters coming in to land a short distance from our burned out light armored vehicle.

Corpsman hustled off the choppers and came running through the dust and sand with medical bags and stretchers in hand. I immediately went to the men. It was only a matter of minutes before each of them was placed on the stretchers and was taken to the choppers. Cpl. O'Neill was very weak. He could not talk, but he managed to lift his head and wink at me. Pfc. Smith gave me a thumbs up as the Corpsman carried him by. I put my Saint Anthony metal in the pocket of Lieutenant Hadad as he entered one of the choppers.

Lieutenant Hadad could barely speak. "You saved my life, Marine. I will see that you are rewarded for this," he whispered.

I was the last of the men to get medical attention. The Corpsman, who looked at my arm, decided to clean the wound with some sort of solution and dressed it with clean bandages. He also put my arm in a sling, and then he gave me a shot that killed the pain. I was also the last of the wounded to get on a chopper.

Before doing so, I looked back at the LAV. I then took one last look at the dead Iraqi soldiers, which Sergeant Dower's men had lined up against the wall. Despite all that, I was excited, as this was my first time flying on a helicopter. I waved to Amber and the other women as we took off. The people on the ground got smaller as we went higher, and the desert looked like a beige blanket covering the enormous barren region.

My thoughts soon shifted though. There was a little flourish of confidence mounting within me. I felt like I was grown, and I were a man of greatness. I had been among the foe and they were not as elite as I was told. Actually, they seemed to be unclear. They were not monsters. Sure, they were trying to kill me, but they were human, and not as gruesome, as I thought they would be. My aim was true and better than theirs. My combative knowledge, skills and ability was better than theirs was. I felt like a warrior, a feeling usually only known by the infantry Marines, who were in great numbers, the men who stayed in foxholes, and went on patrols and fought on the front line. Then, I came back to earth as I remembered the Senior Drill Instructor who was a cook in Vietnam and who during the Tet Offensive, left the kitchen and killed the enemy. At that point, I simply felt like a Marine again. I realized that I was not different from any other Marine, because every Marine is willing to fight, as well as give up his or her life for their America. Moreover, every Marine is willing to give up his or her life to save another Marine, no matter what their job was. Then, I literally did come back to earth as the helicopter touched down.

· · ·

I was in total confusion when I awoke the next day. I was groggy as I was coming to. I had the strangest sensation. I smelled and tasted the aroma in my mother's kitchen. The taste was heavy with tomato sauce, fresh baked bread, and for a moment, I thought that I was home until I focused on a doctor and nurse hovering over me.

"Who are you people, and where am I?" I asked.

"Take it easy young man. I am Doctor Carthen. You are back at the base, and you are being treated at the Naval Field Hospital."

"I gathered myself for a moment and then realized that I had no feeling in my arm. My arm, where is my arm. I can't feel it. You didn't cut it off did you?"

"Relax Marine, your arm is in a sling under your pajamas. It is in a steel brace and it is numb. That is why you cannot see or feel it. Your arm sustained a great deal of bone damage and we need to send you to Landsthul Hospital in Germany, where surgery will be done to replace a portion of your bone with a steel rod."

"Where are the other wounded Marines who where with me? Are they okay? I must see them. I must see them right now, and then I have to call home. My parents are worried about me. They must know that I am alive and that I am going to be okay."

"The other men are fine," the doctor said. "They are being treated for their wounds. I can assure you they will be okay. As far as calling your parents, I am afraid that you will have to wait on that. Right now, the nurse is going to give you a shot to calm your nerves and make you sleep some. You need your rest."

The next thing I knew was nothing, as I was out of it. I awoke two days later to the familiar face of Master Sergeant Gaskin. "How are you doing Son?"

"I am doing fine Master Sergeant. How long have I been sleeping?"

"You have been sleeping for two days now."

"How are the men?" I asked with much concern.

"They are fine Marine. The helicopter pilots, as well as Lieutenant Hadad have already been sent to Germany. They will be fine."

"Yes Master Sergeant, but what about Private First Class, Smith and Corporal O'Neill, how are they doing?"

"They are going to be okay. They are both in traction. All of you will be sent to Germany in about a week for medical care. I had a chance to talk with Private First Class Smith, and Corporal O'Neill provided a written statement. They said that you did a fine job out there. They said that your quick action saved their lives. I am proud of you Mommalione," Master Sergeant Gaskin said as he set my Purple Heart Medal on the bed. "I will be proud to serve under you and call you sir when you are an officer."

"Sir, I would like to call my parent's and let them know that I am okay."

"Lance Corporal, I am asking you to refrain from doing that until Smith and O'Neill are able to do so. Besides, your parents were contacted and told of your situation. Your father is okay for a Navy man. Now, open the box and look at your Purple Heart," Master Sergeant Gaskin said as he exited the room.

I opened the box containing my Purple Heart, and out fell a bullet. I assumed it was the bullet that wounded me.

• • •

I faded in and out of consciousness during the next few days and didn't know the extent of damage to my arm. During that time, I held on to the box containing my Purple Heart and bullet. I actually tried to write home, but I just didn't have the strength to do so. I didn't get to see Cpl. O'Neill or Pfc. Smith until February 8th, when we where all brought together by Master Sergeant Gaskin.

"You men got about two minutes to kiss and hug. Mainly what I want you to do is get your story straight. Later in the day, you will be approached by officers from command. Do not tell them that I brought you men together. These officers will instruct you to give an account of what happened out there. So, get your stories straight and make sure they all match," Master Sergeant Gaskin said before walking away.

"You guys look like shit," Cpl. O'Neill wrote on his pad.

Pfc. Smith shook his head and laughed. "That's funny coming from you. With all due respect Corporal O'Neill, any work they do on your face will be an improvement."

"You saved our life's Mommalione," Cpl. O'Neill wrote.

"Hey, if you recall the events of that day, we all saved each other's life at one time or another. One thing I am concerned with though is my killing of the six soldiers outside the yard wall. I think that they were trying to surrender."

Cpl. O'Neill became furious, as he wrote on his pad. "Those six or so Iraqi soldiers fired on us, and you killed them all. Your quick response not only saved our lives, but the lives of the wounded men behind the wall as well. That is my story and I am sticking to it."

"I can't say anything about it." Pfc. Smith said. "I wasn't in position to see the situation."

"Thank you both," I said.

We discussed the mission in detail. The Master Sergeant approached us after about fifteen minutes. All he had to do was give us the look and we knew that it was time to say goodbye.

The next day I sat around and wrote letters to my mother and sister. In the afternoon, an officer visited me from battalion and we talked for about a half of an hour where I gave him a detailed explanation about the mission. I told him that Cpl. O'Neill and I were under attack when I killed the six Iraqi soldiers. I did not say that they could have been surrendering.

On Sunday, February 10th, I finally had a chance to get out of bed, so I went to the mess hall and afterwards, I attended Mass. After church, I sat on a bench outside the chapel. I was sitting there collecting my thoughts when a Marine approached me.

"Well if it ain't Lance Corporal Mommalione, how is the arm?"

I looked up to see Sergeant Dower standing in front of me." My arm is fucked up. We are all going to be shipped out to a military hospital in Germany."

Sgt. Dower sat next to me. "Mommalione, tell me what happened concerning the six dead Iraqi solders outside the wall at the house you were staying in."

"There is nothing much to tell. They came up behind me and I turned and fired. Why do you ask?"

"That was some shooting Lance Corporal. All six of them assholes died from head and heart shots."

"Hey, I'm an expert shot," I said with annoyance in my voice.

"It is just that when we came across the bodies, it was discovered that none of their weapons had been fired."

Oh shit, I thought. "So, what's your point?"

"Relax Mommalione. We are on the same side here. I piled all the weapons and blew them up in place," Sgt. Dower said as he got up and walked away.

"Thanks," I yelled.

"You're welcome." The sergeant then waved without turning around.

I had a funny feeling in my stomach as I got up and started for the field hospital. I knew that Sergeant Dower had covered my ass and by no means was I ungrateful, but he had a strange way of telling me. Soon after I got back in bed, a Colonel and Saudi officer came to see me. Even though I was not in uniform, I immediately stood at attention.

"Are you Joseph Mommalione?"

"Yes Sir," I said to the Colonel.

"My name is Colonel Zeise. I would like to introduce General Hadad of the Saudi Arabian Army."

"It is a pleasure to meet you," I said as I shook the General's hand and then the hand of the Colonel.

"May I have a word alone with the Corporal?" General Hadad asked the Colonel.

I guess no one told the General that I was only a Lance Corporal.

"It is an honor to meet you Sir, and although brief, it was a pleasure serving with your son."

"The honor is mine Corporal Mommalione."

"Please have a seat General."

"Corporal Mommalione. First, I want to thank you for saving my son's life. I understand that you have a powerful uncle in America. I believe his name is Michael Tucci."

"Yes Sir, but how do you know my Uncle Michael?"

"Allow me to say that your uncle and I share some of the same friends in New York City. Corporal Mommalione, it is my honor to give you as a gift of one hundred thousand dollars. This money will be in American currency."

"Sir, with all due respect, to your rank and all, why would you give me such a generous amount of money?"

The general looked at me as if I were crazy. "Of course, I give you this money for saving my son's life."

I wondered what to say. Moreover, I was at a loss as to how to react to his offer. My initial reaction was that I wanted to jump up and down or scream aloud as if I had just won the lottery or hit it big in Atlantic City. However, those thoughts were soon squashed, as I knew that I couldn't accept such a gift. "Sir, I could not accept the money."

Again, the General looked at me as if I were crazy. "Sure you could," he whispered.

"Sir, I am a Marine. I would not think of accepting such a generous reward or any reward for that matter. I could not receive payment for doing my duty. It just wouldn't be right."

"Sure it would young man. You just think of it as my way of saying thank you for doing a good job."

"No Sir, I just can't."

"Could you accept a medal?"

"Yes Sir, a medal would be nice. It would look good on my dress blue uniform. I could impress everyone at home with a medal. Sir, what about Corporal O'Neill and Private First Class Smith, they also had a part in saving the life of your son."

The General shook his head up and down. "I will see what I could do about all of you receiving medals. However, you must take the money. It is all arranged. The money will be delivered in cash to Michael Tucci. He will have it for you when you get home. Please keep this quiet. Good luck Corporal Mommalione and may your God bless you."

I just sat there dumbfounded after the General left. I couldn't believe what happened. All I could think of was that the Mob must be doing business with the Saudi's. Wow, what a small world, and what a long reach of the Black Hand. I sat there for a couple hours trying to justify receiving the money. I concluded that the monetary gift from General Hadad was truly a gift from the heart, and it would be an insult to him if I reused the gift. I changed back into my pajamas and slid back into the rack.

"What the hell was that all about Marine?"

"I looked up to see Master Sergeant Gaskin standing there."

"Hello Master Sergeant," I said with a smile on my face.

Master Sergeant Gaskin looked angry. "I asked you a question Marine, and don't try and bullshit me. I would know if you are giving me a line of crap."

"The General came by to thank me for saving the life of his son, Lieutenant Hadad."

"And?"

"And, that is it. He also mentioned something about seeing that O'Neill, Smith, and I receive medals. That is it, I swear," I said while being too scared of the Master Sergeant to ask him why he wanted to know.

"The General didn't ask you anything about the mission?"

"No he did not, Master Sergeant. I wouldn't tell him anything if he did ask. What happened out there Master Sergeant? Why were we put in a position where our ass was in a sling?"

"Scuttlebutt has it that you, and the other men will be shipped out to Germany in a few days. When you get there, an officer will address that question for you. I won't be here to say goodbye. I am moving out in preparation for the ground war. Good luck to you Mommalione. I am proud of you. You are one gung-ho Marine." The Master Sergeant then headed toward the door, turned and said, "Semper Fidelis Mommalione."

"Semper Fi Master Sergeant," I said somewhat relieved that he was leaving.

•   •   •

Four days later, doctors put us on a C141 and we flew to Germany. An Aero Medical Team of two flight nurses and three medical technicians accompanied us. As the healing process continued, I still had my arm in a sling. Pfc. Smith had a cast on his leg and Cpl. O'Neill had his jaw wired shut.

The men and I hardly seen each other during the flight, and on route to the hospital. On the first day at Landsthul hospital, an Air Force Captain brought us all together.

"How are you doing Mommalione," Cpl. O'Neill wrote on his pad.

"I'm doing okay. How about you, how are you holding up?"

"I'm feeling better," he wrote.

"What about you Smith. How is the leg?"

"The leg will be okay, but O'Neill and I were talking and we were wondering how the Iraqi army was able to attack in Saudi Arabia?"

"Someone screwed up." Cpl. O'Neill wrote.

"Fuckin A. Someone fucked up big time and put our asses in harms way," I said.

"That is why I am here. Welcome Marines, my name is Captain Mitchell, and I am here to answer the very questions that you just discussed amongst yourselves. However, before we get started, I have a statement here that I need each of you to sign."

Cpl. O'Neill started tapping on his tray. "What the hell are these statements for," he wrote in an angry manner.

"What I have gentlemen, are statements of confidentiality. These statements simply state that you will not ever reveal that the U.S.

military did not know that Iraqi forces crossed the border and attacked the village of Al Khafji in Saudi Arabia on January 29, 1991".

"No Sir, I ain't signing anything," Pfc. Smith said.

"Me neither," Cpl. O'Neill wrote.

"Sir, I guess I'm with them. At least until you tell us more," I said.

"Sir, tell us what happened," Cpl. O'Neill wrote.

"Well Marines, as you know, on the evening of January 29.1991, Iraqi forces did indeed invade terrain on the Saudi side of the border. The attack was four-battalion size and took place in three areas. One of the points of attack was Al Khafji."

"Sir, what were the other two places that the Iraqi forces attacked?" Pfc. Smith asked.

"I am not at liberty to say right now, but during the attack, the Iraqis were able to move into the undefended village. They were however stopped on their other areas of attack by Marine and Saudi ground forces. Are there any other questions at this point?"

Cpl. O'Neill raised his hand. The Captain walked over to him as he wrote, "Why would they attack a village of no significance?"

"That is a good question Corporal. We think that the Iraqis believed that the allies would not have the determination to move against the Iraqi assault, but the Iraqi forces that attacked in the Marine sectors were turned back by ground and air attacks."

"Sir, what took the Marines so long to get to Al-Khafji?" I asked.

"It wasn't until early morning of January 30th, that it was obvious to the U.S. and its allies that the Iraqis were in Al-Khafji. Intelligence showed that some of the Iraqi units were moving back north, but there were at least a battalion size force remaining in the Al-Khafji area."

Cpl. O'Neill, Pfc. Smith and I had no idea the attack by the Iraqis was more than just at Al-Khafji.

"So you are asking us to hush up to the fact that the U.S. forces, mainly the Marine Corps were vulnerable to the attack by Iraqi forces in Saudi Arabia because of lack of military intelligence."

The Captain gave me a hard look. "You are correct Lance Corporal Mommalione."

"I could live with that," Cpl. O'Neill wrote.

"Yeah, me too," Pfc. Smith said.

I gave a palms up. "Crissake, me too."

"I have more news for you," Captain Mitchell said. You gentlemen are the first in the campaign to see ground combat, and what I have here are citations for each of you. I am only going to read a paragraph of each."

"What the hell is this all about?" Pfc. Smith commented.

"If I may continue Pfc. Smith? I think that I will start with you."

"Yes Sir," Pfc. Smith said with a little attitude in his voice.

"The quality of mind and courage enabling Private First Class Smith to engage the enemy at Al-Khafji while severely wounded resulted in the saving of the lives of his fellow Marines and a Saudi Officer. In addition, Private First Class Smith went without sleep for forty-eight hours to guard his wounded comrades while his wounds left him immobile. Private First Class Smith, you are awarded the Silver Star for bravery in the face of the enemy."

"Man I don't know what to say," Pfc. Smith said. "I never expected this. People back in Buffalo often said that I would never amount to anything. Just being a Marine earned me respect, but wait until they see my Silver Star."

"Congratulations bro," I said.

"Yes, Congratulations," Cpl. O'Neill wrote on his pad.

Captain Mitchell walked around for a moment shuffling papers. "Gentlemen may I have your attention please. As I said, I am only going to read a paragraph of each of your citations. This will only take a moment and then I will leave you alone so you can get reacquainted. For superb courage and heroic initiative in the face of the enemy, at Al-Khafji while wounded, Corporal O'Neill put his life in danger by acting above and beyond the call of duty by engaging the enemy to protect his fellow wounded Marines and a Saudi Army Officer. For his action, he is awarded the Silver Star."

"Congratulations Corporal," I said. However, Cpl. O'Neill did not share the same enthusiasm that Pfc. Smith did. I looked over at Pfc. Smith waiting for him to offer his congratulations to Cpl. O'Neill, but he said nothing. In fact, he now looked rather sad.

"Last but not least," the Captain said. "For conspicuous valor at the risk of his life, Lance Corporal Mommalione voluntarily attacked a fortified position while wounded, before he could rescue four Marines and one Saudi Army Officer wounded by rocket fire at Al-Khafji. Not only did he rescue the wounded Marines and Saudi Army Officer after attacking a fortified position, he performed first aid on their various wounds, which again saved the lives of each of the wounded men. After applying first aid, Lance Corporal Mommalione once again engaged the enemy while wounded. Because of that action, Lance Corporal Mommalione again saved the lives of the wounded men. In addition, he is credited in saving numerous allied lives by pin pointing enemy location and calling in artillery fire on enemy locations, via radio, while wounded. For his action, he is awarded the Medal of Honor."

"Congratulations Mommalione," Pfc. Smith said with only a little excitement in his voice.

"Congratulations to all of you," Captain Mitchell said. "All of you should be commended for your heroic action. I am not a Marine, and I know that you Marines live by a higher set of standards than other branches of the service, but do not underestimate yourselves. You are hero's and I am proud to be the one standing here informing you of this."

"I don't know about this. A minute ago I was thrilled of the news that I am being awarded the Silver Star. Now, I just don't know. Something just doesn't feel right. I am a Marine who did my job. I don't feel like a hero."

"Don't feel like that Pfc. I don't understand the sad faces. You men are the first to experience hands on fighting. Hell, the ground war hasn't even started yet," the Captain said.

I was shocked. The Medal of Honor, I couldn't believe it. I knew that we would all receive a Purple Heart, but the Medal of Honor, fuhgeddaboudit. I was sure that General Hadad had something to do with it. Moreover, I thought that we all felt that we didn't deserve the medals, especially me. How did I rate the Medal of Honor?

"Captain, I hear what you are saying. May I say something here," I asked. As I was about to ask my question, Cpl. O'Neill waved me off as if he knew what I was about to say.

211

Cpl. O'Neill was writing madly on his pad. "Mommalione, shut the fuck up and take the damn Medal of Honor. It is good propaganda, for America, and it is good for the Corps too. Besides, it will look good on your uniform, as well as your resume."

Major Berwick did tell me that it would be a short war. I was thinking that the Marines have to give out a certain amount of medals being that the war was going to be short, and they only had a limited time to accomplish this, so I kept my opinions to myself.

"What is your question Marine?"

"Sir, I was wondering if we were going to be able to call home."

"I know that you are all anxious to talk to loved ones back home. We have phone calls set up for Wednesday during the awards presentation. Also, please have your uniforms set out so we could send them to the laundry. And, be advised that the press will be present at the awards ceremony."

•   •   •

We received medical treatment over the next few days. I had an operation that included a steel rod inserted to repair the bone damage to my left arm. Pfc. Smith had the cast removed from his leg. He had to have a pin inserted in his right leg and later he would be fitted for a new cast. Cpl. O'Neill had to have his shattered jaw reconstructed and was fitted for new teeth. He was also scheduled to undergo plastic surgery.

On Wednesday, we got up early and had chow. I helped the guys get in their uniforms. Pfc. Smith was in a wheelchair so he was the most difficult to get ready. We all had mixed emotions about receiving the medals, but were excited because all of America would be watching. Captain Mitchell told us that a Navy Liaison Officer contacted our families, so we knew that our people would be watching on the cable and network news. I think that we were more excited about calling home than we were about getting medals. The presentation of awards took place in an auditorium. The place was loaded with military personnel. Everyone from the lowest to highest rank was there. There were even Generals and Admirals present.

We were all somewhat nervous when we took our seats on stage. As soon as I took my seat, I made eye contact with the front row and there seated, were my parents. I fell off the stage and almost broke my good arm trying to get to them.

"Oh my God," I said. I couldn't even talk because my mother was smothering me with kisses.

"I love you, Joseph."

"I love you too, Mom."

"How is the arm Son?"

"It hurts some Dad. I was told that I might never have full strength again. Forget the arm. What a surprise. I can't believe you guys are here. I just can't believe this. Why didn't you tell me that you were coming?"

"We wanted to surprise you, Joseph."

"Well you accomplished that Mom."

"It is not everyday that our son is awarded the Medal of Honor. It goes without saying that the entire family as well as everyone in Trenton and in Jersey is proud of you. Hell, everyone in America is proud of you," my father said.

"Hey you two, this is the best surprise I have ever had."

I looked up at the guys. They were up on the stage waving to me.

"You gave us a real scare Joseph," my mother said.

"I'm sorry that I called like that."

I got a tap on my shoulder and an officer directed me to take my place on stage. Except for Pfc. Smith, we all stood for the National Anthem. The Marine Corps Hymn was played next. Both the Anthem and the Hymn were followed by a speech from a General who was justifying the war. Three officers spoke after him. It seemed like all three said the same thing. The speeches were stopped so Pfc. Smith and Cpl. O'Neill could call home. The calls were broadcasted over loudspeakers. I had the honor of introducing my mother and father, and then I read a statement for Cpl. O'Neill to his parents.

Then, we got the greatest honor of all, as Captain Mitchell put us on a conference call with the President of the United States. What a proud moment. Afterwards, an Admiral read our citations and we received our medals. I felt so proud. I felt like I just won the gold medal at the Olympics.

When the presentation was over, Captain Mitchell led us to a reception room where they had coffee and pastries waiting for us. Everyone was so good to us. There were mostly officers present, and most of them never met a Medal of Honor recipient before.

After about fifteen minutes of people greeting us, my father pulled us aside. "You young men must feel very proud at this moment. How does it feel to be wearing the nation's highest honor around your neck, Son?"

"Dad, standing up on stage, I felt as if I won the gold medal at the Olympics."

I could immediately tell my father was not pleased with my comment. "You do not win medals Marines," he said. "It is not a competition. Medals are something that are earned and oftentimes amid great peril. Just remember that. I am proud of each of you young men. You are welcome in our home anytime."

"That is kind of you Mr. Mommalione. I look forward to it," Pfc. Smith said.

Cpl. O'Neill wrote nothing, but he shook my father's hand, and gave him a thumb up.

My mother started talking to the guys, as I pulled my father to a corner. "Dad, it was good that I called you from Al-Khafji. If I didn't talk to you, I would have told the truth about how I killed those six Iraqi solders that were trying to surrender."

"I know you would have Son. Now this conversation is never to take place again."

"Okay Dad. How long are you and Mom going to stay?"

My father smiled. "Not long Son. We are leaving in a few hours."

"Why are you leaving so soon?" I asked.

"We are on vacation. Your mother and I are going to Sicily to see your grandparents."

"That is great Dad. I am so happy for you guys, but before you go, I need to talk to you about General Hadad, and the money. I assume that you know about the money."

"What do you need to know Son?"

"What is up with him and Uncle Michael?"

"Your Uncle Michael was using his contacts to try and locate you."

The General took advantage of the opportunity and set up the transaction with your uncle."

"Am I doing the right thing by accepting the money?" I asked.

"Do not give it another thought Son. Besides, you really have no choice."

"Dad, I am going to split the money with the guys. I am going to give each of us twenty thousand, and I am going to give Uncle Michael ten thousand as a tribute. I'm then going to put thirty thousand dollars in a safety deposit box in case one of the guys or me gets in trouble and we need to help each other out." It sounds like a plan to me Son. Did you tell them yet?"

"No, but I will soon."

My mother came up to us and stroked my injured arm. "What are you boys talking about?"

"Mom, Dad tells me that you guys are going to Sicily. Give Grandma and Grandpa my love. Speaking of grandparents, how is Grandma Tucci doing?"

"Oh she is just fine, Joseph. She said that she is going to give you a slap on the culo for scaring the blank out of her. She is staying with Uncle Michael and his family while we are away."

My father laughed. "Poor Michael," he said. "Son, we will be home on Friday, March 1st. What is your situation?"

"I don't know Dad. I was told that my arm would never be at full strength, I assume that the Marines will give me, as well as all of us a medical discharge."

My mother pulled out her camera. "Joseph, I must get a picture of you. I always say how handsome you look in your uniform, and that Medal of Honor is something that we are all proud of."

"After you take my picture, take my Medal of Honor and bring it with you to show it to Grandma and Grandpa."

"No Joseph. I will give them a picture of you wearing your Medal. Now the two of you stand by the flag and say cheese."

"Dad, I never had a chance to take that picture of me in my combat gear that you wanted."

"No problem, Son. This one will do just fine," my father proudly said.

My mother took a few more pictures of my father and me. She then took some pictures of Cpl. O'Neill, Pfc. Smith and me. I spent the next few hours clung to my parents as people approached me and congratulated me. After my mother and father left, the guys were teasing me over my mother being so pretty. They were calling me a mama's boy.

On Sunday, February 24th, the ground attack began against Iraq. We watched CNN as much as we could. On the morning of February 27th, reconnaissance Marines entered Kuwait City. It was killing us not to be there.

We were also healing by then. Cpl. O'Neill was talking some, and Pfc. Smith was doing much better with the pin in his leg. My arm was still in a sling, but the cut from the surgery was healing and no one could tell that there was a rod where a bone once was.

I was sitting on my rack writing a letter to my sister when Captain Mitchell approached me. He handed me orders that stated I would be flying out on March 3rd, via commercial airlines to Dover Air Force Base. My orders also stated that effective March 4th, due to medical reasons; I would be officially discharged from the United States Marine Corps.

"Are you okay Lance Corporal?" Captain Mitchell asked.

"Yes Sir, I'll be fine. Who do I report to for my discharge?"

"You are to report to the Marine Corps Recruiting Office located at Trenton, New Jersey Federal Building at 0900 hours on the morning of March 4th to receive your discharge papers. At that time, the recruiter will advise you about your Veteran's Administration compensation, education, and other benefits. You will need to report to a V.A. Regional Office to apply for benefits, and then you will need to report to a V.A. Medical Center to receive treatment for your service-connected disability. You will have a certified copy of your medical records with you. Make sure you receive a certified copy of your discharge papers to take with you to the V.A. Always keep your original discharge papers in a safe place. Do you have any questions?"

"Yes Sir. What is Veteran Administration compensation?"

"I am not an authority on the matter, but all three of you will initially receive one hundred percent disability compensation. I do not know what amount of money you will receive monthly. Periodically, you will receive medical exams and the disability rating will be reduced or stay the same depending on the severity of your disability. You will always receive free treatment for your service connected disability. There are other benefits too. You will receive a benefits package that explains all benefits."

"Thank you Sir, but what about Private First Class Smith and Corporal O'Neill, when will they go home?"

"Private First Class Smith and Corporal O'Neill will have to remain here for a few more weeks, until they are able to travel."

I ran to tell the guys the news. I rounded up Cpl. O'Neill and Pfc. Smith, and we went and sat in the visitor's lounge. "Listen up guys. I got some sad news. Captain Mitchell just informed me that I am going home on March 3rd. The next day, I am to report to the Federal Building in Trenton to receive my honorable discharge."

"You look disappointed," Cpl. O'Neill said.

"Well, I guess that I am."

"Did you think that they were going to let us stay in?" Pfc. Smith added.

"No, you can't be a Marine if you are not one hundred percent physically fit."

"What else is on your mind Mommalione. I know that you didn't gather us in secret to tell us that you are going home."

That Cpl. O'Neill, he knows everything I thought. "Yes, there is more. Back in Saudi, General Hadad visited me. He is giving me one hundred thousand American dollars for saving his son's life."

"The hell you say," Cpl O'Neill said.

"No shit, man. What I am telling you is for real. You both must agree to never repeat what I am about to say." They both shook their heads up and down.

"Do you want us to sign a confidentiality agreement?" Pfc. Smith said.

"No, that will not be necessary. Everything is set up with my Uncle Michael. My uncle will have the money waiting for me when I get home. I will receive one hundred thousand dollars tax-free."

"Why are you telling us this?" Pfc. Smith asked.

"I am going to give each of us twenty thousand dollars. I am going to give my Uncle Michael ten thousand dollars as a formal gesture of appreciation, and I am going to put the remaining thirty thousand dollars in a safety deposit box. The thirty thousand will remain in the safety deposit box. The three of us will have access to it, and the money will only be used if one of us is in trouble and needs it. April 13th is my nineteenth birthday. I would like for both of you to be there to celebrate my birthday with me and that is when I will give you the cash. What do you think?"

"I think that we should form an alliance and swear to always be faithful to one another as well as help each other out in time of need. O'Neill what do you think?" Pfc. Smith said.

Cpl. O'Neill smiled the best that he could. "I agree, Semper Fedilis." Semper Fedilis is the Marine Corps motto meaning always faithful. "Mommalione, is your family in the Mafia?"

"Something like that, O'Neill. But, we all know that the Mafia is a myth."

"Well you are offering me a deal that I can't refuse."

Pfc. Smith and I both laughed at Cpl. O'Neill's borrowed phrase from the Godfather movie.

"Count me in, I like it. From this day forth, we swear to always be there for each other." Cpl.` O'Neill said.

On February 25, 1991, Pfc. Smith, Cpl. O'Neill and I formed a verbal binding agreement to help each other out in time of need. We swore that this agreement would last our entire lives.

I think that I was a little sad to be leaving the Marine Corps in such a fashion. I knew that I would never get a chance to see the Orient like Carmine did, nor will I get a chance to attend Officer Candidate School.

On Wednesday, the doctor informed me that my strength in my left arm was only at fifty percent. The doctor also informed me that I had diabetes, and he gave me medication for it. Even after the doctor explained it to me, I still didn't understand what diabetes was.

Later that day, Captain Mitchell set me up with a phone call home to let my family know when I will be home. Since my parents were in Italy, I called Carmine; he was not home, so I left him all the information on his answering machine.

The guys and I spent as much time as we could together until it was time for me to leave. Early in the morning of March 3rd, Pfc. Smith, Cpl. O'Neill and I met for the last time as Marines.

"You are not going to get mushy on us are you Mommalione?

"Don't make me kick your ass," Cpl. O'Neill said, and then he hugged me. "Thank you for saving my life. We are brothers now. I owe you man, and I will see you in New Jersey for your birthday."

"That goes for me too bro." I bent down and hugged Pfc. Smith. "I too owe you, and I will also see you in New Jersey for your birthday. This kind of commitment is not only for Italians, O'Neill and I mean what we say."

"I know you guys are my brothers. Semper Fi. I will see you in a month," I said as I left.

Thirteen

Bombs exploded all around me. I took cover behind a burned out American tank. I looked around and all I could see was a black fog.

"Hey man," I yelled to a Marine sitting with his back to me. He said nothing. "Marine, I am talking to you," I said as I pushed him with the butt of my rifle. He rolled over to his side. His face was all charred and blackened. I jumped to my feet and ran as fast as I could, and came out of the black fog. I felt as if I were running in slow motion as going was tough in the sand.

Rat-tatatat-tat-ta-ta I heard as bullets were hitting the sand all around me. I ran and ran and ran until I came to a patch of land covered with grass. This grass was well groomed, like the grass one would find on a golf course. I found myself on a small island of green grass in the middle of the desert. I looked up, the sky was blue, and the sun was bright. A huge tree stood in the middle of the island of green. Under the tree was a bathtub. It was one of them old fashioned bathtubs with the animal feet. I knelt down besides the tub and ran my fingers across the cool water. I then took off my helmet and looked at my reflection in the water. What I saw was a man with a grey beard and wrinkled face. The face looked familiar, but I could not place it.

"Scuze me," a voice said. I turned to see an old man approaching me. I studied his face. He had the same face as the old man in the tub.

I raised my rifle and had it fixed on him. He pointed his finger at me and my rifle became hot, so hot that I had to drop it. "Who are you?" I cried out.

"It is me Joseph. It is Papa Joe. I used to cut your hair when you were a little boy."

"Yikes, you are dead. Papa Joe is dead."

"Yes I am Joseph and you must go. It is not your time yet. You must go now."

"Go where?" I asked.

The old man pointed. "Walk that way. Walk with the sun behind you and walk until you come to a village. There you will be safe amongst friends. Go now and keep on walking. Do not stop until you reach the village."

I picked up my rifle. "Will I see you again Papa Joe?"

"No Joseph, but you will take my name."

"Okeydokey then," I said as I turned and walked away with the sun to my back.

I walked and walked for what seemed like hours, but I didn't get tired. Nor, did I perspire or thirst for water. I walked until I seen the village on the horizon. As I got closer, I saw a burned out helicopter and a burned out light armored vehicle. "Omigod, I am back at Amber's house," I yelled. I climbed over the stone wall, but instead of being at the home of Amber, I found myself back home in my backyard.

"Joey, go in the garage and leave your dirty boots and gun," my Grandmother yelled through the window.

I opened the backdoor of the garage to a nasty smell. When I entered the garage, I was shocked to find two bodies. They were on litters that were placed on my father's sawhorses in the middle of the floor. Their uniforms were bloody. I slowly approached one. His face was a pulp.

"God, I'm hurt. Help me Lance Corporal Mommalione."

"O'Neill, is that you?" I asked.

"Help me, I'm hurt too," the other man uttered.

I quickly ran to his side. His face was also a pulp and one leg was shattered and hanging. "Who are you?" I asked. "Just hold on, boy. You are going to be okay."

"Who are you calling boy, you crazy whop you?"

"Smith, is that you?"

"Well who in the hell do you think it is Mommalione? Now give me some help."

"Wake up Marine, you are dreaming."

I had awoken to a flight attendant leaning over me. "You are having a bad dream. Are you okay?" She asked.

"Where am I, and who are you?"

"My name is Peggy. I am a flight attendant. You are on a commercial flight out of Ramstein Air Force Base. Call me if you need anything." She started to turn and then stopped. "What is that blue ribbon for Soldier?"

"I'm not a Soldier Ma'am. I am a Marine," I said with a smile on my face. "That ribbon that you are referring to is the Medal of Honor."

"Holy shit," a Soldier who was sitting next to me said. "Yow man, you have been awarded the Medal of Honor. I heard about you. What is your name?"

"My name is Joseph Mommalione."

"It is an honor to meet you Joseph Mommalione. My name is Marcus Jackson. I have never seen combat," Marcus said with a little disappointment in his voice.

"Well I would say that you are a lucky man Marcus. There is no shame in not seeing combat. Honor comes in our willingness to serve."

"No Joseph. You are lucky. You are a hero."

"I don't feel so lucky," I said. "My arm is in pretty bad shape, and I have two friends still in Germany recovering from their wounds."

"Joseph, may I see your Medal?"

I was starting to draw a crowd as I took out my Medal of Honor and handed it to Marcus. It was odd I thought that no one asked to see my Purple Heart. I guess that my purple heart was overshadowed by the Medal of Honor.

Finally, the man sitting on the other side of me spoke. "Marine allow me to introduce myself. My name is Jack Pierce. I am an independent writer, and I would like to do a story on you."

"Well Mr. Price, my story is already out. I guess I would say that I am old news," I said.

"Not to me. I would write it in the form of an interview," Mr. Pierce said.

"Who would my story reach?"

"Well, let me tell you Joseph. It will be printed in every major newspaper in the country, as well as every major magazine. You would get a great deal of recognition."

"I'm sorry," I said. "The Medal of Honor is enough recognition for me. Besides, it wouldn't be fair to Corporal O'Neill and Private First Class Smith."

"Who are O'Neill and Smith," Mr. Pierce asked.

"They are the two Marines who were with me on the operation at Khafji."

"Joseph, that is no problem, we could make special mention of them."

"No. I'm sorry, but the answer is no."

• • •

It was a long flight, but time passed by rather quickly. I think that I talked to just about everyone on the flight. Even the pilot came out to welcome me. My arm felt okay as I kept it in the sling throughout the flight. About an hour before we landed, I changed into my dress blue uniform. Instead of ribbons, I wore the actual medals that the ribbons represented. I wore my Purple Heart, National Defense, and Persian Gulf Campaign medals. Around my neck, I wore my Medal of Honor. I didn't wear the Combat Action Medal. I was told that I didn't warrant it. It had something to do with the fact that I needed to have a certain amount of consecutive days in combat to be eligible, and I failed to meet the criteria. Go figure. Everyone cheered as I returned to my seat in my dress blues.

• • •

I lost track of time, but it was mid day when we landed at Dover Air Force Base. I was shocked when I exited the plane to the Marine Corps Band detachment playing the Marines' Hymn. There were television cameras from all the networks and dozens of reporters too. A lieutenant greeted me and asked me to address the crowd. I was not prepared to give a speech.

Someone rushed me to the podium. I was lost as to what to say first. I never had any training in public speaking, and public speaking was worse than combat to me. People started yelling for me to give a speech.

I looked down to see Carmine cheering me on. I took a deep breath and let it out slowly. "Ladies and gentlemen, I am overwhelmed. Every man and woman returning home from the war should get such a greeting. God bless America, and God bless all who served her. Semper Fidellis."

I never greeted so many people in such a short period of time in my life. Moreover, I still had to face all my relatives when I got home. It took about twenty minutes of answering questions and greeting people before I could talk to Carmine. Carmine greeted me with a huge Goomba hug. "Welcome home Joe Momma," Carmine said as he hugged me and kissed me on the cheek.

We were immediately interrupted by a hand on my shoulder from behind. "Joseph, I really wish that you world reconsider my offer."

"Who the hell is this," Carmine asked.

"This here is Jack Pierce. He is an independent journalist who wants to do a story on me. He says that he will make me famous."

Carmine gave Jack a shove with both hands to the chest. "Hit the road Jack, my boy ain't interested."

Jack Pierce took off running. "The hell with you Joe Mommalione," he yelled.

I had to get my orders stamped and then we were on our way in a stretch limousine that was provided by the Tooch.

"You are the man Joey," Carmine said.

"No you are the man, Carmine."

"No you."

"No you."

"No you. I am so proud of you Joey. I watched you on television. I cut your picture out of the paper and framed it. It is hanging on the wall in my den. You know, the Town of Hamilton Square wants you to head the Memorial Day Parade, and Mercer County wants to have a hero's welcome for you at the county Veterans Park."

"Carmine, I have something for you," I said as I pulled Carmine's four leaf clover from my pocket.

"No Joey, you keep it. I want you to have it."

"I appreciate it Carmine. This four leaf clover seen me through some tough times, it is something that I will always treasure."

"The Medal of Honor, I can't believe it. You're not even old enough to drink. I am so so proud of you Joey."

"Carmine I need to talk to you about this Medal of Honor and something else too," I said as if I were about to make a confession.

"Fuhgeddaboudit Joey, whatever you did over there is your hell to deal with. You have two choices. You could let it eat at you like a cancer, or you could suck it up and deal with it. You want to know something Joey; sometimes we have to keep secrets to survive. Let me tell you bro, in a couple of years no one will care anyway."

Even though I knew the answer to my next question, I asked it anyway. "Carmine, is everyone at my parent's house?"

"You know it Joey. When we get there, I want you to do me the honor of having a picture taken of you and me."

"It will be my pleasure," I said with pride. I couldn't have made it without you Carmine. The advice you gave me saved my life."

"Joey you told me that when you came home from boot camp."

"Are you kidding me, I think basic training was harder than the mission that was responsible for me being awarded the Medal of Honor." We both laughed. "Would you like to hold it?"

Carmine's eyes lit up. "Yes I would," he said.

Carmine and I talked all the way home. But, he never mentioned the mission or my wound. I had a huge reception waiting for me when I got home. The entire neighborhood was outside. Hundreds of people, including television and newspaper reporters from Trenton, Philadelphia and New York City greeted me. I got so many kisses that my mouth and face hurt. I got so many hugs, that my wounded arm started to hurt. It took a long time for me to get to the front door.

I spotted my grandmother waiting for me. "Where is my grandma? I want my grandma," I yelled. I started for the door and was cut off by a female reporter who stuck a microphone in my face.

"Mr. Mommalione, tell me how it felt to kill somebody," she asked."

My grandmother came running to my aid. "Get the hell out of here you puttana," she demanded.

"What did she call me," the reporter asked.

"Grandma just called you a whore," Carmine said with a smile on his face.

Grandma gave me a big hug. "Joey you scared the cacca out of me. How is the arm? You don't worry about the arm. I will fix it better than new. I have the cure."

My whole family and then some were in the house. Mom and Dad even had tables set up in the basement. I was happy to see the Tooch too. "Uncle Michael, thank you for everything," I said as we embraced. "I know that you sent Mom and Dad to see me and to Sicily too. And, the other business with the General, you make the world small."

"Joseph, you come to my office at the Casa tomorrow. We have business, but for now, we take a picture, and then we eat."

I took a picture with the Tooch, and then with Carmine. I greeted a few more people and made my way through the parlor to see my parents.

"Hello Son," my father said, as we hugged. "How is the wound?"

"It is okay, how was your trip Dad?"

"Oh it was fine. Your grandmother and grandfather send their love. You are even a hero in Sicily."

I looked around and couldn't find my mother. "Where is Mom?"

My father smiled. "Your mother is upstairs with Mark and Roseanne. Go on up and see them."

I was held up a minute talking to my Uncle Mario and then my other uncles and some of my aunts came up to me. After talking to them for a few minutes, I looked into the kitchen at Carmine as he was stirring the sauce. Carmine read my mind and came to my rescue.

"Scuze me," Carmine said. "Joey did you see your mother yet?"

"No she is upstairs with my sister and Mark."

"Well Marine, you better get up there. You don't want to keep your mother waiting. The only one tougher than a Marine is the mother of a Marine."

"Thanks Carmine," I whispered.

I left Carmine to entertain my aunts and uncles. He is a real charmer and has a way with people. I made my way to the stairs, and ran up them. The first to greet me was my dog Lucky. "Hi girl," I said as I went down to one knee to pet her. She was excited as she ran to my room ahead of me I entered my room and there was the three of them looking out of the window, engaged in conversation.

"Excuse me."

"Joseph," Roseanne yelled as she ran and hugged me.

I kissed my sister and hugged Mark. My mother looked tired. "What's wrong, Mom?"

"Come over here Joseph and give your mother a kiss."

I gave my mother a kiss and hug. "What's the matter Mom?"

"Not a thing now that my baby is home. You are home, you are safe now."

"I love you Mom," I said as I hugged her again.

"Joseph, talk to your sister and Mark a minute. I am going to see how your aunts and grandmother are doing with dinner. They all worked hard in cooking at their houses. Some of the neighbors helped too. My God, how are we going to feed all these people?"

"Don't worry Mom. Carmine is downstairs helping, and I could help too."

"Thank you Joseph, but that will not be necessary," my mother said as she exited the room yelling at the dog to get downstairs.

"Little brother, I am going to help mother. It is good to have you home. I will talk to you later."

"Roseanne, what is wrong with Mom?"

"She is just happy to have you home, and she is concerned about your arm."

Mark turned to go with Roseanne. "Hold on Mark. I have something for you." I reached for my wallet and pulled out his phone card.

"No Joey. I want you to keep it," Mark said with palms up. "It is yours. It would be an honor for me to give the card to you for keeps," Mark said as he was starring at my Medal of Honor around my neck.

"Okay my brother. I am going to frame it and hang it on the wall. But, I want to give you something in exchange." I reached in my pocket and pulled out the bullet that the doctor removed from my arm.

"What is that Joey?"

"Mark, this is the bullet that wounded me, and I want you to have it."

"Wow Joey, I can't accept this. This must mean so much to you."

"That is why I want you to have it. You have been so good to me and to my sister too. I am happy that my sister has a good man like you."

Mark was very emotional as he hugged me. "I don't know what to say Joey. I am honored and will cherish this always. I will take good care of it for you and display it with pride, along with the newspaper picture and article of you."

On our way downstairs, I ran into Bria. I gave her a hug and kissed her on the cheek. "Joey, you still owe me a movie."

I went to bed early, because I knew that I had to get up early. Mark and Roseanne had the house clean before they went to Mark's parent's house to sleep. I got up at 0500 hours, took a shower, and shaved. I put on my dress blue uniform for the last time.

"Once a Marine, always a Marine," my father said as he stood in my bedroom doorway.

"This is the last time I will wear this uniform."

"I know Son. Here let me help you with your arm in the sling. Tomorrow I am going to take your blues to Catuzzi's Cleaners in Trenton. He will clean it and box it so it will stay well preserved. This is one handsome uniform."

I went downstairs, where my mother greeted me. "Sit down and have some eggs and sausage," she said as she adjusted my Medal of Honor around my neck. "Joseph pay attention to what they tell you at your meeting. Especially pay attention to what they tell you about medical treatment for your arm, as well as other Veteran's benefits."

"Okay Mom," I said as I dove into my breakfast with Lucky sitting at my side. "I will fill you in when you come home from work."

I reported to the recruiter's office fifteen minutes early and met with a Sergeant Nixon. He first took me around to his office personnel and then he took me to all the other offices of the armed forces. He introduced me to many people who wanted to meet me. Afterwards, he had me sign some papers and then he shared information with me. I had my choice of going to the Veterans Administration Medical Center in East Orange, New Jersey, or the V.A. in Philadelphia, or Wilmington. I chose to go to the V. A. in Wilmington, as there was less traffic in traveling there. The Veterans Administration Regional Office, which handles benefits, is located on the same grounds as the Medical Center.

Sergeant Nixon called a Mr. Branch, who is the Chief of the Veterans Services Division at the Wilmington Veterans Administration Medical and Regional Office Center, and made an appointment for me on Friday, March 8th.

After Sergeant Nixon officially discharged me from the Marine Corps, I went home and changed my clothes. It was a strange feeling being a civilian again. I then met Carmine for lunch, at a diner in Highstown.

"It is so good to be home Carmine. I have to meet with the Tooch later. How are things going for you," I asked.

"Me, don't worry about me. How are you doing? I know this is gotta be rough on you. How did it go downtown?"

"Okay, it went okay. They were real good to me. I have to go to the V.A. I have to go to the V.A. Medical and Regional Office Center in Wilmington, and then I need to check on unemployment benefits too."

"Unemployment, fuhgeddaboudit. You ain't collecting unemployment. That is welfare man. You will be settled down with your comp from the V.A. and working for the Tooch. You will be fine Joey."

"Okay Carmine now back to you. You look like something is bugging you. Come on spit it out."

"Things are going good; except for I am having a small problem with Vito (Big Nose) Barbero. That fat bastard keeps busting my balls and I can't do anything about it."

"Vito is an asshole. Do you want me to talk to my uncle about him?"

"No, no," Carmine yelled. "Vito is a Skipper (Crew Boss), and I don't want to look weak. He only fucks with me more than the others because I am new and I am a former Marine. It is as if he pushes the envelope without directly putting down the Corps, I will handle it. You know me Joey. I would fuck him up or die trying, but you know what the penalty is for striking a made man. Besides, I have a good thing going. I am making good money, and school is going good. Joey, what are your plans now that you are home?"

"I have to meet with the V.A. on Friday to get set up for physical therapy, compensation checks and school. I plan on going to Rutgers starting in September. In the meantime, I will hang with my uncle and learn the ropes a little, if he has plans for me that is."

"The Tooch has plans for you Joey. He will start you out doing his books and being indirectly involved in every operating element of the business. I'm not going to say anymore, but it wouldn't surprise me none if you take over for him one day. He has high hopes for you."

• • •

Later in the afternoon, I went to the Casa-Di-Roma to meet with my Uncle Michael. I went in the restaurant and was taken up to his office on the second floor. It was the first time I ever set foot in his office, and I must say I was totally disappointed. It did not live up to my expectations as it absolutely was lacking in the way of luxuries. It was downright ordinary. There was no bar, hot tub, stereo system, or bed.

"Joseph, come in my boy. Take a seat please," Uncle Michael said. Uncle Michael went into another room and came out a few minutes later with a small leather bag. "Here is your money from the Saudi General, one hundred thousand dollars, in stacks of ten thousand. What are your plans for the money if you don't mine me asking?"

I placed ten thousand dollars on the desk in front of my uncle. "This is for you Uncle Michael."

"What is this for?" My uncle asked with palms up.

"It is tribute to you Uncle Michael."

"Tribute to me?"

"Yes Sir," I said. I then explained how I was going to give O'Neill and Smith some money as well as put some away to help each other out in time of need.

"Well Joseph, I admire your devotion to your friends, but you have family to turn to in time of need."

"It is a Marine thing, Uncle Michael. Like a band of brothers. I was thinking of giving Carmine some money also."

"Never mind about Carmine; he is doing just fine Joseph. He is bringing in a thousand a week and living rent-free too. I will take care of Carmine. You hold on to your money."

"Okay Uncle Michael, but did I do the right thing by everyone?"

"You did very well Joseph. I respect your Marine Corps thing, but let me talk to you about an Italian thing." Uncle Michael then looked at his calendar. "Take a couple of weeks and get settled. Let us say we meet again here on the 28th at 2:00 in the afternoon."

"Thank you Uncle Michael. I will see you on the 28th."

"Joseph, I understand that Roseanne and her husband are leaving for California on Wednesday. Give them my love."

• • •

I spent the next few days hanging with Roseanne and Mark. It was sad to see them go back to California, but I knew that I would see them soon because Roseanne cannot stay away from Jersey very long. Mark is going to have a problem if he wants to settle in California.

On Friday, I drove to the V.A. Medical and Regional Office Center in Wilmington, Delaware. The Veterans Services Officer gave me special treatment. In less than an hour, Mr. Banks had all the compensation papers filled out, and he explained my benefits. I was informed that I would start receiving my compensation checks on April 1st. After that, he took me to the Medical Center and had me registered in a primary care unit. I was scheduled to receive my medical exam for my service connected disability, and physical treatment consultation on March 20th. The people at the V.A. were very good to me. I am sure that my wound and Medal of Honor had much to do with it, because Mr. Banks told me that when I report on the 20th, the Medical Center Director and representatives of the Veterans of Foreign Wars, Am. Vets, Vietnam Veterans of America, Disabled Veterans of America, and the American legion wanted to meet me.

I was busy for the next couple of weeks. The days went quick. My father told me that I could live in the garage apartment if I like. I had the utilities turned on and spent most of my time painting and hanging blinds. Dad built the garage apartment for my grandmother, but she never moved in. It is somewhat cool with all her fabulous fifties furniture in it. I had to work fast to get it ready for Noah Smith and Patrick O'Neill when they came for my birthday. After they go back home, I was going to turn one of the rooms into a den like the one Carmine and my father have. My father told me that I could have Grandpa's antique guns and swords to put in there.

I spent Sundays at church and had dinner with the family. I also spent time looking at new cars. I really had my eye on a new Firebird, like the one Carmine drove. I opened a bank account, and acquired a safety deposit box.

My appointment at the V.A. on the 20th went well. I received a medical exam and made my first appointment for physical therapy, and diabetes treatment. The staff and Veterans Organizations had a reception for me. I wore a Marine Corps jacket and my Medal of Honor.

Tuesday evening, I received phone calls from Patrick and Noah. They advised me that they arrived home on March 17th and already visited their perspective Veterans Administrations. They decided that they would both be in New Jersey on Monday, April 8th. That same evening, I had a bad dream of the event that took place on January 29th. I woke up in a cold sweat. The next day, I mentioned my dream to Carmine while having lunch.

"So, what do you think caused me to have this dream?" I asked Carmine.

"Joey, you are going to be troubled even more when long suppressed memories of your combat experience surface. Little can be done about the illusive mental images of war. You must recognize the meaning of such occurrences. If you need me to, I will go to the V.A. with you and we will get someone for you to talk with who will help you."

• • •

On the 28th, I attended Uncle Michael's meeting. Present were Peter Feragoli, Pascal Tufo, Vito Barbero and Giovanni Fanna. The men took up all the chairs so I sat on a table that had clean towels, napkins, and tablecloths folded on it. I knew all these men since I was a kid. I couldn't help but notice that all the men were older than my Uncle Michael. All the men except for Vito stood and shook my hand. Vito just grunted from his seat. "Joseph, tell the men what is it that you are going to college for?"

"I will be attending Rutgers in the fall and I will study to be an accountant."

"I have big plans for my nephew," Uncle Michael said. "Eventually, he will take over all the bookkeeping and financial record keeping for me and the organization. For now, I will put him on the payroll and assign him to one of you."

"So, he is going to be like your financial advisor, hey Tooch?"

My uncle looked at me as if I were to answer, so I did. "No Vito, I am going to be his accountant."

"You getting smart with me kid?" Vito said in an angry voice.

"No Vito I was just pointing out that there's a difference. That's all."

"Give him to me," Vito said to my uncle as he chomped on an apple. "I will teach him good. The Marines will look easy to him when I am done with him. Hey kid, I was shot three times on the streets and stabbed twice in bars. They didn't give me a Congressional Medal of Honor."

I was waiting for my uncle to step in and quiet Vito down, but he did no such thing. "It is not the Congressional Medal of Honor. It is simply the Medal of Honor. In addition, I'll tell you, I was only shot once and was awarded the Medal of Honor. How do you like them apples?" I said.

Vito put down the apple and gave a palms up as he looked around the room at the other crew bosses. "What's up with this friggin kid? You all see him getting smart with me? Still, my uncle said nothing. "Hey kid don't take me for a Raghead. I'll fuck you up," Vito said with an angry look on his face.

I took a towel from the table and threw it at him. "Here you fat piece of shit, put this on your head and you will look just like one."

All the men started to laugh and Vito went crazy. He jumped out of his seat and came at me. "Whatta smart ass," he yelled, as he came at me.

I jumped off the table, grabbed a paperweight off the top of my uncle's desk and delivered a powerful blow to Vito's forehead. Vito stands six feet, three inches tall and weighs in the neighborhood of three hundred pounds. He is a bear, but I dropped him to one knee. All the men came to his aid.

"Joseph, do you know what the penalty is for striking a made man?"

"I'm sorry Uncle Michael."

"Don't apologize to me, apologize to Vito," Uncle Michael said.

I went over to where Vito was sitting. All the men put the ice from their drinks in the towel that I threw at him. They kept pushing me away as Vito put the towel to his head. He was already getting a bump.

"Vito, I'm sorry for hitting you. I thought that you were going to kill me."

Giovanni pulled me back. "You should go downstairs. This is not a good time to be talking to Vito."

"I am only trying to apologize."

"Fuhgeddaboudit kid," Vito said.

"Joseph, go downstairs and wait for me at the bar."

"Yes Uncle Michael." I said as I headed for the door. I ran down the stairs as fast as I could.

"Carmine, give me a coke. I need a drink."

"What happened up there Joe Momma? I heard yelling going on."

"That big nose motherfucker. I had a problem with him."

"With Vito, what happed?" Carmine asked with much concern in his voice.

"Oh Carmine, you know how he is."

"You didn't get smart with him, did you? You know how he hates it when someone gets smart with him."

"No I didn't get smart with him, I just popped him one."

"Holy shit man, you hit Vito?"

"Yes, I planted a paperweight in his forehead," I said as the men came down. Vito gave me a mean look when he passed me.

"Joseph, get up here," Uncle Michael yelled. I went up the stairs, not knowing what to expect. "Jesus Christ, Joseph. You clocked him a good one. Watch that temper in the future."

"Sorry Uncle Michael."

"Don't ever say you're sorry. It is a sign of weakness. Besides, your Uncle Michael rather enjoyed it. That fracicone had it coming." A fracicone is a man that talks or acts as if he has balls. He does this to make himself look important and look smarter than he really is. I think.

"It won't happen again Uncle Michael."

"Good, starting sometime next week, I am going to have you work with Giovanni (Little John) Fanna. He is responsible for the area of city and local government, state wide. You know construction contracts, building inspections, licenses, certifications, city and town council influence, parks, sanitation and things of that nature. Make me proud boy. By the way, we are having your birthday party at my beach house. I want to entertain your Marine friends. Now get out of here."

"Thank you Uncle Michael," I yelled as I ran down the steps.

Carmine was waiting at the end of the bar.

"How did it go Joe Momma?"

"It went okay. Uncle Michael told me to watch my temper."

"Joey you are lucky he is the Godfather. There could be serious consequences to pay for hitting a made man."

"Like what, Carmine," I said in a smart tone.

"Like death, Joey. Hey Joey, I forget to tell you. I got news."

"Forgot to tell me what Carmine?"

"Sally, that old girlfriend of yours, is going to college to be a nurse."

"So what, she ain't my girlfriend anymore."

"She is also working at the Quackerbridge Mall on the weekends. You should go and see her. She works at the popcorn stand."

"I don't know Carmine."

"Joe Momma, you are a war hero. You got the Medal of Honor and you never been with a girl. Go see her. Have some fun for crissake."

"Yes Carmine, you are right. You know if I didn't get wounded, I would be going to Officer Candidate School right now. After that, I would be on a Navy ship with the fleet Marine Force touring the Orient. I would be getting all the pussy I want. I see what you mean; I should be out having some fun."

"You're a good looking guy Joe Momma. You are going to meet a lot of girls at the shore this summer and when you go to college too. But, go see her anyway."

• • •

I took Carmine's advice and on Saturday, I went to the mall. I walked around a little until I got up enough nerve to see Sally. I walked up to the popcorn stand to place an order and Sally's face lit up when she seen me.

"Hi Sally girl, I was just passing by and I thought that I would say hello."

"Joey, meet me at the food court in five minutes. I have my lunch break then and I would like to talk to you."

"Okeydokey," I said. I bought some buttered popcorn and a coke. I then headed for the food court and took a seat. I watched for Sally until I saw her coming and then I pretended I was not looking in her direction.

"Hi Joey, it was so nice of you to come and see me," Sally said as we hugged. "Joey about what happened between us, I was foolish and I am sorry."

"Fuhgeddaboudit girl, it don't mean nothing."

"Joey, I can't believe that you were wounded in the war. One day you were home and six months later, you got wounded and you won the Congressional Medal of Honor too. I watched you on television."

I was quickly getting uneasy, and was afraid I would say something stupid. "Look Sally, I have to go," I said. "I just wanted to say hello."

"Joey, will you call me? It was good seeing you. Call me; I would love to talk to you."

"Okay Sally, I will call you on Wednesday."

I pulled out of the parking lot at the mall and headed for my favorite diner in Highstown. After I ate, I went to the discount movie theater. I saw "Dances with Wolves," and then I saw "Misery," and then I saw "Dances with Wolves" again.

• • •

The week of March 31st was excessively filled with chores. On Monday, I took Grandma for her doctor appointments and grocery shopping. I went to the bank and discovered that my V.A. check was directly deposited. On Tuesday, I worked on the apartment with my father. He took the day off to tile the bathroom. Wednesday, was my physical therapy appointment, and my first diabetes clinic appointment. After my appointments, I stopped at the pharmacy and then in the Regional Office and thanked Mr. Banks for adjudicating and expediting my claim. I called Sally in the evening, and she agreed to go to dinner with me Saturday evening. Thursday, I worked on the apartment again. My cousin, Tony, who has a heating and air conditioning business looked over the furnace, hot water tank and central air conditioning system in the garage apartment. On Friday, I had to wait for the phone company to connect the phone in the apartment, and the appliance store delivered my refrigerator. I took Mom, Grandma and Dad for dinner at the Casa. I hardly got to eat or talk to my parents as people were all over me, congratulating me on my Medal of Honor. I must say that I enjoyed the attention. And, I didn't feel too bad about not talking with my parent's and Grandmother because I had been spending a lot of time with them in the evening. Saturday, I waited around for my new washer and dryer to arrive, and I went out with Sally in the evening.

My date with Sally went well. We talked about her education for nursing and her future plans. Mostly she wanted to talk about the day I received my wound. I tried to explain to her that it was not that big of a deal. I avoided explaining in detail. I told her that although my three day ordeal was horrible, it was unlike the guys who fought in Vietnam and other wars who had to worry about killing or being killed on a daily basis for months.

Sally and I talked for hours. I told her about out my plans for attending Rutgers. We made out a little when I took her home to her parent's house. I explained that Patrick and Noah were coming so I would be busy during the week. I invited her to my birthday party though. Sally stated that she had to work until 4:30. We worked it out whereas I would leave the party and pick her up from work.

• • •

The April 7th, Sunday dinner was at the house of Aunt Connie and Uncle Michael. Bria did not attend and I was at ease. After dinner, Uncle Michael took me into his study.

"Joseph, I understand that your friends are coming to Jersey tomorrow. I got a limousine for you to pick them up in."

"Wow, thanks Uncle Michael." I said with much excitement.

He then went on to talk business. "Joseph, I have you scheduled to spend some time with Giovanni on the week of the 21st."

"That will be great, Uncle Michael."

"I have big plans for you Joseph. We will take it slow though," Uncle Michael said as we walked to the dinning room.

Dinner with my large family was always great. When I left Uncle Michael's house, I felt like Joe somebody. I couldn't wait until the guys seen the limo.

I had a hard time sleeping. I was excited Monday when I left for the Philadelphia Airport. I knew that Noah was scheduled to arrive at 12:30 and Patrick would not arrive until 2:00. I entered the terminal at noon, and waited at the gate for Noah to arrive. It was good to see him. He had a walking cast on his leg, and walked with a cane, but he looked good. I was thrilled when he walked through the gate. "Hey Smith, it is good to see you," I said as we embraced in a Goomba hug. I was so happy that he didn't lay one of them black hand greetings on me because I would have surely messed it up.

"How is the arm Mommalione, you crazy Italian."

"It is getting stronger. How is your leg?"

"It is getting stronger too. It may never get back to normal, but let's not talk about that shit. In fact I talked with O'Neill and he agrees that we should not talk at all about war, medals, combat, being heroes or any of that stuff."

We had time to kill and we were not old enough to go to one of the several airport bars, so we got Noah's luggage and checked out the shops, and talked about family. We also talked about the Cincinnati Reds beating the Oakland A's in the 1990 World Series, as well as how the Superbowl passed us by when we were in Saudi Arabia. We then waited at the gate for Patrick to arrive. Patrick came out of the gate grinning from the side of his face. His face looked much better. His wound was much noticeable, but I could tell that the doctors did a remarkable job in such a short period of time.

"What a sorry site you two are."

"Well it is good to see you too, O'Neill," I said. "Come on, lets get your luggage. I hope that you guys are hungry."

"I could use a bite to eat," Patrick said.

Noah rubbed his stomach, "Me too."

"Good, I am taking you guys to lunch at my Uncle Michael's place."

The guys were excited when they saw the limo. "This is class Mommalione," Patrick said.

"This is great man. I feel like a movie star in this ride," Noah added.

We talked about our wounds, treatment, and future plans on the way to the restaurant, promising each other that we will not dwell on the negative issues. Uncle Michael and Carmine were happy to meet them. Carmine even took off from school to be there.

Uncle Michael threw his arms in the air. "Gentlemen, it is an honor to be in the presence of four war heroes. Carmine, please get a bottle of wine from my private stock. We are going to have a toast."

Carmine came back with a bottle of red wine. While he opened and poured it, I introduced everyone. We all stood for the toast from Uncle Michael. "I make this salute to four Marines who won the hearts of America."

"Each of us responded with, "Semper Fi." It was nice of Uncle Michael to include Carmine. After all, he is a former Marine and he did see combat during the 1989 intervention in Panama.

Lunch was great. Uncle Michael served the classic spaghetti with meatballs, along with bread. And, he kept it coming. The conversation included everything from family to football, mostly football. With Uncle Michael being a New York Giants fan, Noah a Buffalo Bills fan, Carmine a New York Jets fan, Patrick a New England Patriots fan, and me being a Philadelphia Eagles fan, we had plenty to talk about. The guys really enjoyed their lunch and meeting Uncle Michael and Carmine. Uncle Michael had something in common with Noah. It turns out that the Tooch makes several business trips a year to Buffalo, New York.

Afterwards, the limousine took us to the house, and we went up to the garage apartment. "This is where you guys are staying. Make yourselves at home and be down at the house at 7:00 for dinner," I said.

"Mommalione this is a nice place you got here. Is this where you stay?" Noah asked.

"I haven't stayed here yet. I have been fixing it up. This is my grandmother's original furniture from thirty or forty years ago."

"Mommalione, are you sure that we are not putting you out?"

"No way O'Neill," I said. "Make yourself at home. I am going to see if Grandma needs help with dinner."

My mother was just pulling in the driveway when I exited the apartment. "Are your friends here Joseph?"

"Yes Mom they will be down at 7:00."

My father arrived home shortly after. Grandma and I set the table while my mother put the final touches on dinner. She was serving an antipasto followed by her famous homemade ravioli.

Noah and Patrick came down at exactly 7:00. My mother greeted them with hugs. "You boys go and have a seat in the dinning room. Dinner will be served shortly," she said with a huge smile on her face.

"Grandma, I would like you to meet Noah Smith and Patrick O'Neill. O'Neill is from Boston, and Smith is from Buffalo," I said. Grandma was in her glory. She is the biggest flirt that I have ever seen.

I helped Mom put the dinner on the table. Diner was terrific. I was amazed to see how much the guys ate, especially after the huge lunch at the Casa-di-Roma. I was so embarrassed though. My family talked about everything they should not have. They talked about family, religion, and politics. The guys were very respectful. They even stood when my mother and grandmother got up to get the dessert. I was not sure what to do when they did that, so I stood also. While I was up, I figured I would help out so I followed Mom and Grandma into the kitchen.

"Joseph, these boys are so polite. Are all Marines that polite," my mother asked.

"Yes Mom, most of them are."

"I like the black boy," Grandma said, "You know what they say about black men, don't you?" My mother just rolled her eyes and made the sign of the cross.

When we got back to the table, Mom asked, "How come you boys do not call each other by your first name?" We looked at each other and we all did a palms up, as we didn't have an answer.

After dinner, the guys helped clear the table and clean up. Then, my father showed them his den. Both Noah and Patrick were proud to see their pictures from the news clipping hanging on the wall, as well as the picture my mother took of them while in Germany.

On Tuesday, I took them on a tour of Trenton. We visited the State House, Old barracks and the Planetarium. We then stopped at the bank and I gave them their money and registered them for access to the safety deposit box.

"Joe, you really don't have to do this."

"We are brothers Pat," I responded with in all sincerity.

Noah laughed. "Do you guys realize that you addressed each other by your first names?"

On Wednesday, we went into the city via train from Princeton Junction. We walked from Penn Station on 34th street to Times Square, and then to Radio City Music Hall. After that, we went to Rockefeller Center at 50th, and 5th. Afterwards, we walked down 5th Avenue to Central Park.

After we took in the sights, we went to Little Italy for dinner. We were unsure of the subway, so we took a taxi. We had dinner at Lombardo's. Uncle Michael called ahead and told them we were coming. Needless to say, we got the royal treatment. In the evening, we went atop the Empire State Building.

The next day, we were off to the shore. I took them to Belmar and then to Point Pleasant. The beach was quiet because it was only April, but it was a nice day so we walked along the beach. I showed them Uncle Michael's beach house.

"Man, this house is huge. Three floors with an observation deck on top. I can't believe it," Noah said.

"What do you think?" I asked Patrick.

"I think that this place must have cost millions."

It was late when we got home. Grandma told me that Sally called and that she was looking forward to attending my birthday party.

On Friday, we went to Washington Crossing. The guys were impressed to actually be standing in the very spot where George Washington crossed the Delaware. In the evening, we went to a party at Princeton where a friend of mine from high school was attending college. Again, we got extravagant treatment.

We were dragging Saturday morning. We were on the road to Uncle Michael's beach house in Point Pleasant at 9:00, as my mother and my grandmother wanted to get things started early. Patrick, Noah and I set up tables. By noon, the house was crowded as most of my family was already there. All the crew Bosses were there with their families, including Vito.

It was about 2:30 when Grandma told me that Uncle Michael wanted to see me in his game room. The game room was located on the third floor. When I walked in, I found all the crew bosses sitting at the bar. My uncles were standing around drinking and talking. Patrick and Noah were playing pool and my dad was behind the bar with Carmine, serving drinks. Uncle Michael walked in with a small cake and everyone broke out singing happy birthday, including Vito. After that, all the crew bosses, as well as Carmine and my uncles handed me envelopes containing money. Noah and Patrick gave me a beautiful gold Marine Corps ring.

"Wait, there is more over there on the table," said Uncle Michael.

I went over to the table and picked up a small bundle wrapped in plain brown paper. "Open it, open it up," everyone was yelling.

I quickly opened it, and found a colt.45. The 24KT gold plated pistol gleamed like a large gold nugget. I found the grips to be custom finished in rosewood with miniature Purple Heart Medals on each. The pistol had personalized engraving in black. One side of the barrel had L/Cpl. Mommalione, Medal of Honor Recipient 1991 engraved on it. Near the hammer was an engraved Medal of Honor. The other side of the barrel had the Marine Corps emblem engraved in the center of it, with ribbons coming off from right and left. The right side of the ribbon read, "Semper Fidelis," which is the Marine Corps motto meaning always faithful. The left side of the ribbon read "United States Marine Corps." Each side of the muzzle had "10 Nov 1775 engraved, which is the birth date of the Marine Corps. I removed the magazine from the pistol and found a round in it. I then checked the chamber to make sure that it was empty.

"Uncle Michael, this weapon is loaded," I said with surprise in my voice.

"Of course, it is like giving someone a new wallet. It would mean bad luck if one didn't put at least a dollar in it."

I put the magazine in my pocket. Everyone admired the pistol as I passed it around. I went up to Uncle Michael and gave him a big hug. I then thanked Patrick and Noah for the ring and being present at my party. When the gun came back around, my father whipped it down with a silicone cloth that my uncle had wrapped with the pistol.

"Do you like it, Dad?"

"It is a beautiful piece Son, a real collector's item. That had to set your uncle back a couple thousand dollars. In addition, Noah and Patrick gave you a sharp looking ring. Next week I will build a nice case for you to display your pistol in."

I put down my glass of wine and took the pistol from my dad. "Shit, I got to get going; I have to pick up Sally."

"Here Joseph, take my BMW." Uncle Michael said, as he threw his keys to me.

"Son, why don't you take and drop the pistol off at home before you come back, and be careful with your uncle's car. Which way are you going?"

"I am going to take Route 35 to route 33 and cut through Windsor and Hightstown."

"Just drive slowly and be very careful with that BMW," my father said with much concern.

I put all the envelopes of money in my inside pocket of my leather jacket. "Hey guys, I will be back soon," I yelled across the room. Both Patrick and Noah waved.

I put the magazine back in the pistol, tucked it in my belt under my leather jacket and ran to the car. I then put the pistol on the passenger seat as I started the car. What a car. One day I would own a BMW I thought.

I was cruising along, not far from home, and listening to a tune on the radio when I spotted a Windsor cop parked in a motel parking lot. I checked my speed. I was fine so I made nothing of it. Before I knew it, he came up on my ass, and then his lights went on. "Shit, what is this all about." I took the pistol and tucked it in my back belt line under my jacket and pulled off to the side of the road.

I opened the window. "What is the problem, Officer?"

"You were going a little fast back there. Hand me your license and registration please."

I handed him my license, searched the glove compartment, and found the registration.

"Did you steal this car Son?"

"No Sir."

"Have you been drinking boy? It smells like you have been drinking."

"I had a glass of wine Sir."

"Do you have drugs in the car?"

"No Sir, why would you ask me such a stupid question," I asked in a sarcastic tone.

"We have had problems with people of the Hispanic race running drugs."

"My race, I am Italian, and do you know who this car belongs to?"

He looked at the registration. "I do now."

"Are you sure that you have not been drinking?"

I was getting angry. "What the fuck did I just tell you? I said that I had one drink. If you look at my license, you would see that today is my birthday," I yelled.

"Step out of the car. I am going to give you a sobriety test."

"No Sir, I refuse to take a sobriety test."

"Do you have a weapon in the car?"

I didn't respond. By now, the cop was getting red in the face. He stepped back a few feet. "Put your hands on the wheel," he said as he drew his gun.

"Why are you fucking with me?"

"Exit the vehicle, place your hands high over your head and face the vehicle."

I did what he commanded. As soon as I raised my arms above my head, he noticed my gold plated pistol. "Now listen to me boy, and listen very carefully. I want you to reach behind your back with your left hand, get a hold of that gun and put in on the ground. Once you do that, I want you to kick it over to me with your left foot and lean into the car.

"No Sir, I cannot do that."

"You will, or I swear, I will shoot."

"Shoot if you must. I can't reach with my left arm on account of I was shot there."

"When were you shot?"

"During the war," I said loudly.

"What war?"

"The Gulf War, you stupid ass. I will take the pistol with my right hand, and I will place it on the car. This is a gold plated hand engraved Colt.45. I will not ruin it."

"I will shoot boy."

Fourteen

There was silence. During, which I stupidly addressed the thought of falling to the ground, removing the gun from by back, chamber the round, and taking the shot. I was confident that I could drop the cop, but I quickly dismissed that plan, because it was stupid.

"So what is it going to be?" I asked.

"Shut up boy, I'm thinking here."

Again there was silence which seemed to last forever. "Well," I yelled.

"Like I told you, I will shoot," the cop yelled.

"Like I told you, shoot if you must, but if you do, you had better kill me, because there is no doubt in my military mind that I will kill you if you fail to kill me."

"I'm not kidding," the officer said in an insecure voice.

"Officer, what is your name?"

"Shut up boy."

"Officer, what we have here is a mistake in identity."

"What do you mean?"

"Well think about it," I said. "It is obvious that you profiled the wrong guy. Granted, it doesn't look good that I have a gun on me here. But, I am not the Hispanic man that you are accustomed to harassing, and now you are in a difficult and embarrassing situation."

"How do you figure that? The way I see it, you are the one in the predicament."

I was really getting pissed off by then. This redneck cop must really be stupid, or he must have balls of steel I imagined.

"You dumb ass cop. Do you know who you are dealing with here? I am the nephew of Michael Tucci, the most well known and powerful man in all of New Jersey."

"Just hold on kid. I need a moment to think about this."

247

"Look, you don't have a moment. Just let me go. In a matter of minutes, we are going to have about five cops here."

No sooner did I get done speaking, when I heard sirens blaring. Windsor sucks as it pertains to cops. They have a cop positioned every half of a mile. Windsor is like a friggin police state. I tried to listen as the cops huddled to discuss the circumstance. I just stood there frozen with my hands glued to the top of the car.

"Joseph Mommalione, this is Sergeant Wigger of the Windsor Police Department speaking. I want you to remove the pistol with your left hand and place it on the ground and then with your left foot, kick the pistol off to your left side."

I started to laugh hysterically. "Wigger, your name is really Wigger. Get the fuck out of here. You gotta be shitting me. You must have caught hell growing up with that name."

"Joseph, this is no joke. Do as you are instructed, or I will shoot."

"Shit Wigger, as I explained to the other officer. I cannot do that on account of my wound."

"Joseph, I am aware of who you are. I am aware that you are the nephew of Michael Tucci, and that you are a former Marine. I am also aware that due to your training, you are a lethal weapon in your own right, and that you are deadly with a firearm. Let's end this now and get you to the police station where we can sort things out."

"Sir, as I told the other officer, what I have here is a custom made gold platted, hand engraved Colt 45 pistol. I will not damage it. What I will do, is remove it with my right hand and place it on top of the car."

Again there was silence for a few minutes. "Okay Joseph, grab hold of the weapon with your right hand using your finger tips only. Place the weapon on the top of the car and then kiss the pavement. Once you do, lock your hands together in the back of your head."

I was feeling weak. Maybe it was the combination of pills for my diabetes, or pain pills for my arm that made me feel that way, but I managed to do what he said. However, I couldn't get my wounded arm back far enough to lock my hands behind my head.

"Lock your hands behind your head," the officer commanded.

"I can't"

"Do it, or I will shoot."

"Fuck you, if you were going to shoot me, you would have done so by now. You are right; you do know who I am. You also know that you crossed the line with my people and you are now in a world of shit."

Three officers jumped on my back. "Yow," I screamed. "Jeez, watch the arm."

The three officers got me to my feet, searched me and placed me in the back of a squad car. Once they did so, they called for yet another cop. One pulled up in no more than three minutes, and they transferred me to his car. My arm was killing me. I kept my mouth shut all the way to the town police station. It was a short ride. The cop transporting me never tried to make conversation with me. I must say, I was somewhat nervous wondering what was going to happen to me once I got there, but I was also confident that my Uncle Michael would intervene and I would be back home in a matter of hours.

When we got to the police station, the officer pulled in a long narrow driveway that had a door at the end. He took me in that door and escorted me down a long narrow hallway to a room with no windows, where an officer sat behind a desk. He didn't look much older than me.

"Look man could you take the cuffs off, my arm is killing me," I cried out.

"I think I could do that," the officer declared in a kind voice. Besides, I will need your belt, ring and shoelaces. My name is Officer Keller."

"Thank you for letting me keep my watch." I said as I rubbed my arm. I kept rubbing my arm as he asked me my name, address, etc.

"Why do you keep rubbing your arm? Do you need medical attention?"

"No, it just hurts, that's all. I was wounded in the war, due to the nature of the wound, and my diabetes, it is taking a long time to heal."

"No shit, you are him! You are the guy that won the Medal of Honor. It is a pleasure to meet you," Officer Keller expressed as he stood and shook my hand. "What the hell did you do to get in here?"

"I don't really know, ask the big John Wayne, looking motherfucker who arrested me."

As I said that, the arresting officer entered the room. "How come this man is not in cuffs?"

"Look man if I wanted to fuck you up, I would have done it by now," I alleged.

"Oh and how do you suppose you would do that?"

"With that big ass led pencil sticking out of your left breast pocket. Where is my gun and money?"

I saw steam coming out of the officer's nose, as he said, "It is all locked up. Now sit down and shut up. You are in enough trouble as it is. Don't let that mouth of your get you in more trouble."

"Sergeant, do you know who this man is?" The younger officer asked."

"Yes, I know who he is. Now, get your report done."

"He is Joseph Mommalione, the Marine who won the Medal of Honor," Officer Keller announced.

"You didn't win the Medal of Honor," I said. "It is not a competition. It is something that is earned. Now here are my ring, belt and shoelaces. I want to make a phone call."

I mulled over who to call. Everyone was at the shore, and I didn't know the number there. For a minute there I thought of calling Roseanne. However, why bother her I thought. If I call her, she would have been on the next flight to Philadelphia. I called home and left a message on the answering machine. I finished answering the officer's questions and he took me to lock up. Poor Sally, she probably thought that I stiffed her, I thought. The cell was small. It had a steel sink and shitter in it. The bunk had a thin mattress and blanket on it. It was hard as concrete. The town jail smelled like a mixture of bleach and cleaning detergent.

I sat there in isolation. The only sounds I heard where cell doors opening and closing on occasion. The process of thinking so much was making me tired. I could only imagine how my family and friends were going to take the news of my arrest. My poor mother, if going to the Marines, and combat did not kill her, the word of my arrest sure will.

After sitting and pacing for about four hours, an officer came to my cell. "What is going on?" I inquired.

"My name is Officer Agar. I wanted to meet and shake the hand of a hero. I was in the Army and was discharged two years ago."

I got to my feet and shook his hand. "Nice to meet you Officer Agar, it is a pleasure to meet a fellow Veteran," I said. "Could you try to contact my parents for me? I am sure they are worried about me."

• • •

Another two hours or so went by when Officer Agar came back with the Trenton Times newspaper, a couple of hamburgers and a coke. "Joseph, I contacted your parents and talked to your father. He is bringing your medication."

"Will I be able to see my father?"

"I am afraid not."

"Officer Agar, when will I be able to get out of here?"

"You need to go in front of the town judge first. I imagine he will set bail and then you could go home."

"Officer, what is the story on that Sergeant Miller who arrested me?"

"Well I'll tell you Joe, he is a real prick. Everyone hates him around here. You didn't hear this from me, but he is under suspicion of profiling?"

I knew the answer to my next question, but I wanted to hear it from Officer Agar. "What do you mean by profiling?"

Officer Agar looked over his right and then left shoulder. "Officer Miller picks out Black's and Hispanics stops them and harasses them by searching their cars for drugs and guns," he whispered. "He has a real hatred for minorities."

"So that's what he did, he took me for a Puerto Rican? He took me for a Puerto Rican driving a beamer."

"One could only assume so. Joseph Mommalione. I will be back and check on you in a little while."

I tried to sleep some, but I was restless and could not. I read the paper. I must say, that was the first time that I ever read the newspaper from cover to cover.

I looked at my watch; it was just before midnight when he came back. "Here is your medication Joe. Your father says not to worry. He also asked for your ring and wallet so I gave them to him. My wife stopped in for a few minutes and brought you some sandwiches and a diet coke. She said that she got you diet because of your diabetes."

"That is great. Please thank her for me. Officer Agar, when will I be able to see the judge?"

"It won't be until sometime on Monday, Joe."

"What do you think man?"

"It doesn't look good Joe. You know with the gun and the large some of money in envelopes on you. In addition, you had four one hundred dollar bills and change in your wallet. You have some explaining to do, but I am confident that he will set bail and that you will be home soon. I saw the gun Joe. What a beauty. Oh, and happy birthday man."

"The gun was a birthday present," I said as the officer walked away.

• • •

It was Monday afternoon, when I went in front of the judge. The officer cuffed my hands behind my back before he took me into court, and my arm was killing me. There I stood in the middle of the courtroom floor with my hands behind my back looking up at the judge sitting behind his desk, shuffling papers.

"Joseph Mommalione, I am Judge Bradley. I am puzzled here young man. You were arrested with a loaded gun, and a lot of envelopes containing cash. And, that does not include the large sum of money in your wallet. What do I have here? Do I have a drug dealer, a hit man, an irate Veteran, a terrorist, or a member of the Mafia?"

"Excuse me Judge, these accusations are bad enough, but did you call me a terrorist? How the fuck would you even consider me a terrorist. First of all, you could see that the gun is a collector's item with only one bullet. And, the bullet is like giving someone a wallet without at least putting a dollar in if for good luck. Do you know who the hell I am? I fought for my country. I am a Marine. I have been awarded the Medal of Honor for crissake?"

"Judge Bradley was vigorously striking his gavel on the desk. "I am very aware of who you are Mr. Mommalione, and what you have been through. If you do not watch your use of language and control yourself in my court, I will find you in contempt."

"Fuck you. What branch of the service were you in Sir? The Judge didn't respond. He just sat there starring at me with an angry look on his face. "I'll bet you weren't ever in the service, were you."

"That is it young man, you are in contempt. Shut your mouth and only speak when I request you do so, or I will gag you."

"Sorry Judge," I said.

"That is better young man. What is your relationship with reputed mobster boss Michael Tucci?"

"He is my uncle and godfather sir."

"What we have here Mr. Mommalione is possession of a loaded firearm, driving under the influence, resisting arrest, threatening the life of a police officer, and contempt of court, as well as the possibility of drug dealing."

"No Sir, what we have here is a cop who profiles individuals. He had no probable cause to stop me and search me or the vehicle I was driving. I was stopped because he thought I was a friggin Puerto Rican and you must be sucking his dick because you sure as hell are in bed with the motherfucker. What about bail?"

"That is it, get him out of my courtroom," the Judge screamed.

"There will be no bail. I am sending this case to the Mercer County Prosecutor. You will get a bail hearing in the near future."

It was about 3:30 in the afternoon, April 15, 1991, when a Windsor Cop took me to the Mason County Correctional Facility on Route 29. As we drove, I watched the Delaware River follow alongside of me. Again I was handcuffed and my arm hurt. When we got to the jail, I noticed the Delaware River disappear as we drove up the long driveway. The officer pulled up to a door; got me out of the car, talked into a phone and a guard buzzed us in. There was a female guard sitting behind the cage. It seemed routine to her as she barely looked up. The guard instructed me to sit on a wooden bench as the officer gave her some paperwork and an envelope containing my personal effects. Once I entered the jail, an inmate working in admissions led me to a clothing room where I was instructed to strip and place my clothing in a bag. I was then instructed to take a shower and put on an orange jump suit. After that, the same inmate took me to administrations in the next room where a guard took my picture. He then put a bracelet on my left wrist. When the paperwork was completed, and my picture was taken, the guard issued me prisoner number 522347. I could see immediately that the County Jail was a shithole and the admissions area was an unorganized clusterfuck.

After all of that bullshit, another inmate issued me a blanket, toothbrush, plastic cup, toilet paper, and a towel. They then gave me a cheese sandwich with grape juice for lunch. I ate my sandwich, drank my juice, and a guard took me to see the doctor. The doctor did not have my medications. He checked my eyes, ears, nose and throat. He grabbed my balls and told me to cough. He moved my arm, my wounded arm up and down and told an assistant to order a copy of my medical record to include x-rays from the VA Medical Center in Wilmington. How he knew I was being treated at the VA in Wilmington was beyond me. When my physical was completed another guard took me to the gym on the first floor where I was issued a plastic boat looking thing with a thin mattress. I found a spot and put my things in place.

A sick feeling suddenly came over me. It was the same feeling I had when I entered the Receiving Barracks to boot camp. I looked around at the forty or so inmates. They looked intimidating. There were only five white guys in the gym. I noticed about ten phones on the wall. I picked up the receiver on one. It did not work. I went to another and it did not work.

"They don't work man," an inmate yelled out. "Only those two over there work," he said as he pointed to the far wall where two lines were formed to use the phones.

I got in the line behind about fifteen others. It should have been obvious to me that these were the only phones working. But, what the hell did I know.

"You got any smokes man?"

"No, I don't. Do you have a name?" I asked

"Yeah, my name is Antonio Amandia. What is yours?"

"My name is Joe Momma, how do I work the phones?"

"Well Joe Momma, you have to punch in your I.D. number to get a dial tone. Then you dial the number you want. Your call will only go through as a collect call. Your people must accept the call on the other end."

"Thanks for the info Amanda. I will talk to you later."

I waited in line for about forty minutes. When I called home, my father answered. "Dad, I'm so glad to hear your voice," I uttered.

"How are you holding up Son?" How is your arm? Are you in pain?"

"I'm okay Dad. I am in some pain. The only medication I got was when I first saw the doctor for my physical. I know my pills are here, because the cop gave it to them when I came in. How are Mom and Grandma doing?"

"They are doing fine. They are worried about you. Noah and Patrick are worried too. Everyone is worried."

"Dad, I need a lawyer, call Uncle Pauly."

"Your Uncle Michael took care of that already. He got you a lawyer. His name is Kenneth Maggio from Newark."

"Patrick and Noah know where to get the money."

"Don't worry about it boy. Uncle Michael has it covered. If we need money, I will let you know."

"Did Mom go to work?"

"Yes."

"Are the guys around?"

"No Son, they are out with Grandma. They said that they are going to stay in town until you get home."

"That may be awhile Dad. I will try and call again later."

• • •

For the next three days, I sat with my back to the wall and talked to no one. I called home at least twice a day. My mother was taking it hard. I told her that I only had a few minutes to use the phone so we kept our conversations short. I thought that it was better that way. The second day I was in jail, some idiot lit up a joint, so there was a shake down and strip search. We had to bend over and spread our ass cheeks. How humiliating it was.

On Thursday, my name came up to leave the gym and go to a wing. A guard took me to the west wing on the second floor. Once there, I could see how old the jail is. I was told by the guard that occasionally one could see roaches and rats running around. The dormitory housed about thirty inmates. I immediately saw that I was one of a few white inmates, which cannot be good I thought. The dorm was about forty-feet long and about twenty feet wide. And it smelled like assholes and feet. The dorm had two toilets and one was broke. There were two showers, one of them was broke. I was happy to see that the two sinks worked. There was no bunk available for me on the first night, so I had to put my mattress on the floor just outside the bathroom. My first meal on the wing consisted of a bologna sandwich and some chips. I had to sit on the floor to eat it. My second meal also sucked. The first night on the wing really sucked. There were two fights, and someone plugged up the toilet. Human waste came within a foot of my mattress. I folded my mattress and move against the bars where I sat awake for the remainder of the night.

On Friday, I got my bunk. I also got into my first fight. I got into it with a huge black guy who was testing the water with me. He never said a word to me. I went up front of the dorm to get my noon meal and when I turned to go back to my bunk, he cold-cocked me in the mouth. I only remembered seeing stars, and that my meal was gone when I awoke. He split my lip good, but I got him back. While he was washing his face, I walked into the bathroom and whacked him three times in the back of the head. I then kicked him several times while he was down.

By Saturday, all the inmates had the word on me. The word on me was that my arrest had to do with weapons charges, and that I was Mob connected. They also knew about my Marine Corps service and about me receiving the Medal of Honor. Without delay, the inmates treated me with respect.

On Sunday, I had my first visit. I only had my father on the visitor list. The gym also served as a visitor-gathering place. The inmates temporarily housed in the gym had to go to the wings during Sunday visits.

My dad was waiting for me. I swear I jumped in his arms when I seen him. My dad brought me four cartons of cigarettes, soap, a brush, and a mirror. Cigarettes are like gold in jail. My dad also put a few hundred dollars in my account so I could order from the jail store.

He took one look at me. "Son, tell me what happened to you."

"Oh it is nothing Dad. Some guy had a bug up his ass and he took it out on me."

"Did you fight back? You know you have to standup for yourself in here. You cannot back down."

"Don't worry; I got him back real good. Dad I am worried about Mom. I am not going to talk to her on the phone no more. All she does is cry. Besides, I could be home soon."

"Your mother will be fine, now just tell me again what happened when you were arrested."

"It was profiling Dad. That Officer Miller is known for profiling. He took me for a P.R. A Puerto Rican driving a BMW just had to be a drug dealer to him. He searched me and found the gun. I told him it was a birthday gift, and that anyone could see that it was a collector's item, but it meant nothing to him. The envelopes containing the money did not help either. I have a bail hearing tomorrow. I have to get out of here Dad. There is nothing but eggplants and P.R.'s in here."

"I checked on your medication. You will start receiving it tomorrow. There was a mix-up with your records, so they say."

"Thanks Dad. I am sorry to put you and mom through so much worry, first the Marine Corps, and now this."

"Don't worry abut that Son. This was not your fault. I must say though, your Marine Buddies are very worried about you."

"I am worried about them too," I said in a concerned way. "I am worried about their Veterans Administration treatment."

"Oh yes, Carmine called Sally and told her what happened. She says that she understands, but Carmine doesn't think that she really does."

"I am not too concerned about Sally anyway. I just don't think that Sally and I are meant to be."

"Uncle Michael told me to tell you that your lawyer, Mr. Maggio is coming to see you on Wednesday. Just hang in there Son. Everyone is praying for you. I am sorry that I told you to take the gun home. I should have taken it."

"Oh no Dad, fuhgeddaboudit, give Mom and Grandma and Lucky my love and take care of Noah and Patrick for me."

"The boys are going to be fine. Uncle Michael already has work lined up for them. They are welcome to stay in the garage apartment as long as they like. Call me after your bail hearing. I have plenty of annual leave to use or loose for work, so I will be home anxious to hear from you."

• • •

Back at the cell block, all the inmates were waiting. Word had gotten to them that I had smokes, and plenty of them. I went up to that big guy I had the fight with. "Here James, you are in charge of these. Please make sure that everyone gets at least a pack." He was delighted. Moreover, it let him know that I was not questioning his authority. I spent the remainder of the day writing a letter to my mother and reading. The air was so thick with smoking that one could cut it with a knife.

I was up and dressed before the lights went on Monday morning. I sat up front and waited for the guard to call my name for court. A guard took me to the administration area with five other inmates. They gave us toast, cereal and milk for breakfast while we waited for transport. All the other inmates had to sit in a locked waiting room, but not me, I sat with one of the guards who asked me about my Medal of Honor. During those twenty-minutes or so, I fixed my eyes on the security monitors overseeing the outside of the jail and the inside waiting area where inmates are bought into the jail. First thing I noticed, was that I was the only one looking at it. The second thing that I noticed, was that the inside camera did not cover the door where guards moved prisoners from police cars or vans into the inside staging area. There was a blind spot. The security camera mainly covered the secured area behind the cage. The third thing I observed, was the outside camera. There I watched a van as it was bringing prisoners back to the jail. I saw the van pull up the long driveway, but it was not in sight when it stopped at the entrance to staging area. There was another blind spot, I thought.

When the guard took us to the staging area, he instructed us to kneel on the wooden bench facing the wall while he shackled our feet. As I turned to get my hands cuffed, I looked up at the security camera. It was not moving from side to side. It was definitely fixed in a still position; I was more convinced that it didn't cover the door leading to the outside.

Unexpectedly the door opened and a guard came in from outside. "Put that cigarette out," the guard behind the cage yelled. "This is a non-smoking area."

We were then transported by van to the courthouse in downtown Trenton. As I looked out the window at the Delaware River on my right, I remembered going to Washington Crossing with Noah and Patrick. I wasn't too down though, because I was on my way to a bail hearing and if all went well, I would be out on bail soon.

When we reached our destination, the van pulled into a garage under the courthouse. We had to go to a holding area, which consisted of two tiers. The guard took off the shackles, and took me to a cell on the second tier. When I entered the cell, there was a Black man standing there with a crazed look on his face. All of a sudden he took his penis out. I swear, it went down to his friggin knees. "What is your problem?" I asked.

"Do you want some of this white boy?"

I gave him a smile and licked my lips. As he came to me, I put my right arm around him. I then put my hand on the back of his head and put my right foot in from of him. With all my power, I slammed his face into the bars. He let out a grunt and fell to the floor. He was knocked out. The guards were there in seconds.

"What is going on here?" One guard asked.

"It was an accident," I said.

"I am going to ask you one more time. What happened here, Mommalione?"

"He tripped over his dick," I yelled.

The guards removed the man from the cell and about fifteen minutes later, the shackles went back on and a guard took me up to another cell outside the court. I sat there for about an hour when a County Sheriff came to get me.

"Mommalione, there will be no hearing for you today. I am taking you back downstairs to the holding cells." I was at awe, but I didn't question him. I sat there scared and confused wondering why I was not granted a bail hearing.

I fell asleep on the way back to the County Jail, and was woken up when it was time to exit the van. As I exited the van, I looked up at the security camera mounted above the entrance to the staging area of the jail. It was pointed outward and to the right. I was correct, there was no way the camera could pickup the van parked in front of the door.

I sat around in a depressed state all morning. And, in the afternoon, I used the phone in the front of the dorm to call home. My dad must have run to the store or had business to attend to, so I left a message on the answering machine explaining what happened at court. I then tried to call the garage apartment, but the guys were out because no one answered there either.

In the evening, a guard instructed me to go down the hall to the clinic.

"Good evening Joseph, my name is Doctor Sheila Stewart. You may call me Sheila or Doctor if you like. Because you need your blood checked daily, your medication will not be brought to you at the wing. You will see me every evening to receive you medication, have your blood checked, and receive physical therapy on your arm. I am off on the weekends. On the weekends, a nurse will issue your medication in the front of the dorm at the same time the other inmates receive meds. The only difference in your case is that yours will be taken in the presence of a guard who will verify and document that you swallowed your pain medication. Your blood testing will not be done on the weekends. Do you have any question?"

"No Ma'am," I said.

I found Sheila to be plain looking women of about thirty-five years old. I also noticed that she was skinny and seemed fragile. My first impression of her was that of a tall bird. Her speech and voice seemed soft. She wore her hair pulled up in a bun and wore no makeup, but she had an attractive way about her. If she were to loose the big ass glasses and let her hair down, she would look okay to me. Oh yes, I would like to get me some of that I thought.

Doctor Sheila issued my medication and checked my blood. "Your sugar count is high, Joseph. It is 191. We will have to work on that." She then checked my wounded arm. "Does this hurt?" She said as she stretched my arm.

"No Ma'am, it only hurts when I put pressure on it by pulling or pushing something." Her touch was soft. In addition, she smelled great.

"I would like to run some tests when I see you tomorrow."

I went back to the wing and I couldn't get my mind off her. I found myself even more attracted to her the next day.

On Wednesday, a guard took me to a meeting room to meet with my lawyer. In walked a dick with a suitcase. "Hello Joseph, my name is Kenneth Maggio. Michael Tucci has retained me. How are you today?"

"Cut the bullshit Ken. Why didn't I get my bail hearing?"

"Joseph, I have been informed that the authorities are concerned that drugs are involved. This is due to the money found in your possession."

"The money was a fuckin birthday gift."

"I know Joseph. I know that, there is talk of moving you to the Trenton State Prison next month."

"What! What the hell for Ken?"

"Joseph did you ever hear of the RICO Laws?"

"No, what is that?"

"RICO stands for Racketeer Influenced and Corrupt Organizations. The federal RICO law is an element of the 1970 Organized Crime Control Act. RICO has been established to deprive organized crime from the shelter it could obtain due to their involvement with legitimate business. RICO also allows prosecution against association's who have involved themselves in racketeering goings-on in order to get hold of or control a business."

I was puzzled as to what he was talking about. "What does that have to do with me?" I asked.

"It really has nothing to do with you. It has to do with your Uncle Michael's business."

"But, I know nothing of my uncle's business, and I don't understand what in the hell you are talking about."

"Listen to me Joseph. The stipulations of RICO are wide-ranging and left open to interpretation. Even the meaning of racketeering is liable to more than one interpretation." I am trying Joseph. In the meanwhile, your uncle wants to know what we can do to make your life more comfortable."

"I need some smokes and magazines. Also I would like to work in the admissions area processing inmates or something. Christ man I'm going crazy sitting around all day. I also need physical therapy on my arm. I have it set up in the evening with the doctor, but I may need an occasional visit to the VA medical Center."

"You will definitely get physical therapy for your arm, and I will see what I could do about getting you some work."

"In the admissions area Ken, it is important that I work in the admissions area. When will I see you again?"

"I will see you next week, Joseph."

• • •

Other than my nightly visits with Doctor Stewart, life in jail really sucked. I missed Easter with my family, and jail was really getting to me. I called my parents, Carmine and the guys in moderation. I just couldn't take my mother's crying, and there was less and less to talk about. However, things started to look up on May 1st. My lawyer brought me five more cartons of cigarettes and informed me that I would be working daily, Monday through Friday in the mailroom which is located in the admissions area. Things were different with Sheila too. In the evening on Wednesday, May 1st, I went to see her for my medication and to get my blood tested as usual.

"Joseph, I am going to step up your physical therapy treatment in addition to administering medication and testing your blood for diabetes control. I have arranged it whereas you will be the last person I see in the evening. I talked with the resident doctor, and he informed me that he received your medical records from the Veterans Administration." Out of the blue, the phone rang and it sounded like Doctor Sheila was having a conversation with her child.

"Is that an outside line," I asked when she hung-up.

262

"Why yes it is Joseph. I need it for my other patients. You know in case of an emergency. I only work here part time. Now I want you to sit on the table."

Sheila finished with my medication and testing my blood. She then started on my physical therapy. "Joseph I need you to strip to your shorts. It is too hard for me to work with you while you are wearing the jumper."

I sat on the table. The doctor pushed on my chest while she pulled on my left arm. She could see in my face that it really hurt. "Joseph, I want you to put your arms on my shoulders and lean into me."

As I did, our lips were only inches apart. Then it happened, our lips met. I took a deep breath as she passionately kissed me. She laid me down. My back was on the table. Her fingers were tracing the line around my lips. As she straddled me, I unbuttoned her blouse and took her bra off. Her full beautiful milky white breasts fell into my face. She let down her hair, leaned over me and her mouth found mine again. I whimpered like a baby. She seemed to sense what was about to happen and quickly started to grind me. It was all I could stand. I spurt gallons into my underpants. I was so embarrassed. I think that she knew it was my first time. She was so thoughtful, polite and considerate by not talking about what happened as we started to get dressed. I wondered if she knew that is was my first time.

I put one leg into my jumper and said, "Sheila, I have never had sex before."

She put her hand across my mouth. "Get dressed, Joseph and I will see you tomorrow. You may use the phone if you like."

I declined the use of the phone. I couldn't believe that the first women I was ever with took place in jail. I felt wonderful. I quickly dismissed the thought that our love making never quite reached the point of intercourse, because I was confident that it would take place the next night, and it did.

On Friday, a guard took me to the meeting room to see my lawyer again. However, instead of seeing my lawyer, two men were waiting. They introduced themselves as FBI.

"What the hell do you guys want?" I questioned.

The one of the agents started talking. "Joseph, I am Special Agent Stanley. You are in a bad situation here and we are going to offer you a way out of it. Please be advised that if you do not cooperate, we are prepared to add additional charges of racketeering and drug dealing to your list of crimes, so it would behoove you to work with us."

"Oh yeah, well fuck you. I never used or sold drugs in my life, and I don't even know the meaning of racketeering. My lawyer tried to explain it to me, but I couldn't get it."

"I am Agent Farley," the other one said. "Just listen to us Joseph. We are in a position to dismiss all charges against you in exchange for information about your Uncle Michael."

"Look you guys, I don't know anything, and if I did, I would not tell you even if I were facing life in prison."

"We are sorry to hear that," Farley said. "We have information connecting you with the organization. As it stands, you are now facing three to five years for possession of an unregistered firearm, threatening the life of a police officer, resisting arrest, etc. You will be facing fifteen to twenty years when we are done adding charges."

"Tell us what you know. You could start with names, information of cash flow, and the layout of organized crime in the Trenton area and we could take it from there."

"Why don't you tell me what you already know Agent Stanley, because you know that I don't know anything?"

"We know everything Joseph. We only need you to confirm it."

"So, I should lie if I have to, in turn for my freedom, because I really don't have any information for you."

"Now you are getting it Joseph," Stanley said.

"Look," Farley said. "We know that Michael Tucci is the Godfather of New Jersey."

"You are scared Farley," I said as I smiled.

Farley looked puzzled. "What do you base that on young man?"

"You are scared. You are so scared that you won't even mention what New York family my uncle is a member of. You may know everything about Michael Tucci, but proving it is another matter. Your people come here in your cheap-ass department store suits and tell me that you know everything."

"That is right Joe Momma," Stanly said with a smirk on his face.

"Wow, you even know that I am called Joe Momma. I am impressed. If you know everything, like you claim you do, then tell me the other meaning of the FBI."

"That is easy," Stanley said. "It means Female Body Inspector." They both laughed.

"Wrong," I said. "It means Forever Bothering Italians." Farley stood and slammed his hand down hard on the table. "You Goomba's are real smartasses."

I was really pissed off by then. "We Goomba's are a certain kind of Italian American. Some people may call us crazy, and some may call us lazy. Hell, we love our women even though we have another one on the side. Many of us may have even been to jail at one time or another. Some of us may even have nicknames, like me for instance. Shit man some of us may even have connections with the mob, but not any of those things make us wiseguys. Now get the fuck out of my face."

"Think about what we said," Agent Farley said. "Oh, and remember we will have no sympathy on you just because you won the Medal of Honor."

"I don't want any," I yelled. "And, you don't win the Medal of Honor, you earn it."

My lawyer walked in as the FBI men were leaving. "What was that all about Joseph?"

"Why don't you tell me Ken? They were the FBI. Ken, they claim that they are going to charge me with drug trafficking. They can't make that stick. I didn't do that."

"Joseph, they claim that they have someone who will testify that you sold drugs."

"That is bullshit man. Talk to me Ken. What is going on here?"

"Okay Joseph, let me explain. The only plea bargain that you are going to be offered is what the FBI just explained to you. The gun possession, threatening the life of an officer, and contempt of court, and obstruction of justice are going to stick. You cannot deny the gun. For those charges, you are looking at three to five years in prison. With additional fabricated charges of drug trafficking and racketeering, you are looking at possibly ten years or more if the jury convicts you of that."

"What about a lenient jury. After all, I am a wounded Medal of Honor recipient and war hero. That should mean something to a jury."

"Don't count on it Joseph. People have short memories, and when it comes to threatening the life of one of their police officers, and carrying a concealed loaded weapon, and drug charges that don't help matters either, not to mention your affiliation with organized crime, you could be up the creek without a paddle. It does not look good Joseph."

"What are my options here?"

"Now listen to me Joseph, you cannot tell what you know about your uncle, and if they connect your Uncle Michael to the gun, he is fucked. It looks like you are going to do some time at Trenton State Penitentiary. How much, I do not know."

"No, no, no. You tell my uncle that under no circumstances will I sing to the Feds. I am no rat, not in a hundred years. Nor, will I make up anything to keep my ass from being jammed up." Ken gave me an odd look. "Prison Ken, jammed up means going to prison. You tell my uncle what I said. Tell him I said, Semper Fidelis."

"What does Semper Fidelis mean, Joseph?"

"It is the Marine Corps Motto. It means always faithful. This is bullshit man. This mess is all because of a prick of a cop profiling me. Ken what is the worse case scenario. If I were to get ten years for example, what does that really mean in time I will have to serve?"

"It means you will serve at least seven years. Joseph it could be worse. The judge may give a fifteen to twenty year sentence if the jury finds you guilty of all charges. Drugs and racketeering are serious crimes. At the least, I would say that you are going to serve five years in prison, possibly more if you are found guilty of drug trafficking and racketeering. The judge will give no leniency at sentencing because you did not plea bargain. I will do everything I could for you. You have got to believe in me Joseph."

"What about bail? I would like to spend time with my family and friends before I go to trial."

"I am working on the bail for you," Ken said as he stood and headed for the door.

"Be sure you tell my uncle what I said," I yelled.

Fifteen

I spent the next two weeks working in the admissions area, mainly in the mailroom. During that time, I got to be friends with the guy who brings the mail from the post office. I had one visit from my father. He brought me more cigarettes and magazines, which I shared with the guys in the dorm. I had one meeting with my lawyer, who told me nothing. Much had gone through my head during that time. For the most part, I was worried about what was going to happen to me. I hardly called home. My evenings with Sheila kept me going, But, the other thing that kept me going, was planning an escape. I had one hell of a plan brewing in my head. I worked on this plan day and night, as well as the period in-between.

On May 20, 1991 I had a bail hearing. I was not nearly as enthused about this one as I was the last, because I was expecting only bad news, and I got it. The judge decided not to set bail pending new charges. However, one good thing did come out of it. My mother was in attendance and I had a chance to speak with her. I was embarrassed though as she had to see me in handcuffs and leg irons. My father stayed back as my mother approached me.

"Joseph, my baby, I love you so much," she said as she hugged me tightly.

"How are you Mother?" I think that was the first time I had ever addressed her as Mother.

Tears were flowing down her face. I only wished that I could wipe them. I also wished that I could hug her. "Look at you Joseph, and look at your hair, it is so long. Look at all them curls. It reminds me of when you were a little boy and you used to twirl your hair."

"I know Mom; I am going to have one of the brothers cut it for me, I love you Mom. I have to go now," I said as the Deputy Sheriff was leading me away by the arm.

"Call me, Joseph. You do not call home enough, and do not worry, as your Uncle Michael will take care of everything."

"I know Mom. I am not worried," I yelled to her as I was led out of the courtroom.

• • •

My next few nights with Sheila were awesome. I was getting to be really good at lovemaking. On the 23rd, the preppy looking FBI men came back to see me. They asked me where I got the gun. I told them to fuck off. Agent Stanley informed me that I have five weeks to change my mind about helping them. That must be when I was going to trial I thought. After they left, I was more convinced that I must escape, but I needed Sheila's help. I waited anxiously to see her that evening.

Sheila could tell that something was on my mind when I reported to her for my pills and treatment. "Joseph, what is the matter?"

"Oh, it is nothing," I said. "My hip bones are hurting. That is all."

"It is from those thin mattresses. I will give you some cream for it that will help. But, I feel that something is really bothering you. Although our lovemaking has been great, you have not been yourself for the last few days."

"Sheila, before we get started, I need to ask you something."

"What is it, Joey," Sheila asked with concern in her voice.

"Why are you here, why me, and why do you not recognize your worth, your quality, and importance? You are educated. You are successful, and you would be pretty if you would loose those big ass glasses and big hair."

Sheila looked surprised that I would talk to her in such a fashion. "Well Joey, it is because of my husband. My husband was into drugs big time. He also had a gambling problem and he was into this guy for a lot of money. The bastard took off and this gangster holds me responsible for my husband's debt. My life has been such a mess, both financially and emotionally. I was lucky to land this part time job at the jail which pays very well."

"Why didn't you tell me this before?"

"Joey you have your own problems and you were already helping me by the attention that you give me every time I see you."

I was getting real angry. "Who is this guy? Is he Italian?" I asked.

"No he is Hispanic, from Cuba I think. His name is Rocco Hernandez."

"Sheila I am going to take care of this problem for you, but I need your help on something too. Is this phone line clean?"

"Yes I think so. I lock up the phone every night, and it is a direct line."

"Good, I am going to have to take my chances."

"Here, take this number. When you get home, call my friend Carmine. Explain who you are and ask him to be at your house tomorrow. Tell him to call me on this phone at 8:00. I am going to need you to let my boys come to your house one or two nights a week to call me here on this line."

Friday evening, I waited patiently for the phone to ring, and at exactly 8:00, it did. Sheila answered it.

"Joey, it is him," Sheila said as she handed me the phone.

"Joe Momma here, did I take you away from anything?"

"Only from my job at the Casa, but I explained to the Tooch that I need time to talk to you and he said okay. What is going on Joey?"

"Oh, yeah Carmine I didn't give any thought to the fact that you would be tending bar tonight. Sorry about that. Carmine you are calling on a direct line to the doctor's office at the county jail. I want all the calls from you to come from her house only on this line. The line is clean and Sheila receives calls from her babysitter every evening. If the phone records are checked, everything will look normal."

"Are you with me so far?"

"Yeah bro, I am listening."

"We are going to communicate twice a week. The doctor is a friend of mine. Let me just say that I am no longer a cherry boy." Carmine started to laugh. "Sheila has agreed to help me with my plan which I will explain later. In turn for her help, I agreed to help her."

"I am still listening bro," Carmine said.

"Good, did you ever hear of a Rocco Hernandez?"

"Yeah, he is a real pig. What about him?"

"My girl is into him for a lot of money. A never-ending situation if you know what I mean. Are we doing business with him?"

"No, he is heavily into dealing drugs. He gets the stuff from Miami and runs it up I-95. We don't touch the stuff. That shit will only get you a lot of years in the joint."

"Good, I need her debt erased."

"You want that I should whack the bastard?" Carmine said with a chuckle."

"No, Sheila's debt will only continue with whoever takes over. You know the routine. Get pictures of his wife and kids, roll up under his garage door when he pulls in, and show him the pictures. Tell him that this is personal and has nothing to do with his business. Tell him the debt isn't worth his family getting hurt. I am confident that he will understand."

"Okay Joey, will do, but be advised that I have to run this by the Tooch. I am sure that he will give his blessing. Your Uncle Michael will do anything for you Joe Momma. Is there anything else you will need?"

"I will need a gun, a powerful gun. I think that a 357 magnum will do. I will need it in about two to three weeks. I am busting out. Tell the guys that I will need their help. I will fill you in on the details later. Oh yeah, I will need you to do some reconnaissance for me on the cop who arrested me. I need his daily routine, and address. I also need information on his wife, kids, kid's school etc. And, a car, I will need a car too."

"I got it my brother, and can do. I will talk to you on Monday at 7:15."

Sheila looked baffled. "Joseph, are you going to be okay? Are you sure you know what you are doing."

"Yes Sheila, and your debt will be cleared next week. Don't worry about the calls. All my communication with my boys will come from this line and only from your house to here. As I said, if the records are checked, they will show nothing out of the ordinary. What is your neighborhood like?"

"It is a young business type community. No one knows each other and people are coming and going all the time. Are you going to be okay, Joey?"

"I will be once I am out of here. Have a good weekend. I will see you Monday evening." Sheila kissed me hard, and then I left. All I wanted to do was go back to the dorm, take a shower since they were both fixed, hand wash my underwear and socks, and do some planning on my escape.

When I got to the shower, there was a blanket hanging across the shower entrance. Who knows what was going on in there, so I took a sponge bath and washed my socks and short at the sink?

About an hour later, they brought a white kid in. He started walking and talking as if he were black. Well the brothers didn't like that, so they beat the hell out of him. I picked him up, brought him up front to where the guards sit and told them to get him out of the dorm. They took him to isolation where he would be safe.

On Saturday, while the inmates were watching television, I asked one of the brothers to give me a haircut. The guard gave him the hair cutting tools and he did a good job on my hair. I spent the remainder of the day playing cards and working on my plan of escape.

Sunday really sucked because they put some of the new arrivals from the gym in the dorm while the gym was being used for visits. There were enough black guys in the dorm to make a Tarzan movie. I did get a visit though. It was from my lawyer who only repeated what he told me in past visits. The only thing good about his visit was that I got out of the dorm for awhile.

Finally, it was Monday. I actually enjoyed working in the mailroom, and I welcomed the short, but friendly visit from Smitty the mailman. In the evening, I went for my medication and visit with Sheila. Carmine called. "Listen, I said. Let's get our next communication time set. What is good for you?"

"Well, I plan on taking care of that problem with the Cuban on Wednesday," Carmine Said. "Thursday is good for me. I will call you then."

"Okay, Thursday is good. Call me at the same time. Are you ready to hear my plan?"

"Yeah bro, give it to me."

"I am setting the date for June 13th. The man who delivers the mail to the jail is going to take me out only he doesn't know it yet. We have sort of become friends. He is twenty-five years old and is a real nice guy who adores his wife and kid, as well as his grandmother. His grandmother lives on Pleasant Valley Road about a mile or two from the jail. He stops to see her everyday, like clockwork."

"I will recon it bro."

"Good Carmine, that is good. Get me the rundown on his kid and wife too, in case we need it."

"Don't worry Joey, I know exactly what to do."

"He is saving up his money, as he plans on buying his granny new parlor furniture. He showed me a picture of the furniture. It is a dark green material. Now listen closely, we are going to buy him the furniture. Pick out a nice couch, loveseat, recliner, end tables, and a coffee table. On the 13th, Noah and Patrick are going to deliver the furniture, via a rental truck. They are going to pull in after Smitty the mailman arrives. You will follow them with my getaway car. Once there, you will approach Smitty before he enters the house and convince him to comply by using usual tactics of threats against granny and his family. Tell him that he must deliver the mail at exactly three thirty. That is when the guards change shifts. This place is a clusterfuck when that happens. I will meet him as I always do. He will deliver the mail as usual plus one guard uniform in a mail bag for me with a pair of sunglasses. I need the kind of sunglasses that the cops use. I will escort Smitty out. There is a blind spot where he parks. The cameras don't cover it. I will light up a smoke before I exit, as if I am going outside to smoke me one. I will then get into the mail vehicle and leave. It will be 7:00 before they realize I am missing. Now listen to this part closely. There is a store in the route 33 flea market that sells military stuff, as well as police, firefighter, state corrections, and county correction guard patches and uniforms. They also sell the shoes that the cops and guards where. I need you to get a complete uniform, including the hat for me."

"I know the place well. I assume that the patches are sewed for fingers down from the top of the sleeve just like we did in the Corps."

"You got it Carmine. Don't forget the hat and the patch on the hat too."

"What is your plan for the cop?" Carmine asked me with concern.

"I will fill you in on that later. What do you think of my plan?"

"I think that it is brilliant. I will run it past your boys and we will go over it to see if we have any ideas. I know that I will have to do a selling job on that mail carrier, which will not be a problem. I will call you on Thursday."

Thursday couldn't come fast enough. I kept busy working in the mailroom. I guess I was doing a great job. I was told by the Chief of Administration Services that since I was on the job, productivity and effectiveness had increased. I didn't know what that meant, but it sure sounded good. I also kept busy by setting up my escape. I made it a point to get more close and personal with Smitty the mailman. He made it certain that he never misses a day of work. That put a smile on my face for sure. My lovemaking with Sheila really intensified. Boy, I knew that I was going to miss her. Carmine called me on Thursday as scheduled, and Sheila answered. She smiled as she handed me the phone.

"What's up," I asked

"Tell Sheila that her problem is resolved. Hernandez said that she is not worth any interference in his business or getting his family hurt. He took me and the boys serious. I explained that it was personal. Now listen, the boys and I have some concerns."

"I am listening," I said.

"Why are you busting out on the 13th?"

"I don't really know. Maybe it is because I was arrested on the 13th and I was born on the 13th, and the 13th is my lucky number."

"Make sure you bring out the orange jail suit. Put it in one of the mail bags and have your boy take it out with him. Don't leave it behind."

"Good point."

Carmine hesitated a moment. "What are you going to do to the cop?"

"I am going to whack him."

"We advise against that. We think that you should get out of the area as fast as you can. I wish you would leave him to us, but if you must get vengeance, only fuck him up."

"Another good idea, what else do you want to know?"

"Why are you buying this Smitty guy all this furniture?"

"Because I like the guy, he is a good family man and he loves his grandmother. Besides, the furniture delivery is good cover if anyone stops by or gets nosey. And, the old lady will not get suspicious."

"What do you need in the way of clothes and money?"

"I need about three changes of casual clothes. No suits. Only what I could carry in a bag. As far as money goes, I need about ten thousand."

"We will put everything in a bag, including the gun. Joey, when do you sort the mail at the jail?"

"It is sorted the next day."

"One big question, we want to run this by the Tooch. What do you think of that?"

"Well I must tell you Carmine, I am very disappointed that my Uncle never made an effort to contact me."

"Joey that is not the way business is done when a man gets jammed up (goes to prison). I really do want your Uncle's blessing on this."

"Sorry Carmine. I mean no disrespect. You got to do what you got to do. I respect that, and I will respect his decision. Abort the mission if the Tooch says that this is a no go."

"You are right on bro," Carmine said with a chuckle. "You just said what I was trusting you would say. I already asked him. He said it is an excellent plan. He said you are smart. The authorities will look at this as an inside connection pulled off by one or more of the guards."

I was a little pissed off. "If you already asked him, then why are you busting my balls here?"

"Because Joey, this is the way the Tooch wanted me to present this to you."

"That prick," I said in a polite way. "He is testing me."

"Joey, I have one other thing. Your Uncle Michael wants us to use your grandmother as an alibi. Her lady friend is remodeling her beauty parlor and we are doing the work, if you know what I mean."

"I really don't like getting my grandmother involved, but it will work. Does she agree to it?" I asked with great concern.

"Yes, it is all set. I will call you next Thursday. By then, I will have completed my recon on the cop and the mailman."

•   •   •

I went over the plan of escape at least one hundred times during the next week. I blueprinted it in my mind. I talked more with Smitty. He gave no indication of not being at work on June 13th. I was starting to form a strategy for when I got out. I needed a plan that did not include my family. I was thinking of going back to Twentynine Palms, California. I entertained the thought of getting some bullshit job there and becoming lost in the desert.

Sheila and I made every minute count. I knew that I would miss her a lot, but I was happy for the time I had with her and that I was able to help her out with her problem with the Cuban. I pictured Carmine and the guys talking to him in resolving Sheila's problem.

I prayed more during the week too. I thanked God for putting the Marine Corps in my life, because no matter how things turned out, I was already successful. I also thanked him for giving me such a good family and friends. I am a Marine I thought and that is something that no one could ever take away from me. They say that once a Marine, always a Marine and I believed it.

On June 3rd, there was a stabbing in another wing and we were under a twenty-four hour lock down. God, I hoped that nothing like that happened on the 13th. When Carmine called me on the 6th, he had all the information on the cop who arrested me.

Carmine was excited. "Bro, I have the entire scoop on the Cop. I talked to a person who turned me on to a Trenton Cop who is on the same bowling league with him. The bastard lives at number 10, Easton Road in Windsor. I suggest that you take care of him at his house. He resides in an old farmhouse, and he has no alarm system. There are no other houses around him, only an old barn a quarter mile away. You will pass it on the way to his house. I checked it out. You could hide the car there. This dick is a real looser. He is thirty-eight years old, divorced, and he lives alone. He gets home at exactly 6:10 every night."

"What approach should I use in entry to the house?" I eagerly asked.

"Use the basement window closest to the right corner as you are looking at the back of the house. Bushes cover it, and the lock is broken on it. I broke it for you. I also left a baseball bat at the bottom of the stairs in case you should need it. Once you go up the stairs, you will find a door. It could be opened with a credit card. Speaking of credit cards, you will find a wallet in your bag with a Pennsylvania driver's license and a credit card. You will also find a Bucks County library card, as well as a Social Security card. The address on the license is to a motel on Route 202 between New Hope and Lahaska. The directions will be in the bag. The owner is the son of a made man in our family."

"I know the place," I said.

"Joe Momma, you are actually registered with the Pennsylvania Department of Motor Vehicle's and the credit card and Social Security card are real. I will tell you your new name when I see you. A train ticket will be in the bag. You are to take the train to Philadelphia. In your wallet, you will find a picture of a baby. On the back of the picture, there is a phone number you must call to have one of our contacts will pick you up at the Market Street Station. He will take you to South Philadelphia and hide you in an apartment at the Italian Market. After things cool down, he will take you to a U-Hall rental place. You are to rent a van, drive it to New Hope and turn it in across from the New Hope Community Center. The address is also in the bag."

"Wow Carmine how did you do all this so quickly. I am shocked. I love you bro."

"We didn't do this quickly. Planning like this takes time. Don't thank me, thank the Tooch. It was all his idea. We had the ball rolling the day you were pinched. Your Uncle Michael knew that the Fed's would get involved and you would be jammed up for at least ten years for not working with them. We had other plans. Our plans included Patrick and Noah, along with five others busting you out on route to court, but your plan was better. I couldn't say anything to you when you started calling from jail. The Tooch is proud of you for your smarts, and loyalty to him. Oh yeah, this line is definitely clean. The authorities at the jail don't even know that it exists. We had our people put it in, so we could coordinate with you. One other thing, we had your girl Sheila in our back pocket all along, We knew of her problem with the Cuban before you did. Why do you think it took you so long to start receiving your medication and therapy? We were negotiating with her. The doctor that she replaced suddenly took a leave of absence if you know what I mean. Taking care of her debt was a part of our approach to getting her to help us by taking the job and putting in the phone line hookup. We were never even at her house when we called you. I am not there now. Noah and Patrick are going to call you next week. How was your first piece of ass bro?"

"You sons of bitches, I really do love you people. No wonder Sheila was so eager to jump my bones, and she did tell me that she locked up the phone every night. You set it up, you bastard you." Sheila was laughing her ass off as she was listening to me talk.

"I got one other surprise for you Joey. Noah and Patrick bought you a new 1991 black Pontiac Firebird. It will be waiting for you at the motel. One other thing Joey and this is real important. The Tooch understands your business with the Cop who arrested you but under no circumstances are you to whack him. Fuck him up if you must, but do not kill him."

"Are there any other surprises?" I asked.

"Actually there is, I was going to tell you this on Tuesday, but I will tell you now. Smitty says that he should deliver the mail at 3:20 on the 13th instead of 3:30. He says that 3:20 will work better for you because the guards are not paying attention to detail during the change of shift goings on. He is concerned that the change of guard will be completed by 3:30 and things will be settled down by then. I will call you on Tuesday, Joey." I hung up the phone and I couldn't believe that Carmine did.

"That is some family you got there Joseph. They really love you very much," Sheila said.

"Yes they are, and you rank right up there with them. I can't believe that you were in on this all along."

"Then why do you look so disappointed Joseph?" Are you disappointed in me?"

"Oh no Sheila, not at all, it is just that I am going to miss you," I said as I followed the phone cord. "Where does this go?"

Sheila looked just as confused as I. "I don't know Joseph, behind the wall I think. Listen to me." Sheila said as she pulled me into her. "Forget about the damn phone line. You will never forget your first time with a woman. I am proud to be the first for you. You are a great lover, and you got heart."

We hugged hard. "I'm sorry that we didn't get a chance to make love tonight. Time is running out for us," I said with a tear in my eye.

Sheila wiped away the tear. "Joseph I have to take off tomorrow and you know that I will not be here for the weekend, but we still have a few nights to be together next week."

I was not aware that Sheila was taking off on Friday. "Okay Sheila you have a good weekend and I will see you on Monday," I said in a disappointing tone as I started to leave.

"Hey young man, I want my kiss," Sheila demanded. Needless to say, it was a passionate one.

It was weird seeing Smitty on Friday. He made as if nothing was going on. It was even weirder seeing the nurse for my medication and blood test. Usually I only see the nurse on the weekends.

The weekend was long. Someone different delivered the mail on Saturday, which concerned me some.

Saturday was my fourth week in jail. It seemed like I was there for six months. Sunday I just sat around and wrote letters to my sister and mother. I had a meeting with my lawyer on Monday. If he knew what was going on, he sure didn't act like it. Again it was weird seeing Smitty. Again he was cool. In the evening, Sheila and I made love for an hour and a half.

Noah called Tuesday evening. "How are you Lance Corporal Mommalione? It sure has been a long time. I hear good things are about to happen for you."

"Hi Noah I can't thank you guys enough for everything you done for me, and for the car too. I just can't believe you guys. Thanks man."

"Hey you saved my life man, but I would have done this for you anyway."

"Noah do you really think that we deserved the medals we were awarded?"

"Why do you ask?"

"I don't know," I said. "I guess that it has just been on my mind now and then."

"Hell no Joe Momma, we did not deserve the medals, but what the hell."

"Yeah, you are right. How is the leg?"

"The wounded one is a little shorter that the other. Both Pat and I are now getting treatment at the V.A, way up East Orange."

"Speaking of the crazy Irishman put him on."

"He is not here Joe. He is with Carmine. They went to pick up your new car and drop it off with some cloths at the motel. You will see him on Thursday."

"Why didn't you go?"

"Because you were expecting a call, and I wanted to be the one to call as I wanted to talk to you, you dumb ass."

"Oh yeah, that makes sense," I told him as I gave myself a head slap. "I will see you on Thursday Noah. Make sure that they disconnect this phone."

"It will be done tomorrow. Good luck Joe Momma," Noah said as he hung up.

"Are you getting nervous yet?" Sheila asked.

"Are you kidding me? I cannot sleep, not that I could sleep at night anyway."

"Listen Joey, tomorrow is our last night together, and I want it to be special."

"What do you have in mind Sheila?"

"I'm going to bring in dinner and bottle of wine."

Our conversation was interrupted by a knock at the door. "What do you want?" Sheila yelled in an angry tone.

"Sorry to interrupt your session Doctor, but we are having a routine shakedown and I must escort prisoner Mommalione back to the dorm," the guard yelled through the locked door.

"I must go," I sadly told Sheila.

"It is okay Joseph, I will see you tomorrow and we will have our special evening together."

I was really anxious all day Wednesday. I must say that again Smitty was calm when I saw him. I seemed to calm down by the time the guard called me up front to report to the doctor.

"Hi handsome, first thing first," Sheila said with a smile. I thought that she was referring to sex, but she took out my medication and the machine for checking my blood count. "I have a great dinner for you Joseph. How is your arm feeling today?"

"It feels okay, but I still have that itchy, tingling feeling inside where the rod was put in."

"Actually that is a good sign Joseph. It means that it is healing. I instructed Carmine where he could pickup pain medication for your arm, as well as medication for your diabetes."

"Sheila, where is the phone?"

"I don't know. It was gone when I got here."

Sheila heated up a couple of plates in the microwave. She made a roast with potatoes. It was so good. I even had a couple glasses of wine. Dinner was topped off with a short but dynamic lovemaking. Afterwards, we were quiet. As I sat on the desk holding her in my arms with her breast in my face, I broke the silence. "You know that they are going to question you."

"I know, but don't worry Joseph. I only see you for an hour or so a night. My written records end the same way after each session. I always write that the patient is withdrawn, and did not talk tonight. In my later reports, I wrote that I am concerned about his depression. Today's report will say that I am considering getting him professional counseling and I recommend medication for the slump he is in. My wordings were and will be something to that effect, so don't worry."

"I am just worried about you Sheila," I said as we were getting dressed.

"Don't worry my love. I will be fine. Losing a prisoner is their screw up. Not mine." A few minutes later, it was time to go. We both had tears in our eyes. "Joseph, you taught me to have a higher opinion toward myself. You also taught me to work on my personal development and I needed that. Now, I want you to realize that you

280

must move on no matter how painful separation may feel. Take a look at what you are really leaving behind." We both laughed.

"I love you Sheila."

Sheila gave me a loving smile. "I love you too. You have your whole life ahead of you, and I will see you again. You can count on it." With that said, we kissed and parted.

The strangest thing happened that night. With the pain of leaving Sheila, and the anxiety of my big jailbreak, I slept all night. Go figure, it must have been the wine, because I never slept at night while in the joint.

At 11:00, I left the wing as usual to report for my clerical duties. Everything was going just fine. I even ate lunch with the guards. As we talked, joked, and laughed. I noticed that none of them were minding the security monitors. Not that it really mattered, because of the blind spots. As I was sorting mail, I thought that not only did my Marine Corps training help me survive in here, but also the discipline I received in the Corps helped me remain composed at such a stressful time. I sure as hell adapted, improvised and overcome like I was taught.

It was 2:45 when I glanced up at the clock. Then it was 3:00, and then it was 3:13. At exactly 3:20, Smitty came in the administration area with two bags of mail, and dropped them at the mailroom door. "I will be right back. I got another bag to get," Smitty yelled out. As usual, no one paid him any attention. I picked up the bags and took them into the mailroom. I checked the first bag and there was my guard uniform, hat and shoes. I changed into the uniform in what had to be record time. The uniform looked and fit great.

Smitty came back and entered the mailroom as I was putting on my sunglasses. He took my arm and cut off the identification bracelet. We didn't say a word to each other. Outside the mailroom a change of the guard was going on. Smitty and I exited the mailroom together and I locked the door behind me. Smitty had my jail suit and shoes in a mailbag. I threw the keys on the desk and started down the hallway to the holding area door. I took out a cigarette, and Smitty hit the buzzer on the door. The door unlocked and we exited. As we exited, I fired up the cigarette.

"Take that cigarette outside," the guard in the cage declared without looking at me. I got outside and there was the truck. I was careful not to cross the invisible line where the security camera would pick me up. I looked around. It was clear so I entered the side of the mail truck. I assumed the prone position. Smitty drove off. We still didn't speak at that time. I must say that I was relatively calm. I could feel us heading down the long winding driveway. Then the truck came to a stop. I heard the turn signal clicking and Smitty made the left hand turn onto Route 29. I let out a sigh of relief.

"Joey, is my family going to be okay now?"

"As long as you don't open your mouth and fuck me over, they will be. Watch the news tonight. You will see reports of a dead cop. If I have no trouble whacking a cop, I could assure you that I have no problem whacking you or your family. And, if I am incarcerated, a member of my family will do it."

"I hate you for putting me through this Joey, but I do wish you luck. I wish you luck, but I hate you."

"I understand," I said.

We drove for a short while and then we made a left turn and headed down Pleasant Valley Road and a minute later, I could see a rental truck in a driveway. Carmine was leaning against it. Smitty pulled up behind it. I exited with the mailbag containing the jail suit. Carmine jumped in the back of the rental truck as Smitty ran into the house.

"It is good to see you, Joe Momma."

"It is good to see you." I said as I joined Carmine in the back of the truck, and gave him a Goomba hug.

"Joey get out of the monkey suit and put these on. Listen to me as you are changing. In this leather bag, you will find one wallet. In the wallet you will find a drivers license, social security card, credit card, library card, family pictures, and three hundred dollars in twenties, tens and fives. On the back of the baby picture, you will find the contact phone number. In the side pocket of the bag, you will find a train ticket to Philadelphia, and directions to the motel in New Hope. In the bag, you will find a change of clothes for a few days, a 357 S&W, with six hollow point rounds in it. You will also find a flashlight, and a windbreaker jacket containing the keys to your new car. The ten thousand dollars you requested is in the trunk of your new car. Your grandmother put a stick of pepperoni in the bag with Italian bread and a diet coke. We used your picture from your Jersey license for our connections in the Pennsylvania Department of Motor Vehicles to make up the Pennsylvania drivers license. At the motel, you will find clothes, and toiletries, also in the trunk of your new car. The person that you need to make contact with at the motel is one of us. His name is Robert Peppi. You are to give him the gun once you make contact. You already have your instructions for when you get to Philadelphia. Do you have any questions?"

"Yeah, is that the car I am using," I said as I pointed to a 1988 Dodge.

"Yes Joey, here are the keys. Ditch the car at the Princeton Junction Train Station."

"Carmine how is my mother?"

"She is okay. She knows nothing of today. We will tell her later. Don't worry about your mother right now."

"Where are Pat and Noah?"

"They are in the house eating cake, and having coffee with the old lady. I will get them in a minute. Make sure you leave me the bag with the jail suit and guard uniform. I will get rid of it."

"Hey Carmine, the uniform was perfect."

"You want to know something Joey; you could thank your grandmother for that. I am going to say goodbye now Joe Momma. Don't call us, we will call you."

Carmine hugged me hard and kissed me on the cheek." Carmine please thank my uncle for me, and give my parents as well as my grandmother my love."

"You are now known as Joe Papa, and as I said, do not call us, we will call you. I will see you soon Joe Papa," Carmine said as he put my Medal of Honor in my hand, with my lucky four-leaf clover.

Carmine jumped off the back of the truck and headed for the house. Suddenly it hit me. "Hey Carmine," I yelled. "Do you remember Papa Joe, the guy that use to cut our hair when we were kids?"

"Yeah, he is long dead. What about him?"

"He came to me in a dream, and he told me that on day I will bear his name, and now my name is Joe Papa."

"Joey, you and your dreams, we are going to change your name from Joe Momma to Joe the Dreamer."

I put my medal to my lips before putting it in the side pocket of the gym bag. The guys came running out. "Hey I really missed you guys," I said. Noah was still walking with a cane and I could tell that Patrick recently had plastic surgery done on his face.

"Hey Joe, how does it feel to be sprung?"

"It feels great Pat. I feel the same as I did the day I flew back to the world on the freedom bird."

"I'll never forget the day I came back. It was Saint Patrick's day when I came home," Patrick said.

"I see that the V.A. is doing a good job on you. You look better than you did the day I met you."

Patrick started laughing as he said, "I think they are doing a pretty good job."

"Joe, was you nervous during the escape?"

"Not as much as I was in combat Noah. It is so good to see you guys."

"We are thinking of staying in the area." Noah said.

"You got a great family, and we like it here. Your uncle said that he has work for us, so we are giving it some thought. We are also thinking of enrolling at Mercer Community College too," Patrick said as he handed me the Marine Corps ring that he and Noah bought me for my birthday.

"I am so glad that you guys brought me my ring, and I am also glad that you are considering staying in the Trenton area. I am not going to say good-bye because I know that I will see you soon and thanks for the new car."

"Speaking of cars, drive slowly, and remember that you were profiled once before."

"I know Noah, that is why I got to settle with this asshole cop."

"Joe, I know that this thing with the cop is an Italian thing, but I wish you would leave him for us to get your revenge for you."

"I appreciate it Patrick, but this is something I got to do."

Noah and Patrick walked me to the stolen car and we didn't say good-bye. We knew that it was just a matter of time before we seen each other again.

• • •

I saw the State Capital Buildings on my left, as I drove through Trenton. I turned down Cass Street and got an eerie feeling as I drove past the large gray walls of the Trenton State Prison. I caught route 129 and got on the I-195, which I took to Route 133. It was 5:15 when I turned on Easton Road. I drove slowly past the old barn and turned around at Officer Miller's house. I then made my way back to the barn. There were no doors on it. I pulled in and took the credit card out of the wallet. I then removed the gun and flashlight from the leather bag and exited the car. I cut through the woods and came out behind Officer Miller's house. I crawled behind the bushes and found the window with the broken lock. I opened it and dropped into the basement. I shined the light on my watch to check the time. I got a warm feeling thinking of Christmas day with Mark and Roseanne when I looked at the time. Moreover, I realized how happy I felt when they gave me the watch as a Christmas gift.

I found the baseball bat that Carmine left and I made my way up the stairs with the bat in one hand and the flashlight in the other. I then removed the credit card from my back pocket and used it to open the basement door. I carefully placed the card back in one back pocket and the flashlight in the other back pocket and adjusted the gun in my belt line. I entered the house and cased it thoroughly. I saw that he had a cluster of junk in the hallway of the front door which partly blocked the door, so I positioned myself in-between the refrigerator and the washing machine, where the back entrance was and bided my time. I didn't move for at least thirty minutes as I waited to attack suddenly and without warning.

I waited patiently. Beads of sweat were forming on my forehead. I was determined not to move or even look at my watch. I refused to entertain any thought of him not coming home on time.

After what seemed like I was in a state of endless time, I heard a car pull in the driveway. A few minutes later, I heard the back door open to the kitchen. I was calm as I had on my Marine war face.

Officer Miller entered the house through the kitchen door. I stepped out from the side of the refrigerator. His mistake was that he went for his gun. As he did so, I swung the bat and struck him in the hand. He then grabbed his right injured hand with his left hand. I lifted the bat high over my head and came down with great force, striking him on top of his left shoulder. As he fell against the stove, I kicked him between the legs and slammed the bat down on the top of his head afflicting damage to his skull. He was out cold. I quickly removed his gun and threw it in the sink. I didn't want to kill him so I was decisive in not using my gun unless I had to, and to that point, I did not need to use my gun. I firmly bound his hands behind his back with his handcuffs. I then tied his feet with a lamp cord.

All that waiting and energetic physical action made me thirsty so I got a beer out of the refrigerator and pulled up a kitchen chair. As I was sitting there waiting for him to come to, I realized that my left arm was numb.

He was not coming around fast enough so I threw some beer in his face. That did the trick. He opened his eyes and I could tell that he was overcome with intense dismay when he realized that it was me standing over him.

"What are you dong in my house?" Officer Miller said.

"Fucking you up, that's what I'm doing in your house. You looked like a monster in your uniform on the day that you arrested me. Now here you are in the same uniform and you look like a helpless pig. Do you realize what you put me through by profiling me. I had my hand engraved Colt .45 gold plated Marine Corps pistol taken away from me. Other than my Medal of Honor, that pistol was my prize possession. You put my family through hell, and made me eat and sleep with the scum of the earth. Why did you profile me and take me for a Puerto Rican? A P.R. driving a BMW must have been up to no good in your book."

"What are you going to do to me?" Officer Miller cried out.

I pulled out my 357 magnum. "I am going to kill you motherfucker." I pointed my pistol at his face and pulled the hammer back. He turned his face and his head started to shrink in-between his shoulders.

"No wait, don't kill me!"

I put the heel of my shoe to his mouth and grinded it into his lips. "Shut the hell up asshole. There ain't anything you could say that would make me spare your miserable life."

"Yes, yes there is. Please listen to me," Officer Miller appealed.

"What do you have to say? You got about a minute before I whack you."

"It wasn't me Joseph. It was Vito. He called me from the shore on his car phone and told me that you were coming by in a beamer. He said that you were dressed heavy (carrying a gun) and I was to pinch (arrest) you. Those were his exact words. He said that it had something to do with revenge for you striking him, and he said that you must pay for striking a made man (member of the Mafia). I swear to you Joseph, that is what he told me. Being that I was on his payroll, I had to do what he ordered. It was business Joseph, nothing but business."

I was furious as I paced around the kitchen waving the gun around. "That cazzo (prick), my uncle is going to be very interested in this," I yelled. I was about six feet away from Officer Miller when I pointed the gun at his left knee.

"No don't Joseph, don't do it."

An earsplitting explosive noise was the next thing heard. Flames came out the muzzle of the 357 magnum. Officer Miller was screaming as he rolled around on the floor. There was blood, flesh, and bone splattered all over him. I blew the shit out of his knee. I then put the gun to the back of his bloody head.

"Why, why," I yelled.

"Joseph, I told you why." Officer Miller cried out. "He doesn't like you. You are a threat to him. He said no one talks to a Skipper (Crew Boss) like you did. He said that you are a loose cannon that had to be dealt with."

At that point, I was feeling intensely violent. I was seeing red. All I could think about was whacking Vito. "Okay Joe, get grip. Let the Tooch handle this," I said aloud, as I walked into the dinning room. I turned and looked back at Officer Miller. I aimed the gun at his head. He wasn't looking at me. I pulled back the hammer and in a split second I dropped my aim down to his right elbow and squeezed off a round. Again flames came out the muzzle of the powerful handgun.

Again Officer Miller let out a scream. I walked up to him. Officer Miller had his eyes closed. I looked down at his right elbow. It was a direct hit. His right elbow and left knee were gone.

Officer Miller had passed out. I kicked him in the ribs. "You just retired motherfucker." I no longer felt emotionally agitated as I tucked the pistol in my belt. I exited the house through the back door and made my way back through the woods to the old barn. When I got to the car, I carefully put the credit card back in my wallet and placed the wallet, flashlight, and gun back in the leather bag.

I looked at my watch. It was 6:40 when I pulled out of the barn and made my way down Conover Road back to Route 130. I made a right on Route 130 and drove to Route 571 which I took to the Princeton Junction Train Station. I parked the car and headed toward the platform. Once there, I checked the departure schedule for Philadelphia. I was in luck as I made it in time to catch the 7:20 train with time to spare. I then went to a pay phone and called an ambulance for Officer Miller.

A crowd started to form on the platform as I waited. I had a tight hold to the railing as I wondered if the authorities at the jail discovered my escape yet. I quickly changed my thoughts to New Hope. New Hope, Pennsylvania is located along the Delaware River directly across from Lambertville New Jersey. Ironically, it is located only a few miles from the Mercy County Correction Center. New Hope has always been a place for my family to get away to. The town has history dating back to before the time of George Washington. Although it is located in a country setting, the town offers the arts as well as history. My dad told me that it was hippy community back in the late 1960's and early 1970's.

My daydreaming became disrupted by a man who looked just a little older than my father. "That is a good looking Marine Corps ring you have there young man. Semper Fidelis."

"Semper Fi" I said, and slowly moved away from him. I heard the whistle of a train, but it happened to be a shuttle train pulling in on one of the tracks. As I looked to my right, I noticed two uniform police officers coming up a set of steps about forty feet away. All of a sudden great agitation and anxiety started to set in, and crazy thoughts were going through my head. Were they looking for me?

Did Officer Miller tip them off? He could not have, I just called for the ambulance not ten minutes before I spotted the cops. However, the ambulance company could have alerted the police who could have could have gone to Miller's house. Or, maybe the cops noticed the stolen car? Did the jail discover my absence? No, they would be checking the jail first before they sound the alarm. Either way, I thought that I could not take the chance. Besides, I had to consider that I had the gun in my bag, and the cops were getting closer. I should have left the gun at Officer Miller's house I thought, but I was under orders to turn it over to my contact at the motel in New Hope. I had too many negative thoughts going through my head. I knew that I had to regroup or my uncertainty could draw attention from the cops.

I turned and passed the man who told me Semper Fidelis just minutes before. By then, the crowd was exiting the shuttle car. I noticed two cop cars in the parking lot. My mind was racing as the train for Philadelphia pulled up. I then mingled with the crowd exiting the shuttle train and started walking through the parking lot behind the cop cars.

Maybe they were looking for someone else I thought, but I already was committed to a course of action that I stayed with. I figured that I would catch a later train if the coast was clear. There was another train for Philadelphia in about twenty minutes. I knew that I could double back and recon the area before I waited up on the platform. If it didn't look good, I could always improvise with another plan. I noticed several cars start to leave the parking lot as I walked toward Alexander Road. I walked along when a vehicle behind me started to beep. I turned and looked. I noticed a large pickup truck with a red front plate with yellow letters that read, "USMC." When the truck pulled along side me, I saw the former Marine I met while waiting for the train. The sign on the door of the truck read, "Greentree Stables, Upper Madefield, Pennsylvania."

"Hello there. Do you need a lift?" The former Marine said.

Immediately, my eyes became fixed on a beautiful girl sitting on the passenger side. "Are you going to Pennsylvania?" I asked.

"Yes, as a matter of fact, we are. Jump in." The girl with the long straight black hair and beautiful green eyes slid over as I got in the truck and put my leather bag behind the seat. "Where are you headed to young man?"

"I am trying to make my way to New Hope."

The man smiled. "We could take you there. We are going in that direction. My name is Hank Dupree and this is my daughter Star. Actually her name is Bright Star in the Sky."

"But I prefer being called Star," she said.

My daughter, Bright Star, is attending Columbia University in the city. I just picked her up for a long weekend."

"Yes, I do not have any classes until next Wednesday and I try and come home every chance I get," Star said.

She was so beautiful and I got a tingling feeling as my leg was pressed against hers.

"I have a horse ranch in Upper Makefield. It is located on Stoney Brook road off route 32," Mr. Dupree said.

"I'm going to a motel about a mile or so outside of New Hope. Sir, does this mean that you will be taking Route 32 on Pennsylvania side of the river to get there?" I was hoping to avoid the Jersey side of the Delaware that would put us on Route 29. We would pass the County Correction Center if we were to take Route 29. As we were talking, we were getting close to Route 1.

"Would you like me to take the Pennsylvania side, of the Delaware River?"

As I turned to face Mr. Dupree, Star turned her head and looked directly in my eyes. Oh my God, I was in love. A funny feeling settled in my stomach as I said, "I just think that the Pennsylvania side has more of a scenic countryside view."

"I will cut through Trenton and cross the Delaware. I agree that the Pennsylvania side of the river is more beautiful. And, this way I could take you past my ranch and we will take the back roads to the motel."

It was almost as if Hank Dupree could read my mind. "I think that it is great that former Marines greet each other with Semper Fi," I said.

"Daddy what does Semper Fi mean?" Star asked.

"Actually it is pronounced Semper Fidelis dear. It is Latin, and it is the Marine Corps motto meaning Always Faithful."

For the next twenty minutes, Hank talked about his family business and his love for horses. He explained how he raises and trains horses for racing. He also explained that he rents stable space and provides rentals for the public who are interested in going horse back riding. He went on to say that he even has staff that teaches how to ride, and they train people and horses for competition.

I was touched when Star said, "We buy old horses that are slated to be put to sleep and those horses live out the remainder of their lives on the ranch. We are American Indian and very fond of horses."

We were then silent until we crossed into Pennsylvania and headed north on Route 32 when the topic got back to the Marine Corps.

"Did you know that Many American Indian's served in the Marine Corp?" Henry said. "I was awarded the bronze star in 1968 for bravery during the battle of Hue City during the Vietnam War."

I reached behind the seat and into the side pocket of the leather bag and pulled out my Medal of Honor and said, "I was awarded this, along with the Purple Heart for bravery during the battle of Khafji City during the Gulf War."

"Oh my God," Hank expressed. "I have never met anyone who was awarded the Medal of Honor. May I have the privilege of holding your Medal?"

"Yes Sir," I said. As I handed the medal to Star, I almost melted when our hands touched. I noticed that she could feel the vibes too.

Hank pulled the truck over to the side of the road. As his eyes positioned on the Medal of Honor, Star's eyes were steadfast on mine. "Do you have a name, Marine?"

"Yes, my name is Joseph Papa."

Hank handed the Medal back to me. "It is an honor to meet you, Joseph."

"That goes for me too," said Star.

Hank continued driving on route 32. We traveled a little further when he turned left onto Stony Brook Road. A weird feeling came over me when I realized that we were a stone throw away from the Correction Center on the Jersey side of the Delaware River. After we drove for a couple of miles, Hank pointed to his right. "This is where she starts. This is where Greentree Stables starts, and goes on for the next three miles."

"My father met my mother while riding his horse on this very road."

Star's statement made me think of my mother. I really missed her. I missed her hug. Her arms always held me tight when I was a kid and needed to feel safe. I wondered how she was going to handle writing the news of my escape for the radio news program where she works.

I knew that we were getting close to New Hope and I didn't want the ride to end. The back roads of eastern Pennsylvania take you through some of the most beautiful countryside in all of America, but is wasn't the ride that I was interested in, it was Star.

We were all quiet for the next few miles. Then, I saw the motel on my left, and I seen a car with a car cover on it. I was sure that it was mine, but at that point, it didn't mean so much to me. I looked at Star and she at me. We kept our eyes locked on each other until Henry pulled into the parking lot. My heart hurt when he came to a stop.

"Thank you very much. You are special people." I said as I opened the door and exited the truck with bag in hand.

Henry got out of the truck as I walked toward the motel, he yelled, "Joseph, please wait."

I stopped and walked back to him. "What is it Sir?"

He had a newspaper clipping in his hand." Listen to me Son. You could stop me if I am out of line. It did not take much for me to notice that you are in some kind of trouble, and I know that the only person awarded the Medal of Honor from Trenton, New Jersey is one Joseph Mommalione." He held up a newspaper clipping. "You are somewhat of a hero to me boy. I cut out this article from the newspaper and keep in my wallet." I was stunned and there was silence for a few seconds. Hank broke the silence. "How would you like a job?" I need help at the ranch. You could start tomorrow morning at 7:00 if you like. The job doesn't pay very much and it is dirty work. I am not promising you a rose garden here. It is hard work. What do you say?"

I looked at Star as she exited the truck and stood off to the side behind her father. Her big green eyes were wide open as she shook her head up and down as if to say, "Please take the offer?"

"Sir, I think I would like that," I said with much excitement in my voice. "You will not regret it Mr. Dupree. I will work very hard. Yes Sir, I think that I would like that very much." I then turned and walked toward the motel office.

Printed in the United States
200266BV00005B/1-84/A

9 781434 336873